THE ENDLESS KNOT

THE ENDLESS KNOT

by

WILLIAM L. BIERSACH

TUMBLAR HOUSE

Bona Tempora Volvant

Arcadia
MMVI

Nihil Obstat: *Huh?*

✝   Imprimatur: *Are you kidding!?!?*

ISBN: 978-0-9791600-2-8

First printing: 2001
Second printing: 2004

All rights reserved.
Manufactured in the U.S.A.
by
Tumblar House
2500 S. Fourth Ave.
Arcadia, CA 91006
www.tumblarhouse.com

THE ENDLESS KNOT

*The first book in the continuing saga of
Fr. John Baptist, the cop-turned-priest, and
Martin Feeney, his gardener-turned-chronicler.*

Other books by

William L. Biersach

∞

Published by Tumblar House

Fiction

The Darkness Did Not
The Search for Saint Valeria
Out of the Depths

Nonfiction

While the Eyes of the Great are Elsewhere

∞

Published by Catholic Treasures

Nonfiction

Of Mary There Is Never Enough

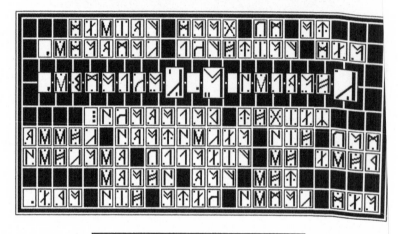

FROM THE COLLECTION OF
GUILLAUME DU CRANE
CRISTAL

AUTHOR'S NOTE: The claim of the Catholic Church to the pentangle, as described in this story, is authentic, historically accurate, and easily verifiable, as are all traditional Roman references throughout. That part, at least, is reliable.

However, for those readers interested in the occult arts, be advised that with regard to every other aspect of magick, ceremonial or wiccan, this book is riddled with "fool's traps." No user's guide is this, but a veritable minefield of mystical misinformation. Beware, take care.

It should be further emphasized that Los Angeles could not possibly be the city in which these events took place. No one in their right mind would think for a second that such ecclesiastical and civil travesties as described in this journal could occur in the sacred City of the Angels, renowned the world over for her noble shepherds, saintly clergy, and honorable citizenry! Besides, the Archdiocese of Los Angeles has seven, count 'em, seven auxiliary bishops—not four. Now, scrupulous readers may find clues throughout as to the actual identity of Archbishop Fulbright's domain, but the author refuses to deny or confirm any and all suppositions. I trust I have made my position sufficiently obscure.

—WLB3

N.B.: I would like to extend special thanks and a garland of "periwinkies" to those who believed in and helped with my work: Julia Ulano, Anne Hale, Lila Karpf, Beverly Dykes, Charles A. Coulombe, and Jeannette Coyne.

Also special mention to FJB, Brother Leonard Mary MICM, Brother Thomas Aquinas MICM, Mark Alessio, Annie Witz my "KS," Michael Dykes and rest of the Drones Club—and a rubberized "Goolgol" toy to Bonnie Callahan for the cover art.

Lastly, a bottle of vintage Dom Perignon to Stephen Frankini for starting Tumblar House at a most propitious moment. *"Bona tempora volvant!"*

Wednesday, June Seventh

Feast Day of Saint Robert of Newminster, Abbot (1159 AD)

1

"FATHER BAPTIST," I HUFFED as I hobbled up the brick walkway to the shaded, mossy spot between the church and the rectory where he liked to meditate after morning Mass. I huff and hobble everywhere because I walk with a pronounced limp—well, more like a reeling lurch followed by a teetering pause during which equilibrium is tentatively restored until the ungainly perambulatory cycle repeats. It's quite a sight, scary really, and amazing that I manage to get anywhere. For me, just going from one end of the garden to the other is a major production, and I had just returned from a trek all the way to the corner for a morning newspaper. "Father Baptist, you won't believe this—"

He was seated in his neat but somewhat threadbare cassock on the wooden bench facing the statue of Saint Thérèse the Little Flower, a moldy old book spread open on his lap. He looked up at me with those unnerving eyes that seemed to whisper, tired yet patiently, "Considering all that I do believe, Martin, do you really think you could come up with something that is beyond me?" Exhaling slowly, he rolled the flimsy cover of the book closed and folded his hands on top. "Hm?"

"What I mean is—" I was lowering myself onto the edge of the cement birdbath, taking care not to knock the rigid, porous bird perched on the pockmarked rim with the handle of my cane. The stony little fellow had been broken off before and poorly repaired. "—that is—"

"If you're talking about Bishop Brassorie," said Father, " I
received word just before Mass. A special messenger from the
Chancery Office."

"Messenger?"

"You were busy lighting the altar candles. He came
through the side door into the sacristy." Father began pulling
a note from the pocket of his cassock, thought better of it, and
shoved it back in. "Wry-looking fellow, probably a seminarian. Didn't stay for Mass."

"Why would they notify you about Brassorie?" I was
shifting myself around, trying to find a comfortable position.
No chance. Nasty critter, arthritis, especially of the spine. A
grouchy companion even on warm summer mornings. "And
by special messenger, yet."

Father Baptist shifted his shoulders, that disconcerting shrug
that seemed to whisper, exhausted but bravely, "Considering
all the crap"—no, he wouldn't have said "crap," not even in
a whisper, "crap" is my word—"Considering all the nasty
and dubious directives that have come to me from the Chancery Office in the last three years, what's one more?" But all
he actually said was, "Hm." Then he reconsidered and
added, "Whatever it is, they want me to come at once. 'They'
meaning the archbishop."

"At once?" My cane, which I'd leaned against the rim of
the birdbath, began to slide away from me. As I grabbed for
it with my right hand, the newspaper wedged under my left
arm slipped and fell to the ground. It landed face down on
the mossy bricks between us. Great. With a back like mine, a
stoop and a reach is an awesome undertaking. "You mean as
in 'right now'?"

"I believe that's what 'at once' means."

"But you're persona non grata. In fact, you're the most
non grata persona in the archdiocese as far as
they're—he's—concerned. Why would they—he—send for
you?"

Hating royal plurals—in application, not concept—I heaved
myself off the birdbath and began descending slowly, back
straight, knees doing all the hydraulic work, just as my physi-
cal therapist had advised. The good Father didn't do the obviously charitable thing and retrieve the paper for me because
we had made an agreement long ago that I was not an invalid
and was perfectly capable of picking up after myself. Besides,
I'm lazy, and if I don't keep my swollen joints moving I'll
freeze up like a department store mannequin. Therefore, the

truly charitable thing for Father to do was to look on unhelp-
fully and dispassionately while I grunted and groaned my way
onto my haunches and scooped up the morning news. It was
a long way down, but it was even a longer way back up.

By the time I'd hoisted myself back onto the rim of the
birdbath, I'd forgotten what we'd been talking about. A
glance at the newspaper in my hand brought it all back.
Wednesday, June seventh. There was a picture in the lower left
corner of the front page, rather small and not very flattering,
taken during a speech Bishop Brassorie had made at some
high school commencement a year or so before. His mouth
was open and his eyes bulged—normal, for him. Underneath
was a caption in bold letters: AUX BISHOP BRASSORIE
FOUND DEAD; MURDERED, SAY POLICE.

GARDENING TIPS: For those of you who aren't Catho-

lic or for modern Catholics who don't appreciate

authority figures, auxiliary bishops are the as-

sistant bishops under an archbishop who govern as-

signed regions of a large archdiocese. Bishop

Brassorie was, or had been, one of four in our

city. And, as you'll see, one closely connected

to St. Philomena's Church.

                                      --M.F.

"Old Brassiere," I mumbled, synopsizing the brief article in
my own, somewhat biased style, "croaked while conducting a
'sunset liturgy' alone in his private chapel. No real specifics,
there never are." I handed the paper to Father. "Can't say
I'm moved."

"We haven't the privilege not to be," he countered, raising
his eyebrows as he scanned the page. He did not appreciate
my word-play with respect to the late auxiliary bishop's name.
"The man had an eternal soul, after all. Still, there was a time

when the death of a bishop would demand a headline. Now it's a tiny article in the lower left corner, three inches in one column. Shows you how far the stature of the Church has diminished. We should be grateful it made the front page at all."

I nodded sadly, knowingly, and silently while he read. When he looked up from the article I ventured, "You still haven't told me why."

"Hm?"

"Why do they want you?" I decided not to buck the royal plural. Too much effort.

He folded the paper and handed it back to me. "Not to give me Brassiere—Brassorie's job, I assure you."

I contorted my lips in what I thought was an expression of cautious thought, a failed attempt at hiding a smirk. "Don't be so certain. Maybe they think you'd follow suit."

"You mean I might have the good grace to get myself murdered, too?"

"Uh-huh. It would sure make their lives easier."

"Anything's possible, I suppose, especially these days. But a promotion, no, not conceivable. Not me, not this archbishop, not this century. I wouldn't want it anyway, even in a saner era."

"The message said 'at once'?"

He nodded. "The nerve. The wording smells of that new monsignor, whatsizname, Goolgol. The archbishop's new lackey. One opinion too many, one principle too few."

"Are you going?"

"Certainly," he said, a secretive smile forming on his lips.

"You mean you're not going."

"No, I mean I am going." The smile remained. "No choice."

"Well." I positioned my cane to start the awesome commotion of rising to my feet. "We haven't had breakfast. We haven't even had our morning coffee. But duty calls, so I'll bring the car around front."

"No. I will go alone."

For a moment I teetered between elation at not having to get up, and devastation at feeling left out. "But you never go anywhere without me."

"This time, yes."

"But I'm your chauffeur, your valet, your right-hand man, your cook when Millie's away, your—"

"According to parish records, you're my gardener; and these roses around St. Thérèse appear to be wilting."

Roses? As in work? He knew darn well I hadn't tended the garden for over a year, not since several grateful but impoverished parishioners started donating their time in lieu of cash in the plate. The very thought of getting down on my hands and knees, never to get up again; why it sent shivers down my already traumatized spine. And my hips—ah, what arthritis does to hips! "But—"

"This errand is not for you. It shouldn't even be for me, but I will do what I can to set that straight."

"I don't understand."

"And I don't want you to. Please." He was rising. "Tend St. Thérèse's roses, will you? And don't forget to water the gardenias around St. Joseph."

2

THE MOST EVIDENT MARK OF GOD'S ANGER, announced the gilded letters in the simulated gold-framed plaque beside the door to Father Baptist's study. Perhaps it wasn't so much a plaque as a piece of hand-lettered posterboard in a glass frame, but "plaque" sounds better than "cheap-o sign" or "budget escutcheon." In any case, I don't think I ever entered that room, day or night, serene or brimming mad, that those words didn't jump out at me, distracting me from my purpose by going for the throat. They went on thus:

The most evident mark of God's anger, and the most terrible castigation He can inflict upon the world, is manifest when He permits His people to fall into the hands of a clergy who are more in name than in deed, priests who practice the cruelty of ravening wolves rather than the charity and affection of devoted shepherds. They abandon the things of God to devote themselves to the things of the world and, in their saintly calling of holiness, they spend their time in profane and worldly pursuits. When God permits such things, it is a very positive proof that He is thoroughly angry with His people, and is visiting His most dreadful wrath upon them.

—St. John Eudes

Father Baptist had his reasons for hanging it there in plainly obvious sight, impossible for any visitor to miss—reasons he never elucidated, at least not to me. It guarded the doorway to his study, or office, or whatever you call the room where a priest sits, reads, writes, pays bills, and speaks with people who come to him with problems. Opposite his writing desk were a couple of old but comfortable padded leather chairs, chocolate brown in their youth, all visible splits held together with gray duct tape. Between Father's desk and the chairs, opposite the door, was a sumptuous fire place, all stern and made of large granite stones set by a mason who treated cement like vanilla icing on an ostentatious layer cake. On the uneven mantelpiece was another plaque, its message framed in simulated silver, and every bit as unnerving as the one by the doorway.

> I do not speak rashly, but as I feel and think. I do not think that many priests are saved, but that those who perish are far more numerous. The reason is that the office requires a great soul. For there are many things to make a priest swerve from rectitude, and he requires great vigilance on every side.
>
> —St. John Chrysostom

Many were the times I'd asked Father Baptist about those plaques. Why those quotations in particular? Was he trying to scare people away? Or were they meant for himself?

His response was always the same. A wink. Just a wink. But an unsettling wink it was, and it seemed to whisper, serene but somewhat seriously, "Considering that I am a priest, is it not a good idea to put a warning label on the bottle?" But of course all he ever did was wink. Once he cleared his throat knowingly, but never satisfied my curiosity.

Actually, there was a third plaque, a small one only a few inches high in a copper frame—real copper, I think—tilted on the far edge of his desk between hand-carved statues of St. Anthony of Padua and St. Thomas More, where he or his visitors could easily see it. It was no secret that he had inked all these plaques himself. The strokes had that intense wobbliness of the amateur calligrapher.

"Do we walk in legends or on the green earth in the day-time?"

"A man may do both," said Aragorn. "For not we but those who come after will make the legends of our time. The green earth, you say? That is a mighty matter of legend, though you tread it under the light of day!"

—J. R. R. Tolkien
The Lord of the Rings

About that quotation he had spoken freely and often, and will do so later in this story, so I will leave it for now.

Anyway, I was standing at the window, my left hand resting on the desk for support, just inches away from DO WE WALK IN LEGENDS. My back was to I DO NOT SPEAK RASHLY, but for reasons I couldn't explain I couldn't get THE MOST EVIDENT MARK OF GOD'S ANGER out of my head. I was watching kind Mr. Folkstone out in the garden through the window. He was tending St. Thérèse's roses with more care and wisdom than I'd ever mustered when I used to do those sorts of chores. Mr. Folkstone, one of those "in lieu of" parishioners I mentioned above, had arrived providentially minutes after Father Baptist rumbled away in the '57 Buick. Whew. He had just turned his attention to the problem of St. Joseph's gardenias when the doorbell rang.

It being Millie's morning off, I hobbled and huffed to the front door and found two moderately dressed, broad-shouldered, stern-faced men on the stoop. One was older than the other by at least ten years, and the one he was older than couldn't have been more than thirty, thirty-five. The older one opened his mouth as if he was going to say something but the younger one cut him off.

"You Father John Baptist?"

I noticed the older one scrunching his lips.

"Do I look like a priest?" I asked.

"I don't know," said the younger guy. "What's a priest look like?"

"You see a collar?" I asked, pointing to my neck.

"Yeah," said the young guy, scratching his own.

"I mean a Roman collar."

"Huh?"

The older one rolled his eyes.

"Never mind," I said. "No, I'm not Father Baptist. He's out. Who may I say called?"

"Sergeant Wickes," said the younger man, flashing me his badge. "This is Lieutenant Taper. Homicide. And you are ...?"

"Martin the gardener," I said. "Also chauffeur, chief cook and bottle washer when Millie the regular cook and house-keeper is out, which she is, and—"

"May we come in?" Still the younger guy. I wondered what the older one's voice would sound like if he ever got a word in. His eyes were so articulate. "We would like to ask you a few questions."

Knowing and caring nothing about laws, rights, all that kind of stuff, I showed them into Father Baptist's study. The older guy, Taper, paused for a moment before entering, his eyes fixed on THE MOST EVIDENT MARK OF GOD'S ANGER by the door. As they seated themselves, the younger one pulled out a notebook and licked the tip of his pencil—the eraser end. The older guy considered the ceiling as an apparent source of patience.

"Last name?" barked Sergeant Wickes.

"Mine? Feeney. That's with an E-Y."

"Mm-hm. You worked here long?"

"Going on thirty years."

"That make you about fifty?"

"Almost."

"How long has Father Baptist been assigned to this parish?"

"He wasn't assigned." I tried resting my right hip on Father's desk, but found the maneuver uncomfortable. "He bought it."

"Beg your pardon?"

"He purchased this property shortly after Bishop Brassorie was promoted. Let me explain. Monsignor Brassorie—that was his title before the archbishop gave him a pointed hat—was the pastor here. Had been for years. Before that he was the assistant pastor, and before that he was just a twerp fresh out of the seminary on the heels of Vatican II."

"I thought they, you know, move these priests around every so often."

"Usually, but not in Brassorie's case. I don't think he ever worked in another parish. Why, he was here back when I started working as the maintenance superintendent for the parish school, too, back when we had a parish school, back when there was still a convent behind the rectory, back before the nuns went coo-coo—"

"Coo-coo."

"You know, took off their habits, abandoned prayer and embraced self-fulfillment seminars."

The sergeant grimaced. His older partner grimaced, too, but the effect was not the same.

"So," sniffed Sergeant Wickes, "you knew Bishop Brassorie."

"No."

"Huh?"

"I knew him when he was a priest and then monsignor. I've never spoken to him since he left St. Philomena's and became a bishop, and he's never tried to stay in touch with me."

"I see. Bad blood?"

"Meaning?"

"Were you on bad terms with him? Did you have a falling out?"

I shifted my weight to my other leg, and fumbled with my cane. My fidgeting probably made me look nervous, suspicious, even guilty of something; but I couldn't help it. "Sort of. When the 'New Mass' came in I gave him a hard time. And I really griped when— Are you a Catholic?"

Sergeant Wickes glanced over at his older partner. It was the first time he'd taken his eyes off me. Again the grimaces, and again the effect was not the same. "Uh, well—"

"I knew it," I said, even though I didn't; but it always makes them wonder. "I can spot an ex-Catholic a mile away."

His eyes jolted back to me. "How could you—?"

"Never mind. Remember when the word went out in the mid-sixties that the Mass was going to be changed from Latin to English? Not all at once; but bit by bit. I thought it was silly, like putting a happy face on a Rembrandt with a crayon, but nobody asked me. Some of the parishioners seemed to like hearing the Mass prayers in English, but what English! My nephew from the Bronx speaks better than the Liturgical Commission. Even he would know that 'all glory and honor *is* yours' is bad grammar. Don't get me started. None of us knew where it was heading. Then directives started coming from the Chancery to move the Tabernacle from the center of the church to the side altar—"

Grimaces and knowing nods. The effect continued to be disparate.

"—and then the Communion rails came out. Well, guess who was assigned those nasty chores? Never have I been so

ashamed, but Monsignor Brassorie thought it was the best
thing since plaid paint. Then, when they brought in a demoli-
tion crew with jackhammers to demolish the high altar and
replace it with a picnic table, I finally started making noises.
Big noises. No, ol' Monsignor Brassorie and I did not get
along."

"You fought a lot?"

"Yep."

"Why didn't he fire you?"

I probably should have kept my yap shut, but as I said, at
the time I didn't worry much about laws and rights and such.
"He wouldn't have dared."

"Why?"

"Because I caught him the night he snuck in and hauled the
statue of St. Rita off in a wheelbarrow."

"He what?"

"He had decided that statues of Saints were passé. He said
they had to go, but even the parish liberals were reluctant to
trash them. After all, most of them were donated by their parents and pioneer families before them that helped build this
city around us. But Old Brassie—er—Monsignor Brassorie
was on a roll. One evening I saw him sneaking into the
church with the wheelbarrow from the garden. Naturally I
suspected he was up to no good—who needs a wheelbarrow in
a church in the middle of the night? I zipped to my room—I
could zip in those days—the same room I still occupy in the
south corner of the rectory with my very own entrance—and
got out my old Kodak with a whaduhyuhcallit lens and crept
in the side door of the church. It was too dark for pictures,
but I saw the whole thing."

"What was he doing?"

"Pulling down her statue from the side altar. He dumped
her in the wheelbarrow and rolled her right down the aisle and
out the front door."

"You're kidding."

"No. I followed him all the way to the Hyperion Bridge. It
was there on the bridge, under one of those bright new street
lamps, just as he was about to throw poor St. Rita over the side,
that I broke cover, got up close, and used the flash."

"What did he do?" Sergeant Wickes was into my story, I
could tell, in spite of himself.

"Blew his top. He turned red, then blue, then a shade of
green I didn't know he had in him. He demanded my camera, of course, and I wouldn't let him have it. I told him if St.

Rita wasn't back in her proper place at Mass the next morning, I was going to give the story to the *Times*. After that, he never crossed me, the innovations dwindled to a trickle and he and I spoke as little as possible."

"And the film?"

"What film?"

"The film in the camera."

"I never said anything about film."

"But—"

"It was just a bluff, but it kept him in line till his promotion."

"Are you making this up?"

"No. This kind of thing I could never make up."

"Then why do you look so nervous?"

"Because my back is killing me and I'm really uncomfortable. Nasty critter, arthritis. Would you mind if I went to the kitchen for some water and aspirin?"

"In a minute," said Wickes. "So how long after that incident did Brassorie make bishop?"

"Not long. Less than a year, I guess." The pain, the pain. "Shows you."

"Shows me what?"

The pain, the pain. "What kind of men get promoted in today's Church."

Wickes blinked. "When Brassorie became auxiliary bishop, was this parish within his jurisdiction?"

"Yes, of course. What do you expect? Peace on earth?" Pain, pain, pain. I pushed off from the desk and massaged my lower back. "Only to men of Good Will. Sergeant, I really do need that aspirin."

The older guy, Lieutenant Taper, stood up and spoke for the first time. "Mind if I come with you? I could use a glass of water myself."

"Sure," I said, reluctantly.

"You stay here," he told his partner.

Taper followed me as I huffed and hobbled out to the kitchen. I pointed to the glasses in the cupboard for him as I reached for the blue one I always leave on the counter next to the Arrowhead Water dispenser. It was one of the few extravagances in which Father Baptist indulged, and it was all on my account. He'd read somewhere that distilled water was good for arthritis sufferers.

GARDENING TIPS: Millie read somewhere that a ta-

blespoon of fruit pectin in a glass of unsweetened

grape juice twice a day is also good for arthritis

pain, but that's another story. And Mr. Folkstone

occasionally brewed a sickening tea made from

herbs grown in the church yard, but that's yet an-

other story. Better stick to this one ...

                                        --M.F.

"Sorry about my partner," said the lieutenant. "He's young."

"I know: he'll learn."

"Uh-huh. Anyway, my name's Lawrence J. Taper." He casually offered his badge for examination. "You can call me Larry."

"Lieutenant," I countered as I placed the bitter pills on my tongue. "And you're still a practicing Catholic—I can tell."

He seemed unimpressed with my insight.

I swallowed half a glass of water in one loud gulp. "I suspect, however, that you have gone along with all the changes since Vatican II."

He gave me a look that almost stopped the aspirin on its way down. For a second I almost thought I was playing eye-chicken with Father Baptist. "When you're in a rowboat," he said, "caught in a hurricane, can you really say you're going along with the storm? Isn't it, rather, the storm that is going along with you?"

I took another gulp and waited as the analgesic wave surged down my esophagus and broke on the welcoming beaches of my stomach. "So what did you follow me in here to ask me?"

"How is Father Baptist? How's he doing?"

I emptied the glass down my gullet and wiped my lips. "Why? Do you know him?"

"I thought I did," he said, filling his own glass. "Once upon a time."

3

"IF YOU PLANT AN ACORN," I was explaining to Lieutenant Taper, "don't be surprised if you get an oak tree." We were talking about the end result of the last thirty years of values-free education. Before that we had talked about all sorts of innocuous topics, from local politics through garlic festivals to traffic jams. I assumed that he was playing "good cop" to Wicke's "bad cop," buttering me up for more information on Bishop Brassorie and—much to my rising consternation—Father Baptist. "Funny how that works."

Just then I heard the front door open and close. It had to be either Millie returning from her morning shopping or Father Baptist returning from the Chancery.

"I understand your point," said Lieutenant Taper. "But see here—"

I missed what he said next because my attention was focused on the heavy footsteps in the entry hall. Definitely Father Baptist. While the lieutenant jabbered on, I poured myself another glass of water, listening all the while to the footsteps as they came down the hall and turned into the study.

"What did the Zen Buddhist say to the hotdog vendor?" I asked, counting down silently. Ten, nine.

"What?" blinked Lieutenant Taper.

"The Zen Buddhist," I said. Eight, seven, six. "To the hotdog vendor."

"I don't know."

Five, four.

"What?" asked Taper.

"What?" I asked.

"What the Zen Buddhist said. To the hotdog vendor."

Three. "Oh him."

"Yeah, him."

Two. "He said, 'Make me one with everything.'"

One.

"What the hell—?"

That wasn't Taper. That was Wickes. A sudden commotion erupted in Father Baptist's study.

Taper, unhampered by a disgruntled spine and an unco-operative walking stick, beat me there with ease. I came lumbering up behind him just as Wickes backed out the study door, his face pink and his eyes livid.

"That sanctimonious son-of-a-bitch in a cassock!" he was bellowing at his senior partner. "Spot an ex-Catholic a mile away? Him, too? What is it about me—? I'm trying to carry on an investigation, and he's trying to convert me back to the Faith."

"Just doing my job," came a voice from inside the study.

Taper stepped past Wickes into the room and approached Father Baptist who was standing by the fireplace, one hand resting on the mantel not far from I DO NOT SPEAK RASHLY. Their eyes met and locked as I limped toward the desk and leaned against it.

"Hi, Jack," said Lieutenant Taper.

"Larry," nodded Father Baptist.

"Huh?" gaped Sergeant Wickes from the safety of the doorway. "You know this guy?"

"Up until ten years ago," said Taper to his partner, "he was my superior officer."

Wickes made a sound. It was something like an old fashioned vacuum cleaner. I thought he was having a stroke, but when he didn't collapse I turned my attention back to *my* superior officer. Father Baptist a cop? I was as shocked as Wickes, but chose to contain myself and not aggravate my beleaguered vertebrae.

"It's been a long time," the lieutenant was saying.

"It sure has," said Father. "You're looking, well, not so well."

"I wouldn't talk. You look like ... bloody hell."

Father Baptist laughed. Not the deep, robust outburst of a man delighted with a hilarious notion; but rather the perplexed sigh of a man caught in a trap about which he has chosen to laugh rather than cry. "I've just come from a brief visit with the archbishop," he said, fingering the loose buttons of his cassock. "And do you know what he wants me to do?"

"Don't tell me," said Taper. "Let me guess. He wants you to start using altar girls."

"Heavens, if that was all. I'd have grounds for appeal. He wants me to conduct my own inquiry, under the auspices of the archdiocese of course. He wants me to come out of retirement and conduct a private murder investigation on behalf of the Church."

"The newspapers will love that. Chief Billowack will have a cow. What did you say?"

"I told him, respectfully of course, that it simply wasn't possible."

"And what did he say?"
"That all things are possible with God."

4

"I DON'T GET IT." Wickes didn't get much. "If collections were falling off to the point where they were gonna shut this parish down, why did Brassorie get promoted to bishop?"

Father Baptist heaved his shoulders. He was seated behind his desk with his hands folded on his abdomen. "That's 're-newal' for you."

"Being pals with the archbishop didn't hurt," I quipped from my corner.

"Is this true?" said Wickes, licking his eraser again. "Were Brassorie and Fulbright —?"

"Monsignor Brassorie and Archbishop Fulbright," said Father, clearing his throat loudly, "were in the seminary together." He emphasized proper titles, in spite of his personal disregard for the characters that held them. "You will have to discuss the depth of their relationship with the archbishop himself."

"But surely you had perceptions," said Wickes. "And if you're going to be butting into this case, you—"

"I am not butting in, as you put it. The archbishop requested my services—authoritatively, I'll grant—and I have until this afternoon to give him my answer, subordinately of course. Perhaps you can help me with that, Larry."

The lieutenant, seated next to Wickes, roused himself from some private reverie. "How so?"

"Tell me how Bishop Brassorie died. Precisely. The newspaper account was vague."

"That's our doing. We're keeping a lid on things for the moment. The circumstances are a bit, shall we say, bizarre."

"Indeed. You and I worked on a lot of strange cases, once upon a time. Surely the world has gotten worse in the last ten years. What do you classify as bizarre?"

Lieutenant Taper leaned forward. "Brassorie was found dead in the private chapel at his residence at St. Philip's Church. You know the place?"

Father Baptist and I exchanged glances. A private joke.

"Yes," he said. "The so-called church, anyway. I've never been inside the bishop's residence."

"Hm." The lieutenant was fishing for words. "He was lying face up on the floor, arms and legs spread wide."

"Tied down?"

"No. Positioned. He was clubbed on the back of the head, then arranged that way on the floor."

"A ritual killing?" said Father.

"Seems to be," said Taper.

"I am still waiting." Father brought his hands up to his face and rested his chin on his knuckles. "For bizarre."

"The blow to the head was not the cause of death. That was just to render him unconscious."

Sergeant Wickes opened his mouth to speak but Taper raised his hand to silence him. Taper was enjoying the prolongation.

"And?" said Father, shifting in his chair.

Their eyes met and held.

"The murderer then carved a triangle in the palm of the victim's left hand. About two inches tall, base toward the palm, apex toward the fingers. The amount of bleeding indicates the victim was still alive when it was done."

"A knife?"

"Yes. It was left on the altar, blood on the blade. Smudges, but no fingerprints—the killer probably wore gloves. Fancy little thing, beveled edge, like a miniature scimitar. Curlicues and bat's wings on the handle. We're checking to see if it was purchased locally."

"And the cause of death?"

"He drowned," said Taper.

Father's eyebrows went up. "Holy water?"

"Jägermeister."

"You're serious."

"Yes. Apparently the bishop's favorite beverage. His liquor cabinet was stocked with it."

Father grimaced. "Grisly."

"The murder?"

"Jägermeister."

"Don't like it myself. Apparently the murderer poured it down the victim's gullet until his stomach was full. It backed up into his lungs. Completely saturated."

Their eyes remained locked.

"Sounds like your kind of murderer," said Taper.

Father Baptist sighed, a long thoughtful sigh as if to whisper, agitated but sadly, "Considering our past escapades, Larry, you're really enjoying this, aren't you?" But all he said was, "Yes."

5

A NEW PLAQUE APPEARED in the rectory later that morning. Well, not exactly a plaque. Just a piece of cardboard stuck on the refrigerator door with a magnet shaped like a pair of praying hands. Now here was a meditation just before lunch:

> As a dog that returneth to his vomit, so is the fool that re-peateth his folly.
> —Proverbs XXVI:11

Millie didn't like it much, either. Back from her grocery run, and feeling as she did that no priest could survive more than a few hours without a woman's ministrations, she hrumphed as only Millie can. She, like everyone connected with St. Philomena's, was of the old school. "I hope that isn't permanent," she scowled, pouring our coffee as we sat at the tiny, wobbly table in the almost-as-tiny dining nook.

"I'll move it to my study," said Father, buttering his toast, "Just as soon as I get a frame for it."

"Framing vomit," she muttered contemptuously, going back to the stove. "What next?" She was an "in lieu of" cook and housekeeper, so she didn't fear being sacked for mouthing off.

"Speaking of vomit," I said, peppering my stew. "Are—"

"Grace," he interrupted, crossing himself. "Almost forgot. Shows you how distracted I am. Bless us, O Lord, and these Thy gifts, which we are about to receive from Thy bounty, through Christ our Lord. Amen."

"Amen."

"May the Divine Assistance be always with us."

"And may the souls of the faithful departed through the mercy of God rest in peace."

"Amen. St. Philomena."

"Pray for us."

"And St. Rita."

"Pray for us."

"In the name of the Father, and of the Son, and of the Holy Ghost."

"Amen."   I unfolded my napkin.   "As I was saying, speaking of vomit, are you ever going to tell me how you went from chief of homicide in one of the fastest-growing cities on earth to being a priest in one of the poorest, most run-down, ramshackle parishes just ten blocks from where you used to work?"

"A longer journey than you think."   Father was shaking salt on his buttered toast. He's the only one I've ever seen do that, other than myself when I tried it once and gagged. "Is it so important?"

"Oh, I guess not. It's just that if our lives are going to be turned upside down and inside out over the next who-knows-how-long, it would be nice to know. Besides, I thought we were friends."

"Have you ever told me what you did before you became the gardener here at St. Philomena's?"

"I've told you everything bad I've ever done. You're my confessor."

"Of course. But I make it a habit to forget everything I hear in the confessional."

"Great, than you know less about me than I do about you."

"No doubt."

"Actually, I'm a sultan escaped from the Arian inquisition in Baghdad."

"Oh really. I'd forgotten."

"So are you going to tell me or not?"

He put down his fork, risking Millie's wrath. She expected full-blown concentrated eating from the men in her domain. To her, setting down a fork was like the US leaving a war un-finished—as it had all too often in recent years, in her con-certed opinion—or Washington only going half-way across the Delaware and deciding that revolution wasn't his Bailiwick after all.

"Yes," he said, locking his fingers in a tight knot over his steaming cup of coffee. "I was Jack Lombard, Chief of Homicide, for almost ten years. Then came the Morgenstern-Barclay case—ugly, violent, and scandalous. So many 're-spectable' citizens involved, so many bloody hands, such sinister motivations. When it was over I took a vacation, and never returned."

"You couldn't take the heat?"

"No, I couldn't understand how people could be so utterly evil, and how God could let it be so. My wife, Christine, had died the year before, and I had much to think about. It's the same question wiser men than I have been pondering for centuries on end: why are things the way they are, and if there is a God, why does He allow it? Why does a good woman die of cancer while despicable men prosper in their corporate palaces? So I decided to put my detective skills to work on the bigger problem."

"And?"

He brought his locked fingers up to his neck and pointed to his Roman collar with his thumbs. "This."

It was my turn to say, "Hm."

"The five years I spent in the diocesan seminary were the worst in my life. I was the token 'late vocation' amidst a gaggle of twerps. What they teach young priests, these days! They would have kicked me out for sure if I'd revealed my mind, but I kept silent. Ordination was my goal, so I answered the examination questions with their modern heresies, lied my way through the orals, and buttered up the overbearing matrons who run the place. The night before my ordination I made a general confession to old Father Riley that almost gave him a heart attack. Thank goodness the confessional is still sacred. And then, Heaven help me, a month later—"

"You bolted."

"—I came out of the closet. Me, a Traditionalist. I was kicked out of my first three parish assignments for preaching about Hell from the pulpit. The archbishop almost took my faculties away. Then I took my pension from the police department and bought this old church which was about to be sold by the archdiocese to a Pentecostal sect. From that point on you know more than anyone."

"Well, sort of."

"You know enough for the moment, at any rate. As soon as you finish, we've got an appointment with the archbishop."

"We? Now I'm included?"

He unlocked his fingers and gave me a look that seemed to whisper, vacant but knowingly, "You are my chauffeur, my right-hand-man, my chief cook and bottle washer when Millie's away." But all he said was, "Of course."

6

PROPER ETIQUETTE REQUIRED that visitors kiss the ring on an archbishop's hand.   His Grace, Archbishop Morley Psalmellus Fulbright, did not dispense with this formality as we entered his office. One of the country's most liberal prelates, he was renowned for his innovative ideas and his consummate dislike of anything that smacked of pre-Vatican II thinking. Begone, reverence to God, the Saints, Angels or Man—except himself, of course, and his bloody ring.

The Chancery building in which we met him was a three-story brick affair, an elegant edifice with a long and charming history—and therefore destined for the iron ball of renovation by year's end. An architect's mock-up of the structure intended to replace it was on display in the foyer. It looked to me like a bunch of sky-blue twisto-matic ice cube trays carefully stacked up and then shaken into disarray by an earthquake.

The circular foyer with its echoing marble floors was the hub of the Chancery building, just as the Chancery was the administrative hub of the archdiocese. From the center rose a sweeping, spiraling stairway which wound its way up through the buzzing hive of ecclesiastical activity, with scores of offices emanating from the central core like spokes in Ezechiel's wheel. As Father Baptist and I ascended the stone steps, we rose through layer upon layer of imposing offices, their hidden activities announced in gold-leaf letters on frosted glass set in thick mahogany doors.   SECRETARIAT FOR MINISTERIAL SERVICES, SECRETARIAT FOR PARISHES AND PASTORAL SERVICES, UNDERSECRETARIAT FOR EDUCATIONAL AND FORMATIONAL SERVICES, and so on.   The higher we climbed, the bigger the doors became, the more I wished we had taken an elevator, and the more the departmental efflorescence took on a judicial bouquet.   ARCHDIOCESAN TRIBUNAL, announced a double-wide door with an ornate brass knob, followed by SYNODAL AND PRO-SYNODAL JUDGES, PROMOTERS OF JUSTICE, and DEFENDER OF THE BOND. The sheer weight of the bureaucracy was dizzying, not to mention my hyperventilation and spinal traumatization from the steep ascent.

When we finally reached the monumental portcullis of the huger-than-huge OFFICE OF THE ARCHBISHOP, Father paused.

"Nervous?" I rasped, and then wished I hadn't.

Father Baptist glanced at me with those unnerving eyes which seemed to whisper, reserved but profoundly, "Considering that in my past life I perused the oily machines of power daily, Martin, and considering further that every morning in my present station I call God down from Heaven onto the altar at Mass, do you really think that anything beyond these ostentatious doors could intimidate me?" But what he said was, "Place on thy heart one drop of the Precious Blood of Jesus and fear nothing."

"Hrm," I mumbled, examining my shoe laces.

"Pope Pius IX," he added, hand on the doorknob. "And remember what we discussed in the car on the way over here."

One of them had come untied.

GARDENING TIPS: Among the things Father Baptist and I had discussed "on the way over" was the matter of proper forms of address with respect to ecclesiastical higher-ups.

A priest, he explained, should be called "Father," and a monsignor "Monsignor." That much I already knew.

A bishop, he continued up the ladder, is normally referred to as "Your Lordship" or "My Lord" in other countries where they're not self-conscious about a revolution. In the United States, however, the appellation has become "Your Excellency"--obviously an Americanism cooked up in order to allow us to pretend that we don't have an aristocracy. ("Your Excellency," by the way, is also applied to governors, ambassadors, and even the president of the country at formal functions.)

An archbishop, on the other hand, rules over the ecclesiastical equivalent of a Duchy and is therefore formally addressed as "Your Grace." Naturally, in the United States, where the theories of power-flow have become somewhat convoluted, an archbishop is often referred to as "Your Excellency" by those who are not "in the know," as I hadn't been before "the ride over" in the car.

We needn't deal with cardinals since there wasn't one in the archdiocese at the time. We'll leave "Your Eminence" for another story—perhaps the sequel, if we ever get that far.

Of course, another thing that Father Baptist and I discussed "on the way over" was the matter of the size of my mouth, the flavor of my comments, and what I might consider doing with them in the interest of smooth sailing in turbulent waters. The above lesson in ecclesial etiquette, in other words, was rendered unnecessary—but nevertheless provided a stimulating backdrop to the meeting. Observe:

—M.F.

The waiting room beyond was a pretentious display of arched ceilings, looped curtains, pulpous carpets, and gaudy estate-sale paintings. It all went swirling by like a bad dream. A squat little receptionist with vertically-mounted nostrils honked an unintelligible greeting and motioned for us to follow her down a wood-paneled hallway to a solemn-looking door marked CONFERENCE ROOM. Inside awaited the archbishop's precious kiss-me ring and a curious assortment of people who will have a lot to do with the rest of this story.

"Ah," said the archbishop, extending his ring in our direction as we entered. The humungous amethyst glittered coldly under the fluorescent lights, much like his citrine eyes. "Father Baptist."

"Your Grace," said Father, reverently osculating the orb.

"And this is my associate, Mr. Martin Feeney."

I cringed as the ring homed in on me like the giant squid stalking the Nautilus. Oh well, I had promised to behave.

"Mister ... Feeney," said the archbishop.

I bowed, much as it pained me, gave his precious gem a reluctant snaky smack while mumbling something between "Your humble servant" and "Don't touch my mustache." As I straightened, two things happened. First, one of my vertebrae slipped with an audible thunk. Second, my eyes locked for a heart-cinching second with His Grace's. Did I imagine it, or was he regarding me with the same frigid loathing he had just lavished upon Father Baptist? Guilt by association and amalgamation. I was honored.

"I've heard of you," said the archbishop.

I almost answered, "And I of you," but caught myself, true to my word. What did he mean, he'd heard of me? The answer dawned as he detached himself from my ring-lapping duties and turned to face his entourage, but never mind.

"Let us all be seated," he said, indicating a round table the size of the carousel at the Santa Monica Pier. Instead of mounting painted horses impaled on posts that went up and down, those in attendance arranged themselves in high-backed leather chairs around the rim of the table. The effect was the same. The archbishop and his cronies sat around the far hemisphere so they could focus their collective dislike at the two of us at our lonely end. I kept track on a scratch pad:

Their Side: (The New World)

Our Side: (The Old World)

GARDENING TIPS: I'll grant that my notion of "taking the minutes" is perhaps unique, but the similarity of the situation to a grossly mismatched
chess game was all too obvious. All the king's
horses, men, women, and jackals against two lonely
pawns.

(Yes, yes, I know: chessboards are not round,
and players on each side share the same color.
All these considerations are discarded in my
sketch in favor of balance, subtlety, and my desire to draw a collar on Father Baptist's pawn
while keeping myself pure.)

                                        --M.F.

"Allow me to introduce everyone," the archbishop began. "Father John Baptist, Mr. Martin Feeney: surely you know my auxiliary bishops. Allow me to present His Excellency, Bishop Jeremiah Ravenshorst—"

"Your Lordship," nodded Father.

"Jerry," nodded back Bishop Ravenshorst with a sociable though vaguely German rasp.

"—and His Excellency, Molmar Mgumba."

"My Lord," said Father.

"Mole," smiled Bishop Mgumba, his deep voice resonating like an African drum.

I suppose this was an attempt to put us on a first-name basis. Fat chance.

The archbishop came to an empty chair. He glared at his watch, hrumphed, then addressed the cream-skinned redhead seated at his far left. "Cheryl, still no word from Bishop Silverspur?"

She shook her head no, her long hair gracefully swirling around her slender, ivory neck. The gesture reminded me of sea birds flying in slow motion. "I'm worried. I called his hotel in Toluca Springs, but the clerk said he hasn't checked in."

"You mean hasn't checked his messages."

"No, he never checked in."

"That is strange," hrumphed the archbishop. "Marsha, have you had any luck?"

Across the table from the redhead, a long-legged vamp with pallid white skin and lacquered black tresses shook her head no, too. But the effect was entirely different. She looked more like a porcupine doing the twist. "He isn't answering his cell phone."

"I wonder what's become of him." Shrugging, he went on with his introductions. "In any case, Cheryl Farnsworth is Bishop Silverspur's personal secretary. I've asked her to attend in his absence. And Ms. Marsha Dukes is my administrative assistant."

A polite round of appropriate nods.

"Next to Marsha we have Ms. Madeline Sugarman, my chief parish advisor, and my liturgical coordinator, Ms. Stephanie Fury."

I couldn't help but notice the similarity of style and manner of the three women on the archbishop's right—our left. It was more than a mere proliferation of S's and M's, but a distinctive *esprit de corps*, a mutually-held agenda if you will.

They were skirting fifty and shared a predilection for post-industrial chill: dark colors, shellacked hair, somber makeup, stainless steel necklaces, and triple-D shoulder pads. I've always questioned shoulder pads on women as a fashion statement, since the male equivalent would be hip-cushions—and one can only imagine the hideous implications of something as nightmarish as that.

Offsetting the dominatrixes was Miss—no ring, I noticed, and no pads—Cheryl Farnsworth, the only woman present who had not been introduced as "Ms." Later-mid-forties, and wearing her years warmly, she was also the only female present who wore pastel colors, daybreak makeup, and a gold charm around her neck on a fine chain. She seemed out of place, on this chessboard anyway.

While my eyes darted back and forth between these female forces, it suddenly dawned on me that I knew one of them, and only too well. Snatching my pencil, I jotted a note to Father Baptist:

Ms. Stephanie Fury used to be Sister Veronica Marie!!!!

He nodded but made no comment.

"Monsignor Goolgol."

Monsignor Goolgol, of "one principle too few" fame, was—um—perhaps a mahjongg tile or a tiddlywink someone had left behind on the chessboard by mistake. He didn't seem to belong, either.

"And finally, co-counsels for the archdiocese, Mr. Shlomo Brennan—"

Jewish mother, Irish father—now there's a couple of laps in the ol' gene pool for you.

"—and Mr. Guilio Gerezanno."

GG for short? I didn't know the Mafia had made inroads into the Los Angeles hierarchy.

These two men nodded gruffly. Rooks, obviously. Castles of cold stone.

The two pawns at this end of the table nodded back in silence, Father Baptist out of a serene lack of being impressed, and me because I had promised to keep a lid on. Nonetheless, my lid slipped a bit whenever I glanced at Sister Veronica Marie, who now called herself Ms. Stephanie Fury. She and I went way back to the days when she was principal of the grammar school at St. Philomena's, back before the nuns went coo-coo.

There was a prolonged silence as both sides sized up each other.

Finally the archbishop spoke. "I have met with all my available staff and auxiliaries, and we agree."

Monsignor Goolgol cleared his throat with a spasm of his protruding Adam's apple.

"We agree," repeated the archbishop sternly. "Father Baptist, have you reconsidered my proposal?"

Father Baptist nodded.

His Grace—Morley to his associates, and Psam (spelled "Psalm" and pronounced "Sam") to his confederates—shifted his bulk in his high-backed throne. "And?"

"You are technically my superior," began Father Baptist, "even though I have been officially on leave for over three years."

"Yet," blurted Goolgol, "you continue your nefarious activities at St. Philomena's."

"I fulfill my vocation to the best of my abilities," said Father, "yes."

"Still pushing the Tridentine Mass, I hear." Ms. Stephanie Fury made a face as if she'd just found a cockroach between her molars with her tongue.

"As per the directives of Pope Pius V, yes. The right of every Catholic priest to say it has never been abrogated."

"And what of the Mass of Paul VI?" sneered Marsha Dukes.

"That is not the matter under discussion," said Father calmly. "My opinions on the subject are no secret. Some day I will have to give account not just for my opinions, but for my actions, to Almighty God—"

"As you say," interrupted the archbishop, aware that his lackeys were shifting nervously, their angry movements making burping noises in their soft leather chairs. "That discussion will keep for another time. For the present, I want to know if you'll take this assignment."

"As my superior you may order it," said Father Baptist. "And I will, of course, obey. I have spoken with the police and the crime you wish me to investigate is certainly stimu-

lating. I would like to settle two things, however, at the onset."

"Yes?"

"First, why do you want an internal investigation? The police are more than adequate for the task."

His Graciousness began contemplating his fingernails.
"There are certain, ahem, sensitive issues surrounding Bishop
Brassorie's, shall we say, private life."

"I was not aware that bishops have a private life," said Father Baptist, his voice raised perhaps one eighth of a semitone.

"Well, he did. And it is to remain private. We cannot have
a cold-blooded killer running loose in the Chancery, and we
certainly can't risk any more scandals."

"Yes," nodded Father Baptist, his voice back to its original,
even pitch. "Scandal seems to have become Mother Church's
middle name."

Again with the burping chairs.

"Hrmph," muttered the archbishop. "You will be discreet
as befits your office, and if you live up to your reputation,
you will find the killer."

"I will be discreet within the law," countered Father Baptist.
"And I will do my best to uncover the murderer's identity,
but I will not withhold evidence from the police if justice will
be hampered by such omission, or if the law so requires. And
be clear on this point: I will not protect the murderer, no matter who he or she may turn out to be, no matter who is implicated, no matter whose heads will roll."

The archbishop glared at him, veins popping all over the
whites of his eyes. "Agreed, of course." Which meant he
most certainly did not, but that's prelate-speak. "Your second point?"

"There is the matter of my fee."

My cane almost slipped from my hand. The archbishop
almost slipped out of his skin. His lackeys almost slipped out
of their chairs in a fanfare of leathery belches.

"What's this?" said Monsignor Goolgol, pushing his sinking glasses back up his nose. "How dare you?"

"I dare nothing," said Father Baptist matter-of-factly. " I
am on leave, and have been for several years. I get no salary
from the archdiocese to run my church—"

"That's because you don't officially have a church,"
snapped Sister Veronica Marie, lately Ms. Stephanie Fury.

Well, well, well. Sister hadn't changed much since I'd last had dealings with her. Some habits, if you'll excuse the pun, are hard to break.

"I have a flock," said Father Baptist, his eyes riveted on his superior. "And they are faithful Catholics all. As am I. And if I am to take time away from my duty—my sworn duty—I expect to be paid. Otherwise, I'm still on leave."

"Preposterous," sneered Monsignor Goolgol.

"The worker deserves just wages," countered Father Baptist. "My rate will be three hundred dollars per diem. That means per day."

"We know what it means," snapped Monsignor Goolgol. "And I object wholeheartedly."

Father Baptist ignored him, keeping his eyes on the archbishop. "Plus expenses. To be paid at the end of each business week. We'll forgo the retainer up front. I do not work Sundays under any circumstances, nor will I be deterred from carrying out my parish obligations—unless you wish to assign me an assistant who wants to say the Latin Mass on weekdays? Confessions every evening, also according to the Old Rite? No, I didn't think so."

"Have you no Eucharistic ministers," glared Ms. Fury, "to conduct communion services in your absence?"

Wrong question, Stephanie. I held my breath. Father swallowed perspicaciously, a dissolving kind of gulp which seemed to whisper, stern yet evenly, "Considering that in 1344 King Philip of Valois had to receive a special dispensation from Pope Clement VI just to touch the sacred vessels, Madam, what do you think my opinion regarding the handling of the Blessed Sacrament by lay men and women would be?" But he simply ignored her.

"I also will require," he continued, "a letter over your signature ordering all Catholics in good standing—lay, clerics, nuns, former nuns, whatever—to give me their full cooperation."

The archbishop sighed. "Anything else?"

"I would appreciate the use of a new car with automatic transmission. My driver, Mr. Feeney, has severe arthritis and the clutch on our old Buick is killing him."

I was still holding my breath, my heart pounding against my ribs.

There was a long silence, like the kind that enshrouds a cemetery, the subliminal but distinct rattling of old bones permeating the peace.

"Done," said the archbishop, much to the gasps of his entourage. "Pick up what you need at the motor pool tomorrow."

I exhaled.

Father Baptist and I rose to leave. No one spoke further.

Down in the foyer, I regarded Father Baptist with renewed respect. "You were rather bold in there."

"You were uncommonly silent."

"It was almost as if you had something on the old goat, blackmail of such an insidious nature—"

"You know perfectly well the cards I hold. You supplied them."

Just at that moment, Ms. Stephanie Fury came striding by, casting a glance our way that could freeze the San Gabriel River. I couldn't resist, having been seated on my tongue for almost half an hour.

"Oh Sister Veronica Marie," I called to her back.

She whirled. "That's not my name any more, Mr. Feeney."

"It's what God calls you, Sister."

I watched her rigid, padded shoulders disappear through a door marked PRIVATE.

7

"BLESS ME, FATHER, FOR I HAVE SINNED; it has been forty-six, no, forty-seven hours—"

"Yes, yes."

"—since my last confession."

I peered at the little window, his diffused shadow playing eerily against the grill cloth. I could imagine him looking down at his hands as if to whisper, alert but wearily, "Considering that you're really talking to God, vile creature of earth, you'd better make this good." What he actually said was, "Go ahead, Martin."

"Well, I didn't tend the roses like you told me to. Mr. Folkstone came along just after you left, and he was so anxious to help, and—"

"Disobedience toward your lawful superior," he summarized. Unlike most priests, he was in no mood for spurious details and lame excuses. He was no counselor. With him it was just the sins, Mack, just the sins. "Yes, go on."

"I also disobeyed you four, no, five times by badgering you about why you had never told me you were once a big shot homicide detective—"

"Yes, yes."

"—before you became a priest. And you gotta'dmit—"

"I gotta'dmit nothing." Whenever he mimics my peculiar contractions, I know he's getting furious, even though he'd never'dmit it. "Further acts of disobedience. Continue."

"And I lied to that police detective about the photograph of St. Rita about to be tossed off the bridge—"

"You lied about who was in it?"

"Only partly, but more so about its existence."

"Explain."

"I told him I snapped the picture but implied that I didn't have film in the camera. And I just conveniently forgot to mention who else was in the picture, helping Monsignor Brassorie that night."

I heard a muffled sound through the grill. It almost sounded like approval, but then he said, "Bearing false witness. Anything else?"

"Uh, no. That's it."

There was a long pause. "Are you sorry for your sins?"

"Well ... Yes. I am sorry, at least for disobeying you. As for lying to the cops, I guess I am, but—"

"Are you truly sorry?"

"... Yes, Father."

"Okay. Regarding your dishonesty and rampant disobedience, say the Stations of the Cross."

"But Father—!"

"You need the exercise, not to mention humility. In addition, regarding the police, you will make reparation by telling the truth—"

"But—!"

"—but only at such time as I tell you to do so. Do you understand? Only when I tell you, and not before."

"Yes, Father."

"Now make a good act of contrition. We'll pursue moral theology regarding the lesser of two evils at another time."

As he began the Absolution in Latin, I recited the same prayer I'd said in confession since I was seven, paying close attention to each word that I spoke. "Oh my God, I am heartily sorry for having offended Thee; and I detest all my sins because of Thy just punishments; but most of all because they offend Thee, my God, who art all good and deserving of all my love." The final words promised the impossible, but as Our Lord assured us, nothing is impossible with God. " I firmly resolve with the help of Thy Grace to sin no more, and to avoid the near occasion of sin."

GARDENING TIPS: Someone once asked Father why

Catholics go to confession over and over again,

knowing that we're going to continue sinning. His

answer: "You take a shower every day, don't you?"

—M.F.

As usual, we concluded our prayers in unison. "Amen."
"Go in peace," he said.
"Thanks a lot," I said, commencing the agonizing process of getting up from the kneeler, just so I could go out and subject myself to the torture of clumping up and down the length of the church, following Jesus to Calvary.
Twenty minutes later, as I hobbled and huffed to the four-teenth and last Station, JESUS IS LAID IN THE TOMB, I saw Father Baptist kneeling at the step between the gates of the altar rail, the same rail I had helped him re-install three years ago when he first came to St. Philomena's. Between my sanc-timonious mumblings, I caught a few snatches of his prayer to Almighty God:
"I loved it so, and the thought of it excites me even now, even though I left it all behind for You. Is it now Your Will that I take up the torch again, or am I just being tempted by my old ways? Please show me what You want of me, and help me to obey. Not my will, but Thine be done."
As quietly as I could, which admittedly is on par with a three-legged elephant dancing on a bowling ball, I came up beside him, not understanding his prayer, but keenly aware that he was in turmoil. I'd never heard such distress in his voice. Anger, yes. Disgust, yes. Fury, regret, even a tinge of bitterness now and then. But such poignant self-searching distress, never.

"Whatever's on Father's mind," I whispered at his side. "Amen."

"Thank-you, Martin."

"Thank God, Father."

"Amen."

Thursday, June Eighth

Feast Day of Saints Medard and Gildard, Twin Brothers, Bishops, and Martyrs (558 AD)

8

ALL OF WHAT I'VE RECOUNTED so far took place on Wednesday, June seventh, the day after the murder. The following morning, Father said morning Mass wearing black vestments, much to the surprise of the score or so of parishioners in attendance.

"This will be a Requiem Mass offered for the repose of the soul of Bishop Eugene Brassorie," he announced at the foot of the altar stairs, "formerly pastor of this parish."

Mr. Turnbuckle, a venerable gentleman who had been a parishioner at St. Philomena's during Old Brassiere's pastorate, rose from his pew in a huff and stomped out. The rest of those present dutifully riffled the pages of their missals in search of the text of the Mass for the Dead. The deceased, of course, was in absentia, residing in the police morgue.

"In nomine Patris," intoned Father, making the Sign of the Cross as he turned to face the altar, "et Filii, et Spiritus Sancti. Amen."

GARDENING TIPS: Most modern Catholics, used as

they are to funerals presented in sweetness and

white, thoroughly basted in the assumption that

just about everyone goes to Heaven, would find the

Traditional Requiem Mass with all its references

to the possibilities of Purgatory and Hell dis-

turbing, if not downright barbaric. Funny, it was

to the tune of this ancient, foreboding Rite that

our greatest and most beloved Saints shuffled off

their mortal coils, not assuming for a moment that

Heaven was theirs, but working out their Salvation

in fear and trembling to the last breath ...

Sorry I mentioned it. Death bothers us all, no

matter how we wrap it and tie the bow.

--M.F.

In any case, Bishop Brassorie got a Requiem complete with Dies Irae whether he liked it or not. Perhaps on the Day of Judgment he'll let us know.

An hour later, as Father Baptist and I were settling down to Millie's diligently supervised breakfast of bacon, eggs, and her secret biscuits with bits of corn and onion throughout, the doorbell rang.

"That will be Lieutenant Taper and his agitated young partner," said Father, pouring cream into his coffee. "I told you to expect them, Millie."

"And what are you going to do for breakfast tomorrow if I feed them today?" she grumbled crossly, lifting several bacon strips from the frying pan with a pair of tongs and setting them on a paper towel to suck up the grease.

"The Curé of Ars lived on a couple of potatoes a day," said Father, sipping his coffee. "Three on special occasions."

"And how long did he live?" I asked over my shoulder as I hobbled from the kitchen to get the front door, not at all sure I would welcome such a regimen.

"Into his seventies, I believe."

"At least he had potatoes," I heard Millie growling as I went down the hall. A woman who always has the last word, our Millie.

Lieutenant Taper was at the door, but with his back to me. He was looking down the front steps to the curb where Sergeant Wickes was talking to two men and a woman who were attired in those slick, broad-shouldered jackets peculiar to newscasters. A van with a big eyeball painted on the side pulled up across the street, and out popped a guy toting a video camera.

"The press," explained Taper over his shoulder. "You'll be seeing more of them."

The reporters caught sight of me and bolted past Wickes, rushing up the steps as a single, hungry organism. Taper whirled and pushed me inside, a maneuver which felt to my spine like an inept recruit being surprised inadvertently at the wrong end of a cannon. I oomphed, but kept my balance. Taper shut the door in the encroaching faces of inquiring minds.

"Sorry," he said, seeing me still frozen in my oomph.

"Me too."

The doorknob rattled a few times, then stopped. Then came a peculiar knock—three shorts, two longs, and two shorts. Winking at me, Taper opened the door, allowing Wickes to slip inside. "Hey!" yelped one of the reporters outside as Wickes slammed the door behind himself with perturbed finality.

"Twede and Sumpf of the *Times*," he grimaced, "and that woman is Tylie Lee of the *Reader*. Two more TV units just pulled up."

"Have you seen the morning paper?" asked Taper, helping me to straighten.

"Yup—ulp!" As I said before, the way up is invariably longer than the way down.

COP-TURNED-PRIEST TURNS COP announced the article—two columns, five or so inches, just right of center, blurry photo of Father Baptist and my right leg leaving the Chancery, page one (continued on page three). The Church was regaining Her stature, albeit via a persona non grata. The newspaper was spread open on the kitchen table, Jacco Babs' by-line bisected by a brown arch left by Father's coffee cup. Jacco Babs was a Pulitzer contender who always covered the really sensational murders.

"So much for the solitude of my rectory," sighed Father, retrieving the last strip of bacon from his plate as Millie snatched it from the table. "Did you guys leak the story about me?"

"You know better than that," huffed Taper, adjusting his pants indignantly. "That's a Chancery spill, oily and everything."

"You gents seat yourselves," said Millie, motioning with her full hands. It was an order, not a suggestion. "I'll get you some coffee."

"Thank-you," said Taper, settling down opposite Father.

I maneuvered myself into my customary chair at Father's left elbow, leaving Wickes the spot by Father's right. Wickes looked nervous—proximity to the sanctimonious son-of-a-bitch in a cassock, no doubt.

"As soon as we finish, we'll go to St. Philip's," said Taper, gently rolling the silverware off his napkin and spreading the cloth on his lap. Rather cultivated for a cop. I thought police detectives ate with a paper napkin crushed in one hand, a plastic fork in the other, a gob of mustard lodged in the the corner of their mouth, and a couple of toothpicks sticking out of their breast pocket. "You'll want to see the murder site."

"How many people reside there?" asked Father, slipping the bacon half-way into his mouth and biting down with a loud crunch.

"Aside from the bishop," said Wickes, "twelve, but most were away at the time." He fidgeted, cleared his throat, then pulled out a small spiral notebook and started sifting through the pages. Really nervous.

"Of the three resident priests," explained Taper, "only the pastor, Havermeyer, was there. The other two were away at some sort of archdiocesan retreat in Toluca Springs. A big deal. Fulbright ordered almost all his minions to attend, leaving most parishes without priests from Thursday of last week until they meander home sometime today."

"So Catholics throughout the archdiocese went without Mass on Sunday," winced Father, chewing noisily. "Just lay-run communion services."

"Yeah," said Taper. "That's all we had at my parish. You'd think Mass would be more important than some work-shop—"

"Seminar on the fairway," I interjected. "The latest in ecclesiastical innovation. Mass pales to insignificance by comparison. It's called 'sand trap theology,' or 'putter stutter.'"

"Of the five nuns who live at St. Philips," continued Taper, smiling, "only one stuck around. The other four were also at the Springs—"

"—for the special workshop on Eucharistic caddies," I interrupted. "Extraordinary Eucharistic caddies. They pass out golf balls while the priests get lost in the woods."

"Anyone else?" asked Father, ignoring me.

"Two seminarians," concluded Taper, "helping out while on temporary leave from their studies—reconsidering their vocations or something like that. We talked to one, David Smoley—he was the one who found the body, by the way—but the other one, Joel Maruppa, has been missing since the night of the murder. His family hasn't heard from him. We're making inquiries."

"The cook and the housekeeper had the night off," added Wickes. "And the housekeeper, a Latino woman, probably illegal, quit the morning after the murder—scared stiff."

"Joel Maruppa," said Father, swallowing pensively. "That sounds familiar. Is his father's name Albert?"

Wickes rattled his pages and then tapped one with inflated definitude. "Yes, that's right. You know him?"

"Albert Maruppa was the electrician who installed the new lights in the sanctuary when I first came to St. Philomena's. Devout man, devoted wife, large family, active in the parish. His sons helped him. I suspected that the youngest had a vocation. Albert moved his family to the other side of town—near the coast, I think, when the Barkinbay Beach housing development opened up. He still attends Mass here occasionally."

"Yeah, that's him," said Wickes.

Father Baptist was reviewing the math in his head as he inserted the rest of the bacon strip into his mouth. "So only three, perhaps four people were there the night of the murder. I don't suppose they saw or heard anything?"

"Nope."

"And the murder took place at what time?"

"Between six and eight," said Wickes, consulting another page of his notebook, "best we can figure."

"Any hunches?" asked Father, wiping his fingers on a napkin.

"Not really," said Taper. "A few vague suspicions, nothing concrete."

"I used to value your vague suspicions almost as highly as hard evidence. One usually led to the other."

"Not this time."

"Anything else?"

"Well," said Taper, reaching into his breast pocket and pulling out a color photograph, "there is this. I couldn't show you until your connection with the case became official, at least at your end. You understand that, from ours, Billowack considers you persona non grata. Mucho non grata."

"A designation with which I am all too familiar," said Father. "What do you have there?"

The lieutenant handed him the photo. "We found a piece of cloth clutched in the victim's right hand. Raw cotton, probably hand-woven. The pattern's embroidered with needle and thread. The colors in the fibers are uneven, and the lab says the dyes are homemade, distilled from flowers and plants."

Father laid the photo flat before him. The legs of my chair squawked as I shifted myself into a better position to see the curious clue.

"The actual size of each square is two inches on a side," said Taper. "The photograph makes them look smaller. I recognized those characters in the second and third row as runes—surely you remember the Morgenstern-Barclay case—so I called in that witchcraft specialist—"

"Not that Ambuliella woman," said Father.

"Yeah," said Taper, "the same one we used before. Ambuliella Beryl Smith."

Father looked up at me and sighed. "A real gem in the methodological tiara of scientific criminology."

"I thought so," said Wickes, unaware of Father's sarcasm. "She explained everything. First she clarified that there is white magic and black magic, and good witches and bad witches."

"According to A. E. Waite," said Father, "in his *Book of Black Magic and of Pacts*, there is no such distinction between the white and black arts."

"You've read such a book?" asked Taper.

"It's on the shelf in my study," said Father. "To be forewarned is to be forearmed."

"And having wrists isn't a bad idea either," added the gardener. Boom cheesh.

"But," said Wickes, "Ambuliella is an expert, a professional, and she said there's a big difference—"

"I can imagine," said Father. "Listen, Sergeant. I, too, am
a professional. Magick—spelled with a final K to distinguish
it from sleight-of-hand parlor tricks—is the attempt to make
circumstance conform to the human will, using means impro-
portionate to the end. In this sense, the saying of a few
words—HOC EST ENIM CORPUS MEUM, from which our detractors derive the slur, 'Hocus Pocus'—is the highest form of
magick. A mere piece of bread is transformed into the Body,
Blood, Soul, and Divinity of Our Lord Jesus Christ. The same
is true of all the Sacraments. A thimble of water transforms a
damned creature into a Son of God. A few words clean a
man's soul of mortal sin, and so on."

"But—" said Wickes.

"But there are lower forms of magick, too," continued Father. "The kinds A. E. Waite was talking about. Some be-
nign, some not. In its basest form, black magick, it becomes
the antithesis of the prayer of Jesus, 'Not My will, but Thine
be done.' Every valid prayer to Almighty God must be uttered with this underlying assumption. I say Mass each day
because I choose to do so, but only because He has made it
clear that it is His Will that I do so. It is He, not I, Who is in
charge. Recognizing this fact is the second step toward wisdom, fear of the Lord being first. Any magick, pagan or
ceremonial, which seeks to circumvent the divine plan is therefore antagonistic toward it. All such magick is irrevocably
black."

"Clearly," said Wickes, "aside from your brand of 'Hocus
Pocus,' there are good magical intentions and evil ones—"

"Clearly," said Father, "'good' must be defined as that
which is in accordance with God's Will. Try that definition
out on your Ambuliella woman and see where it gets you. No,
Sergeant, pursuing God's Will at the expense of one's own is
the proper vehicle for Man's efforts. Nothing else can be
called 'good.' In every other instance, only one power is in-
voked. But let us not drive the point into the ground."

"It always seemed funny to me," I mused, being a gardener
and very adept at driving things into the ground, "that in the
movie, *The Wizard of Oz*, after the Good Witch of the North

asked Dorothy, 'Are you a good witch or a bad witch?' she
went on to explain that good witches are beautiful and only
bad witches are ugly."

"Martin," said Father.

"Which either means the Good Witch was terribly near-
sighted, or Dorothy was obviously—"

"Martin," said Father again.

"But let us not drive the point into the ground."

Father rolled his eyes, then turned them toward Wickes. " I
interrupted   you,   Sergeant.   What   did   Miss
Smith—Ambuliella—have to say about this swatch of cloth?"

Wickes opened his mouth to speak, then thought better of it
and closed it. Then, throwing caution to the wind, he opened
it again. "At first she was reluctant to talk about it, but then
she relented." Oh yeah, right, as if he broke down her resistance. "For one thing, she told us which end is up. We'd
been turning it around for hours trying to make sense of it.
Secondly, the runes in the second and third row stand for R-E
and R-T-H respectively. That fancier symbol in the upper
right corner is a combination of two runes, back to back—P
and S, both inverted sideways. That's how witches sometimes
combine their initials into a single character. Sort of like a
trademark or signature."

He pulled a gold felt-tipped pen from his coat pocket and
jotted some squiggles authoritatively on a blank sheet in his
notebook. Then he spun it around for us to see.

$$P + S = ꟼ + Ɔ = ꟼƆ = ꟼⱣ$$

$$ᛕ + ᛝ = ᛩ + ᚠ = ᛪ = ᛟ$$

"Nice pen," said Father.

"Huh?"

"You were using a pencil yesterday."

Wickes looked dumbfounded. "I forgot my pen yesterday.
Now, as for these runes —"

"The symbol in the upper right corner of the cloth obviously stands for PS or SP," said Father. "The five dots
around it are merely ornamental. Notice also the downward-

pointed triangle in the top row. The ancient symbol for the hermetic element, water. And of course, there is the pentagram."

"You understand all this stuff?" asked Taper, amused.

Father smiled, also amused. "I do remember the Morgenstern-Barclay case, and since then my research has taken me down many curious paths. Besides, anyone who's read Tolkien's *Lord of the Rings* is bound to be familiar with runes. What surprised me is that you didn't observe that I immediately knew which way to turn this photograph when you handed it to me."

"I must be slipping," said Taper.

Irritated, Sergeant Wickes slapped his notebook shut and jammed it into his jacket pocket.

The lieutenant pulled a sheet of paper from his pocket and unfolded it. "Sybil, one of the lab gals, generated this translation on her computer using some kind of graphics program. The image is almost identical except the runes have been replaced with English letters. You're welcome to this copy, but I guess you don't need it."

"Actually," said Father, glancing at it and handing it to me, "it might prove useful."

As I examined the peculiar pattern, I was reminded of many wars of Boggle waged between Father Baptist and myself on cold winter nights before the fireplace. I didn't recall a single time that I had won a match. A single round, occasionally, but never a game.

I was also aware that my eyes kept being drawn to the symbol at the bottom like a moth flirting with a candle, fluttering this way and that but always drifting inexorably a little bit closer—

—entranced by the bobbing light, fascinated with the deadly flame.

Father's voice intruded upon my reverie, even though he was speaking to the police officers. "Did Miss Smith offer any suggestions as to the meaning of this pattern?"

"Part of some kind of spell," said Taper. "You talked to her at greater length, Sergeant."

Wickes cleared his throat, wary of Father's uncanny ability to cut him off at the pass. "Apparently in something called 'Pentoven Magick,' a witch or warlock weaves their heart's desire symbolically into a cloth. It's important that conjurers make all magical objects by hand so as to impart something of themselves into the talisman. Don't let the idea of embroidery lead to the assumption that the perpetrator is a woman. This could have been done by a man."

"Quite right," said Father.

Wickes gulped, encouraged but wary. "In fact, according to Ambuliella, since the lines on this cloth are pretty straightforward—no extemporaneous frills, no decorations or embellishments around the edge—she thought this looked more like a man's effort than a woman's."

"Hrmph," snorted Father.

Wickes gulped again.

"I have a question," said I. "Or rather an observation. I am no expert, but at the risk of driving something even further into the ground, I've always heard that a pentagram with one angle pointed up is good or white or whatever, while an inverted pentagram denotes evil."

"What's your point?" asked Taper.

"It's just that the pentagram on this cloth is pointing up, and yet this spell seems to be connected with a murder. Maybe I'm just still stranded in Oz."

"May be," said Father.

Taper nodded his agreement.

"The word 'Pentoven' is new to me," said Father, "but not the practice of a 'casting cloth' or 'witching quilt.' They are generally round or square. From the irregular shape and incomplete words on this cloth, we can assume this to be a fragment cut from a larger pattern. This is only part of a puzzle. Assuming we are indeed dealing with a witch or warlock—"

Just then Millie arrived with two plates balanced on her left arm and two coffee mugs tangled in the fingers of her right hand. Somehow she got it all on the table without a spill.

"Anything else?" she said, blowing a wisp of gray-streaked hair from her rosy face.

"More than enough," said Taper graciously. "This is wonderful."

There was a thump under the table. Wickes perked up, first glaring at Taper and then smiling up at Millie. "Oh yes, wonderful."

She looked down on them fiercely. "It would've been better if we had potatoes."

"Then potatoes you shall have," said Taper, prying apart one of her secret biscuits and savoring the steam. He shoveled some butter in with a knife. "My wife, Lucille, is quite a gardener. She should get a ribbon or something. Got a whole produce section in the back yard. Wait'll you see her russets. Huge, like footballs, and more than we'll ever eat. Great for soup or stew. I'll bring some the next time I come over." His last sentence was muffled by the biscuit in his mouth. Not so cultivated after all—but charming nonetheless.

Millie stood like a frying pan Amazon, sizing up our guests. "Hrmph," she said as she turned to strut away, wiping her hands on her checkered apron. "And where are we going to get leeks?"

That's our Millie.

9

BISHOP BRASSORIE'S RESIDENCE was at one of those relatively new church structures distinguished from a savings and loan only by the corpus-less cross over the main entrance.

About that private joke that passed between Father and me at the mention of St. Philip's a few pages back. First, it must be remembered that Father Baptist had a life before he became a priest—a career in homicide, a wife, and who knows what else he never told me. In his present status, he considered it pious and prudent to avoid off-color jokes and innuendoes. As for me, I've admitted that I was a sultan escaped from the Arian inquisition in Baghdad—which is to say I've never married and don't intend to but always leave the door ajar for the unexpected. In working and living so closely with Father a lot of his pious prudence inevitably rubbed off onto me. I can only hope that unsavory conclusions won't be drawn regarding two men, albeit experienced in the ways of the world and having left most of it behind, who nonetheless shared the perception that the church at the corner of Dominion and Delmonico was shaped like ... uh...

Let me put it this way. The joke was that the first time we saw the place after its construction, we had just gone through a drive-thru for lunch and Father was sipping a soft drink through a straw. We were passing by in the car when I looked up and said, "Ah, that must be St. Fallopia's." Coke came out his nose.

The anterior looked exactly like a biology textbook frontal cross-section illustration of the human female reproduction facility—right down to the bell-tower bulges which were dead ringers for ovaries. I can't imagine anyone seeing the structure and thinking otherwise, yet I've never heard anyone else mention it. One of our city's most glaring and obviously cherished secrets.

The rectory was a wing of that very building, a sprained limb sprawling off to the left in a conundrum of the slanted beams and skewed lines so favored by aficionados of ultra-modern post-mortem architecture.

I think Wickes kind of liked the place. As we climbed the steps in front, cement slabs embedded with rainbow sparkles, he kept eyeing the splatter-pattern windows and zigzagging quarry work with a glint of appreciation. Either that or he was still dazed from that knock he got on the head when we left the rectory at St. Philomena's and had to push our way through the microphones and video cameras to the black and white police car parked at the curb.

"Of course," Father Baptist was saying, "we both know I have no official capacity, even with all the archbishop's posturing."

"There was a time," mused Lieutenant Taper, "when the archbishop of so great a diocese could summon the mayor to his office and bawl him out for a misplaced expletive in a speech before the barkeeper's association; or stop the presses to prevent scandal; or even halt production of a morally objectionable movie with a phone call. But that was four prelates back and before Vatican II."

"You're beginning to sound like him," spat Wickes, jerking his head in Father's direction with a crack of his neck. I wished I could do that. "Are you going Trad, too?"

"Careful, Sergeant," said the lieutenant. "You're revealing your age."

Wickes puffed his cheeks and fell silent.

I was never the kind of kid who nursed injured birds back to health, and I've never been accused of an excess of compassion except with respect to my own miseries, but I was starting to feel a bit sorry for Sergeant Wickes. He really couldn't seem to keep his foot out of his mouth. And that weighty ecclesial chip on his shoulder made him as lopsided as me, only with me it's spinal and with him it's personal. For the moment, however, I was mainly occupied with grunting my way up the glittering stairs, wishing I'd taken the wheelchair ramp instead.

The summit achieved, Taper turned left and led the way around the side of the nave—or what might have been called the nave if such terms still applied—toward the rectory, or what might now be called the "presiders' residence." The cement path slithered along the side of the building, circumventing clusters of inconveniently-planted palm trees, then moseyed around a ten-foot quartzite obeliskish sculpture with a spear through it entitled THOUGHT, and finally arrived at a door under a tilted triangular arch.

The lieutenant pressed the button, and something that sounded like a rusty gong in a manhole bonged inside.

After about a minute the door was opened by a woman dressed in a gray sweater and blue plaid skirt whose mouth was so tight I couldn't see how sound got out. "Oh," she squinted, if the verb could somehow be applied to speech. She looked from Taper to Wickes and back again. "It's you again."

She turned away, leaving us to close the door behind ourselves. A fly got in but I didn't mind. Without a word she disappeared down one of several hallways spraying off from the polyhedral entrance hall. The receding shuffle of her shoes on the thick carpet quickly merged with the pervasive undertones of the central air conditioning system.

"Housekeeper?" asked Father Baptist.

"Nun," said Taper. "The housekeeper quit yesterday, remember? This way."

"Wait a minute," said Father, pulling the front door open again. He dropped to one knee, his attention caught by something on the floor, a little patch of light brown wedged between the metal sill and the thick fibers of the deep-pile carpet.

"Looks like a small clod of earth," said Taper, kneeling beside him.

"Yes," said Father, peering at the little lump from various angles. "Would you mind having it checked?"

"No problem." Taper pulled a small plastic bag from his pants pocket and, using the back of his fingernail as a pusher, shoved the little lump inside. "May I ask what for?"

"Mineral content," said Father, rising to his feet. "Possible chemical flags, plant seeds, spores, anything to identify an area in the city where it might have come from."

"Do you know how many people come in and out this door each day?" said Wickes.

"No doubt many," said Father. "Now, which way did you say?"

"There," said Taper, motioning toward the passage on the right.

It was a long, arched tubular sort of affair with irregularly spaced doors on both sides. After fifty feet or so it opened up in a huge atrium. More like paradise in a biosphere, complete with towering trees and hanging vines that would have pleased Tarzan. Immense tinted glass skylights glimmered four stories above our heads, and hidden valves sprayed jets of water in fine mists to keep all the leaves glistening and the humidity equatorial.

We followed a path of crunchy Hawaiian black sand that weaved among tangles of colorful tropical plants, crossed a wooden bridge over a noisy brook, and came upon a man in a Giants sweatshirt standing in a small graveled clearing between two claws of coiling hybrid plants from another planet. His jeans were either old and faded or new and pre-faded, and on his feet he wore a pair of those Mexican sandals with tire treads for soles.

"Hello," he said, looking up from the book in his hand. "I'm Monsignor Havermeyer. I've already met the gentlemen from the police. You must be Father Baptist."

"Yes," said Father, "and this is my associate, Martin."

"Associate pastor?"

"No, I just associate," I said, shaking his hand.

The monsignor looked puzzled for one second and then turned back to Father Baptist. "May I have a word with you?"

"Of course."

The monsignor gave the rest of us a look that said go away. Taper and Wickes complied. Habitually disobedient, I just shuffled a few steps back to the bridge and pretended to meditate on guppies amidst the bubbles in the gurgling brook.

"This is terrible," said the monsignor.

"Did you know the bishop well?" asked Father.

"No." The monsignor ran his fingers back through his whitening hair. He was no older than Father Baptist, but he wasn't wearing his years as well. "Rarely saw him. He never offered to say Mass, or to help with anything for that matter. Scooting around town on Chancery business most of the time. When he was here at all, he kept to his suite of rooms upstairs. And, uh—"

"Yes, Monsignor?"

"As for his evenings, well, I've heard—you know, just talk—that he went out a lot at night. Often on foot, not in clerical garb. I never saw this personally, you understand. In a building as big and sprawling as this, it's very possible not to see someone coming or going. David and Joel—"

"The seminarians."

"—yes, they would know more about his activities than I. It was David that found him, poor kid. When he came and got me the other night he was white as a sheet."

"Where were you?"

"In the library, watching television."

"I see."

"Madeline Sugarman, the archbishop's parish advisor, has a talk show on cable every Tuesday and Thursday night. It's called 'Spotlight on Community.'"

"I didn't know that."

"Yeah, well, it's nothing spectacular but I was bored—plus I knew I'd be asked how it went. Most of the regular residents were in Toluca Springs that night."

"So I understand."

"I had a touch of flu so I bowed out. They've been trickling in all morning from the retreat, but naturally they can't help you. There weren't many of us here when Bishop Brassorie, you know, uh—"

"Yes, I know."

"Sister Charleen didn't go to the Springs with the others, but she was out that night. She works on Madeline Sugarman's show. That leaves myself, David, and Joel, and Joel has disappeared. I'm worried about him. What if whoever murdered the bishop, uh, did something to him, too? How did they get in? And there I was, just watching television while the bishop was, while the murderer was—"

"And you heard nothing unusual."

"As you'll see, the bishop's quarters are up there on the top floor, and the library is over there at the other end of the building on the ground floor. No, I didn't hear a thing."

"Any idea why Bishop Brassorie was here and not in Toluca Springs for the retreat?"

"No. He never told me, not that we spoke much."

"I have some questions I'd like to ask Sister Charleen and David Smoley. Is there some place I could use? An office perhaps."

"Use mine—I rarely do. It's over thataway."

"Thank-you. I'm on my way to see the bishop's quarters. Would you be so kind as to tell them to meet me at your office in, say, twenty minutes? I'll speak to them individually."

"Surely. Oh, and Father Baptist—" Havermeyer puffed his cheeks and let them collapse. Then he rubbed his chin, scratched his ear, and massaged his neck. Then he repeated the cheek inflation exercise. I got the impression he was finally about to say what he'd been waiting to say in the atrium since before our arrival.

"Monsignor?"

"I understand you say the, uh, Tridentine Mass." He whispered the word, "Tridentine."

"Yes."

The monsignor wrapped his arms around himself, just above his middle. "I was ordained just as the Novus Ordo came in, but I remember the Old Mass from before, ever since I was a kid. I wish ... that is, I'm just curious. How do you get away with it?"

"I don't know what you mean. I simply follow the directives of Saint Pope Pius V as he clearly stated them in *Quo primum*. Every priest of the Catholic Church has the right to say the Tridentine Mass in perpetuity. No bishop can overturn a papal privilege, even if the Pope in question lived four centuries ago."

"Really," gurgled the monsignor, surprised.

"Really," said Father. "So I'm not getting away with anything, as you put it. In fact, you could follow suit."

"I'd, uh, it's just that, well—" The monsignor coughed to clear an obstruction in his throat.

Father Baptist lowered his voice until it was hard for me to hear, but I got the gist. "Why don't you come by St. Philomena's, just to observe? Mass every weekday at six thirty, Sundays at eight, and a High Mass at ten-thirty—"

"Heavens," sputtered Monsignor Havermeyer, examining his Tijuana road-hugger all-weather-tread sandals. He had to bend over somewhat to do so. "I couldn't risk being ... if the archbishop ever ... I mean, I have my pension to consider."

"Well, there is that."

"I'm just, uh, sorry, you understand, um ..." His words faded into an inarticulate mumble. He was really fond of those sandals. They had ten thousand miles left in them at least.

"In that case, confessions are every day at five-thirty," said Father Baptist. "Except Sunday."

Monsignor Havermeyer looked up with a start, the muscles of his face coiling in outrage. But when their eyes met, and he saw that Father Baptist was dead serious—and deadly compassionate—his ire subsided.

"Maybe we can talk about this later," said Father. "If my rectory is too hazardous for your pension, I'll meet you somewhere else. For now, I'd better move on with these police officers."

"Quite right," said the monsignor, a wistful look in his eyes. "Of course."

Havermeyer wandered off thataway, leaving deep tread marks on the sandy path. The rest of us groped through the remainder of the jungle till we emerged at the bottom of a ramp that sloped upward in a gentle curve to the second floor—or was it the third? It was hard to tell in a building where concepts of perspective and balance had gotten snarled in the architect's convoluted mental blender.

The top of the ramp opened onto a kind of verandah overlooking the atrium through which we had just safaried. It reminded me of the Tomorrowland Terrace at Disneyland, a few plastic trapezoidal chairs and rhomboidal tables dotting the rubberized surface, facing no particular direction. At the far end was a large door crisscrossed with yellow police tape. As we approached I noticed an illuminated ten-digit keypad to the right of the doorway, and above it an engraved brass sign: BISHOP'S RESIDENCE, PRIVATE—NO ADMITTANCE.

"A real man of the people," I said under my breath.

"That's an electronic combination lock," said Taper.

"Nine-nine-nine," said Wickes, tapping the keypad. "Not very imaginative."

"Isn't that six-six-six upside down?" I asked, but was ignored.

The door popped open with an electric poof and then swung slowly and smoothly inward.

"No way to open this without the combination?" asked Father.

"Not without tools that would have left marks," said Taper. "See? No keyhole, no doorknob, nothing but a smooth hardwood door set in a metal frame. It's like a vault."

"Any other entrance?"

"An exterior door, just like this one, with an outside stairway. Lots of windows, but it would take a ladder to reach them, and none of them open—climate control, and all that."

"Both doors have the same combination?"

"Uh-huh."

"And who gave it to you?"

"The seminarian, David Smoley."

"And how did he come to know it?"

"He says he was Bishop Brassorie's assistant."

"I'll have some questions to ask him."

"Sure."

"Who else had access to the bishop's quarters?"

"We're working on that," said Taper. "Who knew the combination, and who knew who knew."

Father Baptist, then Wickes, ducked under the police tape. Taper, seeing me hesitate—ducking requires a nimble spine—kindly detached the strands from one side of the doorway and motioned me through. I nodded gratefully as I passed into the nether realms of Brassorieland.

10

"YOU'VE GOT TO BE KIDDING." The words just popped out of my mouth at the sight of the huge oil painting hanging on the wall in the living room. *The Rape of the Sabine Women* was a tea party by comparison. Patrons at a triple-X feature at "The Keep" on Sunset—never been there myself, but I've heard tales—would have blushed at the lascivious orgy portrayed above the marble fireplace ... well, maybe.

"Private life indeed," said Father Baptist, shaking his head sadly.

"And there's more to come," said Wickes, unable to keep a touch of adolescence out of his voice.

My eyes traveled around the room. It was beyond plush. It was downright sensuous. Silk drapes, humungous satin pillows scattered on enormous couches with billowing cushions and carpet piled so deep the Marianas Trench conceded defeat. There was a mirrored bar, a fountain encircling a buxom alabaster lass endlessly pouring water from a bronze jug, massive electrostatic stereo speakers, huge TV screen with ceiling-mounted video projector. And on the walls, paintings and more paintings.

Father Baptist averted his eyes. He bowed his head in what I thought was a moment of prayer. But after a long moment, I realized something on the carpeted floor had caught his attention. He began making little circular motions in the piles with the toe of his shoe, working his way back toward the entrance. There he knelt down and ran his fingers through the fabric.

"More dirt?" asked Taper.

"No," said Father, pulling the front door open by means of a recessed handle on the inside and looking at the rubber-nubbed welcome mat outside. "If you haven't done so, would you have your guys vacuum that mat and this area of the carpet just inside the front door?"

"I haven't, but I will."

"Where did the Bishop keep his shoes? The bedroom closet?"

"Funny you should ask," said Wickes. "He kept his shoes in this entry closet, right next to the front door. Apparently didn't like shoes indoors. I understand he made his guests take theirs off, too."

"Interesting." Father was already in the closet, massaging the carpet. Then he began rummaging through the bishop's dozen or so pairs of shoes, footwear for every occasion. "Would you have all these checked, too?"

"For what?"

"Whatever's on them."

"Okay."

"I take it, then," said Father, straightening, "that the bishop was not wearing shoes when he died."

"Indoor sandals. Sort of quasi-Japanese style."

"What days does the housekeeper—you said she quit?—what days did she vacuum the carpets?"

"We'll have to check."

"Do you want to see the bedroom?" asked Wickes, waving his arm vaguely in the direction of an arched double door.

"That can wait," said Father Baptist, adjusting his collar. "The chapel?"

"Over there," pointed Taper. "The blue door."

Father Baptist pushed through and we followed.

I didn't know what to expect, but I wasn't surprised. Bishop Brassorie's private chapel was roughly twenty by thirty, or fifteen by thirty-five, depending on what axis you measured—and that depended on what you defined as an axis. None of the porous cement walls—I counted seven—were straight, or even, or rectangular. I felt like I was in a collapsing egg carton. There were no religious paintings, statues, or Stations. No images at all save a splash of phosphorescent paint on the far wall that might suggest a soaring bird to a mind fluttering high on artificial flight-inducing substances. No Tabernacle, Sanctuary lamp, or any candles at all save one gnarly wax stump at one corner of the altar. Oh yes, the altar: a block of irregular basaltic rubble captured in cement with occasional swirls of graphite throughout for contrast. I've seen more inspiring drinking fountains at the city zoo. No missal lay upon it, nor altar cloth, nor anything that would give a hint as to its purpose.

The arched ceiling had a puckered appearance, dollops of mismatched lumps and chunks folding and stretching like chewing gum and culminating in an elliptical skylight of stained glass—sort of a sunburp pattern. The midmorning sun cast a splash of clashing colors on the floor, right on the spot where the deceased bishop's splayed outline was marked with police chalk. The mauve carpet was darkly stained around the head and torso, and the reek of stale liquor was downright invidious.

Father Baptist crouched beside the outline, searching. Then he was on his hands and knees, his nose almost touching the floor. "Any idea how many bottles it took to drown him? Looks like he coughed up a lot before he succumbed."

"We found over twenty empty bottles in the trash," said Taper, "but it's hard to say how many were already there before the murder. My guess, considering the size of the stain on the carpet, is a dozen or more."

"When was the trash emptied last?"

"I'll check on it." The lieutenant indicated a spot with his toe. "His chalice was right about here. The lab boys have it now."

Father moved down to the feet area, his fingers massaging the carpet as though coaxing evidence from the fibers. "Chalice, did you say?"

"The newspaper said something about a 'sundown liturgy,'" I commented. "Was he saying Mass?"

Taper tugged on his right earlobe. "We're not sure what he was doing. Mention a chalice and the newspapers make assumptions. That's why we didn't tell them about the witching quilt, or the knife on the altar. Imagine what they would have done with that. You'll want to see those items, of course, when the lab tests are finished. We'll have to release the exact cause of death to the press, which means Jägermeister will get some unwanted advertising."

"Uh-huh." Father was crawling around the base of the altar, nose to the floor. I'd never seen him in such a pose. "Your guys were thorough?"

"You bet."

Father Baptist froze. "Then how did they miss this?"

Taper and Wickes crouched down beside him. I peered over their shoulders, but couldn't see what they were gawking at.

"They didn't," said Taper, relieved. "There was more of it, which was tagged and taken to the lab. This little sprig just got left behind."

"Do you know what it is?" said Wickes. "Some kind of weed?"

"Parsley?" said Taper. "Perhaps rosemary. It has an interesting smell when you crush it." He pulled a handkerchief from his hip pocket and used it as a makeshift glove, pinching the specimen with his fingers through the cloth and lifting it from the indentation where the heavy altar met the carpeted floor. As he rocked back on his haunches I could see the little dry cluster of pale green leaves against the white cloth.

"Hyssop," I said.

The policemen looked up at me.

"I am an altar boy—and a gardener."

11

"ARE YOU THROUGH?"

Sister Squint, or rather Sister Charleen Vickers, was rising from her chair in Monsignor Havermeyer's office. She was fingering the quartz crystal hanging from a chain around her neck. It was not in the shape of a cross. "I've answered all this before. The police know I was not here at the time the bishop was murdered. I was at the television studio. I see no reason—"

"What day is the trash collected?" asked Father Baptist, oblivious to her impatience.

She gave him an irked but quizzical look. "Fridays. Why?"

"Did the housekeeper collect it all throughout the residence?"

"I don't know. I suppose she did. I've never noticed. Now I'd really like to—"

"Have you ever been inside Bishop Brassorie's quarters?"

"No." She scrunched up her face even more than it was already, and repeated a little louder than necessary. "No. If you don't mind—"

"Sister, you seem surprisingly uncooperative. Doesn't it concern you that a murder has taken place within the building in which you dwell?"

She looked from Father Baptist to Lieutenant Taper to Sergeant Wickes, skipped me, and went back to Father Baptist. " I don't see—"

"Neither do I," said Father, leaning back in his chair. "Since you're in such a hurry, we'll just have to continue this later."

She hesitated, started for the door, hesitated again, then stomped out.

"Maybe she doesn't like priests," commented Taper.

"Or Bishop Brassorie," said Father, scratching his chin.

"Or men in general."

Wickes was looking through his pockets. "Lieutenant, have you seen my pen—you know, the gold one?"

"No," said Taper.

"Sure you didn't borrow it or something?"

"Quite sure."

"Hm. I wonder where I could have left it."

"Upstairs?"

"Don't think so. No."

"You wrote in your notebook with it this morning," said Father.

"I did? I don't remember."

"At the breakfast table," I said. "The runic lesson."

"It'll turn up," said Father. "Let's see. Is that seminarian out there? Sergeant, please show him in."

David Smoley was a soft, chubby, pinkish, sweaty sort of lad, twenty-two, who looked like he could use a slice of chocolate cake for positive reinforcement right about then. He took his seat opposite the semicircle of caloric—I mean, choleric—inquisitors.

Father smiled, calm and cordial, yet firm. "I believe you've met Lieutenant Taper and Sergeant Wickes. That's my assistant, Martin. I'm Father John Baptist."

"Yes, I know. I've heard a lot about you."

"Really. What have you heard?"

The boy swallowed. "That you're, you know, a throwback."

"And what would that make Bishop Brassorie?"

David Smoley swallowed again. "Uh, I don't know what you mean."

"I'm curious as to your duties as Bishop Brassorie's assistant."

"I just, you know, did things for him."

"Office work?"

"Yes."

"Errands?"

"Uh-huh."

"Didn't he have a secretary?"

"Two. Mrs. Sapperstein and Ms. Brinkley."

Father turned to Lieutenant Taper. "Did they go to Toluca Springs?"

Taper nodded.

Father continued. "Regarding Mrs. Sapperstein and Ms. Brinkley, did the bishop have more work for them than they could handle?"

"I don't know what you mean."

"I mean, why did he need you?"

Smoley swallowed uncomfortably. "He didn't need me. I'm on leave, and he just, you know, gave me things to do."

"To fill up your time."

"Yes."

"While you considered your vocation."

"Yes."

"Ever polish his shoes? I mean that literally, of course, as in did he ever ask you to clean his shoes, take them out for repair, that sort of thing?"

"No."

I remember seeing a photograph once in *National Geographic* of a toad sitting on a hot plate—reptile sweat is considered a powerful aphrodisiac in some culturally-challenged parts of the world. I think it was Connecticut. Anyway, the expression of David Smoley's face reminded me of that poor critter. Funny, the questions didn't seem all that hard to me.

"Where were you Tuesday night, between six and eight?"

"I already told the police. I went to see a movie—two blocks away."

"That checks out," said Wickes.

"I'm sure it does," said Father. "Tell me, David, did the housekeeper have a regular schedule for cleaning the bishop's suite?"

"What? Oh, um, Thursday. No, Friday. I'm not sure."

"How did she get access?"

"Huh?"

"I can't imagine, with all this high-tech security, that the housekeeper would be given the combination to the bishop's front door."

David was kneading his knuckles. "Actually, Joel and me did most of the cleaning."

"Most?"

"Well, all."

"Good for humility and all that, I suppose."

"Yeah. And Mrs. Nulato—the housekeeper—refused to go in there."

"Did she?"

"She said the paintings were, um, kind of sinful."

"Ah, there is that. So when was the carpet vacuumed last?"

"I guess it was Friday."

"This is important. We need to know for sure."

"It was Joel's turn. You'll have to ask him."

"I counted seven wastebaskets in the bishop's suite. Who last emptied them?"

"I—I don't know. Joel, I guess. It was—"

"His turn."

"Yes."

"When was it going to be your turn again?"

David swallowed again. This time it almost didn't go down. "Uh —"

"How often did you go into the bishop's suite?"

"Oh, just about every day, I guess."

"Were you in there on Tuesday—the day before yesterday?"

"That was the day—yes."

"When did you last see the bishop alive?"

"'Round five-thirty, when I told him I was going out."

"Was anyone with him?"

David licked his lips. "Joel was."

"And when you came back after the show?"

"I went in to see if there was anything he needed before I —"

"Did Bishop Brassorie ever send you out to buy hyssop?"

"Huh?"

"Hyssop."

"Uh, I don't know what that is."

"Did Bishop Brassorie attend any kind of ground-breaking ceremony in the past, say, three days?"

"What? No, I don't think so."

"Construction site, something like that?"

"Not that I know of."

"Are there any buildings going up around this neighborhood?"

"Sure, next block east of here there's a new office building—almost completed. Over on Third."

"And where is Joel Maruppa right now?"

The seminarian's eyes went momentarily wide. "I don't—I don't know."

"David, is there anything you want to tell me?"

Something caught in the kid's throat, something thick and gooey. He shook his head.

Father sat back in his chair. "No doubt we'll be talking again."

Lieutenant Taper shut the door behind the lad. "I'd forgotten your peculiar style of interrogation, poking here, groping there. No apparent pattern. What did you used to call it?"

"Fishing," said Father Baptist. "Just fishing."

12

"SO WHAT DO YOU THINK?" said Taper as Wickes pulled the police car out of the parking lot.

"I don't know yet," said Father next to me in the back seat. "Will Chief Billowack let me look at your official files? The lab reports?"

"He'll huff and he'll puff, but he'll never forget that you were once his superior officer. Of course, he is a Methodist. Let me butter him up and see if he's approachable tomorrow."

"What about the hyssop?" asked Wickes, looking over his shoulder at me. I hate it when drivers do that. "What's that have to do with being an altar boy?"

"You should come to High Mass," I said, my eyes riveted to his eyes which should have been on the road but weren't. "Father begins by intoning the Asperges."

"The what?"

"The blessing of the people with holy water before Mass." I wanted to lean forward, grab his head, give it a sharp turn frontward, and hammer it into place, but just then he remembered that he was driving a car and turned toward the windshield without my assistance. Relieved, I took a deep breath and sang, "Asperges me," and then the choir's response, "Domine, hyssopo, et mundabor; lavabis me et super nivem dealbabor."

Of course, the effect was not the same as when Father and the all-volunteer "in lieu of" choir at St. Philomena's have a fire under them, which is just about every Sunday. My rendition was more like a fireplace bellows with a squeaky hinge.

"Meaning?" asked Wickes, just as glad that I had stopped singing as I was that he was watching the road.

"Thou shalt sprinkle me with hyssop, O Lord," said Father, "and I shall be cleansed; Thou shalt wash me, and I shall be made whiter than snow."

"In the Old Testament," I explained, "the high priests used hyssop branches to sprinkle sacrificial blood on the people. The words of the Asperges are from Psalm Fifty—Vulgate reckoning, the Protestant Bibles and the new twisted Catholic Bibles count the Psalms differently. Today priests use a metal sprinkler and holy water, but the words are the same."

"So it's unusual to find a sprig of hyssop in the bishop's chapel?" asked Wickes.

"Very unusual. Like I said, priests today don't use it any-more. In fact, most priests don't even use holy water. In fact, most priests don't even know their—"

"Then how do you know what it looks like?"

"Mr. Folkstone has been attempting to get an herb garden started under the kitchen window at the rectory. Basil, oreg-ano, parsley, that sort of thing. Hyssop is a mint, and I don't much like the taste—neither does Millie, thank Heaven—but it does smell nice in boiling water. Sort of a natural air fresh-ener. I use it now and then in my room when the rain seeps in and the rugs mildew."

"It has all kinds of religious significance," added Father. "As Christ was dying on the cross, He was offered a sponge dipped in vinegar on a branch of hyssop."

I nodded. "And it was often used by painters of religious art as a symbol of humility."

"You might have your men look around the bishop's suite for more," said Father.

"You think the killer left it," said Taper.

"I think we'd better find out."

13

"THANKS FOR THE LIFT," I said as I closed the police car door in front of the Chancery motor pool.

"If you're coming for breakfast tomorrow," said Father, crouching so he could address the detectives at eye level through the side window, "be sure to bring those potatoes."

"Gotcha," said Taper. "I won't forget. And I'll have Wickes stop for leeks on the way home."

"Right," said Wickes sarcastically, putting their car into drive.

"That would be wise," said Father, waving them off.

The motor pool was really just a public parking structure near the Chancery that had been purchased and enclosed by the archdiocese when its automotive needs had expanded in direct disproportion to church attendance. Funny how that works.

"Yeah, I got the memo," said Freddie, the cigar-sucking Coke-sipping ice-chomping overall-wearing stump of muscle

as he wiped his greasy hands on an even greasier rag. " I
pulled out that '93 Camry for you."

"Excuse me," I said, a bit wary of guys who chew ice.
"Do you have something higher?"

"Whadduya want, Bub, a Cadillac?"

"No, I mean higher off the ground. It's my back, you
see. Arthritis. I know Camry's are good cars but they're low
to the ground. You have to crouch to get in, and bend your
head down, and I can't do either. I need something I can step
up into."

"Hm," he said, looking around his domain. "Ain't got
no vans right now. They all got checked out for the party in
Toluca Springs, and haven't been returned yet. They should
be dribbling in throughout the day. Maybe tomorrow."

"A van would be overkill," I said. "We don't need anything that big."

"There's the Jeep, but—"

"That Cherokee?" Metallic gold, four-wheel drive,
enormous all-weather tires, automatic transmission, way up off
the ground and—best of all—fun. "That would be great."

"Hold your horses. Father Spindle up at St. Cyprian's
uses that buggy a lot when he goes skiing."

"It looks like a '93."

"'94, but—"

"Maybe it's time for Father Spindle to requisition a '95,"
I said. "All right with you, Father?"

Long pause. For a moment I thought he was going to
give me a spiel about how off-road vehicles and the duties and
dignity of a priest could not coexist in the same sentence.
Then I realized he was simply lost in thought.

"What? Oh, sure, Martin. Whatever makes you comfortable."

"Done," I said.

"But—" butted Fred. Then he smiled, his incisors worn
clear away by glaciation. "Oh hell, let Father Spindle brave
the mountain roads in a Honda Civic, for all I care. Father
Baptist, I've heard about you."

"The murder investigation?"

"Naw—I mean yeah—but what I mean is your little
church and going back to the Latin and all. I'd like to come
over on Sunday but my wife, you know, she plays guitar in
our parish's so-called music ministry. Don't tell her I told
you this, but I heard one of the parish kids call them the
'Ever-Twangin' Mostly-Saggin' Steel-Pluckers.'"

"Perhaps you'll get away some day," said Father. "When you do, come pay us a visit. Thank-you, Freddie, for all your help."

"Ah, skip it. Father, could I have your blessing?"

"Of course."

14

I PARKED THE JEEP NEXT TO THE BUICK in the little parking lot behind the rectory at St. Philomena's. There was no garage, or even a carport, just five parking spots marked CLERGY—a reference to a long-gone day when St. Philomena's actually had that many priests on hand. Father was already out of his side, through the wrought-iron gate, past the tangled jungle of untamed vegetation behind the church, and well on his way up the brick path that wound through the garden by the time I had grunted and groaned my way to a standing position next to the car. As I crouched back inside to grope for my cane, I noticed a motion out of the corner of my eye.

A reporter, I thought.

As I straightened, cane in hand, I took a long look across the lot toward the two-story building that had once been the convent and was now a Best Western motel. The cypress bush at the near corner was still waving slightly. There was no breeze.

Someone had been there, watching us. I was sure of it.

15

"TO THE EMPRESS OF ALL THE AMERICAS," said Father, holding up a flute glass brimming with champagne.

"To Our Lady," said Pierre and Edward and Arthur and Jonathan, hoisting their glasses high. I took the pledge years ago, so I was drinking ginger ale—but in a flute glass, it was close enough. "To Our Blessed Mother."

The glasses clinked, the beverages sipped, and the Mother of God so honored, we settled back down into our seats. It was a few minutes before nine o'clock Thursday evening, and we were in Father's study. Kitchen chairs had been brought from the dining nook to accommodate everyone. A small but inviting fire crackled in the fireplace, even though it was summer—rain or shine, the rectory tended to be chilly at night.

Millie, of course, had retired.

"As I was saying, Father," said Edward. "Ever since I read that book, I look at everything differently."

"I agree," said Arthur. "When you look at life through the lens of true doctrine, nothing will ever be the same again." He took a deep, noisy sip and laughed broadly. "It's great."

"Emperors and paupers," intoned Pierre with a far-off twinkle in his eye and a lofty lilt in his voice, "queens and chambermaids, philosophers and simpletons. The spell of the True Faith has ever captivated the minds of the high and the low."

"The Church ennobles everything She touches," said Jonathan, continuing the incantation in the same exalted tone, "transforming pagan warlords with all their debaucheries into gallant knights with their golden codes of chivalry."

"To the doctrine," said Jonathan.

"The doctrine," said Edward.

"Extra ecclesiam nulla salus," said they all. Me, too.

This, I'll grant you, is not the kind of conversation in which four single men—not to mention a priest and a gardener—generally engage on a Thursday evening over drinks, but that's what was so interesting about these fellows. Even though there was a grandeur to their tone, perhaps even a hint of condescension in their manner, they were absolutely sincere.

"The part about Father Michael Mueller," said Edward, "it's just amazing. The fight he had with the Paulists. Then being silenced by his own order, the Redemptorists."

"And how Cardinal Gibbons futzed with the Baltimore Catechism," added Jonathan. "And got away with it."

"I loved the author's reply to charges of intolerance," said Arthur. "'It is not intolerant at all to insist that words mean what they say.'"

"To words meaning what they say," toasted Edward.

"Amen to that," said they all.

"I've said it before and it's worth repeating," said Father, leaning back in his chair and savoring a moment of paternal pride. He really enjoyed their company, and more so their zest for the Faith. "*Desire and Deception* by Thomas A. Hutchinson is the most important book to be published in the

last hundred years. Charlemagne Press should be congratu-
lated for their courage in bringing it to light. You've done
yourselves a great service by reading it, and more so by ab-
sorbing it."

"To 'D & D,'" toasted Pierre.

"To 'D & D,'" cheered the rest. Clink.

Before I go on, I should explain about Jonathan Clubb, Edward Strypes Wyndham, Pierre Bontemps and Arthur von Derschmidt. They were single men, ages twenty-five through
forty (I just listed them in age order, Jonathan being the
youngest), who came to drink champagne—port on cold rainy
nights and scotch on special occasions—smoke cigars, and
talk Church with Father Baptist. None of them lived close to
St. Philomena's, but they came to Father's Latin Mass every
Sunday and on Holy Days of Obligation. They came
promptly at eight on Thursday evenings—several bottles in
hand—chatted until nine, sang songs until nine-thirty or so,
and then went out bar-hopping. Ah, the stamina of youth.
Oh, and they invariably wore tuxedoes in the evenings.

"To the Knights," toasted Jonathan.

"The Knights Tumblar," cheered the rest.

Actually, it was their peculiar pronunciation of "Tumbler."
That's what they called their little gentlemen's club.

"How about a song?" announced Jonathan, clearing his
throat with a swish of bubbly.

"In a moment," said Father, rising from his chair. "First I
want to talk with you good fellows about something. Something important. I need your help."

They lowered their glasses and listened respectfully. There
was no mistaking the tone of Father's voice and the look in
his eye. They were accustomed to slipping from frivolity to
solemnity and back again.

"As you're aware," began Father, "my services have been
requested by the archbishop in the matter of the death of
Auxiliary Bishop Brassorie. I have appreciated, by the way,
your self-control in keeping jokes on the matter to a minimum."

"All except Pierre," said Edward. "He can't help himself."

A chuckle made its way around the room, but they settled
quickly back into attentive silence.

"There was a time," said Father, "when I had a whole division of detectives working under me, and boy did we get
things done. Now I have no staff other than Martin, whose

loyalty and character are above reproach, but who will agree when I say he's limited in legwork and short on investigative skills. Still, I am not without assets—angelic, not bureaucratic—and as for resources, I have some of the most remarkable comrades a detective could ever imagine. You gentlemen are a most valuable resource to me. You have given me much hope in these dire times, and now I must ask for more. Call it a favor."

"You name it," said Jonathan. "We'll move Heaven and earth to do it."

Father Baptist eased himself back into his chair. "Are you gents familiar with the Palmetto district? The area around St. Philip's."

"Not exactly our part of town," said Edward. "Or is it?"

"Having never been there," said Arthur, "how would we know?"

"I sense an adventure," said Pierre. "It's in the air."

"Of a sort," said Father. "What I want you to do is concentrate your drinking efforts in the bars in that district for the next week or so."

"Not exactly the kinds of places we'd normally go," said Jonathan.

"I realize that," said Father. "I hate to say it, but your formal wear may not be appropriate in this instance."

"Then you'll need to give us your dispensation," said Pierre, fingering his lapel.

"Granted," said Father. "You'll have to play the apparel game by ear. Mainly what I want you to do is listen."

"For what?" asked Jonathan.

"A few key words and names. Look, it would not be prudent for me to fill you in on all the facts of this case. It would color your perceptions, perhaps make you hear things that aren't there. No, no, believe me, I've worked with witnesses too long to think otherwise. Trust me on this. I'll tell you this much: Monsignor Havermeyer mentioned that Bishop Brassorie often went out on foot at night in plain clothes. The question presents itself: where did he go? Perhaps someone met him with a car. If not, what was his destination? A possible answer is the local bars."

"A bishop that hung out in bars," mused Jonathan.

"A true man of the people," added Pierre sarcastically.

"Perhaps," said Father. "What I want you to do is visit the lounges and just listen for a few key words, and if you hear them, note who said them. Perhaps engage whoever said them in light conversation, find out a little about them casually. Underline casually. Do not probe for their names, do not inquire about their places of employment, do not ask anything specific. There's no quicker way to arouse suspicion. Let them do the talking. I needn't remind you that we're looking for a murderer, so be careful. I suggest we meet here again on Saturday evening, two days hence, this time, to compare notes."

"What key words?" asked Arthur.

Father opened the desk drawer and pulled out four slips of paper. "I've made a list for each of you. Memorize it, don't carry it."

"Hm," said Pierre, studying his. "Bishop Brassorie, Saint Philip's, Charleen Vickers, Bishop Silverspur, Bishop Ravenshorst, Stephanie Fury, Marsha Dukes, Madeline Sugarman, Ol' Archbishop Morley— indeed?—hyssop, pentagrams, witching quilts, and—huh?—Jägermeister in connection with any of the above?"

"Yuck," said Arthur.

They all knew about Jägermeister.

No one asked about hyssop.

"Done," said Pierre, slipping the paper into his vest pocket. "Now for a song."

"First a Hail Mary," said Father, "in honor of St. Anthony of Padua, requesting his aid in this endeavor. Then a song. Let's make it a mighty song indeed."

Friday, June Ninth

Feast Day of Saints Ephrem,
Father and Doctor of the Church (373 AD) and
Columbkille, Apostle to Scotland (597 AD)

∞ Day of Abstinence ∞

16

FRIDAY WAS FULL OF SURPRISES. The first came early in the morning during Mass.

On weekends there is never a shortage of altar boys. I have actually broken up fights in the sacristy over who gets to serve High Mass on Sunday—specifically, who gets to swing the censer. Kids love those fumes. On weekdays, however, altar boys are at a premium, and since Father will never permit altar girls—not to mention liturgical dancers, lady Scripture readers, devout mimes in divine tights, or any female presence within the sanctuary—the job invariably falls to me.

Not that I mind. In my heart of hearts, I enjoy nothing better than mumbling the Latin responses and ringing the bells at the appropriate awesome moments. I do tend to lurch awkwardly when I have to heft the altar missal around since I can't carry the book and use my cane at the same time. There are rarely more than a score of parishioners in attendance, and even my humungous ego can tolerate—indeed, would welcome—the derision of any bunch of people who consider the Mass important enough to make it their first priority each and every day.

GARDENING TIPS: In the Traditional Rite the priest

and server face the altar with their backs to the

congregation. In other words, with their focus on

God. Student savant of human nature that She was,

the historical Church understood that if the

priest faced the people he would soon become a

game show host. In times past such a possibility

was considered undesirable, ludicrous, and offen-

sive to Almighty God. Today's priests, by con-

trast, go to workshops in Toluca Springs to prac-

tice sincere smiles, hone up on spontaneous jocu-

larity, and receive free samples of teeth-whiten-

ing dental products. Which is one of the many

reasons I prefer the Traditional Rite. I hate

game shows.

—M.F.

There were only a couple of moments when I was turned around to glimpse the attendees, like when I moved the altar missal from the Epistle side to the Gospel side, and when going to a side table to fetch the cruets at the Offertory. It was during those brief instances that I saw a new face—or at least in that dim lighting, a new outline—seated half-way back in the nave, roughly even with the side chapel dedicated to St. Jude. I wouldn't have given it a second thought if I hadn't noticed her again while I was holding the golden paten under each communicant's chin as they received the Blessed Sacrament on their tongue. A woman without a veil, sitting not kneeling, arms folded across her chest, form-fitting pantsuit rather than a dress, shoulder-pads a linebacker would covet; such a woman was rather conspicuous at a "Trad haven" like St. Philomena's. The thought occurred to me that she might be a reporter who had come inside to observe the throwback priest in his natural habitat. Father had already asked some of the larger men present to usher out anyone with a video camera growing out of the side of their neck.

The woman was still sitting there in the shadows after Mass as I extinguished the candles. Seeing her again gave me the creeps, and I almost jumped out of my skin a few minutes later when she came up to me as I was hobbling across the garden toward the rectory, and I finally got a good look at her.

"Some things never change," she said as a crisp breeze rippled through St. Thérèse's roses. It felt like a lizard skittering across my grave.

"Sister Veronica Marie," I said, nodding my head in scaled respect. Formal bows were beyond me, especially early in the morning, and never when someone's messing with my grave. "How nice of you to pay us a visit after all these years. I still don't recognize you without your habit."

Lightning flickered across her storm cloud eyes. "It's barbaric," she said icily.

"What is?"

"The Old Mass. I'd almost forgotten how archaic and chauvinistic it was."

"Is," I corrected her.

Thunderheads were crossing her corneas, illuminated by pitchforks of lightning. "True religion," she said, "is rightfully a woman's domain."

"Oh," I said. "Chauvinism in reverse. If you really believe that, why don't you leave the Church founded by Jesus Christ, the God Man, and join a coven dedicated to the goddess-marm of feminist wishful thinking? I hear paganism is doing well these days."

"Because I'm a woman," she said.

I scratched my head. "Ah, that explains it."

"The Church has controlled us, manipulated us into submission, made us feel sinister and inferior. But the pendulum swings. Women are the source of life, the wellspring of love, the fountain of peace."

"'Women are random clusters of vagaries,'" I quoted. Sorry, it just slipped out. It happens sometimes.

"Shakespeare via Caliban?" she said, her eyelids frosting.

"Rex Stout via Nero Wolfe," I answered. "Of course, Archie Goodwin's response is worth noting: 'Not that random.'"

"'Pfui,'" she hissed, quoting Stout whether she knew it or not. "You can never understand."

"Then why not leave me alone?"

"You don't see it. Your insufferable species never does. Women have been subjugated for centuries because of biological restrictions. But now those fetters have been severed. Women are no longer merely incubators, we are free. Even the Bible predicted it. 'And the earth helped the woman.' That's in Revelations."

"Out of context," I countered, "and the book is properly called the Apocalypse. 'Wellsprings of love,' you think? I'd say you're the fulfillment of an earlier prophecy:

> And those merciless murderers of their own children, and
> eaters of men's bowels, and devourers of blood from the midst
> of thy consecration, and those parents sacrificing with their
> own hands helpless souls, it was thy will to destroy ...

Okay, I'll admit it wasn't really a prophecy but a prayer of historical recollection, but even so, it had the desired effect. She started to back away.

"'Source of life'?" I was on a roll, and on the verge of bellowing. "You said it, Sister. And so did St. Paul, concerning womankind:

> Yet she shall be saved through childbearing; if she continue
> in faith, and love, and sanctification, with sobriety.

"We will win," she said, turning away like an iceberg cutting loose from an arctic shelf. "Your kind will go the way of the dinosaur."

"Look who's talking," I shouted at her retreating back. "You're the ones who aren't procreating. 'Fountains of peace,' my eye."

I stood there, huffing and puffing for a minute or two, first congratulating myself, then wishing I'd kept my yap shut. Ms. Stephanie Fury was a headstrong woman with a lot of clout. Of course, what had just occurred was only a continuation of the only conversation she and I had ever had.

Gathering my wits and gripping my cane, I limped toward the outside kitchen door. The window over the sink was slightly ajar, and I could hear Millie humming as she put the coffee on. A smile blossomed on my face as I realized what she was singing, drawing her lyric from the twenty-fifth chapter of Ecclesiasticus in conjunction with a melody loosely derived from the national anthem:

> And there is no anger
> above the anger of a woman.
> It will be more agreeable
> to abide with a lion and a dragon,
> Than to dwell with a wicked woman ...

That's our Millie. I would have kissed her, except she would have dented my skull with a cast-iron skillet. God bless her.

17

BREAKFAST WAS ALMOST A HALF HOUR LATER than usual that morning. Millie kept us waiting while she conjured up something special with the organic loot Lieutenant Taper brought from his wife's garden.

"Symbolism in ritual," Father was saying after grace while we were all waiting in the dining nook, "is incredibly powerful, a universe of meaning distilled into a single object or action." He wasn't talking about the Mass, but rather the murder of Bishop Brassorie—but he *could* have been talking about the Mass. "And we mustn't forget that this crime was performed with all the trappings of ritual."

"The triangle carved on the palm of the hand," nodded Taper.

"Positioning the victim that way on the floor," added myself.

"The witching quilt," said Taper.

"And the Jägermeister?" asked Wickes.

"That could be a red herring," said Father. "Just something that was handy, or some kind of private vendetta: 'You like Jägermeister so much, Your Lordship? Here, choke on it.' But it could also have had deep significance, personal or even spiritual, both for the murderer and the victim. By the way—"

There was a loud clang from the direction of the stove. Millie was in full form.

"—did you ever find your pen, Sergeant?" Father leaned forward in his chair, his stomach grumbling sanctimoniously as he sipped his umpteenth cup of coffee. Millie had been making occasional surgical sweeps to the dining nook, keeping the caffeine coming between valiant forays back into the thunderous cacophony of her culinary battlefield. All the while she spitted and sputtered something about how one of us must have prayed for patience, since the Lord was calling upon us to exercise it.

"My pen?" asked Wickes, lamely rechecking the same pockets he'd just been checking. "No."

"We have a sure-fire method for finding lost objects around here," said Father. "Would you like to know what it is?"

"Uh, sure," he said skeptically. "I guess so."

"In the name of the Father and of the Son and of the Holy Ghost," began Father. I complied, as did Lieutenant Taper, though his Sign of the Cross was one of those wrist-flick jobs where his hand never moved more than an inch from his belly button. Wickes' hands remained motionless, his lips rigid, and his eyes stiffly staring.

"In honor of St. Anthony of Padua," said Father. "Hail Mary, full of grace, the Lord is with Thee, blessed art Thou among women, and blessed is the fruit of Thy womb, Jesus."

"Holy Mary, Mother of God," answered Taper and I, though he kept his voice down to a half mumble, "pray for us sinners, now and at the hour of our death. Amen." Wickes remained conspicuously silent.

After we crossed ourselves in completion—again, Taper getting by with the wrist-flick and Wickes encoring his impression of a pillar of salt—Father sat back confidently, his hands folded on his stomach. "Now, Sergeant, take another look around."

"I already have."

"Look again."

Wickes shifted in his chair. "Why should I—?"

There was a tiny metallic scrape under the table. Startled, Wickes lifted the table cloth and looked down at what he had just nudged with his shoe.

"I'll be damned," he said.

"Saint Anthony never lets us down," said Father matter-of-
factly. "Why, just the other day—"

"Soup's on," roared Millie, brandishing a large platter of
steaming victualic creativity. "I call it 'Surprise des
Anges'—'Surprise of the Angels.'"

I don't know if that made her an angel for cooking it, or
Lucille Taper an angel for growing it, or Lieutenant Taper an
angel for bringing it, or all of us for eating it, but it was without doubt a most pleasant surprise. Potatoes, celery, red and
green bell peppers, onions, chunks of elephant garlic that
zinged the tongue just right, a touch of parsley, and the whole
ballet laced with melted cheddar cheese—and a hint of par-
mesan, if my taste buds haven't lost their discrimination. The
mushroom omelet was but an afterthought. In the three years
since Father Baptist bought St. Philomena's we'd never had
such a feast for breakfast.

Our cries of bravo and thanks were countered by Millie's
growl that any respectable kitchen should have an automatic
dishwasher.

We slurped and chomped for a few minutes, passing this
condiment and that, until we reached that euphoric state where
the forks move of their own accord and conversation kicks in.

"What do you know about Jägermeister, Jack?" asked Taper.

I wondered for a moment if Father objected to the lieutenant's continued use of his former, personal, non-clerical
nickname. He made no comment, but focused on the subject
at hand.

"Horrid stuff," he said. "Some kind of herbal liquor—made from fermented cabbage, I believe. Europeans
drink it hot, I understand, before a hunt. It's becoming
popular over here, but Heaven knows why."

"Do you know the label has a cross on it?" asked Taper.

"Between the horns of a goat," said Wickes.

"Not a goat," said Father, a momentary smile on his lips.
"A stag. It's a reference to Saint Hubert, the Patron Saint of
Hunters. In the year 685 he was out in the forest of Arden-
nes—where the Battle of the Bulge would take place centuries
later—and he saw a vision of a cross between the antlers of a
deer. He abandoned the hunt and became a monk, and eventually the bishop of Liège in Belgium."

"Could that be part of the murderer's symbolism?" asked
Taper. "The hunt, the killing of animals, the spilling of
blood, some kind of death token?"

"To our forebears," said Father, wiping his mouth with a napkin, "the hunt rather roused images of life."

"I don't get you," said Wickes.

"In our modern culture," said Father, "man has been disassociated from the source of his nourishment. We no longer grow our own food—except for a few marvelous exceptions like Mrs. Taper—nor hunt our own meat. But in times past an unsuccessful hunt meant an empty table. The hunt was the enactment of the drama of life, and by extension, the drama of man's quest for Salvation—and the quest of God for man's Salvation."

Silence settled on the breakfast table. Father let it hang there just long enough for the right effect, and then continued. "It is disconcerting, I know, to think of ourselves as God's prey, that He hunts us down, corners us, brings us to ground—but the imagery is well worth considering. Martin, who was it who said, 'The hunt is the relaxation of the Christian'?"

"St. Francis de Sales," I said offhandedly, grateful for the chance to show off, "in his *Introduction to the Devout Life.*"

"Interesting," said Taper.

Wickes mumbled something under his breath. I only caught the last word, "weird."

"Whether the murderer knew any of this," said Father, "when he decided upon Jägermeister as a lethal weapon, is still to be determined."

"If so," said Taper, "the killer could be a macho type for whom the Jägermeister symbolized something distinctly heroic. Or the killer could be an incensed murderess, a vegetarian Gaea-worshipping eco-maniac giving the man his carnivorous comeuppance. In either case, he or she certainly has a flair for imagery."

"Maybe," said Wickes, "he or she finds significance in the orange and green colors on the label, or the brown color of the liquor."

"Or maybe," said the gardener, "he or she just used what was handy. You said the bishop had a large supply of the stuff."

"Maybe," said Father. "Maybe. We don't know enough about the murderer to even hazard a guess as to his or her sex. Gentlemen, if you don't mind, I will dispense with gender pronouns and resort to the use of 'he' in the collective sense."

"I don't mind," said Taper. "But don't talk that way to
the reporters."

"I don't intend to talk to them at all," said Father. "Now,
have you learned anything else? The missing seminarian,
Joel?"

"No sign of him," said Wickes.

"His parents are worried sick," said Taper.

"I must remember to give Albert Maruppa a call," said Father. "Anything else of interest?"

"Archbishop Fulbright and Bishop Brassorie went way
back," said Taper. "Buddies even before the seminary. High
school. That accounts for the promotion of an unsuccessful
parish priest to bishop. We're still looking, as discreety as
possible, into the backgrounds of everyone close to the archbishop."

"Is he a suspect?" I asked, picturing His Graciousness and
his precious ring on his magnificent throne mounted in a gas
chamber.

"We're just being thorough," shrugged Taper. "He was in
town at the time of the murder—alone in his residence, no
witnesses."

"And his middle name is Psalmellus," said Wickes. "That
would match the PS on the witching quilt."

"Meanwhile," continued Taper, "by the archbishop's own
orders, most of his people were in Toluca Springs for that lav-
ish diocesan retreat. The Toluca sheriffs have tried at their
end, but everybody's already back here now, or dawdling
along the way. It will take a while to pin down everyone's
whereabouts on Tuesday. Bishop Zia Silverspur, curiously, is
missing. No one's seen him since last Thursday when he set
out for the Springs, five days before the murder."

"That's certainly cause for concern," said Father. "One
bishop dead, one missing. Where was Bishop Silverspur seen
last?"

"Leaving his residence at St. Michael's just after lunch,"
said Taper. "Bags in the car, apparently heading for the
Springs. His personal secretary, Cheryl Farnsworth, saw him
off, but no one saw him arrive. We're working on it. By the
way, Jack, why didn't you go?"

"To Toluca Springs? I wasn't invited."

"Hm. Should have guessed. Speaking of being thorough, I
understand that Stephanie Fury, who is now the liturgical coordinator for the archdiocese, used to live just in back of this
rectory."

"In the convent," I said, "when she was Sister Veronica Marie, principal of the parish grammar school."

"Before my time," said Father.

"Thanks to her," I said, "the convent is now a motel and the school was bulldozed so we could have a gas station on the corner. She was just here a little while ago."

"Really," said Taper. "What did she want?"

"Oh, she and I just had a little Bible study in the garden. She hit me with the Apocalypse, chapter twelve, verse sixteen."

"That isolated verse," noted Father. "Entirely out of context."

"Right, so I hit her with Wisdom twelve, five and six. She balked. Then I smacked her with—"

"Not," said Father, eyebrows raised half an inch, "First Timothy."

"Yes, Father, First Timothy."

"Two fifteen?"

"The same."

Father stared at me, one of those unsettling scowls that seemed to whisper, cautiously yet redressingly, "Considering the power that woman wields, Martin, do you think it was wise to provoke her?" Or perhaps it was charitably yet sacerdotally, "Considering you and your fiery tongue—James three six—confession is at five-thirty. Be there. I suggest you bring kneepads." But all he said was, "Oh."

"I take it," said Taper, pointing his potato-logged fork in my direction, "you get along with her as well as you did with Monsignor Brassorie?"

"I'd say about par. She was his—how do I put this?—his right-hand man. When the changes came in and the habits came off, she mutated from an austere but quietly dingie nun to an austere but loudly bloodthirsty lioness with an agenda."

"You didn't like her," observed Wickes. Give the man a promotion.

"I don't like stupidity," I answered. "She restructured the school curriculum, threw out all the old religion textbooks, ordered her nuns to teach syrupy psycho-soft drivel instead of solid doctrine, and drove most of those kids right out of the Faith. She actually brought in a bona fide witch to give a presentation. Someone actually dingier than herself: crescent moon on her forehead, bells on her toes, called herself Starfire or something. Imagine that: bringing an avowed pagan to St. Philomena's to raise the children's 'goddess consciousness.'

And out of two hundred families, only one parent complained—Albert Maruppa. Sister Veronica accused him of being close-minded at the next parent-teachers' meeting."

Wickes, no doubt a product of such nunnery nincompoopery, shifted uneasily in his chair. "How did she and Brassorie get along?"

I hesitated. I'm still not sure if I was honestly avoiding the issue or trying to bait them into prying it out of me with all the dramatic uproar of a pneumatic drill. No doubt at the Last Judgment all will be made clear.

"Well?" said Taper.

"There was talk," I mumbled. "Talk, mind you, that the two of them were, um, perhaps closer than was considered proper."

"Talk," said Taper.

"I just did," I said.

"I mean, what kind of talk? Rumors, accusations, someone in the parish seeing them at a ski lodge together?"

"All of the above," I said. "Except it was at the marina, not a ski lodge. I forget who said they saw them. Like I said, it was talk. Gossip. I don't trust gossip, even when it's good."

"So you got a kick out of what you heard," said Wickes.

"In the sense that I hoped Old Brassiere would get canned for inappropriate behavior, yes. In the sense of relishing a scandal, no—at least, not much."

18

"AND THEN," SAID TAPER, shoving his plate away, "there is the matter of the pentagram on the cloth."

"A veritable can of worms," said Father Baptist, rising from the table. "It may mean any number of things."

"Witchcraft," said Wickes. "Obviously."

"Perhaps," said Father, "but as I was about to say—"

"I know something of the occult, too," said the sergeant, a bit too authoritatively for someone who thought that talking with a so-called witchcraft specialist for an hour amounted to knowing something. "The five-pointed star stands for the five extremities of the human body, or more specifically, the empowered man—or woman, as the case may be. Enlightenment is the key to power. Wiccans—that's what real witches and warlocks call themselves—use the pentagram in their rituals as a symbol of directed power."

"If the murderer was wiccan, perhaps," said Father, leading the way to his study. "But we do not know that. And we must remember that what we of European stock would recognize as a witch would be considerably different than what, say, a Navajo would call a witch. By the way, Millie, a thousand thanks for that marvelous repast."

"Glad you liked it, Father," she called down the hallway, the muscles of her forearms bulging with the weight of our dirty dishes. "Expect to see the leftovers in the form of soup this evening."

"I cannot wait," called Father, easing himself into his chair behind the desk, the statues of Sts. Anthony and Thomas More close at hand, not to mention DO WE WALK IN LEGENDS and the freshly-framed AS A DOG THAT RETURNETH TO HIS VOMIT.

"As I was saying," said Wickes, again with that authoritative tone, "real wiccans, of European descent at least, believe the pentagram to be—"

"Real wiccans?" said Father. "Just because someone professes authenticity, Sergeant, doesn't make the claim true. Besides, we haven't yet established beyond all doubt that the murderer is wiccan."

"But—"

"Hear me, please. The pentagram in and of itself does not prove anything. The culprit may be using a symbol about which he understands little or nothing, even if he thinks his knowledge is comprehensive. Maybe he's seen too many B movies, or takes rock album covers too seriously. You would do well to remember that we live in a culture that is the product of the Reformation: a society in which old forms, though maintained superficially, have become detached from their original European, and therefore Catholic, meaning."

"I don't follow you," said Wickes, visibly irked. "Real witches—"

"Modern witchcraft," said Father, leaning forward and resting his elbows on the desk, "was the fabrication of one Gerald Gardner who, with the clandestine help of Aleister Crowley, a renowned Satanist and infamous trickster, cooked up a bunch of bogus rituals and ignited the synthetic revival of witchcraft in England in the nineteen thirties. Gardner's associates suspected that starting a coven was merely his scam for encouraging pretty unclad girls to dance around a fire. Real witches my eye."

"But—"

"Most claims of hereditary witchcraft are spurious at best. Witches and warlocks of centuries past were culturally isolated and literally illiterate. There was no 'network' of witches spread across Europe, as some of these modern wiccans claim, and what far-flung witches there were certainly left no written records. In any case, twentieth century wiccans have no original claim to the pentagram. I wonder how they would react, along with so many rock groups who have adorned their album covers with the design, if they knew that the Church's claim to the symbol predates theirs."

Wickes was on the verge of making vacuum cleaner sounds again as Father pulled a copy of J. R. R. Tolkien's translation of *Sir Gawain and the Green Knight* from a nearby shelf and opened it with aplomb. "These words are from the time of King Arthur:

> Then they brought him his blazon that was of brilliant gules
> with the pentangle depicted in pure hue of gold.
> By the baldric he caught it and about his neck he cast it:
> right well and worthy it went with the knight.
> And why the pentangle is proper to that prince so noble
> I intend now to tell you, though it may tarry my story.
> It is a sign that Solomon once set on a time
> to betoken Troth, as it is entitled to do;
> for it is a figure that in it five points holdeth,
> and each line overlaps and is linked with another,
> and every way it is endless; and the English, I hear,
> everywhere name it the Endless Knot.

"So you see," said Father, closing the book with finality, "the pentagram was the Church's first—a symbol honorable for a good knight to wear—and has been perverted in the public perception, like so much else that was once holy."

"Is there anything that isn't related to the Church in your mind?" rasped Wickes, slapping the desk with his hand.

"Can't think of anything," said Father calmly. "It's where all roads eventually lead."

"Bosh," said Wickes, pulling back into his chair.

"Be that as it may," said Taper, patiently trying to carry on, "only a handful of people would know any of this."

"Only one person," said Father, "killed Bishop Brassorie. It is his mind we must fathom. The murderer may be wiccan, or may simply want us to think he is. I'm simply saying that we must not permit ourselves to assume anything with regard to the murderer's use of symbols—at least, not yet."

Wickes mumbled something else, and I didn't catch the last word.

19

SURPRISE NUMBER WHATEVER—I've lost count—came moments later in the form of a loud knock at the front door. Millie brushed by the study to answer it, wiping her hands on her apron.

A sound like a dragon with a stubbed toe rumbled down the hallway.

"Billowack," said Taper, cringing. "He said he might drop by."

"The Bulldog Billowack I knew," commented Father, "would never just 'drop by.'"

"True," said Taper. "Perhaps I should have said 'drop upon.'"

"Lombard," came a marrow-melding roar. The sound and the shape were reminiscent of the radioactive star of a Godzilla movie. He was mean, he was wide, he was towering in the doorway. The citizens of Tokyo were scattering across the carpet in terror at his feet.

"Montgomery," said Father Baptist, rising from his chair. Montgomery!? "Good to see you."

"No it ain't," bellowed Billowack. "And you're the last person I want to deal with at the end of a miserable week."

Wickes offered the Chief of Homicide his chair, or rather leapt out of the way to avoid being crushed. Father settled back behind his desk, and Taper did his best to cross his legs casually.

"Who does the archbishop think he is?" boomed Billowack.

"He thinks he's the archbishop," said Father.

"Well he can take a flying leap."

"I've said that for years."

"Don't be cute."

"Wouldn't occur to me. I take it you don't appreciate my involvement in this case."

"Haw!"

"I'm not doing handstands myself, but orders are orders."

"Pshaw!"

"If you'll excuse me," I mumbled, imagining the relief that might be achieved by stuffing cotton in my ears. "I'll just—"

"I'll have you know your lackey, Quasimodo here, is a suspect," bawled Billowack. "Whudduya think of that?"

"—tend to my duties," I whispered, slinking in stiff lurches out the door. Quasimodo? Ouch.

"And you, Taper, you want me to let this mackerel-snapping priest and his deformed sidekick have access to official police files?"

I was half-way to the kitchen when I realized there were footsteps right behind mine. Sergeant Wickes.

20

SOMETIMES A SEEMINGLY LITTLE THING can change your mind about someone, or at least begin to. In the case of mine with respect to Sergeant Wickes, it was the matter of his pager.

He had followed me out through the garden to my room at the far corner of the rectory while Billowack was having it out with Father Baptist. I had left the carnage to avoid being scalded by flying Godzilla phlegm, and I guess Wickes wanted to hide, too.

"Not a long tour," I said, flipping the light switch. "That's my bed, my aspirin supply on the night stand, that's my desk, my armchair where I like to read at night, my type-writer—Dad's portable Underwood, it still works—bookshelves, and the bathroom is in there, complete with my tooth brush and toenail clippers."

"And you've been living here for thirty years?" He was eyeing my little library. Dad always said you could tell a lot about a man by the books on his shelves. By the way Wickes was examining mine, his dad must have given him the same sagacious advice.

"More like three decades," I said. "No ambition. Never wanted to be anything else. As you can see, it all worked out. Gardening suits me, or at least it did until the arthritis got really bad two years ago."

"You don't talk like a gardener."

What an opening, but I decided not to draw a parallel with him and his profession.

"Ah," he said, pulling a sketch pad out from between two large volumes. He flipped through the pages. "You're an artist I see."

"Putting a lump of charcoal in a orangutan's paw doesn't make him an artist."

"But these aren't charcoal drawings," said Wickes. He examined one of the pages more closely. Then he sniffed it. "What do you draw with?"

"Crayons," I coughed.

He looked at me, smiling. "Crayons?"

"As you can see, I only use two colors: black and green."

"But crayons?"

"Years ago," I sighed, "when the nuns and the school were still here, Sister Cecilia asked me to help her unpack a case of crayons she'd ordered for the first graders. You remember how they come, sixteen colors to a box. Well, someone at the factory fell asleep at the controls because every pack of crayons in that carton had only two colors."

"Black and green," said Wickes, closing the sketch pad. "You have a unique—what's the word I want?—a unique, uh ..."

"I still have about a third of the case left," I said, accepting it from him and slipping it back to its place on the shelf. "Maybe by the time I've exhausted my supply an appropriate word will present itself."

"And what's this?" He pulled a comb-bound manuscript from the top shelf. "And this?" The one next to it.

I admit I cringed—as "all the skin on my scalp, face, shoulders and back tightening, warping, buckling, shriveling, and shrinking right down into my underwear"—but there was no help for it. "Oh," I tried to say disinterestedly, "I dabble at the typewriter a bit."

"A bit? You've got three, four, five manuscripts here. Anything published?"

"Naw."

"I like this title, 'The Wicked West of the Which?' What's that about?"

"Nothing. Really, it's stupid. Every agent I sent it to said so. The last one wrote his comments on the title page. See for yourself."

"'Dear Martin,'" he read, "'You write like a guy slugging martinis and having a laugh, and no one else in the whole world sees what's so funny. Not interested, but keep 'em coming. Yours, Sal Silverstein.'"

I sighed with relief as he put the manuscript back in its place rather than embarrass me further by starting to read it. Then he embarrassed me even worse by spying the page sticking out of the typewriter.

"What's this?"

"Oh, nothing."

"Nothing my eye." He read aloud:

"Father Baptist," I huffed as I hobbled up the
brick walkway to the shaded, mossy spot between
the church and the rectory where he liked to meditate after morning Mass. I huff and hobble everywhere because I walk with a pronounced limp ...

Sergeant Wickes looked up at me with impish eyes. "You're writing a book about him?"

"Just a rough draft," I replied. "Very rough."

"So you're his Doctor Watson?"

"Or Archie Goodwin. Who knows? I'll probably change all the proper names. Wouldn't want to get sued. I just figured that when Father cracks this case—"

"You really think he will?"

"I know he will."

"And you'll be there with your memoirs ready."

I felt like crawling under the carpet. It sounded so lame coming from his lips. Besides, I am just a gardener, and how many folks out there are secretly writing books, hoping to be published? The gangrenous image of me lurching around a posh book-signing party flickered through my head, children fleeing in terror from my unintentional imitation of the

Hunchback of Notre Dame. I shook my head wearily. "I just don't get much sleep. The ol' spine keeps me up, so I ..." I waved my hand in the general direction of the typewriter.

"Hm." He cranked more of the page into view.

```
... He looked up at me with those unnerving eyes

that seemed to whisper, tired yet patiently, "Con-

sidering all that I do believe, Martin, do you

really think you could come up with something that

is beyond me?"
```

Sergeant Wickes straightened. "Do you really know what he's thinking? I mean, like you've written here?"

"I never have a clue what's going on in Father Baptist's mind unless he spells it out, and even then I'm not sure. But conjecture has always been my specialty." I looked at a growing stack of pages on the desk. "There's more, but I've been concentrating on trying to get the beginning right."

He was looking at me like a man looks when he's trying to change his assessment of the man he's looking at, but with equivocal success. "You know," he said at last, "I have a sister-in-law who works for a publisher in New York—"

Just then his pager beeped.

That's when I had the opportunity to try to change my mind about him, too. It's been my experience that whenever anybody's pager beeps, they think it gives them a license to use your telephone. No matter what area code, county or country, it's suddenly, "Hey, my beeper just beeped and, like, I've gotta return this call and—aha!—there's your phone. Outa my way." Any suggestion that they seek out the nearest pay phone invariably results in a wide-eyed look of infuriated bewilderment: "But my beeper just beeped. I gotta call now! Now, do you hear? Now!"

"'Scuse me," said Sergeant Wickes, digging his pager out of his breast pocket. "Oh, that's my other sister-in-law in 'Frisco. Darned if I didn't leave my cellular phone in the car."

Bowing to what I thought was the inevitable, I was just raising my hand to point to the telephone on my night stand when he stuffed the thing back into his pocket. "I'll call her later."

"Go ahead," I said magnanimously, except it was a test, so I wasn't really being all that generous.

"Naw. It's long distance and prime time."

"Really. Go ahead."

"Thanks, but it'll keep."

"You're sure." One last try.

"Positive." He passed.

I'm no friend of technology, and I'd rather eat raw sweetbreads than have a pager clipped to my belt, but I did appreciate the fact that if this guy was going to carry one of those little demanding pager banshees, he also had the decency to return calls on his own phone.

A spark—not a fire, but a clearly visible, albeit tiny, spark—of class.

I decided then and there that this man was worth a second chance.

21

"ONE MORE THING," I said, cranking the page back down into the typewriter, "before we venture back to the land of the bellowing bulldog."

"What?"

"A glimpse into the landscape left behind by the likes of Sister Veronica Marie, currently passing herself as Ms. Stephanie Fury."

I drew his attention to an old dusty glass frame on the wall opposite my bed. It was a child's watercolor, sixteen by twenty, with a few words superimposed in blobby ink in the lower right corner.

"This was given to me by a little girl named Frances Marie Thompson," I explained. "I'm not big on kids, you understand, but she was a truly sweet child, the kind that makes a bachelor wish he were married. You know the kind: sixth grader, springy curls, sunrise smile, and convent eyes. Surprisingly, or perhaps not surprisingly, she became attached to Sister Veronica Marie. Kids are funny that way. They meet an adult that has the same name, or even the same middle name, and that becomes sufficient basis for adoration. In spite of Sister's, shall we say, disagreeable disposition and chiseled fangs, in Frances' eyes she could do no wrong."

"I've got a five-year-old niece who's like that with me," said Wickes, grinning at the thought. When his smile was genuine, it was okay.

"Then you know what I mean. One time Sister got her Rosary caught in a classroom door—you know those huge Rosaries nuns used to wear? The crucifix was shattered beyond repair. Well, Frances spent at least a week whittling a new one. And, since Sister Veronica Marie was so fond of Monsignor Eugene Brassorie, our Frances—unlike some children who would develop thorns of jealousy—found it in her generous heart to be equally devoted to him. She was always leaving flowers on his windowsill, things like that. Little did she know. Anyway, the day came when the convent held some kind of a nuns' union rally. It was unanimous: all previously professed promises went out the window, along with their devotions, Rosaries, and habits."

Sergeant Wickes made an uncomfortable hrmph. The sound of sensitive nerves being prodded by a gardener's tool.

"It wasn't long before Sister invited a witch to talk to the children. I told you about that. Anyway, I found little Frances Marie hiding in the garden one day, right over there by the birdbath, crying her poor little heart out. When I asked her what was wrong, she just blubbered all the harder. 'Oh Mr. Marty,' was all she could say—that's what the school kids used to call me—'Oh, oh, oh Mr. Marty.' I didn't know what to do or say, so I just sat with her for a long, long time. A while later, Sister Veronica Marie came looking for her. She'd missed several classes."

Wickes was examining the watercolor, eyebrows furrowed. "And?"

"Frances acted like a mouse backed into a corner by a hungry cat. She actually cowered behind me while I explained to Sister that Frances had apparently had a dizzy spell. Sister was not pleased. She insisted on taking Frances to class, but I told her I would take care of things. The hotter she got, the colder I became. You get the idea."

"So what happened?"

"The same thing that happens when you pour boiling water on a glacier: the ice melts at first, but wins in the end. Sister Veronica Marie went away, and Frances and I became fast friends.   She often spent morning breaks and lunch time talking to me while I tended the garden or clipped the hedges. I showed her some books of poetry, and she started writing verses herself.   Sad stuff, all of it.   Full of dark shadows and spiteful verbs.   For reasons she would not explain, she stopped attending Mass here at school.   They used to have Mass every First Friday and on Holy Days of Obligation for the children. She refused to go.   I thought at the time it was because the changes had just come in, the English replacing the Latin, but there had to be more.   She was, after all, a devout child.   But she wouldn't have anything whatsoever to do with Monsignor Brassorie or Sister Veronica Marie.   I had the distinct impression that Sister and Monsignor were trying to make amends to her for something, but I never knew for what.   Her grades began to suffer, and she became thin and pale.   And then ..."

Wickes was running his finger down the edge of the frame. He paused to rub a clod of dust between his thumb and forefinger.   "Yes?"

"Then," I swallowed hard, "one morning, the first of May to be exact, I found this picture rolled up and attached to my doorknob with a rubber band.   I never saw Frances Marie Thompson again."

"You mean she disappeared?"

"Yup."   I sighed heavily.   "The police checked into the matter, of course.   Her parents were both dead, and the aunt she was living with held down two jobs, and wasn't aware she was missing for several days.   None of her schoolmates—not that she had any really close friends, but you know, kids who went to class with her—had any idea she was planning to run away or where she might go if she did.   It certainly shocked me.   In another month school would have let out for summer vacation, and I had been saving some money to send her to a summer camp, you know, to kind of get away from all her ..."   My voice trailed off.

"And you say she left this watercolor on your door?   Any idea when?   What time?"

The questions were familiar.   The police had asked them almost thirty years ago.   "I went to my room early," I said. "'Round seven, seven-thirty.   It had been a long day.   I fell asleep reading in my armchair, maybe nine, nine-thirty.   I couldn't be sure.   It certainly wasn't on my door when I came in, and I never heard a sound."

"Hm," said the sergeant, rubbing his chin.

The watercolor was an eerie picture, the frightening sort of image that could only erupt from a tormented spirit—formless but not quite, hinting of quasi-solid things that go rampaging through impressionable children's nightmares. In all the years it had hung on my wall, I had never been able to figure it out.

There were five black, vaguely-human shapes standing or dancing in a circle around a bright something-or-other, perhaps a campfire. Three of the shapes were turned away from the viewer, and seemed to be draped in robes—or perhaps melting, who knows? The other two were facing the viewer, but, being hooded, their features were hidden in shadow except for red blotches that seemed to be eyes. Of these, one had something white and radiant around its neck, something three-sided and blazing, like a glowing triskelion or a fluorescent cravat.

It was all so nebulous and indistinct. The paints had run together in some places, and the surrounding contours and configurations suggested nothing in particular, or at least nothing in this world. In the lower left corner there seemed to be a smaller humanoid shape outside the circle. It had a pale, round face and three little smears that suggested eyes and mouth opened wide. I've always felt that it was running away from the others, but this was suggested more by the inscription in the opposite corner than the artistry of the drawing itself:

> I fled Him, and in the mist of tears
> I hid from Him, down glooms of fears.
> Running faster than the laughter,
> From the strong Feet that followed, followed after.
>
> —Frances M.T.

"Is that a nun?" asked Wickes, pointing at one of the robed shapes.

"Could be," I shrugged. "The inscription is a reference to a poem by Francis Thompson, sort of her namesake. I have it here in this book." I opened a volume to a familiar place.

Sergeant Wickes looked at the page, lost in thought.

THE HOUND OF HEAVEN

I fled Him, down the nights and down the days;
I fled Him, down the arches of the years;
I fled Him, down the labyrinthine ways
Of my own mind; and in the mist of tears
I hid from Him, and under running laughter.
Up vistaed hopes I sped;
And shot, precipitated,
Adown Titanic glooms of chasmèd fears,
From the strong Feet that followed, followed after.
But with unhurrying chase,
And unperturbed pace,
Deliberate speed, majestic instancy,
They beat—and a Voice beat
More instant than the Feet—
'All things betray thee, who betrayest Me.'

"It goes on for several pages," I said, retrieving the book. "But the first stanza is the gist."

Wickes took his notepad out of his pocket and made a note to himself. "I'll check the files on this," he said. "Maybe she turned up some time later and you weren't told. I expect you'd want to know."

"Thanks," I said. "All these years I've gone to sleep looking at that picture, wondering what became of her. I pray for Frances every night. Whatever it was she was fleeing from, I hope the Hound of Heaven caught her in the end."

Flipping the notebook shut, Wickes turned and strode to the door. He swung it open but didn't leave. He just stood there looking at the birdbath in the garden.

I could almost hear Father Baptist's words reverberating between the church and the rectory, shaking the dust in my little room: *"The hunt was the enactment of the drama of life, and by extension, the drama of man's quest for Salvation—and the quest of God for man's Salvation."*

No matter the century, no matter the circumstance, no matter the shenanigans of the clergy, no matter the treachery and debauchery rampant around us—no matter the eloquence of our excuses—the Hound of Heaven is ever at our heels.

"We'd best be getting back," said Wickes.

"Guess so."

All was silent in the study when we arrived. The bellowing bulldog was gone. Lieutenant Taper and Father Baptist were sitting at the desk, chairs and heads together, perusing the contents of a police file. I could see a photograph of a pale hand with a triangle carved rudely into the palm. There were pages and pages of technical charts, lists of measurements, mineral analyses, chemical breakdowns, and the like.

"He let you have them," I said as I hobbled in. Perhaps I should have put a question mark after "them" because my voice went up at the end of the sentence. Still, it was a statement of the obvious.

Father looked up at me with those unfathomable eyes that seemed to whisper, battle-worn but victoriously, "Considering that Billowack used to be my junior officer, that his ambient bark and his bite have nothing to do with his essential intelligence, and that he knows I'm the superior detective, what did you expect?" But all he actually said was, "Martin, would you please ask Millie to put on some more coffee?"

22

I WAS PUTTERING AROUND IN THE VESTIBULE of the church, restocking the rack with reading materials before locking up for the night. Father Baptist had turned off the light above the confessional twenty-five minutes before and had gone over to the rectory. My knees were still smarting from the Stations. As usual, the slots for *The Magnificent Promises of St. Bridget* and *The Third Secret of Fatima* were empty. Just as usual, the measure of coins in the donation box failed to meet the cost of replenishing the supplies. Oh well.

I was crossing myself at the holy water font when an unkempt man emerged from the shadows. He was in his early twenties. His clothes were soiled and wrinkled, his hair disheveled. His beard—surprisingly dark and dense for one so young—was bent out of shape, as though he'd slept awkwardly upon it. In our poor parish I was used to beggars, but something in his manner made me cautious. And cautiousness in the looker breeds caution in the looked-upon.

"Yes?" I asked warily.

"Excuse me," he said furtively.

I looked at him, he looked at me.

"How can I help you?" I asked, gripping my cane.

He swallowed. "I need to see Father Baptist."

Oh great, I thought, a mass murderer with an unexpected tug of conscience. "He's finished hearing confessions."

He swallowed again, eyeing my cane. "It's not that."

"Oh?"

"I mean, I really need to see him. It's urgent."

Right, I thought, backing away a step. "Urgent."

"Please," he said, stepping forward into a cone of incandescent light under one of the lamps in the arched ceiling.

I looked at him, he looked at me.

I can only imagine what he saw: a bent gatekeeper brandishing a crooked cane. Spooky thought. What I beheld was a scruffy young man with eyes ablaze with terrified determination. Yes, terrified. He was shaking. Strangely, there was something about him that seemed familiar.

He swallowed again. "I'm ... uh ..."

I think the word he was looking for but couldn't find was "desperate." At least, that was my appraisal of him. He didn't look dangerous so much as desperate. I know, I know, one can lead to the other, but as we at St. Philomena's are in the business of trying to save souls, there is always some degree of risk involved.

I relaxed my grip on my cane. "Let's see if we can find him."

He nodded his thank-you and attempted a smile. He didn't really succeed, but I gave him a gold star for effort.

I led him out through the side door of the church and through the garden toward the kitchen. "Let's see. He's probably —"

The kitchen door opened before my hand touched the knob. Father Baptist leaned out and looked past me to my bedraggled companion. "Joel?"

"Y-yes, Father."

"I thought I saw you hovering around the back of the church earlier. Was that you in the parking lot yesterday?"

"Yes, Father."

"I've been expecting you." He stepped back for us to enter. "Millie, could you possibly stretch the soup for our guest?"

There was a huff and a puff from the direction of the stove. "I suppose, if I must. All I have to do is add water."

"Done, then."

Father ushered Joel to the dining nook as Millie banged a few pots to establish her rung in the societal ladder.

"You look hungry."

"I am, Father. How come, how uh, were you expecting me?"

"Just a hunch. That, and I spoke with your father on the phone this afternoon. He is a man of character."

"Yes, sir."

"And very worried. From what he told me of you, I had a feeling you'd seek me out. Where have you been staying?"

"Oh, just around. It's easy to blend in with the homeless. Park benches aren't so bad."

"Your father said you like to go among the poor. I can appreciate that."

The lad shrugged.

"Do sit down," said Father. "Martin?"

I obliged, smarting from the thought of attempting to sleep on a park bench. The more I looked at this young man, peeling away his outer crust in my imagination, the more I saw his father Albert.

"I decided to add milk," said Millie, carrying over a pot of steaming white soup. "You'll have to have your coffee black in the morning."

"No problem," said Father.

"And," Millie was eyeing Joel, "I'll chop up some salad, courtesy of Mrs. Taper, bless her soul."

"Splendid" said Father. "Here, Joel, hand me your bowl."

"I need to talk to you," said the boy, his lips quivering. " I need to tell you—"

"Dinner first," said Father. "And Millie, do bring our guest a glass of wine."

Father crossed himself and we followed suit. "Bless us O Lord ..." Our grace was punctuated with chopping sounds from Millie's cutting board. "... through Christ our Lord. Amen. And thank-you, St. Anthony, for an answer to prayer. In the name of the Father, and of the Son, and of the Holy Ghost."

"Amen."

Joel had manners, I could tell. But he was also ravenous. His bowl was empty before Millie clunked down the wine glass in front of him. His wine glass was empty before the salad arrived. Father played with his food thoughtfully for a while, some form of private polo involving his spoon and a floating lump of carrot in his soup.

Millie had just slammed a refill of the salad bowl on the table and charged off again when there came a tap at the window.

Father glanced at his watch. "Ah, right on time." He
winked at Joel as he leaned over to unlatch the little French
window next to his chair. That particular window was one of
the most charming features of the rectory. The panes were
made of darkly-stained glass depicting a Dove sitting upon a
golden Chalice, a drop of blood dangling from its beak.

"Good ev'nin', Faddah," said a brittle little voice from outside.

"The same to you, Mrs. Magillicuddy."

"Bless me, Faddah, for I have sinned. It's been a week,
y'know."

He knew. I knew. Joel Maruppa was finding out.

"My dear woman," Father said solemnly. "What do you
wish to tell me?"

"It's that Muriel Cladusky," she rasped. "I knowed it's
her, I does. First I jus' 'spected, now I'm abs'lute pos'tive."

"What's she done?"

"Why, she's stealin' me intentions, Faddah. Right out from
under me nose, so t'speak. Right out of me noggin. I goes
ups to Commun'n, an' no sooner does I kneels back down
than she snatches me intentions right out of me prayers, she
does."

"Hm," said Father, dead serious. "And what specific intention has she stolen from you?"

"I've been askin' the Good Lord that I might win the
lott'ry, Faddah. What with Willum ailin' an' all, we needs the
money. But week after week I keep gettin' all the wrong
numbers. So I knows it's her doin'. She's stealin' me intentions right out of me prayers, she is. I sees her lookin' at
me, sometimes, like a cat's watchin' a birdcage. Maybe you
should warn the others. If she's stealin' me own intentions,
mightn't she just as maybe be stealin' theirs?"

"Perhaps," said Father, forming a steeple with his fingers.
"I can't say, but it seems to me if the woman is that desperate
for prayers, she must need them indeed. Perhaps the charitable thing to do is pray for her all the more, that her needs be
met. Remember Our Lord's admonition: if a man steals your
coat, give him your cloak as well. If someone steals your
prayers—"

"Me intentions, Faddah, she's stealin' me intentions right
out of me prayers."

"—then you should give her the intentions of your novenas
as well."

"Hm. That'll be hard, Faddah."

"The road to Calvary is nothing else, I'm afraid."

"Yo're right, of course. You always is. An' me thinkin' of me self as usual. So much for the lott'ry, too, I suppose."

"God's rewards are not always so obvious, but they are all the more real."

The old woman sputtered a bit, then coughed, then swallowed. "If you says so, Faddah."

"Why don't you make that novena to St. Jude, and maybe pick a few flowers to put in front of his statue in the church tomorrow? He'd appreciate that, and maybe he'll do something special for William."

"Okay, Faddah."

"Now make a good act of contrition."

"Angel of God my Guardian dear," she mumbled fervently, hands clasped and knuckles white, "mournin' an' weepin' in this vale of tears, where there is hatred let me sow love, an' the Light shines where there is darkness, light, an' where there is sadness, joy. Amen."

I don't know what Father Baptist was murmuring in Latin.

"Thank-you, Faddah."

"Go in peace, Mrs. Magillicuddy."

"Oh, b'fore I do—go, I means—would you kindly give these here periwinkies to your man, Feeney? I was walkin' in the woods, I was—summer's upon us, it is, an' the faeries are about, you know—an' I thoughts these might cheers him up, him bein' all so dour an' all."

Flashing me a glance that said, "Not a word, Martin," Father Baptist accepted a small bouquet of green fronds from her gnarled hands. "Thank-you, Mrs. Magillicuddy. I'll see that he gets them."

"Cheers him up, they will."

"No doubt, no doubt."

"G'bye, now."

"Good night."

The window closed and latched, and the leafy gift deposited in my water glass, he returned to his cold soup.

"Poor woman," said Joel. "Is there anything that could be done for her husband?"

"William died last year," said Father. "She visits the Blessed Sacrament several times a day, helps Mr. Folkstone with the watering, and taps on my window every Friday at precisely 6:15, rain or shine, just about the time William succumbed."

"I don't know what to say."

"Don't say anything, Joel," said Father. "I expect you to exercise discretion.   True, this wasn't a valid Sacrament—she's hardly what you'd call 'lucid' when she gets in these moods. She's doesn't come here to purge herself of her sins but to work things out in her mind. She knows I'm not alone—she has ears and eyes—but she chooses to ignore Martin and Millie and now you. Her act of contrition is gobbledygook, a hodgepodge of phrases snatched from various devotions. No, this isn't really confession. It's some kind of self-imposed therapy. Nonetheless, anything she said is to be treated as confidential."

"Sure thing, Father."

"Invariably, she snaps out of it and goes about her routine. She goes to regular confession almost every Saturday, and though I can't tell you what transpires there, I can assure you that it's nothing like what just happened here."

"Of course, Father."

"And St. Jude always has fresh flowers."

"Did she say 'periwinkies'?" I asked, examining the fronds in my glass. "If Mrs. Magillicuddy meant 'periwinkle' she's mistaken." I pinched a leaf and sniffed—I am a gardener, after all. "This is sage."

"Her knowledge of horticulture may be lacking," said Father, "but her heart's in the right place."

"And what," I snorted, "did she mean by 'dour'?"

"What," blinked Joel, "did she mean by 'faeries'?"

"Here's dessert," said Millie, setting down a meager portion of her special less-than-scratch cake. "Maybe I can stretch it with ice cream."

"A feast," said Father. "I don't know what we'd do without you."

"I do," she said, snatching up the dirty plates.

23

"SO WHY DID YOU RUN OFF?" asked Father Baptist. "And more important, when?"

We were seated in the study with cups of steaming coffee. For all her blustering, Millie makes the best. And she knows it. And she managed to scrounge up some cream in spite of the rumored dairy shortage.

Joel was gazing at the little steam swirls on the surface of his brew. "It's embarrassing."

"No doubt," said Father. "But better said now to me than to others I can think of in far more uncomfortable settings."

"You know how sometimes something's going on, and you just don't want it to be, so you ignore it, and you go on ignoring it, until it hits you in the face?"

"You have just described life in general," said Father. "And everything in particular. What about you?"

"I should have known. He told me the paintings were art treasures—and that art transcends morality. He told me the rich furnishings were gifts he couldn't refuse from dignitaries who would be offended if they came for a visit and didn't see them in his living room. He told me all kinds of things, and he was a bishop, and so I ignored the obvious." He took a long sip of his coffee, even though it was still too hot to drink.

"And?"

"I come from a very religious family, Father. You know us Maruppas, devout Catholics. I grew up respecting priests, and more so bishops, and, and—"

"It was hard to accept that Bishop Brassorie was not the holy man you acknowledged him to be."

"He wanted me to—you saw the painting in the living room—he wanted—" The coffee was sloshing out of his cup, dribbling down his fingers. He didn't feel it. "Right up to the last second I thought he was joking, or testing me, or I don't know what. You've got to understand."

"I do. And?"

"The moment I knew what he really was up to—what he wanted me to—I ran. Right out of the damn place, right down the street, through the park. I ran until I couldn't run anymore."

"So he was alive when you last saw him."

"Yes."

"And what time was that?"

"I don't know. Six, maybe six fifteen. David poked his head in to say he was going to the movies. A few minutes later, I guess 'cause we were alone and no one about, Brassorie made his move. The last thing he said was, 'You'll be sorry, Joel, when I'm archbishop—'"

"He expected to be the next archbishop?" said Father. "It was my understanding that Morley had as yet appointed no coadjutor."

"Co-what?"

"'Coadjutor with the right of succession.' There are proto-
cols involved, but an archbishop can appoint his successor. I
had no idea Bishop Brassorie was the golden boy."

"I don't know about that. All I know is what he said."

Father Baptist was rubbing his chin. "Joel, did Bishop Brassorie attend a funeral recently, say, within the last week?"

"Not that I'm aware of."

"Hm. Was he perhaps involved in a ground-breaking
ceremony—a new high school gymnasium somewhere? Any
kind of construction site?"

"I don't think so."

"What about hyssop?"

"What's that?"

"Never mind. Why did you end up doing most of the
house chores in Bishop Brassorie's suite?"

Joel gulped. "Uh, that is—"

"Am I safe in assuming that David Smoley was perhaps
more receptive to the bishop's, uh, wishes?"

"I'd rather not say, Father."

"I appreciate that you'd rather not."

Father Baptist folded his arms and bowed his head in deep
thought. "You will spend the night here. No argument. You
need a good night's rest and time to collect your thoughts.
I'll have to tell the police about you, but that can wait till tomorrow. After that, if you have no objections, I'll call Monsignor Havermeyer and tell him you're going to continue considering your vocation while staying here for a while."

"I don't mind."

"In the mean time, I want you to wash up. Martin, see if
you can get Joel some clean clothes. There might be something in the poor bin."

"Will you be going to the funeral tomorrow?" I asked,
struggling to my feet. "They're burying Bishop Brassorie.
Mass at St. Fallopia's at ten-thirty, burial around noon, Sacred
Heart Cemetery."

"St. Fallopia's?" asked Joel.

"Code name for St. Philip's," I answered.

Father rolled his eyes. "It will be dreadful. But you never
know what will turn up at a murder victim's funeral."

And turn up something did. Big time.

Saturday, June Tenth

Feast Day of Saint Margaret of Scotland (1093 AD) and Blessed Diana (1236 AD)

24

YES, SOME REALLY BIG SURPRISES turned up on Saturday.

The funeral Mass at St. Philip's Church was concelebrated by His Gracefulness Archbishop Morley Fulbright and his two available auxiliaries, Their Lordships Bishops Ravenshorst and Mgumba. To the archbishop's obvious ire, Bishop Silverspur did not show for the occasion. He was still missing, apparently lost in the Twilight Zone somewhere between here and Toluca Springs.

Oh, what the heck? Three strong women are more than equal to one flighty bishop, aren't they? Appearing at the ovulating side of the sanctuary were Mss. Margaret Dukes, Madeline Sugarman, and the unsinkable Stephanie Fury as the charcoal-clad squad of extraordinary Eucharistic ministers. They more than filled the vacuum. With what I won't say. The thought occurred to me that they might do a rock video and start a new career as the "Altar Belles."

There stood the archbishop in center stage with an auxi-lackey on each side. They looked so elegant at the front of the church in their nighties—those chiffon drapes the clergy wear nowadays, so unlike the regal vestments worn by their predecessors (and a few throwbacks like Father Baptist). These three could have made the cover of *Vogue*.

Monsignor Havermeyer had been conscripted to read consoling Scriptural passages from the pulpit. His heart didn't appear to be in it.

GARDENING TIPS: When all was said and done, and
the whole case was finally closed, I showed Sergeant Wickes this completed manuscript. He was
not, of course, pleased with my depiction of him
throughout. My promise that I was going to change
all the characters' names and even disguise the
identity of the city in which these events happened did not allay Wickes' indignation in the
slightest, nor did my reminding him that he really
did say the things I said he said. As for this
chapter about Bishop Brassorie's funeral, the sergeant found it "a bit bombastic and declamatory."
I was surprised he knew the words. He probably
had a dictionary up his sleeve.

Later, when I ran the chapter by Father Baptist
for his critique, he just looked at me with those
piercing eyes which seemed to whisper, anes-
thetizing yet surgically, "Considering that St.
Paul admonishes us to walk 'with all humility and
mildness, with patience'--Ephesians chapter four,
verse two--don't forget confession is at five-
thirty. The rack will be oiled and ready." But
all he finally said was, "Actually, Martin, the
church is named after the first bishop of Reuter,

Phillip of Roto, and should be spelled with two

L's." When I looked it up in the phone book there

was only one L, so I don't know what he was talk-

ing about. I found no such personage in <u>Saints</u> <u>to</u>

<u>Remember</u> either.

Anyway, after much hedging and edging, I exed-

out seven pages of my vociferous, opinionated ban-

ter, thus sparing my readers the agony of my com-

mentary regarding the details of the funeral Mass.

Besides, it was at the cemetery that things got

jumping, so I'll skip to that.

                                        --M.F.

I don't know whose idea it was to release a dove at the
grave-side service. Maudlin symbolism—the soul fluttering
up to God—may have a place in the world, but as far as I'm
concerned I'd rather avoid stepping in it. Anyway, more on
the dove in just a moment.
Saturday, June tenth, was a bright, sunny day. The funeral
procession from the church to the cemetery had been somewhat long on cars—my guess was more than fifty—but short
on distance—only five blocks. I managed to squeeze the Jeep
into fourth place behind the hearse, just to irritate their ecclesial majesties, but mainly with hopes of getting our picture in
the paper. It would have worked, too—our picture in the paper—if things that were about to happen hadn't.
There were over a hundred people gathered around the
grave, dealing with death in over a hundred ways. Naturally,
since black is no longer considered requisite attire at such occasions, the crowd might just as well have been assembled for
the grand opening of a new home appliance store. There were
only enough rickety folding chairs provided for a score of the
most prestigious posteriors, so most of the bereaved had to
stand. The casket was draped in white satin, plastered with

lilies, orchids, gardenias, carnations, baby's breath—anything white—and garnished with delicate, silver-flecked ferns. The resulting olfactory admixture was nauseating, overwhelmingly so.

Just about all of the archdiocesen bureaucracy had turned out for the occasion, fresh and renewed from their stint at Toluca Springs. The Altar Belles, of course, were close at hand, tall and silent, austere as stone. Auxiliary Bishops Ravenshorst and Mgumba stood nearby with their assembled staffs of former-priests, ex-nuns, and erstwhile theologians. Monsignor Goolgol was moving in and around the throng, his chiseled alabaster nose poking here and there like the beak of a scavenger in search of carrion.

Father Baptist was the only priest present wearing a cassock and collar, preferring such attire to the latest clerical fashions from Detroit or Oahu. A black note on an otherwise white keyboard, he was quietly yet intently taking it all in.

And yes, I'll admit it, I was on the lookout for Bishop Silverspur's secretary, Miss Cheryl Farnsworth. I hadn't spotted her at the church during Mass. The Altar Belles really needed her womanly warmth to offset their feminist frost. She did finally show up just as the holy water was starting to fly, sporting a simple but attractive blue dress, green scarf, and high heels that made her approach across the cemetery lawn somewhat cumbersome—becomingly so. Somehow her arrival freed my mind to consider other things.

Archbishop Fulbright was giving his "Farewell, good buddy" sermon, blathering on about death being an "expansion of mind." I was leaning on my cane thinking, Yes, finding oneself dangling over the chasm of Hell at the end of a shoestring might, indeed, be a consciousness-augmenting experience.

And then on some cue I didn't catch, one of the funeral directors—also known as "internment facilitators"—popped open a wire cage and shook out the dove. Startled by its sudden, violent release, the little fellow almost flopped to the ground. But, true to its species, it flapped and fluttered frantically, missed the turf by inches, skirted the casket, and then began to ascend. The crowd watched, captivated, as the delicate avian rose, awkwardly at first, and then with amplified confidence. Higher and higher it went—five feet, ten, twenty—escorting Bishop Brassorie's presumably unsullied soul heavenward.

Suddenly, out of nowhere, and with a plasma-clotting shriek, the hawk struck. It came from above, seemingly out of the sun, nabbed the dove with its fierce talons, encored his vein-clogging cry, and streaked off toward a stand of nearby oaks, its broad wings flapping like oiled, leathery membranes as it settled down to engorge its trembling feast.

Two curled white feathers descended in zigzags, coming gently to rest at the head of Bishop Brassorie's bronze coffin.

Two women squealed, one fainted, and several others seemed to sway this way and that, going in and out of focus. Their male escorts were dodging back and forth, trying to catch them whichever way they toppled. Most of the unattached men jammed their hands in their back pockets, rocked back and forth from heel to toe, and mumbled, "Ulp," "Ohhh," or "I'll be damned." One distinguished-looking usher from St. Philip's strutted militarily to a shaded spot behind a cypress tree and loudly lost his breakfast. That already-strained seminarian, David Smoley, didn't exactly faint. He just sort of demonstrated a full-phase particle reversal and blinked into a parallel universe for a few seconds. When his body came back, his eyeballs remained on the other side.

"Did you get that, Ziggie?" I heard a reporter ask his partner with the camera.

"Sure did, Jacco."

"Bingo."

25

"FATHER, WAS THAT A SIGN?"

Funny how people in crisis gravitate toward the man in the collar. Since Father Baptist was the only priest so accoutered, he became an instant bullseye of oracular attention.

"Was that an omen?"

"Does that mean poor Bishop Brassorie's soul went to, you know, to um—?"

"Does that mean the bishop didn't make it to, um, you know—?"

"It must mean something, Father, mustn't it?"

"Of course it does, Abigail. Everything means something, doesn't it, Father?"

"Isn't there something about the sun turning to blood? Or is it the moon?"

"What about the bird? How could God let such a terrible thing happen to dear Bishop Brassorie's soul?"

"Of course, believing as I do in reincarnation, none of this makes any sense, does it, Father?"

"Father?"

"Father!"

How fortunate they were that I was not wearing a collar that day—not that I ever could or would, but just as a matter of imaginative speculation, you understand. I might have hit them with something poignant yet unfathomable, like:

> For the king of Babylon stood in the highway, at the head of two ways, seeking divination, shuffling arrows: he inquired of the idols, and consulted entrails ... And he shall be in their eyes as one consulting the oracle in vain ...

Of course, Ezechiel chapter twenty-one, verses twenty-one and twenty-three had nothing whatsoever to do with the event at hand, but imagine what the talk show hosts would have made out of it—and for weeks to come!

That's why I never could, and never would, ever wear a collar.

Father Baptist answered their urgent pleas with a question of his own. "Was that a hawk or a spotted owl?"

That's why he does wear a collar. He's good.

Anyway, some people went off to get a closer look at the predator on his bloody perch, got one, and then wished they hadn't. One fellow made a dash for a nearby storm drain. Some people wandered in ever-widening circles, gradually disappearing like lost zombies among the grave markers. Others just went straight to their cars and sped off.

The archbishop had already made his exit, having silently shut his prayer book, turned away, and strutted to his limo without further comment. The Altar Belles were almost as swift, and equally silent. Cheryl Farnsworth simply vaporized.

Soon, everyone had dispersed except for a couple of die-hard reporters hoping to get something quotable from Father or myself with respect to Father. Also close at hand were our favorite lieutenant and sergeant from Homicide, and a handful of cemetery workers in denim blues and hard-hats. I recognized the foreman as Roberto Guadalupe, a tobacco-chewing boulder of a man with a mustache he probably set with corn cobs for rollers. He occasionally attended Mass at St. Philomena's, and he more frequently claimed linear descent from Pancho Villa.

"Okay, muchachos," he told the crew, "let's do it."

Like clockwork, they rolled back the fake grass around the casket, revealing the deep rectangular hole underneath. Within seconds they were lowering Old Brassiere into the bowels of the earth with nylon ropes.

Surprise.

"What's wrong?" asked Roberto, stepping up to the edge.

"It is not flat," said one of the workers. The tag above his shirt pocket said DUGGO.

"Whachoo mean, not flat?"

"The coffin, it is not lying flat," said Duggo, scratching his head. "So the bottom of the hole, it must not be level."

"How can the hole not be flat?" asked Roberto. "We don't dig them any other way."

"Maybe a rock fell in just before we lowered the casket."

"Problem?" asked Lieutenant Taper.

"Dunno," shrugged Roberto.

"Who cares?" said another worker. SPADE. "Once we cover it up, what difference does it make?"

Roberto was only a grave digger, but he was descended from Aztecs and Visigoths—not to mention Pancho Villa—and he had his honor to consider, such as it was. This was just a hole, but it was in a very real sense his hole, his responsibility. In a voice that brooked no back-talk, he gave the order, "Lift the coffin back out, amigos."

After a few moments of groans, grunts, and grimaces, the coffin was hauled out and shoved aside on the grass. Roberto slid off the edge of the gaping rectangular chasm and landed gingerly in the depths.

"Officer?" he said after a few moments of prodding and scraping in the deep, dark dirt. "You'd better look at this."

Ten seconds later, Lieutenant Taper was crouching down in there beside Roberto, digging away at the earth with both hands. The rest of us gathered around the rim. The sun was almost overhead, so we saw it all.

"Sergeant," barked the lieutenant, "call Billowack. We've got another homicide."

"Are you getting this, Ziggie?" said the reporter next to me.

"Yup," said his partner.
"Pay dirt."

26

THE CEMETERY WAS CRAWLING WITH COPS. Jacco Babs
and Ziggie Svelte were the only reporters allowed within the
police perimeter because they were witnesses to the discovery,
though they were corralled away from the main hive of forensic activity. Jacco kept stroking Ziggie's camera, looking
more satisfied than the hawk up in the oak tree.

In a nutshell, Bishop Zia Silverspur had finally turned up.

"Damnedest thing I've seen," Solomon Yung-sul Wong,
the coroner, was saying to Lieutenant Taper, "since Tuesday,
anyway. I'd say knocked unconscious and then buried alive.
Death by suffocation."

"How long's he been down in there?"

"Five, six days."

"That long?"

"A preliminary guess. I'll let you know more after the
autopsy."

"Keep your voice down. We don't want those reporters to
hear any of this."

"Right. Gotcha."

"Was there a triangle carved in the victim's left hand?"

"Not in the left hand. It was carved on the sole of his right
foot."

"Right foot?"

"On the fleshy underside between the arch and the toes. If
he hadn't been barefooted, we wouldn't have noticed it till we
got the body back to the forensic lab."

"Which way was it pointed?"

"The foot?"

"The triangle."

"Oh, that. Toward the toes. From the amount of blood on
the skin, also the dirt caked around the wound, I'd say it was
carved while he was still alive—though probably after he was
clubbed unconscious. Like the other one. I found the knife
in his pocket. Same design as the previous case. Smudges but
no prints—caked with dirt, anyway. The murderer might have
been wearing gloves."

Taper grimaced. "And the bottle?"

"Big. Two-liter size. Roughly half empty. Burgundy, I think—the label's been peeled off. Made of green glass. It was set upright in the crook of the victim's right arm. When the murderer covered him with dirt it was still sticking up by about eight inches."

"So that's what prevented the coffin from lying flat when the workers lowered it in."

"Nice little party he was having."

Taper drew close to Mr. Wong's ear. "And was there, you know, a piece of cloth, like the one in the other murder?"

"Yup, clutched in his left hand. We haven't pried it loose yet."

"Well, make sure those reporters don't see it."

"Right."

I figured I'd hear all of this again and in better detail later in Father's study, so I moseyed over to where Father Baptist and Roberto Guadalupe were standing. Their faces were intense and their voices were pitched in low, fierce, escaping-steam whispers.

"As I told you, Father. We got the order to dig the hole on Thursday morning, June first. We dug it that afternoon."

"But Bishop Brassorie wasn't murdered until Tuesday the sixth. There was no need for a grave last week."

Roberto held up his clipboard bulging with swollen pink and yellow forms. "Look, here's the work order. It says what plot to dig up. See? Tier fifteen, row seventeen. The order, it is dated the first of June. Ten days ago."

"Is it signed?"

"Sí. Here."

Father snatched the clipboard out of Roberto's hands. "Has anyone else seen this?"

Roberto hesitated. "Um."

"What aren't you telling me?"

"Father, my job, it is not much. Still, it is all I have to support my family."

"But you did ask questions, didn't you?"

"Sí."

"Tell me."

Roberto twirled the left horn of his enormous mustache and sighed. "Okay. It's all going to come out, no? It's like this: usually the work order comes with a certificate of ownership stapled to it. Like a bill of sale. You know, they treat graves like real estate these days."

"Yes."

"Well, this work order was by itself. I figured it must have become separated somehow from the certificate, though I can see now there are no staple holes or clip marks in the corner. Anyway, the archdiocese owns all the plots in this section of the cemetery. Everything in tiers one through thirty is VIP territory. No one gets buried here unless an order comes down from the Chancery Office."

"The question," said Father. "You asked someone a question."

"Sí. I thought some dignitary had cashed in his chips. And I had this work order but no certificate. Then I noticed the signature, and I've never seen a work order with his name on it. It's always a secretary or some monsignor, but never him. Well, rules are rules, and I figured someone made a mistake up the chute, and I didn't want it to land on me. So I made a phone call to the Chancery."

"Did you talk directly to him?"

"I don't know who I talked to. I called that extension under his name—see? It's printed on the form under the official seal. A man answered. When I explained about the grave he asked who signed the order, just like you did. I told him. He sounded surprised, told me to FAX him a copy."

"Did you?"

"Uh-huh. I didn't even know we had one of those gizmos in the office, but Mrs. Flores—she's the cemetery administrator—worked it for me."

"While the man was still on the phone?"

"Sí."

"Do you still have the cover sheet?"

"The what?"

"The sheet that shows the date and time the FAX was sent."

"Sí, it should be there somewhere." Roberto retrieved the clipboard and flipped through the fan of paperwork pinned beneath the metal clasp. "Here."

Father glared at it for a long moment. "So what did the man say when he received the copy at his end?"

"He sounded, I don't know, kind of nervous. He said he'd look into it. I knew there were no highbrow funerals on the duty roster that week, so I asked if maybe I should fill the hole back up. He just got more upset and said he'd get back to me."

"Did he?"

"No."

"Did anyone?"

"Nope."

"So you left the grave open."

"I had the men cover the pile of raw earth with Astroturf, and we left some saw horses around the grave so no one would accidentally fall in. This VIP section doesn't get a lot of visitors anyway."

"This all happened a week ago Thursday, the day you dug the hole."

"Sí."

"That explains why the grave and the pile beside it are bone dry. Then what happened?"

"On Wednesday, June seventh, I got a new work order, with a certificate attached. It said to dig up tier fifteen—"

"Row seventeen."

"That's right, Father. So I figured you can't dig the same grave twice. That first order, it must have just been a stupid mistake."

"One more thing. Have you seen anyone hanging around this grave, anyone at all?"

"No, but then I've spent almost all my time at St. Gabriel's Corner, the other side of the hill, burying just plain folks. It's been a busy week."

Out of the corner of my eye I saw Taper and Wickes approaching, and looming behind them like a wicked hurricane on the horizon was the ever-popular bellowist, Montgomery "Bulldog" Billowack.

"Got something?" asked Taper.

"Yes," said Father. He put his hand on the foreman's shoulder. "Roberto, you must tell these officers everything you've just told me. Don't leave anything out. You understand?"

"Sí, Father."

"I will do what I can to protect your job."

"Gracias, Father."

Father left Roberto in the capable hands of Taper, Wickes, and tropical storm Billowack. Grabbing my elbow, he directed me towards the Jeep.

"Where to?" I asked, turning the key in the ignition.

"The Chancery. I hope that's where he went from here."

27

I'VE ALWAYS LOVED THE SCENE where the detective with fire in his eyes and gravel in his larynx defiantly pushes his way past the receptionist, through the wide double doors, and into the executive's office. Life might have imitated art if it hadn't been Saturday. As it was, no one was manning—or rather womaning—the desk in the outer office, so Father Baptist met no resistance as he knocked the doors aside and stomped into the inner sanctum.

Monsignor Goolgol's lower jaw dropped to the floor, along with a few dozen sheets of paper which slipped from his hand.

Archbishop Morley "Psalm" (pronounced "Sam") Fulbright, seated behind his desk, looked annoyed. "Father Baptist," he said, "what the devil—?"

"Out," said Father to the monsignor, motioning over his shoulder with his thumb. "Now."

"How dare you?" quivered Goolgol, pushing his glasses back up his nose. I thought of the way a lizard flicks its tongue out and in. Then I thought of what it might look like if the critter accidentally swallowed his tongue. Then I thought how much the monsignor's Adam's apple looked like that as Father closed in on him until their noses almost touched—a hideous thought for both of them, no doubt.

"I said now."

There was a loud gulp, a rustle of hastily gathered papers, a swish of sweet-scented air, and the slam (pronounced "slam") of the door. Good ol' Goolgol could sure move when he had a mind.

"All right," said the archbishop, folding his hands on the desk. "What is the meaning of this intrusion?"

"This is nothing," said Father, "like the invasion that's nipping at my heels. Why didn't you tell me about tier fifteen, row seventeen?"

The archbishop turned as white as the floral array on Bishop Brassorie's coffin. "How did you find out about that?"

"The foreman at Sacred Heart Cemetery called here a week ago Thursday, the first of June, at three fifteen in the afternoon. The receptionist, I figure, was on a break. Perhaps Marsha Dukes, your administrative assistant, was running an errand at the time. Most of your staff was headed for Toluca Springs. Anyway, by whatever circumstance, you answered the call yourself. Mr. Guadalupe wanted to know why your signature was on an order to dig up a grave, a grave for which there was as yet no body."

"What makes you think he spoke with me?"

"Because he phoned the number on the work order—this office. You asked him to FAX you a copy. The FAX number is on all official Chancery stationary, including work orders. The machine itself is right beside the receptionist's desk."

"I repeat, what makes you think he spoke to me?"

Father Baptist set his hands down on the edge of the archbishop's desk and leaned forward on his knuckles. Another pose I'd never seen him assume before. "Why did you summon me the moment you heard that Bishop Brassorie had been murdered? I've been asking myself that, and it hasn't made any sense. You despise me. You abhor everything for which I stand. You've devoted your career to the systematic destruction of everything I represent. You would like nothing better than to drive me from your archdiocese."

"You know I wouldn't do that," said the archbishop, choosing his words carefully. "You know I couldn't, not with what you and your gardener could—"

"Let's stick to the issue at hand. When you saw the work order come over the FAX from the cemetery, you wondered how your signature got on it. Simple. You sign a hundred documents a day. People you trust hand them to you in stacks. The work order looked like any other memo. Your signature could have been procured weeks ago. You were puzzled, but not alarmed."

Morley's cheeks began to blaze. "Now see here—"

"Not alarmed," repeated Father, his tone as steady and inexorable as an oncoming steamroller, "at least, until you got news of Bishop Brassorie's death. Then you knew something was really amiss. Your signature was on a work order to dig up a grave five days before there was a body to put in it. The work order was not a silly mistake, and it was no coincidence. You didn't know what it meant, but you sensed—as I do—that someone in the Chancery is playing games. Deadly games."

"Hrmph," said the archbishop, unconvincingly.

"So," continued Father, "you realized you had the answer to a prayer right under your nose: me, Jack Lombard, cop-turned-priest, eking out a meager existence at St. Philomena's, the very parish your buddy Brassiere almost choked out of existence. If there was going to be trouble, and if someone was trying to implicate you in some way—and especially if you were innocent of his murder—then you knew that having a trained professional with a track record like mine in your court might just save your hide."

The archbishop glared silently.

"As for Eugene Brassorie," said Father, the edge in his voice slashing the air like a glistening knife, "even though you knew him to be a nefarious malefactor, you gave him a bishop's hat and promised him the post of 'coadjutor with the right of succession.' Was that just because you'd been friends since puberty, or did he have something on you?"

"You go too far," said the archbishop.

"I've only started," said Father. "And rest assured, men I personally trained are in charge of the police investigation. What I can figure out, they can figure out."

During the next few seconds of screaming silence, I slowly became aware of my own existence again and was pleased to discover that I was still breathing. Then came a squealing sound through the open window, a car braking to an abrupt halt on the street below. The screech reminded me of that hawk in the cemetery.

"I hope," said Father at last, "you will not make it impracticable for me to help you."

"Well." The archbishop cleared his throat. It sounded like those noises big motor boats make when they're disgorging water. He was either found out and furious about it, or couldn't remember the definition of "impracticable." He attempted an unconvincing smile. "Father Baptist—John—what can I say? You've got me. Need I add, 'again'?"

"You needn't add anything for the moment," said Father straightening, the ferocity of his tone subsiding. He glanced at the window, then at me, and then back to his lawful superior. "I don't think you killed your friend Brassorie, and I'm positive you didn't kill Zia Silverspur."

"Silverspur!"

"Oh didn't I mention it? I did have this other matter on my mind. A short while ago—in fact, just after you left the cemetery—Bishop Silverspur's body was found under a thin layer of earth in the bottom of Bishop Brassorie's grave. Tier fifteen, row seventeen. Buried alive. He's probably been there since the day he disappeared, the same day your signature appeared on the order to dig that very grave."

"Good heavens."

"That's why I said the police will be here momentarily, as in any second now, and I won't be here when they arrive. I just wanted to make sure we both know where we stand. I will solve this perplexing conundrum for you—even in spite of you—and you are expected to be proportionately and fiscally grateful in the end. I should tell you that I suspect it's going to get far worse before it gets better."

Morley moved his lips but no sound came out.

"But I respectfully warn you, Your Grace," said Father, motioning me toward the door. "Don't toy with me again. If you think of anything I should know, anything I'll find out—and you know I'll find out everything—you can reach me at my rectory. Yes?"

The archbishop nodded.

Father started to leave, then hesitated. "Another thing. I strongly suggest that we have another meeting. There are some questions I need to ask, and as soon as possible. You, the remaining auxiliaries, everyone who was present the other day. How soon could that be arranged?"

Archbishop Fulbright consulted his desk calendar. "How about tomorrow, noonish?"

"I don't work on Sundays," said Father Baptist.

"Not even for something as urgent as—?"

Father just sniffed.

"Right," said the archbishop, returning to his calendar. " I imagine Monday is too long to wait. This afternoon, then. Say, four o'clock."

"Fine by me. Rather short notice for them."

"I am the archbishop," said Morley. He drew a deep breath as if to prove it. "They'll be here."

"Fine," said Father, turning to leave, but hesitating yet again. "One more thing. I gave Mr. Guadalupe my assurance that his job security will not be jeopardized by his demonstration of responsibility and loyalty to his employer."

"Of course," said the archbishop, now fully inflated.

"With your permission," said Father, following me out the door.

Approaching footsteps and gruff voices were echoing through the foyer downstairs. We ducked into a side nook where they keep the Coke machines as the storm roared past.

28

"DID YOU SAY ST. BASIL'S, FATHER?" I pulled the Jeep out into traffic. There was a little more prodding in my voice than was necessary. "Going to see Father Nicanor?"

"Mm-hm," said Father Baptist, gazing out the side window.

It was always a treat to take Father Baptist to St. Basil's. I could spend hours there, losing myself among the colonnades, tapestries, arched walkways, and inspiring icons. Father Stephen Nicanor was a Maronite, one of a score of time-honored but inconspicuous Rites within the Roman Catholic Church—perfectly valid, completely loyal to the Pope, and for the most part unravaged by the topsy-turvy changes that have so tarnished the Latin Rite since Vatican II. In these days of post-conciliar spiritual famine, increasing numbers of tradition-minded Catholics have sought refuge in these less auspicious but often more reverent and nourishing folds of the veil of Faith.

Father Nicanor was a tall, thin, sandstone pillar with a thick, bristling beard. His nose and fingers were incredibly long, and his eyes were astonishingly round. There was something constantly-moving yet solidly stationary about him, like fine sand trickling through a ponderous hourglass. He rolled his R's in a manner unlike anyone else I've ever heard: less brittle than a Scot, more precise than a Spaniard, and with more harmonic complexity than a Russian, even an angry Russian. Father Nicanor spoke eleven languages, held five doctorates, and had said Mass on seven continents. Yes, all seven. And he was Father Baptist's confessor.

"Does he ever make you do the Stations?" I asked.

"Who?"

"Father Nicanor."

"What about him, Martin? I was miles away."

"I asked you if Father Nicanor ever makes you do the Stations."

"I suppose he would if he felt my sins required it."

"Have they?—ever required it, I mean."

"Martin, what are you driving at?"

"Oh nothing."

29

"I CAN SEE THE HEADLINES NOW," said Taper, framing the air with his hands. "THE LIQUOR MURDERS."

"FULBRIGHT'S FINEST LICK THE BUCKET," I said, massaging my lower back which was beginning to throb after a long day, a day which was far from over. "WOTTA WAY TO GO."

"Better that than THE QUILT FROM HELL," said Father. "You're sure that details about the casting cloth have been kept from the press—from everyone?"

"Unless Wickes here talks in his sleep."

"To whom?" asked Wickes. "I'm not married."

"Well," said Father, "there is that."

We were standing in front of Auxiliary Bishop Silverspur's residence at St. Michael's at the corner of Third and Euclid. At Father's suggestion, I had stopped at a booth and buzzed Sergeant Wickes on his cellular phone to tell him we were headed there after Father's brief sojourn at St. Basil's.

St. Michael's was nothing like St. Philip's. It was a medium-to-large church in a rather affluent parish, built back in 1965. The effects of Vatican II had not yet had time to infect the diocesan architects—too much.

"So," I said, leaning heavily on my cane, "are you going to make us beg?"

"For what?" said Taper, all innocence.

"For a look at the second part of the quilt, of course."

"Oh," he said nonchalantly. "That."

"Yes," I said a bit chalantly. "That."

He reached into his pocket and brought out a color photo along with a computer print-out. "Here's the second piece, and there's the digitally-generated translation."

I held them side by side while Father stood at my elbow and scrutinized them. I was aware of his breath rustling the hairs on my knuckles.

"Another pentagram," said Wickes, an understandable but unflattering twinge of gloat in his voice.

"Indeed," said Father.

"And the PS is inverted to SP," added the sergeant.

"And this triangle?" said Father. "Pointed down with a horizontal line through it?"

"Earth. It's the Hermetic symbol for earth."

"You've been doing your homework," commented Father. Wickes didn't know whether to bleat, blight, or blither.

"So has Sybil Wexler," said Taper, pulling another computer print-out from another pocket and unfolding it. "The computer whiz at the lab. She's convinced these letters are part of an acrostic, a word puzzle, so she devised a program that systematically fit the two pieces together in every possible way. This is just one page of a whole stack."

"She's assuming, of course," said Father, "that the two pieces we have are adjacent to each other in the complete quilt. It is very possible that they are not. Still, I'm a big fan of initiative."

"I'll tell her that," said Taper, folding it up again. "She's a big fan of yours."

Father leaned thoughtfully against the stone wall by the front gate. "By the way," he said presently, "did you find out anything from the carpets at Bishop Brassorie's residence?"

"Sure," said Wickes, flipping open his trusty notebook. "The dirt you found just inside the entrance to the building turned out to be of a clay-like composition, high feldspar content. Comprehensive mineral and chemical analyses aren't in yet. Preliminary biological tests revealed a high concentration of anaerobic bacteria—dead from contact with the air, but enough residue left for detection under a microscope. This suggests a subterranean origin, and that the clod was recently excavated from a depth of at least three to six feet."

"Like a grave," said Father.

"Like a grave," agreed Wickes. "The lab is already running cross-comparisons from the hole where Bishop Silverspur was discovered this morning."

"I'm almost certain they'll match," said Father. "I've noticed that I sometimes track that kind of soil home from internments. Dirt from several feet down isn't like topsoil—different color and texture. Hard to get out of the rugs. Millie invariably throws a fit."

"That's why you were asking about construction sites," said Taper. "They have to dig down before they lay foundations."

"Did any of that clay turn up on Brassorie's shoes? Or on his carpet?"

"No," said Wickes. "There was nothing at all like what you found downstairs at the front entrance. There were more traces of hyssop on his living room carpet upstairs, but since we already found that in his chapel, it comes as no surprise."

"So," said Father, pushing himself away from the wall, "barring some surprise from the chemical analysis, it would seem that someone who was at the scene of Bishop Silverspur's death also crossed the threshold of St. Philip's rectory, but didn't go as far as Bishop Brassorie's suite."

"So you think someone at St. Philip's murdered Bishop Silverspur?" asked Wickes.

"Thinking is not knowing," said Father. "For all we know, one of the seminarians took an evening stroll through the cemetery sometime last week. It certainly is within walking distance. I suggest you get a warrant and have the shoes and closet floors of everyone at St. Philip's examined."

"Check," said Taper.

"Well," said Wickes, "it looks like I'm involved in my first serial murder case. Brassorie, as it turns out, was the second man murdered in the sequence of events, though he was the first to be discovered. Both men were auxiliaries of Archbishop Fulbright, so my guess is it's two down, two to go. And let's not forget that the archbishop's middle name is Psalmellus. P-S. Maybe he decided to do some episcopal housecleaning."

"I'm sure the archbishop regrets his middle name," said Father, "for many reasons. I doubt that he's fool enough to leave so obvious a signature behind. However, I am inclined to accept your assessment that we're involved in a serial pattern."

"But there is an inconsistency," said Wickes. "The triangle on the right foot instead of the left hand."

Father shrugged. "In both cases the triangle was carved into the soft tissues of an extremity, the palm and the sole. In both cases the base of the triangle faced the torso while the apex pointed toward the digits, be they fingers or toes. I see enough consistency to discern at least the probability of a pattern."

"That seems like a significant consistency," said the gardener thoughtfully.

"By the way," said Father, "was there any hyssop in the grave?"

"Yes, as a matter of fact," said Taper. "The lab boys might have overlooked it if they hadn't been 'keyed in' due to the Brassorie case."

"St. Augustine grass, foxtail weed, sage ..." Wickes was consulting his notebook. "Here it is. Traces of hyssop were found on his moccasins."

"Moccasins?" blinked Father.

"Yeah," said Wickes.

Father Baptist was scratching his chin. "What was Zia Silverspur wearing when he died?"

"Ah," said Wickes, slipping his pages again. "Buckskin jacket with fringes—you know, Buffalo Bill style—matching pants. His feet were bare, but a pair of deerskin moccasins were sort of tossed in along side the body. He also had an amulet of small beads in the shape of an eagle around his neck, a silver ear clip in the shape of a feather, and several turquoise rings on his fingers. Like he was going to a pow-wow."

"From what I hear," said Father, "that's not surprising."

"How so?"

Father Baptist ran his fingers back through his hair. "Bishop Zia Silverspur was apparently of American Indian descent—Gabrielino Tribe, I think. I read something about him a while back in the diocesan newspaper. His blood heritage hadn't mattered much to him as he climbed up the hierarchical ladder, but once he had a bishop's hat—"

"It suddenly dawned on him one day," I interrupted, "while he was shaving, that though he had been rubbing his elbows raw with Kimo Sabe, he had more in common with Tonto. Suddenly he felt compelled to get back to his roots."

"A common compulsion these days," said Taper.

"And not a bad thing," said Father, "if one engages in intelligent research. Unfortunately, Bishop Silverspur fell under the spell of his own imagination. Like so many people in search of the mystical, he just presumed that whatever struck his fancy, whatever fired his imagination, whatever gave him emotional highs, was real. Apparently the thought of conducting something as tedious as historical research didn't appeal to him."

"Got on a lot of talk shows," I said. "Bad-mouthing Blessed Junipero Serra for having the cultural audacity and political poor taste to convert the Indians in California to the Faith. The nerve of that ferocious friar, Serra the Insufferable, browbeating all those helpless Indians—excuse me, Native Americans—forcing them to accept Catholicism by brute force, and all by himself. Kicking and screaming he hauled them to the baptismal font. Thousands of them. Southern California is still crisscrossed with the troughs left by their pathetically dragging feet. That one-man avenging marauder, striking terror into hoards of thunderstruck hearts, Nippo the Nefarious ..."

Sergeant Wickes was giving me a perplexed look, like he knew I was embellishing but didn't know how much, or on what side of the watershed my own opinion flowed. I debated whether to relieve him of the tension of doubt or let him stew a while. I was just deciding to add more salt when Father Baptist turned the conversation.

"In any case, hyssop seems to figure somehow in both crimes."

"Right," said Wickes eagerly. "Another consistency."

"But," said Father, "we don't know why. Let's not be too quick to jump to conclusions. We haven't yet established that the killer carried it into Bishop Brassorie's chapel. For all we know, Brassorie himself purchased it from an herbalist and boiled it as part of a daily regimen of aromatherapy. Nor do we know if Bishop Silverspur picked it up on his moccasins by walking through a patch of it somewhere nearby, or if he used it regularly as part of some Native American ritual."

"Ah," said Taper with a twinkle in his eye, "but wouldn't it be grand if the hyssop is part of the pattern?" He made a frame again in the air with his fingers. "Imagine the headlines: THE AROMA MURDERS."

"Or," said I, "TWO SCENTS IN THE COLLECTION PLATE."

"Jacco Babs could get another Pulitzer," said Taper.

Father was scratching his chin again. "Has it been determined whether Bishop Silverspur was actually drinking the burgundy, and how much?"

"Actually, it wasn't burgundy," said Taper. "The bottle was standard California winery stock, with the glue from the original label on it, but the liquor inside was something else entirely. The assistant coroner, John Holtsclaw—he came aboard a couple of years after you left the force, Jack—he's part Gabrielino Indian or something. He's pretty sure it's a home-brewed concoction made from distilled juniper berries and jimson weed. Real fire water from the reservation. You could pour it in your gas tank and watch your car exceed the speed of sound, but don't get any on the fenders because it will dissolve the paint right off. Holtsclaw gave it an unpronounceable name, but said it's loosely translated, 'Blood catch fire, brain turn ash.' Bootlegged for sure. Impossible to trace."

"Are you going to say this is consistent with Jägermeister?" asked Wickes.

"Not yet," said Father. "Anything on how much he'd consumed?"

"Hard to say," said Taper. "Some. With the body lying there all of nine days, it may be impossible to tell. Why did you ask?"

"Just fishing," said Father. "Any word on Joel Maruppa?"

"The seminarian? Not yet."

"What do you plan to do when you find him?"

Taper folded his arms across his chest. "At the moment we just want him for questioning. He was the last person to see Bishop Brassorie alive."

"That you know of."

"That we know of."

Father pushed the wooden gate open and followed the walkway down the side of St. Michael's toward the bishop's residence. "I have a confession to make, Larry. Joel showed up at my rectory last night, cold, scared, starved, and exhausted. We were able to accommodate all four of his immediate needs."

"Is he there now?" said the lieutenant, halting in his tracks.

"Yes. I thought it best for him to get a good night's rest. He's been through a lot, and I'm convinced he had nothing to do with the murder of Bishop Brassorie."

"Not cool, Jack," said Taper angrily. "You should have called me immediately. We've been wasting man-hours looking for him."

"You're right, of course," said Father, slowing his stride. "I apologize. It's just that if I'd called you last night, you would have come right over and interrogated him—and he was utterly exhausted. And this morning, so much else was going on."

"Billowack will call it harboring a fugitive."

"Joel Maruppa has not been charged with a crime, so he isn't a fugitive. In any case, I'll vouch for him. And I'm inviting you to come and talk with him after we get done here."

Father's hand was on the doorbell.

High-heeled footsteps approached from within. The latch unlocked and the door swung open.

"Oh, hello," said Cheryl Farnsworth.

From her limp red hair, vacuous expression, and collapsed posture, it was obvious she had been informed of her boss's whereabouts.

30

"YOU'VE GOT ME," said Cheryl Farnsworth, pointing to an elaborately decorated cloth hanging on the wall above the late Bishop Silverspur's desk. "I don't know what that's supposed to represent. He was just into cowboys and Indians, big time."

The whole office was something out of a western history museum. The walls were cluttered with spears, arrows, knives, pipes, you name it. The floor was a patchwork of mismatched throw rugs. It was bumpy to walk on. The shelves were void of books but brimming with wood carvings, bleached bones, ceremonial drums and clusters of feathers.

And yes, I'll admit it. I was aware that Miss Farnsworth was still wearing the same blue dress and green scarf she'd worn to the funeral that morning. I also noticed—and not just because I was honing my detective skills—the same gold charm around her neck from the first time I'd met her in the archbishop's office. It looked like a funny zigzag. I wanted to ask her about it, but now was not the time.

"You sound like you didn't approve," I commented, kicking myself for the unwarranted note of authority that had slipped into my tone. Who was I trying to impress, anyway?

She puckered her lips, picking her words carefully. " I hated seeing him parading his mid-life crisis in public. Don't get me wrong, I love the Native Americans. I've visited several reservations in Arizona and New Mexico with him, and I'm currently involved in negotiations with the board of directors at the Old West Museum regarding—well, that's another matter. I got the impression they were embarrassed by his behavior."

"But wasn't he their blood brother?" asked Wickes.

"Only one sixteenth," she said, smiling in spite of the gravity of the moment. "The rest of him was Scottish and Lithuanian."

"When did you last see Bishop Silverspur?" asked Taper.

"The Thursday before last, just after lunch. I helped him carry his bags out to the car."

"And as far as you knew, he was heading for Toluca Springs."

"Yes."

"He didn't mention any stops he intended to make?"

"He did say something about a side trip to Palm Gardens, you know, where they have all those date stands by the highway. But that's almost to the Springs, and now it looks—" She stifled a shudder. "—like he never left the city. It's weird, thinking of him just laying there in that grave since, since—"

"Excuse me," said Father. "When did you find out he was dead?"

"Marsha Dukes called from the archbishop's office a little while ago. But ..." She hesitated, thinking.

"What?"

"In a way, I guess I already knew. I've known it for days."

"How so?"

She sniffed, rubbed her eyes, and reached for her purse on a nearby chair. From inside she produced a small, dark, plastic object.

"A pager," I said. Whoa, give me a medal.

"Yes," she said. "I hate these things. I utterly hate them."

Ah, at last I knew we had something in common.

"But Zia—Bishop Silverspur—insisted I carry one," she continued, "just in case he ever needed to reach me. As my employer he had that right, I guess, but I resisted the idea for a long time. I finally agreed, only under the condition that he never give the number to anyone else. The thought of being pestered everywhere I go—"

"So he was the only person who ever beeped you?" said Wickes.

"That's right."

"And you gave the number to no one else," said Taper, "not even close friends?"

"No one," she said. "Like I said, I hate these things."

"And?" asked Father.

"And." She let out a big sigh. "I haven't heard a peep out of it since the Thursday before last."

"The day he left for Toluca Springs," said Taper.

She nodded, sniffing. "He used to beep me seven, eight, nine times a day. Sometimes more. But since he left for the Springs, nothing. He had a cellular phone which he carried around in his pocket. I've called the number dozens of times, but—" Mascara-tinted tears were leaking from the corners of her eyes.

I wished I had a silk hankie to offer her, but all I had was a travel pack of Kleenex.

"Sergeant Wickes," said Father. "You didn't mention anything about a cellular phone being found on Bishop Silverspur's body."

"That's because there wasn't one," said Wickes. "I'm sure of it."

"Perhaps it's in his car," said Lieutenant Taper, "wherever that is."

"When Marsha called," she said, dabbing her eyes, "she also said you requested another meeting this afternoon at four."

"Yes," said Father.

"That's less than forty-five minutes from now. If you don't mind, I've got a few things to do before I scurry over to the Chancery Office."

"Is it really that late?" blinked Father.

"You know how it is," said Taper. "'Blood catch fire—'"

"'Brain turn ash,'" said Cheryl Farnsworth.

We all looked at her.

"That was Bishop Silverspur's favorite drink," she said. "He always brought some back from his trips to the reservations."

"In burgundy bottles?" asked Taper.

"In all kinds of bottles," said Cheryl Farnsworth. "Whatever the tribal distillers could get their hands on. How did you
know?"

"It's a long story," said Father. "And we have a meeting
to rush off to. Lieutenant, Sergeant, I'd invite you but I think
I'll handle this better if I'm solo. Internal Church business
and all that."

"Fine," said Taper. "Be that way."

"Come, Martin," said Father, heading for the front door.
"See you there, Miss Farnsworth."

"Hi ho, Silver," I said, lassoing my faithful cane. "Away."

31

"I SUGGESTED THIS MEETING," said Father as we seated
ourselves at the archbishop's conference table, "to save
time—and perhaps lives."

It was the lopsided chessboard again.

The archbishop's eyes were funnels of simmering, hierarchical furor and frustration. His episcopal status, I mused,
placed him in the middle of a most perplexing political and
emotional sandwich. The anxious blinks of his pastors below,
the condescending glares of his superiors in Rome, and the
penetrating cathode-ray eyeballs of the meddlesome media
were all upon him. He did not know who to trust—with the
possible exception of Father Baptist, which galled him miserably. And the situation was becoming increasingly intolerable.
Billowack's incursion on the heels of Father Baptist's frontal
assault earlier that afternoon certainly hadn't helped his mood
or outlook any.

Morley's white auxiliary, Bishop Jeremiah Ravenshorst, had
the face of a man strapped to a rack, a swinging pendulum
descending toward him a notch at a time. He looked haunted,
hunted, hewed, and harried. A cruel thought danced through
my mind. I saw myself going up to him and slapping him on
the back while shaking his hand with one of those joke buzzer
rings in each palm. Zzzzing! In his overwrought state, he
would have exploded into a blurry fog of scattering subatomic
particles. Instant annihilation, what fun—at least, until I'd
have to admit the deed in the confessional. Knee pads, indeed.

On the other hand, Morley's other auxiliary, Bishop Molmar Mgumba, looked surprisingly calm, doodling on a notepad with one half of his concentration while fondling something hidden under the folds of his multi-colored coat with the
other. The large white eyes in his burnt umber countenance
seemed focused on something beyond the table, beyond the
room, beyond the walls of the building, beyond the Emerald
City, on beyond Oz. "Are you a good bishop or a bad
bishop?" asked the White Witch of the North.

The Altar Belles were, well, the Altar Belles. No matter the
circumstance, they looked gray and grim. On this occasion
there was also a suggestion of furtive vigilance in their collective, somber stare. They seemed stretched tight, like a mouse-
trap spring when it's pulled into its lethal position. Tension
was running high throughout the Chancery, no doubt. Probably throughout the whole archdiocesan machinery.

Cheryl Farnsworth, sitting opposite them, was still wearing
the same dress and scarf, complimented with a recent splash of
perfume. Gardenia, I think. Her eyes were swollen, and she'd
given up on trying to cover the damage with makeup. More
than anything, she seemed exhausted. Her red hair was a bit
on the droopy side.

The two chairs previously occupied by the lawyers, Shlomo
Brennan and Guilio Gerezanno, were empty. Their absence
was duly noted, but the vacuum left in their wake I found
somehow consoling. The archbishop's power to summon
men to his presence on a moment's notice had limitations.
Hm.

Monsignor Goolgol still looked like a tiddlywink left behind
after the second-grade championship. All sprockets but no
gears.

It was apparent that one of the two pawns at our end of the
chessboard seemed to have grown in stature since the last
match. Can a pawn become a knight, or maybe a rook? Father Baptist was showing them that he could. The other pawn,
well, I just sat there rubbing the handle of my cane, taking it
all in with what I hoped was a sagacious expression on my
face.

"First," said Father, "I need to get a clear picture of where
each of you was at the time of the murders."

"Are we suspects?" asked Ms. Stephanie Fury, her features
taut. I noticed she avoided eye contact with yours truly. And
the world helped the woman, my eye.

"Yes," said Father.

"Like hell," she retorted.

"Preposterous," said Goolgol.

"Father Baptist," hrmphed the archbishop. "I don't see how any of this—"

"Excuse me, Your Grace," said Father. "Two of your auxiliaries are dead. The same shadow may well be hovering above the two who remain, perhaps even over yourself."

"He's right," said Bishop Ravenshorst, twitching anxiously as his private pitty pendulum slipped down another notch. "He's ... right."

"Perhaps," said Bishop Mgumba, still fingering that lump inside his coat. Such serenity in the presence of adversity was most remarkable, surely commendable—for me, it was irksome. I visualized not a sword above his head, but a jack-hammer. And I was beginning to wonder what it was he was so contentedly fondling in there—meditation balls, tranquilizers, Silly Putty perhaps?

"Suspicion is not accusation," said Father. "But like it or not, I need to ask each and all of you about your whereabouts on Thursday June first and Tuesday the sixth. Your Grace."

"Both days," said the archbishop, "I was in my office at the Chancery. Thursday the first was the day most of my staff left for the retreat in Toluca Springs, and Tuesday the sixth they were still away. Marsha Dukes stayed behind, so we can vouch for each other. As for the nights, I was alone in my residence both evenings."

"Do you have a housekeeper?" asked Father.

"She isn't there nights," said the archbishop.

"Any visitors, phone calls?"

"Not that I remember. Just Monsignor Havermeyer Tuesday evening, to inform me that Bishop Brassorie was dead."

"Why didn't you go to Toluca Springs?"

The archbishop blinked. "It never occurred to me. The retreat was for the benefit of all the clergy, religious, and staff in my charge. I figured they needed a vacation, and I needed a break—"

Three high-pitched beeps scissored his sentence. He looked angrily around the table. Marsha Dukes sheepishly held up her pager. "Sorry," she said, clicking it off.

The archbishop hrmphed. He didn't like those nasty things any more than I did. Dear me, that meant we had something in common.

"And Your Lordship?" said Father turning to Bishop Ravenshorst, the white auxiliary.

"W-w-well," he grimaced, cracking his knuckles, "I left for Toluca Springs Thursday morning with Father Spindle from St. Cyprian's. We were in my car, and Father Spindle did the driving. I hate long trips. We left right after breakfast, around nine o'clock. We took our time and got there around two-thirty. Lots of people saw me at the retreat. My whole staff was there, and representatives from all the parishes in my jurisdiction. That's where I was on Tuesday as well. I flew home by myself early Wednesday morning as soon as I heard about Bishop Brassorie."

"The same is true of myself," said Bishop Mgumba, his basso voice as thick, rich, and nauseatingly sweet as an amaretto truffle. "I drove alone both ways, but I attended many workshops and discussions at the retreat. Certainly witnesses can be found to attest to my whereabouts. I, too, returned immediately upon learning of my fellow bishop's demise."

"Did it come as a surprise," asked Father, "that Bishop Brassorie was not in Toluca Springs with you?"

Bishop Mgumba shrugged. "Not really."

"Bishop Ravenshorst?" probed Father.

"Bishop Brassorie," hedged the white auxiliary, "was sort of a lone wolf, if you know what I mean."

Monsignor Goolgol cleared his throat. I thought he was going to up-chuck his Adam's apple. "I was in Toluca Springs from Thursday until Tuesday morning of this week."

"Tuesday morning," remarked Father Baptist. "Where were you in the evening?"

"The time of Bishop Brassorie's murder." The monsignor cleared his throat again. "Let's see. Yes. I came back from the retreat two days early because I just couldn't afford to get behind in my paperwork." He glanced over at the archbishop for approval but got none. "I worked in my study at my residence at St. Damien's until almost nine. Yes, that's about when Archbishop Fulbright phoned to tell me about Bishop Brassorie's, uh, demise."

"Nine," said Father.

"Monsignor Havermeyer phoned me from St. Philip's," the archbishop interjected, "around eight-thirty after discovering Bishop Brassorie's body. First the police, then me."

"And you called Monsignor Goolgol," said Father.

"Yes."

"So you knew he was back in town."

"I must have. Why yes, he'd phoned me that afternoon to let me know where he'd be."

"Monsignor Goolgol, did anyone see you at your residence that night?"

"No, no one was around." The monsignor pulled out a handkerchief and began mopping the bony buttresses of his forehead.

"And the ladies?" said Father, addressing the Altar Belles. They sniffed at the term.

"We were all here in town both days," said Stephanie Fury.

"Someone had to keep the Chancery running," said Marsha Dukes.

"What about in the evenings?" asked Father. "How about Tuesday night between six-thirty and eight, when Bishop Brassorie was murdered?"

"Tuesday," said Ms. Sugarman, glancing expectantly at Mss. Dukes and Fury.

"That was the night of Madeline's TV show," said Ms. Dukes.

"'Spotlight on Community,'" said Ms. Sugarman. She said it with a note of pride, but I caught an underlying subharmonic edge of trepidation in her tone. Was she hiding something?

"The three of us were at the studio," said Ms. Fury, "from five until about ten thirty."

"Closer to eleven," said Ms. Sugarman, again with that hint of apprehension. "And don't forget Sister Charlene."

"Vickers?" asked Father. "From St. Philip's?"

"Yes. She was there, too."

"The four of you," said Father.

"We're it," said Ms. Fury. "We're the entire production staff. I'm the producer-director. Marsha operates the cameras. We've only got two. She just goes back and forth making sure they're aimed right."

"Once in a while I get to do a zoom in or out," said Ms. Dukes with a pinch of sarcasm, "but not often."

"And Charleen works the switchboard," said Ms. Fury. "It's a call-in show, and she screens out the quacks—well, most of them."

"And there is no other staff on hand?" asked Father. "No technicians, electricians, whatever?"

"No," said Ms. Fury. "It's just a cubby-hole studio. If you want to check it out, it's on the second floor of this building."

"Right here in the Chancery?" asked Father.

"Real low-budget," nodded Ms. Fury.

"If anything goes wrong," said Ms. Sugarman, "we just go off the air while we wait for Cheryl to come and fix it."

"Miss Farnsworth?" asked Father.

The lady in the blue dress and green scarf shifted in her chair, sending her little gold charm swinging. "I used to work in music production. I know something about tape machines and video cameras. Sometimes I act as technical troubleshooter."

"Were your services required at any time Tuesday evening?"

"No," said Miss Farnsworth. "I was home alone all night at St. Michael's."

"You have a room there?" asked Father.

"I have my own apartment downtown, but sometimes when I work late Bishop Silverspur lets me use the guest room."

"I see," said Father Baptist. "So except for Miss Farnsworth, you ladies can all account for each other's whereabouts Tuesday evening."

"Yes," they said severally.

"What about the previous Thursday?"

"The same," blurted Ms. Sugarman.

The other Belles exchanged glances.

"We do the show Tuesdays and Thursdays." The faint edge in Ms. Sugarman's voice had become a coarse, rusty blade.

"Yes," said Ms. Fury, soothingly. "That's right. The archdiocese doesn't have its own cable channel, so we do a microwave feed across town to the Rapture Channel—you know, TCN, the Totally Christian Network. We're the only Catholic show on their cable channel."

Father Baptist didn't speak for several seconds. "And you were all occupied at the studio that Thursday evening as well?"

"All of us," said Marsha Dukes.

"You'd all swear to that, of course."

"Of course," said Madeline Sugarman.

"And you, Miss Farnsworth?"

"Home alone I'm afraid," said Cheryl, eyeing the others with an expression I couldn't fathom, "at my own apartment. I guess I've got no provable alibi for either night."

"Alibis are curious things," said Father, easing himself back in his chair.

"How so?" asked Cheryl Farnsworth.
Father Baptist remained silent.

32

"THERE ARE THREE CRITERIA for becoming a Knight of the
Tumblar," Pierre was explaining to Joel Maruppa. "The first,
of course, is that you must be a practicing Roman Catholic,
upholding all that the Church teaches, even those irksome
things which elude your present understanding."

"Father said Joel here is a seminarian," said Jonathan,
pouring himself another glass of champagne.

"Then all the more reason to repeat," said Pierre sternly,
"you must be a practicing Roman Catholic."

Joel looked from Pierre to Jonathan to Edward to Arthur to
me to Father and finally back to Pierre. Then, with a defiant
smirk, he unbuttoned his shirt and revealed something dangling against his chest.

"Hm," said Pierre. "A five-fold scapular. And a St.
Benedict medal. That's a good sign."

"What else?" said Joel, closing his shirt and straightening
his tie. There were, of course, no tuxedoes in the poor bin, but
I had managed to assemble a serviceable black suit for the lad.

"You must enjoy having a good time," said Pierre. " I
can't help it myself. That's my name: Bontemps. Some men
aspire to having a good time, others strive to have a good time,
and a few brave souls even achieve it. But me, I was born to
have a good time. It is my destiny."

"That's why he's our leader," explained Jonathan.

"And we do have a good time," laughed Arthur.

"Boy, do we," said Edward.

"Yes," said Pierre with an air of authority, "a Knight Tumblar must enjoy merrymaking. Drinking and singing are a
major part of our work."

"Work?" asked Joel. "Drinking and singing?"

"Most people today, I'll grant you," said Arthur, eyeing
the bubbles in his glass, "are Puritans. Thou shalt not drink
without guilt—"

"Remember all those alcoholics in China," said Edward.

"Thou shalt not smoke cigars—" continued Arthur.

"Second-hand smoke is politically incorrect," added Jonathan, "except when emitted from Indian smoke-huts, outdoor barbecues, and active volcanoes awaiting human sacrifices."

"But those will go, too," said Pierre. "Just give the legislators time."

"Thou shalt not sing in public," continued Arthur. "Clamorous frivolity is not to be encouraged. The greatest commandment in our 'free society' is this: Thou shalt not have a good time. The Puritans set the tone when they settled in New England, and it persists in our cultural subconscious to this day. Well, we're Catholics, not Calvinists."

"'Where ever Catholic sun doth shine,'" quoted Pierre, raising his glass.

"'There's lots of laughter and good red wine,'" chimed the others, rising to their feet.

"'At least I've always heard it so,'" said Father.

"'Benedicamus domino,'" said we all, clinking our glasses together.

"Hilaire Belloc," explained Pierre. "Historian and poet."

"Do you drink?" asked Jonathan.

Joel eyed everyone again. The wheels were really grinding inside that head of his. "I am a Maruppa, like my father. I can drink any of you under the table."

"I'll take that as a yes," said Arthur.

"Mr. Feeney here doesn't drink," noted Jonathan.

I felt a cold shiver.

"And can therefore never be a Tumblar," said Edward.

"Poor soul," said Pierre. "Dare I say it? He took the pledge."

I felt a hot shiver.

"Imagine that," sighed Arthur. "Never to drink champagne again."

"Perish the thought," shuddered Pierre.

"He's what you call," said Edward sadly, "a teetotaler."

All eyes turned to me in pitiful sympathy.

That did it. I set down my glass hard. "I am not a teetotaler."

"But Mr. Feeney," said Pierre, "Martin old chum, you did swear off drinking. What does that make you if not a teetotaler?"

"Teetotaling," I said gruffly, "is an erroneous Puritan notion, based on the absurd idea that alcohol is evil, as if God would make anything inanimate evil. I thought you understood. It is precisely because alcohol is good that I took the pledge. I gave up one good for a greater good. It's like the difference, Mr. Bontemps, between celibacy and misogyny."

"Quite right," said Pierre. "The old bean must've slipped. My apologies."

"And mine," said Edward.

"Accepted," said the gardener.

"And the third requirement?" asked Joel, his lips tight with indignation.

"Oh that," said Edward. "Unlike other organizations that bow to politically corrective pressures, our third criteria for consideration for membership in the Tumblars is that we have to like you."

"Like me?"

"Why yes," said Jonathan. "We certainly wouldn't want you around if we didn't enjoy your company."

"What's with you guys?" said Joel crossly. "What makes you think I'd want to join your weird little club? Who do you think you are?"

"We're missionaries," said Pierre, "of a fashion."

"You see," said Arthur, "the Fundies and Thumpers have discredited street-corner preaching, the Telly-Vangies have 'one-eight-hundreded' evangelization beyond repair, and the JW's have made everyone afraid to answer their doors. The problem is: how do we get the message out?"

"In the midst of all that flack and confusion," said Edward, "how do we spread the Catholic Faith, as Christ commanded us to do?"

"A real problem in our peculiar times," said Jonathan.

"But," said Pierre, "our dear Hilaire Belloc also said—I'm paraphrasing with abandon, but get used to it, I'm that way—there are only three ways you can convince anyone of anything: coercion, deception, and snobbery. In our mission-ary work, coercion is lost to us, since no one can be forced to embrace the Faith. That would be a violation of Free Will. Deception, of course, is out—Satan being the father of lies and all that. Which leaves us with but one course of action."

"Conversion through snobbery," said Jonathan.

"To snobbery," said the others, clinking their glasses.

"You'd be surprised," said Arthur, "how many people come up to us, wanting to know who we are, why we're all in formal wear—"

"Why *do* you wear tuxedoes?" asked Joel.

Edward swirled the fluid in his glass. "It is after six, isn't it?"

"Yes," said Joel.

Edward nodded, his answer having been given.

Joel did not understand.

He would learn.

"And once the door to conversation is open," said Pierre, "all sentences lead to Rome. You will find us in the most unlikely places, shouting to be heard over the loud music, informing the curious."

"Don't they just think you're a bunch of drunks?" scowled Joel.

"St. Peter was so accused," said Arthur, "on the day of Pentecost, yet thousands were baptized that day. And of course there was—"

"Excuse me, gents," interupted Father. "Before you go further with the, uh, indoctrination, may I remind you that I asked you here for this special meeting to see if you found out anything."

"It has been a mission," said Arthur, "above and beyond the call of duty."

"No doubt," said Father.

The Tumblars settled themselves in their chairs. With the addition of Joel, who kept looking around warily, there was no place for me to sit. No matter. When my back gets as sore as it was that night, I actually prefer to stand.

"There's a place down an alley off Delmonico," began Jonathan. "It's called 'La Hotte Spotte.'"

"A real dive," commented Edward, "in the high-class sense."

"While we were there," said Pierre, "we heard Bishop Brassorie's name several times. Just conversations here and there, regular patrons. Apparently he used to show his face, if not a lot, at least enough to be known."

"And now to be missed," added Arthur.

"Big tipper," said Edward.

"And he was usually there with Ravenshorst and Silverspur," said Jonathan. "None of them has been seen all week. Is it true, what I heard on the radio about Zia Silverspur?"

"I don't know what you heard," said Father. "He was found dead in Bishop Brassorie's grave."

"Wow," said Jonathan. "And just laying there since last week. Must have been pretty ripe when they found him."

"So," said Father, sniffing, "Ravenshorst, Silverspur, and Brassorie frequented—or at least occasioned—'La Hotte Spotte.' Any mention of Molmar Mgumba?"

"Not there," said Pierre. "At the other dive."

A snicker darted around the room.

"Yeah, Pierre," said Edward. "Tell Father about 'The Hole in the Dike.'"

"I'd rather not," said Pierre, a rare blush blossoming on his face.

"The name perhaps says it all," said Father.

"No perhaps about it," said Arthur. "There was Pierre, surrounded by these fierce-looking, uh—"

"You should have seen him," laughed Jonathan.

"Go on," said Edward. "Tell him what you said."

Pierre coughed.

Edward stood and attempted to mimic Pierre's monarchical stance. "He said, 'Excuse me, ladies. You're arguing with the wrong man—'"

Pierre coughed again and stood up. If his words were going to come back upon him, he'd rather utter them himself—accurately. "What I said was, 'Pardon me, mesdames, but you've no quarrel with me. You see, I am a lesbian.'"

Joel let out a laugh and a gasp at the same time. It must have hurt.

"And what did they say?" asked Father.

"Oh, they were dumbfounded," said Pierre. "The important thing, though, is that somewhere in the midst of all that leather and lace, I heard some key words. Namely Brassorie, Mgumba, Fury, and Sugarman. And something else not on your list: Starfire."

"Didn't you mention a Starfire recently?" said Father, turning to me.

"That I did," I said. "She was the witch that Sister Veronica Marie invited here to poison the minds of the children at St. Philomena's grammar school, years ago."

"Well," said Pierre, "she's kept the faith, and she owns some kind of witchery store near Delmonico and Piedmont."

"There were a bunch of these on the bar," said Edward, unfolding a bright yellow flyer cluttered with wavering words. "She's going to be giving a lecture on 'Pentoven Magick' this coming Wednesday evening at the St. Francis of Assisi parish hall."

"That's just about a mile from here," said Arthur.

"Fr. Jay's parish," said Jonathan. "Perhaps we should attend."

"Popinjay," said Pierre, quoting from an imaginary dictionary, "a strutting, supercilious person."

"Sounds like your expedition has been fruitful," said Father. "Tell me Joel, of the following list of people, who would recognize you if they bumped into you: Marsha Dukes, Madeline Sugarman, Stephanie Fury, and Sister Charleen Vickers?"

"Sister Charleen, of course," said Joel. "She lives in the same residence as Bishop Brassorie, er, did. She does, he did. And Stephanie Fury might. She chaired the vocational board that admitted me to the diocesan seminary."

"Did you have a beard then?"

"Yes."

"For a just and serious cause, would you consider shaving it off?"

Joel's eyes widened. "I—I'd have to think about it."

"Please do so," said Father. "And then do so. I want you to accompany these gentlemen on their mission for the next few nights. You are in a better position than they to spot anyone connected with the Chancery."

"And it would give you a chance to see us in action," said Arthur.

"And we you," said Pierre.

"A song," said Edward.

"Yes, a song," said Pierre.

"You're all nuts," said Joel, stroking his beard protectively. "You know that."

"First another prayer to St. Anthony," said Father. "In fact, I'd like to request that you all begin a novena to both St. Anthony and St. Thomas More to help in our endeavors." He indicated the statues on the edge of his desk. "I need their guidance and protection, as do you all."

"Of course," said Arthur.

"Done," said Pierre.

"So let this be the first night of nine days," said Father. "In the name of the Father—"

"—and of the Son," they all intoned, maneuvering off their chairs and onto their knees.

"—and of the Holy Ghost. Amen."

Just then the doorbell rang.

Clutching my cane, I began to rise from the floor, but Pierre in a flurry of exaggerated gallantry jumped up, charged through the doorway, and dashed down the hall, flute glass in hand. He didn't spill a drop.

"If it's the press," I called after him, "don't let 'em in."

We all waited in curious silence as the sound of the latch and the rusty hinges drifted up the hallway from the front porch. A moment or two later, Pierre came striding back into our midst with a courtly flourish.

"Reverend Father," he announced solemnly, "Knights of the Tumblar, beloved non-teetolating friend Martin Feeney, and cherished guest, Joel Maruppa. May I present—"

A shape draped in a long, black topcoat filled the doorway. For a split second I thought it was Billowack playing Hamlet's father's ghost, but the proportions were all wrong.

"—His Grace, Archbishop Morley Psalmellus Fulbright."

The Knights exchanged startled but knowing glances, gripped their glasses, and got upstanding. Father looked at his watch, pursed his lips as though he'd lost a personal bet by a matter of minutes, then rearranged his features to present his superior with a look of strength, confidence, calm, and an acceptable but conservative level of sacerdotal submission. Joel Maruppa looked like he'd swallowed his scapular. He was the last to rise and raise his glass.

"To Holy Mother Church," said Pierre.

"Holy Mother Church," said we all, clinking our glasses.

"And to Her good shepherds," said Pierre. "Long may they reign."

"Long may Her good shepherds reign." Clink, clink, clink.

Generally, unexpected visitors have some kind of reaction to the Tumblars, usually a combination of curious disapproval, encouraging disdain, and charmed envy. The archbishop, however, stood there like a black carnival tent, his office concealed within mysterious dark flaps, glaring first at the plaque just outside the study door, then ominously through us at Father Baptist. At last he spoke. "We need to talk."

"Of course," said Father, setting down his flute glass. "Gentlemen, you must excuse me. Please go on with the prayer, and do choose a good song."

"We will, Father," chimed the Knights as Father escorted his superior out of the room. "Rest assured, we will."

Sunday, June Eleventh

Feast Day of Saint Barnabas, Companion of Saint Paul and Martyr (60 AD)

32

"YOU'RE WALKING ON DANGEROUS GROUND." Mr. Turnbuckle was standing on the steps in front of St. Philomena's, his finger leveled at Father Baptist's nose. "How dare you accuse St. Thomas Aquinas of error, and from the pulpit?"

It was the morning after the archbishop's surprise visit to St. Philomena's. Father had just finished saying High Mass. The collection had been heftier than usual, if the weight of the pouch was any indicator, and the "in lieu of" Gregorian choir had outdone themselves. The ushers had done a good job of keeping intrusive cameramen outside, but there was no denying that the parishioners were enjoying being attached to a pastor who had aroused such attention in the news media. Several reporters, having been banished in no uncertain terms by Father from the church steps after Mass, were milling around the sidewalk beyond the wrought-iron gates, gathering "background material" on the cop-turned-priest-turned-cop.

"Actually," said Father calmly, nodding to other parishioners as they filed past, "the *Summa Theologica* contains a surprising number of blatant errors. Over thirty. Don't forget, St. Thomas denied the Immaculate Conception, thereby delaying its solemn definition by six centuries, so respected was his opinion."

"But he was a Saint."

"He was a man, Mr. Turnbuckle. He was not canonized for his writings, but for heroic virtue. He himself wanted his work burned before his death."

"No."

"Yes, and I quote: 'Everything I have written is as so much straw compared with the realities.' Unfortunately he realized too late that by departing from the ultra-realism of St. Augustine, he had opened a theological Pandora's Box. He attempted to reconcile the teachings of the Church with Aristotle, whose philosophy was based on materialism. It was through the *Summa* that many errors began to seep into the Church. Did you know that St. Thomas' best friend, St. Bonaventure, called him 'the father of all heresies'?"

"No."

"It took a few hundred years, but the seeds planted by St. Thomas have blossomed into the major ills that plague Holy Mother Church, and therefore the world, today."

Mr. Turnbuckle had turned a scary shade of crimson. "You go too far. You should stick to saying the Mass in Latin, and leave theology to theologians."

"And arrogant know-it-alls like Thurgood T. Turnbuckle," I mumbled inaudibly.

"I'm afraid you're missing a critical point, Mr. Turnbuckle," said Father. "We had the Latin Mass, but it didn't stop the Reformation. We had the Latin Mass, but it didn't prevent Vatican II. The Mass is not the issue, but rather the theology it represents. The modernists couldn't have stolen the Latin Mass from us if they hadn't first rewritten theology in the mind of the average Catholic priest and layman. The people would never have stood for the New Mass if they had been brought up with sound Catholic teaching. Unfortunately, most Trads just want to turn the clock back a few decades. What they don't realize is that the poison that produced our present chaos was festering long before this century began."

"Now see here—oomph!"

A plump, juicy plum of a woman bumped Mr. Turnbuckle aside and grasped Father's hands. "I wanna thank you so much, Faddah. My Bennie, he so happy you come to visit him in the hospital last week."

"It was my pleasure, Mrs. Cladusky."

She kissed his hands. "Not one hour after you anoint him, not one, he is better. Did you know that? To this day, on the floor is still the doctor's jaw."

"Extreme Unction often has its medicinal as well as spiritual benefits. I must drop by and see him again, perhaps this afternoon."

"He's home now. You come for dinner. I fix you a feast you never forget."

"Why, thank-you, Mrs. Cladusky."

"Muriel, Father. Please. To you I'm Muriel."

I was standing a few feet away like a scarecrow in the cornfield, propped up with my cane. Sergeant Wickes was at my side, having just experienced his first Latin Mass in decades. The words, "Well, what did you think?" hovered on the tip of my tongue, but my better judgment told me to say instead, "Thank-you for coming, Sergeant."

Wickes obviously wasn't sure what he thought, or how he felt about whatever it was he wasn't thinking, so he changed the subject slightly. "The lieutenant wanted to come, and his wife, too. But you know how it is. He doesn't dare take her anywhere she might come in contact with suspects in a case. He can't risk anyone connected with the investigation in progress gaining access to his family."

"Yeah," I said. "I can see how that could be dangerous."

"Me, I'm single and free. Anyway, I'll probably see you in a day or two as new things develop."

"No doubt." Then I added, "You know, you don't have to wait for new things to develop. Why not just drop by for breakfast? Or coffee? Millie's always got a pot or pan ready to break over your head."

Smiling, he descended the stairs and wandered off through the throng. Just then a pillar of graphite came strolling out of the church, her steel neckware and earware clunking hollowly. "Mr. Feeney," she said stiffly.

"Miss Sugarman." I nodded to her with what I hoped was reptilian respect.

"Stephanie was right. It was archaic and chauvinistic."

"Is," I corrected her. "How nice of His Gracefulness to send you down here for a Catholic experience, Ms. Sugarman. Or are you just doing research for your show? It must be quite a shock after the paganism and liturgical debauchery you're used to."

She looked at me icily. "'And the earth helped the woman,'" she rasped, nudging past and heading down the stairs.

"'Thou shalt not suffer a witch to live," I said, just loud enough for her to hear. Sorry, it just slipped out. That's the Protestant translation of Exodus twenty-two eighteen, which is inaccurate—the proper rendering is "wizards," not "witches." King James had his agenda. Oh well, the moment was irresistible.

"Oh," exclaimed Mrs. Theodora Turpin to her husband, Tanner, who was waiting patiently to shake Father Baptist's hand. "Wasn't that the woman from that cable TV show, 'Spotlight on Community'?"

"Yes, Dear," nodded her husband. "I think it was."

"Fancy her being here at St. Philomena's."

"Yes, Dear, imagine that."

"Do you remember how I tried and tried to call her while she was on the air the other night? And all I kept getting was that awful busy signal?"

"Yes, Dear. A lot of people must have been trying to get through."

"I've never not gotten through before. I was so furious."

"Yes, Dear, I do remember. Oh, good morning, Father Baptist. I just wanted to tell you how much I appreciated your insights on St. Thomas and the rise of rationalism—"

"How can you say such a thing?" Thurgood T. Turnbuckle had turned the turret of his attention and set his sights on Patrick Railsback, our head usher. "The Founding Fathers were inspired by the Holy Spirit to write the Constitution of the United States."

"The Founding Fathers were Freemasons," huffed Patrick Railsback. "What would the Holy Ghost be doing conspiring with heretics?"

"Besides," cut in the jolly voice of Pierre Bontemps, whose face and torso seemed to materialize out of nowhere, "the Founding Fathers were all traitors to the Crown. If things had gone differently, they all would have hanged."

"Now see here—" huffed Mr. Turnbuckle, but Pierre's face vanished amidst the horde again, as if he'd never been there. "—? Ahem. At any rate, George Washington died a Catholic. He was reconciled on his deathbed."

"But he lived as a Mason," countered Mr. Railsback. "And it is upon that foundation that this country was built. Take a close look at the symbols all over the dollar bill—"

"Besides," interrupted Pierre again, the elf of the party, "Pope Leo XIII condemned Americanism as a heresy in 1890."

"What?" barked Mr. Turnbuckle, turning. "Now see here—"

But Pierre had vanished again.

"But he's the pope," snapped Mrs. Dypczyk, brandishing her purse at Freddie Furkin, the cigar-sucking Coke-sipping ice-chomping overall-wearing stump of muscle from the Chancery motor pool. This morning he was sans cigar and Coke, and was sporting a surprisingly smart gabardine suite. Somehow he had eluded the euphonious clutches of his wife and the Ever-Twangin' Mostly-Saggin' Steel-Pluckers to attend Mass at St. Philomena's.   Unfortunately, he was now facing the ire of Irma Dypczyk, one of the more outspoken ladies of our fair parish. Popolatry was her specialty.

"Whatcha talkin' about?" said Freddie, baring his glaciated teeth. "He's still a man."

"He's a holy man. The Holy Ghost wouldn't let the pope say or do anything that might harm the Church."

"Listen, history says otherwise. Like it or not, there have been bad popes—"

"Too true," chimed Jonathan and Arthur, demonstrating their Tumblarish ability to materialize where ever an argument was in progress. I was so used to seeing them in formal wear that I always did a double-take when they wore regular suits and ties.

"Was the Holy Ghost guiding Pope John XII," asked Jonathan, "when he died in the arms of his mistress?"

"Did the Holy Ghost inspire Pope Steven VI," added Arthur, "when he exhumed his predecessor, Pope Formosus, and conducted a mock trial over the corpse?"

"And who prompted Pope John XXIII to convene Vatican II?" said Arthur, grabbing Jonathan's arm.

"Or Pope Paul VI to promulgate the New Mass?" they said together, as if rehearsed, before vanishing like a swirling mist back into the thinning crowd.

"But he's the pope," repeated Mrs. Dypczyk, oblivious to their intervention. "All faithful Catholics are required to recognize his headship."

"Sure," said Freddie. "I agree. He's Peter, and upon this rock Christ built His Church. But Peter wasn't perfect. He denied Christ three times after his appointment. The papacy is no guarantee of moral perfection. The pope still has to go to confession, just like you and me."

"But he's infallible."

"Only when he speaks ex cathedra."

I should add, to catch the flavor of the conversation, that Freddie pronounced it "hex cuh-*thee*-druh," and the look on his face really did require a cigar. Who would have thought this garage mechanic knew so much about theology? Obviously he'd been reading something besides *Camshaft News and Dipstick Report* in his office during breaks.

"And that's only happened once in the last hundred years," he continued. "You can't tell me this New Catechism he's been pushing is inspired by God. Have you read it?"

"I don't have to. I know it's good because he said so."

"Lady, you make about as much sense as my wife."

"I resent that."

"So would she."

"Hogwash." Another country heard from. Over by the little shrine of St. Francis de Sales, Mrs. Patricia Earheart was jabbing her finger at Mr. Gregory Holman's sternum. "How can you say such a thing?"

"Because it's true."

"It can't be."

"But it is."

I wished I was close enough to glean what they were talking about. Jacco Babs and his pal, Ziggie, were close at hand taking notes. I never saw a follow-up in the paper.

"Ah, Mr. Lambert," I heard Father saying. "Good to see you this morning."

"Likewise, Father," said Steve Lambert, shaking his hand. "Enjoyed your sermon. You always make me think."

"That's certainly a good indicator."

"I know this may be a touchy subject at the moment, but have you ever considered video-taping your sermons? Or your Mass? You could be the next Fulton J. Sheen. You could sell the tapes after Mass, or even by mail order. Heck, I bet you could get some air play on some of the local cable stations."

"Heavens. No, I can't say the thought has ever crossed my mind."

"It wouldn't be hard to do. You know, I'm a cameraman at KROM—local news, that sort of thing. I was just thinking that I could rig up a two-camera system at almost no cost. Heck, I could probably borrow the equipment for free."

"I'd have to think about it, Steve."

"Please do. Really, I'm serious—"

"I don't care if you are a Maruppa," Edward was saying to Joel under the shade of the avocado tree.

I almost didn't recognize Joel without his beard.

Having only been around the Tumblars for one evening, he hadn't yet mastered the skill of appearing and vanishing. In

fact, he didn't look like he was in a hurry to come or go anywhere. He just stood there, swaying slightly, his mouth moving but I heard no sound. My guess as an amateur lip reader
is that he was saying something along the order of,
"Ooooooooh, man."

"It's not that you drank too much," said Edward, a fra-
ternal hand on Joel's shoulder. "You just can't mix a zombie
with a whiskey sour and a martini all on top of a Bloody
Mary—"

"I repeat: hogwash." Mrs. Patricia Earheart's finger was
embedded up to the second knuckle in Mr. Gregory Holman's chest. "You don't know what you're talking about."

"I beg to differ."

"But you can't."

"But I do—"

"Excuse me, Martin."

I turned to my right to see the kind face of Mr. Folkstone,
the man who had performed such wonders with St. Thérèse's
roses and St. Joseph's gardenias, relieving me of a lot of
stooping, moaning, and bewailing in the process.

"Good morning, Henry, " I greeted him.

"I've been meaning to ask you." He raised his right hand
and pointed a stubby, callused finger at the pin on my left lapel. "What is that? It looks like a dinosaur of some kind.
Tyrannosaurus, maybe?"

That's exactly what it was, the skull of the great carnivore,
gnarly jagged teeth and all, profiled in silver. Nasty looking
critter. I'd picked it up at an arts and crafts fair a few months
before. I sometimes wore it on Sunday mornings. It seemed
fitting, somehow.

"It's a Tradosaurus," I said, gripping my lapels riverboat
style. "Tradosaurus Rex to be precise."

"I don't understand. Why do you wear such a thing?"

I lowered my voice to a conspiratorial whisper. "Because
Trads are the most obnoxious people in the world."

Mr. Folkstone blinked. Then he blinked again. "But, these
people here, we're Traditionalists."

"Yup," I nodded. "My kind of people."

"Hrmph." He shrugged and turned away. "I don't get
it."

He would learn.

"See you at 'Peanuts'?" asked a sweet voice near my left
ear.

I didn't have to turn to know it was Danielle Parks, our "in lieu of" choir director. And by her side—the wind shifted and my nose picked up an exotic whiff of patchouli—was Wanda Hemmingway, first soprano and former rock vocalist. Danielle and Wanda were close friends, great singers, summery but modest dressers, and consummate Trads.

"Sure," I said. "We should start moseying over there."

"Peanuts" was a coffee shop/beanery/pizzeria/bakery located directly across the street from St. Philomena's. Rumor had it that Toni Gnocchi, the proprietor, was the second-cousin of the great-uncle of the girlfriend of somebody connected with the Mafia. Who's to say? His chef made the best chili for miles. The pancakes were the finest in the city. And the butternut muffins—indescribable.

About twenty or thirty of Father's flock drifted over there after the High Mass each Sunday to settle the world's problems over brunch—sort of a local tradition. Mr. Gnocchi usually cordoned off the banquet room in back and let us bellow, blather, and slaver out of harm's way—and out of earshot of his other customers. Gloria, the Hungarian waitress with the mysterious eyes and bumper-car hips, usually took care of us all by her herself. She once remarked that she found us almost as bizarre as her relatives.

Just as I started my lurching maneuver down the church steps, a face materialized out of the muddle of people below, and it wasn't a Tumblar. Okay, yes, I'll admit it. I was delighted to see Cheryl Farnsworth working her way towards me.

"Well hello," I said, trying but failing to act nonchalant. "Surprised to see you here."

"Really?" she said, ascending the first two steps.

As the saying goes, the eyes are the mirror of the soul. But, as my sagacious dad used to point out, the knee is the fulcrum of the leg. And Cheryl Farnsworth had two of them.

"If you came with Madeline Sugarman," I said, "she went that way." I instantly regretted suggesting that she go any other direction than the one in which she was already headed. Luckily, she did not.

"I came alone," she said, arriving at my step. She gave me a penetrating yet enchanting look that almost cured my arthritis. For the first time I was able to get a close look at the charm she wore around her neck, and I still couldn't figure out what it was. Golden and shiny, the beveled edges caught the light in a peculiar way, hinting at colors that weren't really there.

I was about to mention it when she said, "You don't re-member me, do you?"

A strange choice of words. How could I not? "Remember you?"

After a long moment, she smiled and said, "Hello."

"Hello," I said lamely, then realized with a start that Dan-ielle and Wanda were still standing beside me.

"Oh yes," I ahemed. "Danielle, Wanda, this is Cheryl. She's the—"

"Cheryl Farnsworth?" beamed Wanda. "Didn't you use to work with Bombing Fluid?"

"I was their stage manager for three years," said Cheryl. "On their last tour I was also in charge of lighting and special effects."

"I was in Salvador Dolly," said Wanda. "We were your warm-up band at Algernon Park."

Cheryl's eyes did not register recognition, but her lips tensed. "Oh?"

Wanda touched Cheryl's arm in sympathetic camaraderie. "It was such a terrible shock. No, I mean, um—"

Cheryl's jaw stiffened.

"What a poor choice of words," said Wanda, hand up to her open mouth. "What I meant to say was it was such a horrible tragedy."

Cheryl softened. "I understand. You're not the first to pick those words. Hard not to. Look, someone mentioned going across the street for lunch. I'm starving. How about you?"

"Famished," agreed Wanda.

"Me, too," said Danielle.

"Shall we?" motioned Cheryl.

With that, I watched as three pairs of fulcra turned and started down the steps. The thought crossed my mind that Mrs. Magillicuddy was right: maybe someone was stealing other people's intentions right our of their prayers. Just as they reached the sidewalk, Wanda stopped in her tracks, turned, and bounded back up to where I was standing. Quite a feat in heels as high as hers.

"She's not your type anyway," she whispered into my ear.

I feigned ignorance. "What?"

She just winked, whirled, and trotted back down to her flitting companions.

"'Peanuts'?" asked Father Baptist at my side.

I shrugged. "I'm not sure I'm hungry."

"I could hear your stomach growling all the way up in the pulpit during my sermon. Come on."

Peanuts, I thought.

33

"THEREFORE HE THAT SPEAKETH UNJUST THINGS," announced Father, "cannot be hid, neither shall the chastising judgment pass him by."

I'm skipping now to Sunday evening.

"Wisdom, isn't it?" I said, looking up from the sheets of paper I had spread out on his desk. The room was dark except for the funnel of dusty light under the desk lamp.

"Chapter one," he said, hanging his overcoat on the hook on the back of the door. "Verse eight."

"The Reformers never knew what they were missing when they cut that book from their Bible." I began the arduous process of hoisting myself out of his chair, but he motioned me to stay put.

Father took the visitor's seat across from me. "On the contrary, they knew exactly what they were doing."

"Too bad the Prods today don't know."

"More so Catholics."

I shrugged in acquiescence. "Did you have a nice dinner at the Cladusky's?"

"Stupendous. Her stuffed cabbage is the best, but don't repeat that to Millie. By the way, is she in tonight?"

"I think I saw a light under her door."

"And Joel?"

"Out with the Tumblars again."

"Good, good. I hoped he would find them intriguing, if somewhat perplexing, companions."

"If nothing else, he's learning not to mix his liquors. So why the quote from the Book of Wisdom?"

"It's interesting how the truth always rises to the surface. And if you keep your eyes and ears open, and pray unceasingly to St. Anthony of Padua for assistance, eventually you can skim it off."

I rubbed my weary eyes. "Oh."

"Old Chief Mercer was my mentor," said Father, clasping his fingers behind his neck. "Back when I first transferred to Homicide. He used to say that every murder investigation begins as passive, receptive activity, the gathering of facts. 'Vacuum cleaner mode,' he called it. Things come to you, and you just keep sucking them in and storing them in your pouch. Then comes a moment of turnaround. He called it flipping the switch to 'exhaust mode.' You suddenly realize you have enough facts to put it all together, and then you can finally take action."

"Are you saying you're now in exhaust mode?"

"No, far from it. I'll let you know when something flips my switch. What is interesting is that even here at St. Philomena's, and then at dinner at the Cladusky's, tidbits of useful information came my way today."

"Such as?"

"The fact that several of our parishioners actually watch Madeline Sugarman's show."

"Yeah, strange. It's sort of like Republican volunteers viewing home movies of the Democratic candidate's victory party."

"More important is that I now know of two people—Theodora Turpin and Muriel Cladusky—who attempted to call the show last Tuesday and only got a busy signal."

"Isn't that rather typical of phone-in shows?"

"I wouldn't have thought Ms. Sugarman's show has that large an audience. And both women claim they usually get through."

"Busy signals can be annoying."

"Yes." He scanned the papers under my splayed fingers. "And what has been busying you?"

I adjusted the desk lamp to illuminate a larger area. "I went to the library and conducted some research of my own. These are photocopies from old articles."

"The *Times* ?"

"No, *Rolling Stone*. Something Wanda Hemmingway said to Cheryl Farnsworth on the church steps this morning sparked my curiosity."

"Do tell."

Judiciously, I arranged the sheets on the desk, then rearranged them another way. Then I folded my hands on top and ignored them. "You're aware that our choir director, Wanda, used to be a rock singer. Fronted a band called Salvador Dolly."

"Yes. She left show business shortly after she converted."

"Yeah, well she recognized Cheryl Farnsworth as a member of a group called Bombing Fluid, and in the course of the conversation mentioned that something terrible had happened at a concert at Algernon Park. I found a write-up about it. Seven years ago the Fluid's lead guitarist, Jymmy Thinggob, died right on stage in front of seven thousand people—"

Just then the phone rang.

And me on a roll.

Sighing, I picked up the receiver. "St. Philomena's Rectory."

"Martin," said Sergeant Wickes, urgently. "Looks like something new has developed. Is Father Baptist there?"

"Do you want to speak with him?" I looked at Father across the desk. He had unclasped his hands and was leaning forward, sensing something was wrong.

"No. Just grab him and head for St. Gregory the Wonderworker's rectory. 1634 Raymond, three blocks south of 32nd."

"Why?"

"There's been another murder."

"Who?"

"Bishop Mgumba."

I whispered the information to Father Baptist, then returned my attention to the phone. "When?"

"About an hour ago. And this time the spider got tangled in her own web."

"Her? The murderer is a woman?"

"Yup."

"You're sure."

"Just get down here. Pronto."

"Hold on." I was looking at my watch. "We can't possibly leave sooner than forty-five minutes."

"Why not?" said Wickes on the phone and Father Baptist across the desk simultaneously.

I cupped the receiver with my hand. "Just trying to keep you honest, Father. You distinctly told the archbishop —twice—you don't work on Sundays. It's only eleven-fifteen."

Father thought for a moment, then smiled. "What about Mark two twenty-seven?"

"Ah, gotcha," I said, removing my hand from the phone.

"What's going on?" demanded Wickes.

"No problem," I assured him. "We're leaving right away. 'The Sabbath was made for man, and not man for the Sabbath.'"

"Huh?"

"Never mind." I had already scooped all my busywork into a fairly neat pile. I picked up the statue of St. Thomas More, shoved the pages under his base—leaving him to ponder the matter. "We're leaving immediately."

34

"THIS IS REALLY WEIRD," the assistant coroner, John Holts-claw, was saying. He withdrew a Dunhill cigarette from a flat red box in his shirt pocket and gripped it with his lips. Then he thought better of it and reversed the process. "I mean, the other two were strange, but this is—I don't know how to put it."

"You said it," said the police photographer as he pocketed a roll of film, the fifth since our arrival. "This one takes the cake."

One thing I'll say for Bishop Mgumba: he had one helluva bathroom. It was bigger than my whole apartment at the rectory, and every inch of it lined with sparkling tile, terra cotta bricks, or real marble—like the steps around the gargantuan bathtub. He had a sumptuous toilet, the only one I've ever seen to which such an adjective could be applied, with a seat that looked more comfortable than the cushions of my arm-chair. I've never used a bidet, and I hope I never do, but there it was.

Most impressive of all was the shower. Eight feet deep and six wide, its thick, heavy, crystal clear Plexiglas door was set in a rubberized frame that made a perfect, air-tight seal. This, Sergeant Wickes explained to me, was to contain the steam that

could be directed into the tiled chamber through six strategi-
cally positioned jets. There were also heating elements in the
tiled ceiling, water-proof fans for circulation, and a built-in
marble park bench for stretching out. With a set-up like that,
the bishop could luxuriate in the steam, take a refreshing
shower, then get his whole self blow-dried, and all without
leaving the shower stall.

"Watch your step," said Solomon Yung-sul Wong, the chief
coroner, to his officers. "The floor is slippery in there." He
looked at us and puffed out his cheeks. "I don't know what
the hell to say."

Taper, Wickes, Father Baptist, and myself backed out the
doorway and watched from the hall as several of the lab crew
in plastic smocks and surgical masks stepped gingerly over the
rubber-silled threshold and into the shower. Within, on the
tiled floor, his head under the bench and his feet near the
door, lay Bishop Mgumba. All he had on was a towel around
his middle and a bloody triangle on his right palm, the apex
pointed toward his fingers. I thanked the Angels that his eyes
were closed.

Collapsed face down beside him, head near his feet, arms
still stretched eerily toward the glass door, was the body of a
woman dressed mostly in gray. I thanked the Saints that I
couldn't see her face.

The whole bathroom was redolent with a sweet, pungent,
throat-ticklingly nauseating odor. "That's what you get,"
elucidated Lieutenant Taper, "when you flambé two human
beings in white rum."

I nodded knowingly, grimaced queasily, and blinked in-
comprehensibly.

Father Baptist sniffed and clasped his hands behind his back,
a glare of consternation on his face.

"Did you find a piece of the quilt?" I asked.

"Yeah," said Wickes. "Sybil Wexler is running tests on it
now."

"The way it looks," the lieutenant continued, scratching his
scalp thoughtfully, "Mgumba came in here to take a shower,
and this woman somehow knocked him out—though I'm not
sure how."

"I don't see his clothes anywhere," said Father.

"He undressed in the bedroom. This way."

As impressed as I was by the bathroom, I was glad to get out
of there, away from the hubbub of police lab mites. The vision of that woman's hands—dead fingers curled into pet-

rified talons, skin buckled and stretched in desperate agony—would haunt my daydreams for weeks.

Taper led us down the hallway in a slalom pattern around
the lab boys who were dotting the landscape, and into the
bishop's boudoir. After seeing Bishop Brassorie's residence
and Bishop Silverspur's study, perhaps my expectation nodes
had become jaded. Bishop Molmar Mgumba, not surprisingly, was a collector of Afro-Caribbean artifacts—so many, in
fact, that it was hard to find his bed amidst the visual storm of
masks, carved statues, rattles, drums, staffs, and the like. There
were a number of wrought-iron cages around the room, all of
them inhabited by Technicolor birds amidst a stunning assortment of tropical plants. The police photographer's flashes
made the birds squawk and flutter in avian outrage.

"Another bishop in search of his roots," I observed.

"His clothes are there on the edge of the bed," said Wickes.

Father approached, then stooped to examine the shoes which
were on the floor, partially obscured by the fan of the bed-
spread.

"Don't touch anything in here," said Taper. "This room
hasn't been scrutinized yet."

"Of course," said Father, rising to his feet. "Make a note,
Lieutenant, to check these shoes and the carpet thoroughly. If
I'm not mistaken, there's traces of hyssop on both."

"Hyssop again," said Wickes.

"What's that?" I asked, indicating a dark lump on the carpet.

"I don't know," said Taper. "And I repeat, don't touch."

"It looks like some kind of leather pouch," said Father,
stepping around the corner of the bed to get a better look,
"with long pull-strings."

"Curious," said Father. "It almost reminds me of— Larry,
how do you piece this together so far?"

"Like I said, he undressed in here, then walked down the
hall to the shower. My guess is she was waiting for him in the
bathroom, perhaps behind the door."

"May we go back in there?" asked Father.

No, I thought to myself. No, no, no. Not back in there.
Negatory. Positively absolutely irrevocably not.

"Certainly," said Taper, leading the way back down the
hall.

Several of the lab crew moved aside as we reentered the
bathroom.

"She had quite a murderous imagination," said Taper. "See those empty bottles in that cardboard case next to the tub? Sixteen in all. Sargasso brand white rum, bottled in Haiti. That stuff will dissolve the fillings right out of your teeth. She doused the whole inside of the shower with it, walls and all. Even managed to splash some up on the ceiling. From the smudges on the floor it appears it took her several trips to cart the empty bottles over to where they are now."

"Smudges?" I asked.

"The alcohol in the rum evaporates," said Taper, "but leaves a sticky residue behind. That's what you see tracked across the floor here to the tub and back. I'll thank you not to step there. Anyway, she knocked him out, then dragged the victim inside. She probably did the rum dousing after she'd laid him out in the shower. From the blood on the shower floor it's plain that she carved the triangle on his palm in there. My guess is she planned to step out, toss a match back inside, slam the door, and watch him broil through the glass. But somehow the door swung shut, and something touched off the fumes. Wong says it must have been quite a flash."

The coroner looked up from something he was scribbling on his clipboard. "Yeah. We'll have to do some tests to recreate the event, but I'd say all the oxygen was used up in there in a matter of two to five seconds."

"Normally," added John Holtsclaw, inserting another Dunhill into his mouth, "an instantaneous vacuum like that would have sucked air up the drain—right through the crook in the pipe—but the, uh, the bishop's, uh, derriere was pressed on top of the duct, blocking it." He hesitated, took the cigarette out of his mouth, and put it back in the red box in his pocket. "You can see from those hand-shaped smudges on the inside surface of the glass that she tried to push the door open, but the suction was too strong—"

Just then the lab crew lifted the woman out of the shower. Her steel necklace scraped against the sill as they maneuvered her through the rubber-lined doorway. The bewilderment in her frozen eyes was the stuff of nightmares.

"Madeline Sugarman," said Father, shaking his head slowly as they placed her on a gurney. "She attended Mass at St. Philomena's this morning."

"Yeah," said Wickes.

"You can see," said Solomon Yung-sul Wong, "all short, fine hair was rendered into ash—eyebrows, lashes, delicate facial hair, and along the arms. But the longer hair on top of her head is, for the most part, undamaged. Same for her clothes and the male victim's towel. All lint and surface fibers singed away, but the weave itself is intact. The fire was extremely hot because of the alcohol-rich fumes, but very brief due to the short supply of oxygen. So it wasn't the fire that killed them, but asphyxiation."

"Like I said," concluded John Holtsclaw, starting to reach for his Dunhills again. "This is really weird."

"But at least this clears up a lot of things," said Wickes, clicking his gold pen and closing his notebook with an air of finality.

"You think so?" said Father.

"Sure. She got away with it twice before, but like I said, the spider got tangled in her own web."

"Of course there is a problem," said Father. "In fact, there are several."

We had to move out of the way as the bishop's body was carried out and placed on a second gurney in the hallway.

"Such as?" said Wickes.

"I can think of one," interjected Lieutenant Taper. "At least, regarding the other murders. According to your account of the meeting at the archbishop's office, Jack, Ms. Sugarman had an alibi both evenings. A staff meeting at the time of Bishop Silverspur's demise, and she was on television at the time of Bishop Brassorie's death."

"If," said Father, "that alibi holds up. As for the incident at hand, it's clear to me that Bishop Mgumba was knocked unconscious in the bedroom, not in here."

"What?" said Wickes.

"Step outside into the hallway and walk back into this bathroom. See? The whole wall above the sink is mirrored. From the doorway you can see the reflection of this entire room, even the interior of the shower. There was no way she could hide in here and not be seen by the bishop as he entered."

"Good point," said Taper.

"Furthermore, if you look closely at his shoes in the bedroom you'll see that the laces are still tied. Generally men don't pull their shoes off without first untying them unless their shoes are too big or they're in an awful hurry. Given his standard of living, I'll wager the bishop's shoes fit fine. Whether he was in a hurry or not, we'll never know. But the leather pouch Martin spotted on the floor, unless I miss my guess, is a Voudou charm—considered an extremely potent talisman, at least, to those who believe in such things."

"Can a Catholic bishop," scowled Wickes, "believe in such things?"

"A loaded question," said Father, "along the lines of, 'When did you stop beating your wife?' You might have asked, 'Can a man who believes in such things be a Catholic bishop?' But no matter. All I know is that Bishop Mgumba was fiddling with it under his coat during the meeting yesterday afternoon at the Chancery. And if it means what I think it does, he never would have tossed it carelessly on the floor. I suggest he was struck from behind in the bedroom, and his clothes removed by the perpetrators."

"'Tors,'" said Taper, "as in plural?"

"Yes. There were no signs of a body being dragged down the carpeted hallway. He was a large man. I suggest he was carried, and probably by two people."

"Supposition," said Wickes.

"Conclusion," said Father. "Mr. Wong, there are definitely hand marks on the inside of the shower door, indicating Ms. Sugarman's attempt to push her way out?"

"Yes."

"What about on the outside?"

"Of the door?" He turned to John Holtsclaw. "Did we check that?"

The assistant coroner was already crouching next to the Plexiglas door with a magnifying glass. "You're right. I almost missed it. It's hard to see because the smudges on the inside are so obvious. There are faint smudges on the outside, too. No clear prints, though, as far as I can tell."

"White rum residue?"

"Possibly."

Father Baptist pointed to the door. "Notice, gentlemen, that the shower door is standing open. It does not swing shut on its own. I suspect it was closed from the outside."

"You could be right," said John Holtsclaw, scratching himself just above the Dunhills in his shirt pocket. I was beginning to want one myself. "A second person could have ignited the fumes with, say, a cigarette lighter, then pushed the door shut and held it while the fire did its work."

"You can't prove this," said Wickes.

"Have you found a match inside the shower stall?" asked Father.

"No," said Holtsclaw. "We assumed a spark from the heating elements in the shower ceiling—"

"Who found the bodies?" asked Father.

"The cleaning woman," said Taper, "Mrs. Kindleson."

"That little twig of a woman we met when we first came in?"

"Yes."

"Did she open the shower door when she found them?"

"Yes, that's what she said."

"Did she describe any great effort in doing so?"

"Come to think of it, no." Taper scratched his head. "We figured that, with a sustained suction, after a while air would have leaked into the shower, equalizing the pressure. Then the door could be opened easily."

"Mr. Wong," said Father. "When you run your tests to recreate this incident, I strongly suggest you analyze this door seal to determine exactly how strong the vacuum created in there really was. I'm not a betting man, but I'd lay odds that, though certainly the fire could deplete the shower stall of oxygen, the suction would not have been beyond the strength of Ms. Sugarman to push her way out."

"I think you're reaching," said Wickes. "Those smudges on the outside of the door could have been left by Ms. Sugarman as she tromped back and forth with all that rum. Even if the coroner here proves the suction wasn't all that great, the woman was shocked by the flash and suddenly deprived of oxygen—probably disoriented. I still say she was alone."

"Unless I've missed something," said Father, "there's one item—or the lack of it—which necessitates the presence of a second person."

"What's that?" asked Taper.

"You said the triangle was definitely cut on the bishop's hand while he lay there in the shower. The blood on the tiles proves that. Where is the knife?"

Everyone's eyes darted around the bathroom.

"It's not here," said Taper.

"Exactly," said Father.

Monday, June Twelfth

Feast Day of Saint John of Saint Facundo, Hermit and Patron Saint of Salamanca, Spain (1479 AD)

35

"NO, YOU MAY *NOT* HAVE BREAKFAST," roared Millie, angrily sploshing coffee into my cup from a pot soaring all of two feet above the table. As usual, she didn't spill a drop. "This isn't a restaurant, and I'm not a short-order cook. When His Nibs is through with Mr. Turnbuckle, or vice versa"—she charmingly pronounced it "visa viscera"—"I'll prepare a meal for the both of you, but not one minute before."

It was the morning after the murder of Bishop Mgumba. Father Baptist had said morning Mass on schedule. As I'd had no sleep, my Latin responses had lagged a little, but I managed to get through without curling up and snoring at the foot of the altar.

Father had said another Requiem Mass in black vestments, this time for Bishops Silverspur and Mgumba, and Mr. Turnbuckle had stormed out in a huff.

There were close to a dozen reporters outside, so Father chose to finish his post-Sacrificial meditations in his study. I opted not to lumber off to the corner for a newspaper. Instead, I earned my pay as gardener for the first time in many months by watering St. Thérèse's roses. The fact that several nosy newsmen got hosed down in the process is purely coincidental.

"You'll regret this, Feeney," yelled Jacco Babs, rubbing his face with his red hankie.

"What're you gonna do?" I replied, as I coiled up the hose. "Misspell my name?"

"Worse."

"Misspell your name?"

"Arrgghhh!"

Mission accomplished, I went inside for breakfast, only to discover Millie in the delightful mood I've described.

"Confessions are at five-thirty," she hissed, slamming a kettle down on the stove. "Every single God-fearing day. Who does that insufferable man think he is, coming in and demanding special privileges from Father at breakfast time?"

I considered reminding her that Father often told his parishioners that he was at their disposal to hear confessions any time, night or day, and that if he ever looked annoyed or sounded irritable when they took him up on the offer, they had his permission to rebuke him severely. However, not wanting to explain to Dr. Kaylan Volman, our "in lieu of" parish dentist, how I lost my front teeth in a collision with Millie's eighteen-inch cast-iron skillet, I held my peace and sipped my coffee.

Presently, we heard the door to Father's study open down the hall, and the muffled sounds of Mr. Turnbuckle's gratitude as he was being escorted out the front door. When Father entered the kitchen, he greeted Millie with silent deference, having no more predilection than I for explanations to Dr. Volman.

"Morning," I said.

"Yes," he acknowledged as he seated himself. "It is."

Millie approached threateningly with the coffee pot in her mitted hand. "I was going to make French toast," she growled as she dive-bombed him a cup of Java.

"Wonderful," he said, rubbing his hands together.

"But now it's Portuguese."

Father and I exchanged glances, not wanting to know.

"I don't suppose you got much sleep," I ventured, as Millie attacked her battery of pots and pans with bitter vengeance.

"Well," said Father, dribbling cream into his coffee, "as Father Nicanor has often said (I wish I could roll my R's like he does): 'A priest must pray, and he must pray each and every day. No priest worth his salt can survive without at least two hours of solid daily prayer. But, if you've got a lot of things going on and you just can't find the time, then you need to pray for at least three hours. However, if you're so busy you don't know which end is up, and you can barely fit in the brushing of your teeth, then no doubt about it, you're in the four-hour-per-day prayer bracket.'"

Like so many things spiritual, it made peculiar sense.

"So what bracket are you in?" I asked, before downing my cup.

"I can't stand going around with unbrushed teeth, so I do without sleep."

"You'll do without food before long," spat Millie, attacking some innocent eggs in a steel bowl fiercely with a whisk. "Just wait'll you see if I don't quit."

"Heavens, Millie," said Father. "Don't even think of such a thing. What would we do without you? What is it you want? More pay?"

"More of nothing," she spat, "is still nothing."

"Well," said Father, "there is that. By the way, where is our young refugee from the seminary?"

"As far as I know," I said, "Joel never came home last night."

"Hrmph," snorted Millie. "Probably stayed over with one of those drunken rascals you're so fond of."

"Better them," said Father, spreading a napkin on his lap, "than the misbegotten riffraff in the seminary."

"So tell me," I said, "how is Mr. Turn—"

Millie slammed some butter into a skillet with a metal spatula.

"—buckle?"

Father looked at me with expended eyes that seemed to whisper, tired yet spunkily, "Considering that you know I immediately forget everything about a confession, Martin—even that there has been one—how can you ask such an inane question?" But all he said was, "Oh? Was he here?"

"Ah," I said, acknowledging my stupidity. "Then tell me, what's on our agenda for today?"

"Well, for starters, Lieutenant Taper said he and Sergeant Wickes will be dropping by—"

Millie banged the skillet a few more times with the spatula, demonstrating that butter does indeed melt faster if terrorized.

"—after breakfast with whatever lab results are in. Then you and I have a couple of errands to run. First, we need to buzz by the Times building to place an ad. Second, I want to visit one of our parishioners at his workplace, then I need to see a man who owes me a favor. Maybe, if we have time, we'll swing by the archbishop's office."

Only Millie could make the gentle sizzle of egg-battered bread in a hot skillet sound mean—and smell Portuguese.

"Fine," I said. "Who needs sleep? By the way, have you had any thoughts about the murder last night?"

"You mean murders, plural. What kind of thoughts?"

"Oh, you know, little things—the bizarre concept of using white rum and a shower stall as a murder weapon, for one. All this was planned in intricate detail and well in advance, and mapped out on that witching whatchacallit before the deed was done."

"I don't know about that," said Father. "Granted, the serial murders of the auxiliary bishops were carefully planned—indeed, now that the pattern is unquestionably established, Bishop Ravenshorst is in a most distressing position—but I'm not convinced the murder of Madeline Sugarman was premeditated. It may well have been a crime of the moment. Obviously she was assisting someone else with the murder of Bishop Mgumba. Perhaps her accomplice took an opportunity to silence a woman who was losing her resolve."

"But why was she involved in this murder and not the others?"

"We do not know that. All we know is that she and her lady friends had a mutual alibi for those murders. I've always been leery of such semblances."

"You mean like the husband who says he was home with his wife, and his wife says she was at home alone with her husband, but no one else saw them there."

"Correct."

"Of course, on one night at least—Bishop Brassorie's murder—Ms. Sugarman was on cable. Thousands of viewers saw her. Some even spoke with her on the phone."

"Well, there is that."

"Hmm," I said, finally getting to what I'd wanted to ask all morning, "so what do you think will be on the third piece of the quilt? Which element, I mean."

"There are only four hermetic elements," said Father. "Earth, water, fire and air. In a sense, all the victims in this unsettling sequence died due to a critical lack of air, a condition brought about by the application of another element. Bishop Silverspur was buried alive—earth. Bishop Brassorie was drowned in liqueur—not exactly water but in the same spirit as a murder weapon—a fluid, in other words. The double murder last night presents us with an elemental problem: death was due to oxygen deprivation—air—a situation induced by combustion—fire. Which hermetic element is represented here?"

"I say fire," I said, shifting thoughtfully in my chair.

"I say the devil," said Millie, nudging something around noisily in her skillet.

"A sobering insight, Millie," said Father. "Ultimately, he is our adversary. But as for the element, my hunch is that this next piece of the quilt will have incorporated in its design a triangle with the apex pointed upward and a horizontal line across it."

"Fire?" I asked.

"Air," he answered. "Just a hunch. Everything about this killer is perplexing. His patterns are explicit and daring, yet convoluted and volatile. He boldly leaves a blueprint, yet there's an undercurrent of unpredictability in the way he carries out the plan. There's an underlying flavor to it all, but it's like a taste on the tongue I can't quite place."

"Like trying to pick up mercury," I observed. "It keeps slipping away."

"Exactly."

"The absence of the knife is a break from the pattern. What could it mean?"

"This murderer depends profoundly on symbols. If there is a deviation from the pattern, it is no accident. It has a purpose, though as I was just saying, the design is convoluted, difficult to fathom."

"Or he's just plain insane."

"Well, there is that possibility."

"By the way," I said, "you haven't told me what the archbishop wanted the other night."

He gave me another one of those looks. "Oh? Was he here?"

"You're not going to tell me His Graciousness has appointed you his confessor!"

"No, but I'd rather forget the conversation just the same. Basically, he wanted to know what it would take to persuade you to destroy a certain photograph you have in your possession."

"Me?" I sniffed innocently. "As in my?"

"The same."

I snorted not so innocently. "And what did you tell him?"

"'With men this is impossible'—"

"Matthew nineteen," I nodded. "Verse twenty-six."

"—and with Martin Feeney, even more so."

Just then the doorbell rang.

"You stay put," barked Millie, wiping her hands on her apron. She paused in the doorway before stomping down the hall. "Don't you dare move."

Father and I exchanged glances, sorry for the poor soul on the front porch.

36

"WHO DO YOU THINK YOU ARE?" came Millie's voice, echoing down the hallway like thunder rolling through a craggy sandstone canyon. "Father Baptist and Mr. Feeney have been out all night, doing your job for you, and by holy gum they're going to eat their breakfast in peace."

I gulped. Millie had never, in all the time I'd known her, ever referred to me as Mr. Feeney.

"This warrant says otherwise," came an equally ferocious voice, maybe one and a half octaves lower than hers.

"Over my dead body."

"That can be arranged, lady. Outa my way."

"Eeek!"

I wondered if Jacco and Ziggie were on hand out there to capture the clash of the Titans on the doorstep for the morning edition.

There was a mighty commotion, but Father motioned me to stay put when I started to rise. A moment later, the shadow of Chief Montgomery "Bulldog" Billowack loomed across our humble table. He waved an official-looking piece of paper at Father's face and snorted like a pig who'd just found a fresh bucket of slops. "We're conducting a legal search of the premises," he chortled, a bulb of white saliva quivering on the corner of his contorted mouth.

Squeezing around Billowack's ballooning circumference came Millie, Tesla coils for fists and blowtorches for eyes. She gave him a look that could have curdled concrete, then silently returned to her stove.

"Fine with me, Monty," said Father calmly. "My house is your house. Explore as you will. We don't use any of the rooms upstairs, but you're free to search them along with the rest. But as Millie so astutely pointed out, your business has nothing whatsoever to do with Martin and me finishing our breakfast. And if you're looking for Joel Maruppa, he's not

here. The room in which he slept is down the hall. Will you
please excuse us?"

Billowack huffed, then he puffed, then he thought better of
it and strode out of the kitchen, barking orders to officers
waiting down the hallway.

"You're a brave woman, Millie," said Father.

"Ah, go on," she said, scraping the skillet with the spatula
she no doubt wanted to bury in Billowack's head. The
rhythm of metal against metal reminded me of a sword fight
in a swashbuckler movie.

"I'm serious," said Father. "I've even seen men from the
bomb squad wilt at the approach of Bulldog Billowack, and
they've got nerves of steel."

"Flattery works," she said, tossing two plates down before
us, three slices of perfectly-browned Portuguese toast centered
on each. "Melt some butter on these while I go bury my
head in a pillow and scream."

"Oh, do it here," I said, grabbing her hand in mock gal-
lance. "Shatter every window in the house. You've earned
it."

She yanked her hand away but gave me a rare, though wry,
smile. Then she turned to Father. "What on earth can they
be looking for? Certainly they don't think you or that nice
young man, Joel, had anything to do with these terrible murders—though frankly, killing bishops these days is justifiable
homicide, if you ask me."

"I'd watch what you say," said Father, smothering his
breakfast with a widening mound of dark imitation maple
syrup. "There are policemen swarming all over our house.
But as for the search, I think they are just being thorough."

"We have to be," said an unexpected voice.

Startled, we all turned to see Lieutenant Taper leaning in the
doorway.

He had a manila folder in his hand and a hollow, exhausted
look in his eyes. He needed a shave, a fresh shirt, and his
tongue could have used a cleaning and a pressing, but so far
he was the brightest ray of sunshine in our day. Luckily the
day was young. "Especially after what we found in the archbishop's office less than an hour ago."

"Ah, Larry," said Father, motioning him to sit. "Millie,
please pour the lieutenant some coffee. He is after all, more
than anyone else currently invading our house, on our side.
In a cup, please—not in his lap. Is Sergeant Wickes with
you?"

"No. He's still over at the Chancery Office." The lieuten-ant sank wearily in a chair. The sound of Millie slamming a cup down in front of him opened his eyes—for a moment, anyway. I could tell, from the way she sploshed coffee in his direction, that she liked him.

A couple of loud bumps echoed down the hallway, the sounds of the invasive search in progress. We did our best to ignore them.

"So they found the knife," said Father.

"How did you know?"

"Cops are like bees. A swarm doesn't go on a stinging rampage unless something upsets the hive. I should know, I used to be chief drone. What could better get you guys riled up than finding the knife from last night's murder? I take it you got a search warrant to check out the Chancery, and that's where you found it."

"Billowack woke up Judge Ahern around three this morn-ing. They're also scouring through St. Philip's, St. Michael's, and St. Gregory the Wonderworker's."

"Excellent," said Father. "And no doubt you're checking on the whereabouts last night of everyone connected with this case?"

"Sure. You want to be in on any of the interviews? They'll be going on all day."

"No. I'll trust in your competence. Besides, Martin and I have other things to do. Now the knife. Larry, do you have a photo of it there?"

"What? Oh, yeah. In fact, I have shots of all three. Three murders, three knives." Taper dug around in his manila folder. "Here. You should have a complete set." He glanced nervously over his shoulder, then shrugged. "Bil-lowack told me not to give you any more official stuff, but to hell with him."

Father eyed the photographs and handed them to me. The top one had the word "Mgumba" scribbled in the corner with a black marking pen. It was a little scimitar with a fancy han-dle. The contour of the blade, and the thought of what had been done with it, made my teeth soft. The effect was en-hanced by the design of the handle. Shapes reminiscent of bats in flight swirled their way back from the hilt and termi-nated in a kind of skull-shaped nub at the end of the handle.

"Any leads on where they were purchased?" asked Father.

"Not yet."

I shuffled through the other photographs, "Silverspur" and "Brassorie," but they all looked identical to me. I said, "Hmm," and set them down on the table. I was more interested in something else:

"The quilt."

Lieutenant Taper had drifted out of focus for a moment. "Huh? Oh, yeah." He opened the manila folder and dug wearily around inside for the second time. "Here."

I scooted around the table—well, more like lurched, staggered, and almost knocked over the remaining chair—to look at the new piece of the puzzle in Father's hand.

"Hmm," said Father.

"Triangle with apex up," I said. "Horizontal line through it. Air. By the Incorrupt Tongue of St. Anthony of Padua, you were right, Father."

The lieutenant took a long sip from his cup and swallowed noisily. "I was expecting fire. So was everyone at the lab."

"Hrmph," grunted an angry presence towering over us.

Taper looked up, startled.

"Do you want something to eat?" asked Millie. She was being nice, but it still sounded like a threat. "I've got enough left for a slice or two."

"Yes, please," said Father on the lieutenant's behalf. "And bless you, Millie."

Aware of her disapproving glare, Father handed me the quilt photo and began dutifully slicing up his breakfast. Deftly, he assembled a swaying stack of Portuguese toast segments on his plate. Then, with a mighty thrust of his fork, he lanced them through.

Millie nodded her disowning approval and headed back to the stove.

"A blank square in the top row," I said, maneuvering my chair back to its original position. "That's something new. And what's that symbol in the first square in the second row?"

"An hourglass perhaps," said Taper, blinking drunkenly. "X marks the spot. The Roman numeral 'ten.' I don't know."

"And the runes?" I asked eagerly. "What do they say?"

"SP in the top row," said Father, still balancing the bulging gob of Millie's culinary effort on his fork, "the second row is F-I, and the third is E-A."

"I've got Sybil Wexler's computerization in here somewhere," said Taper, digging around again. "Ah, here."

As he handed it to me, Father plunged the dripping mass on his fork deep into his mouth. He could barely close his lips around it. Millie smiled with satisfaction as she approached for another bombing raid with the coffee pot.

"Devil's work," she grumbled, glaring at the clue in my hands. "And in this house."

"Awrchbishawp's awrders," said Father, cheeks bulging.

There were several loud thumps from the far end of the rectory, and a muffled, slavering noise. That could only be Billowack living up to his nickname.

"Like I said," said Millie, strafing our cups with Java, "devil's work."

37

"I THINK I'VE GOT SOME OF THE WORDS FIGURED OUT," I said, making a left turn on Putnam Drive. "On the quilt I mean. Didn't the section found in Bishop Brassorie's hand have the letters R-E and R-T-H?"

"Yes," said Father, his head lolling as we bounced through a treacherous dip in the road.

"And today's section says F-I and E-A. Sounds like the makings of 'fire' and 'earth' to me."

"Bravo," said Father. "Our Boggle matches have finally paid off." He unfolded three print-outs from his pocket and arranged them in his lap. The jostling of the car made them slip around, but when I glanced over I got the idea:

"Would you mind slowing down for the next dip, Martin? The warning signs are there to suggest deceleration as a wise course of action when traversing transverse troughs in the roadway."

But that's what four-wheel-drives are for. Shucks. I almost dared him to say "traversing transverse troughs" ten times, but only said, "Right."

"No, left at the next street. KROM is down a mile or so on the south side of Palomar."

"Right."

Getting away from the Billowack Brigade at the rectory had been a piece of cake. I simply suggested that Lieutenant Taper make a preliminary search of my private quarters himself. Father Baptist came along as ecclesiastical observer.   Once there, I told the lieutenant that the only way to get inside the mind of a dangerously demented desperado was to walk for a mile in his moccasins. The next best thing, since the bandit in question didn't have any moccasins, was to stretch out for a spell on his bunk.

I don't know what happened first, my turning the key in the Cherokee's ignition, or the sound of Taper's snoring rattling the foundations and thereby attracting the attention of his fellow officers who were still snooping around inside the rectory.

In any case, we made our getaway without incident, leaving Millie to guard the kitchen with her defensive cookware. Our first stop was at the *Times* building, where we made a quick visit to the classified ads department.

"Hey," said the peaches and cream lass behind the counter, "aren't you on our front page today?"

"Could be," shrugged Father, unfolding a piece of paper. "I'd like to run this ad for the next three days. Three columns, prominent on the page."

\$100 • \$100 • \$100 • \$100
"Spotlight on Community" Search
\$100 will be paid to anyone
who spoke on the phone
with Madeline Sugarman
during her final show,
Tuesday, June 6.
Proof required.
Contact FJB at Box 584 ...

"Hot on the trail, eh Father?" she beamed, reaching for her calculator.

"More like warm on the road. Tell me, isn't the Catholic diocesan newspaper printed here?"

"The Flock? Yes. The Chancery Office sends us their camera-ready layouts, and we rent them our presses for each run. Then they pick them up for distribution."

"Could you arrange to get this ad placed in there as well? I believe it comes out on Wednesday."

"Sure, no problem. I deal with them all the time. I'll just phone it in."

"Kind of a hefty reward," I mentioned, looking over his shoulder, "for a man getting by on your lack of salary, even with your per diem from the archbishop—which, by the way, we have yet to see."

"'He who soweth sparingly,'" he said, digging around in his wallet, "'shall also reap sparingly.' Second Corinthians."

"Uh-huh," I nodded. "Nine six. I never thought I'd ever see you placing an ad in *The Crock.*"

"Neither did I, not since they refused to print my Mass schedule. They wouldn't even run an ad for our May Fair last year."

"What will you consider 'proof'?"

"Most people have portable cassette recorders these days, or video machines. I suspect that someone calling in a talk-show would be likely to record themselves one way or another for posterity. If not, I'd accept the testimony of a reliable witness."

"Will that be all?" asked the young lady.

"Yes," said Father.

First errand completed, we headed for the television station.

"So," I said, settling down to thirty-five miles per hour on Palomar Parkway. "Did anything else of interest happen when the archbishop didn't drop in the other night? You know, other than the fact that he did drop in?"

"Did he?"

"Even though you wish he hadn't. Remember? You didn't hand over the photograph."

"Well," said Father, smiling out of the side of his mouth, "it wasn't mine to give."

"Good point," I nodded. "I think I'm going to have it laminated."

"But now that you've brought it up again, he did mention something just as he was leaving."

"You mean after he never arrived in the first place."

"Funny how that works. Anyway, he may have just been making farewell small talk, but he asked my opinion as to whether he should go ahead with the dedication ceremony of the Del Agua Mission a week from this coming Wednesday."

"You mean with his ever-decreasing supply of auxiliaries with which to pad the speaking platform?"

"He was down to two the night he didn't come over, but now he's down to one.

"What did you tell him—the night before there was only one?"

"I told him I don't believe that Feast Days, Holy Days, and commemorative days, be they historical events or birthdays and wedding anniversaries, should ever be celebrated on any day other than the day they appear on the calendar. The feeling is lost and the discipline bypassed when you move them for convenience's sake. In other words, I thought he should proceed as scheduled."

"And what did he say to that—considering that just last month he changed Ascension Thursday to Sunday?"

"He said he'd think about it."

While the archbishop was no doubt continuing to do so, we pulled into the parking lot along side the KROM building. It was shortly after ten.

"I wonder," said Father to the girl at the sign-in desk in the lobby, "if I might see Steve Lambert. He works in the newsroom."

"Sorry," she said, adjusting her hair as she examined her reflection in a blank computer screen. "No visitors without a pass—um—" She caught sight of his collar and cassock. "Say, aren't you that Father Something?"

"Why, yes. So I am. And this is my assistant—"

"Martin O'Ruther," I said, waving with two fingers.

"Do you have an appointment?"

"No," said Father. "But I'm sure Mr. Lambert would okay a pass, and the producer of your news program would be interested in an exclusive interview with me. Would you please call the newsroom and tell them I'm here?"

"Interview?" I squeaked—and I rarely squeak. "But Father—ulp."

The instep of his left shoe made a swift impression on the outstep of my right ankle.

In the time it took an elevator to come down from the third floor, Father and I were suddenly shaking hands with a shirt-sleeved man with eyes that screamed, "Trust me," and long, bony, angular arms that reminded me of the forelegs on a praying mantis.

"So good to meet you," he chortled. "I'm Maurice Morgan Mercedes, the producer of ROMedia News. Call me Mo. Kerry here says you want to do an exclusive, and with us, and here you are."

"I would like to discuss the possibility," said Father. "Where is Mr. Lambert?"

"He's up in the newsroom," chuckled Mo. "Of course, as a cameraman, he would have no say in something like this."

"On the contrary," said Father. "What he has to say has everything to do with it."

"Huh?" Mo almost choked on a titter. "I don't get you."

"Perhaps it will help if I explain—upstairs, of course—and with Mr. Lambert present. Martin? Won't you come along?"

"Hey," I said, hobbling after them. "Why not?"

"Excuse me," called Kerry from her post at the blank computer. "Mr. O'Ruther, you and the, uh, whatayum, you know—"

"Priest," I suggested.

"Yeah, him. You need these passes on your lapels to get through the building."

"Never touch 'em," I called back. "Lapels, I mean."

38

"SO WE HAVE A DEAL," said Father as the elevator settled smoothly on the ground floor again. The doors whispered open, revealing Kerry still monitoring her facial details in the blank computer screen.

"I guess so," chortled Mo the Mantis. "I surely do guess so, and there you are."

"And I want to thank Mr. Lambert in advance for his efforts in bringing this project to fruition," said Father, shaking the glowing cameraman's hand.

Steve Lambert looked like a man who had just been handed a promotion. "Anytime, Father."

"And you're sure," whispered Father, "you can arrange the hook-up?"

"You bet," winked Steve. And a raise.

"We'll have everything ready," chuckled Mo. "I just know you'll be pleased, and with us, and there you are."

"Till tomorrow," said Father.

Steve mouthed, "Thank-you," as Father and I stepped out of the elevator and made our way toward the glass doors across the lobby. Behind us, Mr. Mercedes let loose with a muffled implosion of giggled snorts. Mercifully, the elevator doors hissed closed, cutting him off in mid-snigger.

"That was certainly interesting," I said as I wrenched myself into position behind the steering wheel of the Cherokee. "Now where to?"

"It's almost one o'clock," said Father. "He should be open by now."

"Who should?"

"The man who owes me a favor. Turn left at the light, and then left on Allen."

"Right."

Father guided me through a zigzagging maze of streets. At each turn it seemed the roadway got narrower, the asphalt more irregular, the storefronts shabbier, and the sidewalks gnarlier. Eventually he told me to pull up in front of a crummy little establishment that looked like a cross between a Caribbean haberdashery, a wicker furniture outlet, a taxidermy emporium, a magic shop, a tropical arboretum, and a warehouse for orthopedic props. There was a warped sign hanging over the doorway, painted to resemble an eyeball. Around the cornea were the crooked words, WIDE EYE DO DAT? A cockeyed sign on the door announced:

FORTUNES UNTOLD
∞ BONES READ ∞
POTIONS FOR ALL OCCASIONS
GUILLAUME DU CRANE CRISTAL, PROPRIETOR.

"This," I said as we approached the door, "is the guy who owes you a favor?"

"Certainly," said Father, grasping the doorknob. "Years ago, before I made chief, I saved Monsieur du Crane Cristal from a visit to the gas chamber by proving that, at the time of a murder with which he had been charged, he was behind the curtain at a seance thumping the walls and dragging chains along the floor. He was in the employ of Madame Michelle

Nostalgie de la Boue, a prominent clairvoyant who was at-tempting to pull the ectoplasmic wool over the eyes of a wealthy and pathetically gullible widow. Madame got five years, and Monsieur got two."

The door creaked as he pushed it open.

"I'm sure he appreciated that," I said, peering around the murky shop.

"With all his heart," said Father, closing the door behind us. A funny little out-of-tune bell—if indeed a single note can be out of key with itself, as this one certainly was—tinkled as he did so. "Considering the alternative the DA was offering him."

The narrow room we entered rose to a startling height. The only light came through the front window, which was frosted with years of street soot and city filth. The walls were lined with shelves, and the shelves were cluttered with dark, ominous forms—withered, sickly, dead things that looked as though they'd once been part of bigger, healthier things. There were long, once-regal display cases up and down the room, the kind in which jewelers array their most precious gems. But the items in these glass cases were neither precious, nor anything a sane woman would want set in a brooch. Coiled things, shriv-eled things, odd-shaped stones, extracts and powders, oily utensils of guileful design and unknown purpose.

"Notice this," said Father, pointing to a leather pouch with long pull-strings hanging from a wooden hook.

"A dead ringer for Bishop Mgumba's," I noted.

"Look there," he said, pointing to a collection of ornately-framed witching quilts on the opposite wall. Some were rec-tangular, some were circular, one was trapezoidal. Some were composed of adjacent squares, some of interlocking triangles, one of entangled dodecagons. All were dotted with arcane symbols and crisscrossed with esoteric alphabets—some runes, some hieroglyphs, some cryptic squiggles. One characteristic was consistent: each had one, single, obvious empty space, just like the third piece of our own, ominously growing quilt.

"As I understand it," said Father, "the blank space is the focus of the entire pattern, the locus of intention. Everything else on the casting cloth somehow points to it."

"Do you know what any of these cloths were used for? You know, what the intention of the, uh, artist was?"

"Haven't a clue. As with our own puzzle, the symbols are personal to the one making it."

I wondered, as I examined these marvels of malevolent embroidery, what desires, agendas, and vendettas prompted their conception—what affections were coveted, what plans were instigated, what revenge was savored in the minds of the sorcerers who put their all into the making of these dire cloths? So intriguing was their design, and so captivating the concept, that I had to remind myself that the murderer we sought had not waited for some invisible magical force to eliminate three bishops so far, but had carried out the deeds himself, by his own hand.   Apparently witching quilts helped those who helped themselves.

"Is it typical," I asked, "to cut the cloth up as you kill off your victims?"

"Murder isn't the typical purpose of a witching quilt. Sacrifice may be involved. Conjurers have been known to spill blood, usually animal, as a means of oblation. But generally speaking, the quilt is designed to focus magical power in order to achieve a goal, not to commit an injury. In other words, a junior witch might make a casting cloth in order to get a promotion, but not to kill off the competition."

"Ah, but what if he slits the throat of his competition as an unwilling offering to his, uh, cause?"

"Well, there is that."

"In any case, this collection of witching quilts is most interesting."

These things I might have overlooked, surrounded as they were with eye-snatching grossly-gaudy tapestries, vacantly-staring obligingly-smiling skulls, faintly-glowing wax-sealed peeling-labeled vials, and yellow-gray jerky-dried stretched-and-curled mummified hands. Yes, hands.

"Isn't this the wrong part of the country for Voudou?" I asked.

"Hey, mon," a voice erupted from an arched doorway at the far end. With a scrape and a rattle, a curtain of beaded strings parted and in stepped a lanky rack of ribs blackened and dipped in Cajun sauce, with a sprinkling of exotic feathers in his steel wool dreadlocks. "Hey, mon, whud chu tink yu know whudduh yu talkin' 'bout?"

He came stomping toward us like a Zulu king arriving for a limbo championship. "Dah country may be wrong for dah Voudou, but dah Voudou is ripe for dah soul, mon. Any soul, any one, anywhere. Ha ha. Whud chu want wid me, mon?"

"Cut the rasta, Willie," said Father.

"Hey, mon," cooed the proprietor, whirling around to face Father. "Who you callin' — ?"

"You never were very good at it. You may be able to convince a desperate widow, or attract a few curiosity seekers, or take in some drive-by suckers, but no one with an ear thinks you're really from Haiti, or New Orleans, or even the South for that matter."

"Jack," said the man, wiggling his long, disjointed finger in Father's face. "Oh damn, damn, damn. You again. I should've known you'd come back, Jack."

"You did swear," said Father.

"Arrgh!" the man grimaced. "Yeah, I guess I did. I regretted it then, and I jus' knows I'm about to regret it some more. I've seen you on the news. Everyone on the street thought you was gone for good, but no, you is back on the attack, Jack. An' wearin' black."

Aha, I thought, a title for my book: THE BLACK JACK ATTACK ... Naw.

Father adjusted his collar. "It's Father John Baptist now."

"Ooooooh," groaned the man, sinking to his knees. "Like I'm supposed to cringe and grovel before the Holy Mon."

"Only if you don't want me to tip the vice boys about illicit activities in your back room."

"Ooooooh." He leaned forward and touched his forehead to the floor. It was quite a trick. "Like, how low should I bow, Bwana?"

"Guillaume du Crane Cristal," said Father, turning to me, "means 'William of the Crystal Skull,' if my potholed memory of French hasn't gone completely dim. Back when I had dealings with him he was just Willie Kapps."

"Willie 'Skull' Kapps," said Willie, rising and swatting dust balls from the knees of his baggy trousers. He did not know, or perhaps care, that his eyebrows were also fringed with fluffs of carnivorous lint. "That's what they used to call me, back when this was the seedy part of town. Now there is no seedy part of town."

"Willie's quite an anomaly," explained Father. "His magical shenanigans are phony as a seven-dollar bill. But he knows just about everything there is to know about every form of witchcraft, incantation, and conjuration there is. He has books on his back shelves that would send wiccans screaming back to their church pews."

"Shh, Father Mon," said Willie. "Careful who you tell."

"Willie," said Father, "this is Martin. You can trust him."

Willie and I shook glances.

"The lieutenant doesn't know this," said Father to me, while looking at Mr. Kapps, "but years ago when he was consulting Ambuliella Beryl Smith for information on the occult during the Morgenstern-Barclay case, I was down here pumping Willie for the real scoop."

"Yeah," said Willie to me. "I don't dish out any of that phony-baloney fuzzy-feel-good wickie tripe. You ask me for the scoop, I shovel it at you straight and full-strength. If it give you the nightmares, that your problem."

Surprise, I thought to myself, he'd fit right in with the Trads at St. Philomena's.

"So now you're back on the murder trail," said Willie to Father. "And from what I hear, it's a doozie."

"And what you haven't heard," said Father, "would turn your hair white."

"Just so's it ain't my skin," said Willie, his lips erupting into a engaging, robust smile. "Why don't you gents come into my inner sanctum and tell Monsieur du Crane Cristal all about it?"

"There's only one thing I want to know," I said.

"Yes?" said Father and Monsieur together.

"The sign on the door. How do you 'untell' a fortune?"

"Ah," said Willie, putting his spindly hand on my shoulder and guiding me toward the bead-strung doorway in the back. "I shall put on a pot of mweemuck root tea. I see you have much to learn, Martin Mon, and Guillaume has much to teach."

39

"DON'T BE AN IDIOT," ROARED FATHER BAPTIST, pounding his fist on the corner of Marsha Duke's desk. The clock that almost fell off the edge said 3:15.

Ms. Dukes wasn't behind her desk, and Father wasn't roaring at her. She was standing nearby, over by the water cooler with Archbishop Morley Psalmellus Fulbright, wondering what was going to happen next. Sergeant Wickes, Bulldog Billowack, and our favorite gardener were finding out.

"If you arrest him," continued Father, "you'll only end up looking like a fool."

"Oh," said Billowack, rolling his eyes in mock terror. "And we're supposed to take your word for it?"

"Considering my record in matters of this kind—we'll charitably overlook yours—and the fact that you really don't know what you're up against, I strongly advise you to heed what I say."

Billowack started counting on those gun barrels he called fingers. "One: we found the blood-stained knife here in his office—in his desk drawer for Pete's sake. The lab matched it with Bishop Mgumba's blood type, tying him to last night's murder. Two—"

"On what grounds did you search this office?" interrupted Father.

"Huh?" blinked Billowack. "An anonymous tip. Two—"

"Someone phoned?" asked Father, standing his ground.

"No. I received a typewritten note in today's mail."

"Fortuitous," said Father, "and highly suspicious."

"No matter," huffed Billowack. "Two," he resumed. "We found traces of hyssop on the carpet in the archbishop's office, as well as out here in the reception area, so we've got him linked to the scene of Bishop Brassorie's death and Bishop Mgumba's. Three: Holtsclaw found a clod of dried clay under the desk in the archbishop's office. It matches dirt from the grave where Bishop Silverspur was buried alive. Four: we can prove he signed the work order to dig the grave the same day Silverspur was planted in it. Five: he's got no alibi for the times of either of the murders. Six: ... er ..."

For a half second, Billowack looked puzzled. He'd just run out of bazookas on his right hand, so he had to switch paws in order to continue his arithmetic tirade.

"Six: not nearly as conclusive, but juries love these kinds of things, is the fact that his middle name begins with P-S, like the symbol on that casting kilt. And seven: he had access, or the means to gain access, to every crime scene connected with this case." He blew the smoke from his smoldering canons and shoved them into his oversized holsters. "What more do you want?"

Father rubbed his face with the palm of his hand, as if to wipe stray gun powder from his eyes. "A motive."

Billowack sucked in his cheeks—a stunning effect, sort of like a hot air balloon having a hernia. "We're working on it."

"And," said Father, "how about tangible evidence?"

"Pshaw!" A gooey twirl of Billowack's saliva flew on that one. "We've got this one nailed down tight."

"Oh really," said Father, moving toward the Chief of Homicide and raising his own arsenal of photon torpedoes menacingly. "One: you found no fingerprints on the knife, only smudges which I'll lay odds match those on the other knives in shape, size, and texture. You haven't produced the gloves that made any of those smudges, and any number of people could have planted this knife in the archbishop's drawer. You haven't yet determined how many of the staff have keys to this suite."

"We're working on it—"

"Two: dried hyssop can be purchased at any store that sells incense, herbs, newage books, or bath salts. Have you proved the traces you found here are the same genus as the bunch found in Bishop Brassorie's chapel at St. Philip's? What if further analysis reveals that the sample from the former is *Hyssopus officinalis* and the later is *Hyssopus absinthium?* And how do you know that it was tracked in here on his shoes, and not, say—" Father swung his finger around the room and homed in on a target. "—Marsha Dukes' over there?"

She blinked, made a little chirp, and banged her elbow into the water cooler. It must have hurt.

"Just as a possibility, of course," said Father, nodding to her, then regarding me.

"'Officinalis'?" I was mouthing discretely. "'Absinthium'?"

He gave me a look that seemed to say, confidently yet conspiratorially, "Considering the emotional intensity of the moment, Martin, rather than break my eloquent stride I'll leave it for you to ponder whether I've done my homework or made that up." But all he did was ignore me and return his attention to Billowack.

"Three:" he continued, "the archbishop himself conducted the interment service for his deceased friend, Bishop Brassorie, at the cemetery. Any defense lawyer worth his spittle would ask how you're so sure the archbishop didn't get a bit of graveside clay wedged on his wing tip at that time, only to have it come free later while he sat at this desk, head in hand, lamenting the passing of his cherished friend—pals since the seminary, by all accounts. And bear in mind, in an archdiocese of this size and wealth, he can afford a whole army of world class attorneys, all willing to sell their legal phlegm for outrageous fees, clamoring for the chance to strut up and down before a jury on national television."

Billowack looked like he was working up a few quarts of *Beast from Twenty-Thousand Fathoms*-grade saliva within his wobbling jowls.

Undaunted, Father continued. "If you'd been reading the lab reports, you would know we also found a sample of that same clay just inside the doorstep at St. Philip's rectory—two days before Bishop Brassorie's funeral. Could this mean that Bishop Brassorie killed Bishop Silverspur? Or did David Smoley commit that particular murder? Or Joel Maruppa? Or Sister Charlene Vickers? They all had keys to the front door."

Marsha Dukes made another chirp, but avoided another collision with the water cooler.

"Four: the archbishop signs scores of memos and letters every day, most of them handed to him in stacks. Anyone on his staff could have slipped that work order onto his desk to sign. Five: as for the witching quilt, what makes you think P-S is more significant than S-P? Both combinations are represented on it. Witching quilts are, for want of a better term, a fine art. Have you established that he knows the first thing about them? Have you made comparisons with the sections in our possession and completed quilts done by certified conjurers? Do you know where to find such things?"

"Certified—?"

"Six: alibis—they're only as reliable as the witnesses who provide them. Let's go through some enlightening details about the three nights in question—"

"All right," barked Billowack. "All right. So maybe an arrest would be premature at this stage."

"Not to mention that it would leave you wide open to a false-arrest lawsuit of national-interest proportions," said Father. "Bursting in upon private citizens and ransacking their homes while waving search warrants is one thing, but arresting an archbishop, a prince of the Roman Catholic Church, in one of the country's largest cities is quite another. Speaking of which, did you come up with anything of interest in my rectory?—or St. Philip's—or anywhere else you vandalized this morning?"

Billowack hesitated. "We're still collating."

"Collating," said Father Baptist, shaking his head. "There's a word for you. And to top it all off, you just revealed significant bits of evidence to suspects in this murder investigation."

"Huh?"

"The knives, the clay from the grave, the hyssop, and the witching quilt have all been kept from the media until this afternoon. Now both the archbishop and Marsha Dukes know about them. What if one of them is the murderer? What if either of them is an innocent acquaintance of the murderer and unwittingly divulges the information?"

The fat sacks within Billowack's jowls were quivering violently.

"All because," continued Father, "you got cocky and thought you'd make a name for yourself with a daring arrest of a prominent figure."

"You're way out of line," snarled the chief. "I'm trying to prevent murder number four. Archbishop Fulbright is the most likely perpetrator, no matter what tricks you pull out of your hat. But let's suppose I don't arrest him. What happens if this other guy, Ravenshorst, ends up croaked one of these evenings?"

"If he is next on the murderer's list," said Father, "and it's certainly reasonable to presume so, then he will die whether the archbishop is in custody or not."

"I'm going to put guards around him 'round the clock."

"With all due respect, Chief, it's been my experience that, if someone really wants to kill another person, there's really very little the police or anyone can do to prevent it. There are simply too many ways to kill a human being. Bullets, knives, projectiles, electrical shorts, virulent strains of bacteria left on a toothbrush, or poison swabbed on the silverware—no bodyguard can possibly cover all bases."

I was beginning to feel like I was in a Rex Stout novel, but what the hey.

"The murderer we seek," continued Father, "is clearly resourceful and imaginative. Look at the innovative uses he has found for alcoholic beverages. Notice his flagrant audacity in leaving clues all over the place, confident that, even if we figure them out, the knowledge will do us no good. You may assign as many men as you wish to surround Bishop Ravenshorst—he'll no doubt demand it, and it'll make good copy—but all you'll be doing is providing an ample assortment of witnesses to his demise. You may as well issue Jacco Babs and his cameraman an engraved invitation."

"But we know the next weapon will somehow involve fire," said Billowack. "All we've got to do is keep lots of extinguishers handy."

"The murder last night," said Father, "also involved fire—but in the murderer's mind the deed was more related to air. What if, within our killer's nebulous grasp of metaphysics, fire is akin to something you can't anticipate? Say, explosives, or the agony of a thousand bee stings. What good will your fire extinguishers be then?"

"So you're saying Bishop Ravenshorst doesn't stand a chance," said Marsha Dukes, rubbing her elbow.

Father turned to leave. "Let's just say I hope the remaining auxiliary bishop is prepared to meet his Maker."

40

"AH, WHAT HAVE WE HERE?" said Pierre, rubbing his hands together eagerly in the study. "Father Baptist is expanding his libationary horizons, perhaps?"

"Not exactly," said Father.

Pierre picked up the first of the four bottles from the desk. "Hmm. Burgundy, a blood red wine. The blood is the life, after all. However, this brand is completely beneath you, Father, if you don't mind my saying so. But wait, what's this? The cork has been breached and—whoa!—that's certainly not wine within. Smells more like kerosene."

"Close," said Father. "John Holtsclaw, the assistant coroner, managed to procure from his uncle on the Gabrielino reservation something similar to what was actually in Bishop Silverspur's bottle at the time of his death. It's distilled from juniper berries and jimson weed. The Indians call it, 'Blood catch fire, brain turn ash.' I wouldn't taste it if I were you, not if I valued my fillings."

"And this," said Jonathan, hefting the second bottle. "We all know about Jägermeister. Yecch."

"And—phew!" Arthur's neck bones cracked as his head jerked away from the mouth of the third bottle. "Strongest rum to ever singe my nostril hairs."

"Sargasso white rum," explained Father. "In the Voudou religion they drink white rum to St. John the Baptist."

"Cheers," said Arthur, raising the bottle in salute while rubbing his tender neck.

"However," said Father, "in Haiti, where religions meld like molten alloys, they call him Baron Samedi, the God of Death."

"Then not so cheerful," said Arthur, setting the third bottle down. "I take it back."

"And what's this for?" asked Joel, handling the fourth. "'Evian'?"

"For the moment," said Father, "bottled water is standing in for the fourth brand of peculiar liquor that, I fear, will soon take its place."

"I get it," said Arthur, fetching a bottle of champagne from the official Tumblar bucket—courtesy of Millie's broom closet—near the fireplace, much to the delight and approval of everyone present. "You're trying to get into the mind of the murderer."

"Something like that," nodded Father, holding out his fluted glass for a splosh.

"And these?" asked Edward, pointing to three photographs under the desk lamp. "Murder weapons?"

"No," said Father, turning the photos around so the Tumblars could better see the ornate scimitars. "Not murder weapons. But each was used for, shall we say, a ceremonial purpose at one of the crime scenes."

"May I?" asked Edward, indicating the magnifying glass near Father's elbow.

"Of course."

The other Tumblars looked on as Edward took the photos, one by one, examining them meticulously. In matters of conversation, the Knights were all outspoken. In matters of individual expertise, they deferred to one another. Edward, as they all knew, had the best eye for detail. They always let him scrutinize restaurant checks and bar bills.

"This is blood on the blades," he said presently. "Isn't it?"

Jonathan ulped.

Father nodded. "Notice anything else?"

"They seem to be identical, except for these—what?—serial numbers on the nub at the end of each handle. Roman numerals. XXXVI on this one—thirty-six. LXXII here on the second one—seventy-two. And the third is, uh, LXXII—seventy-two again. That's odd. Serial numbers don't repeat."

"Very good," said Father. "You caught that."

"What does it mean?" asked Arthur, looking over Edward's shoulder.

"I don't know," said Father. "The murderer is setting up all kinds of symbolic detail. There's more, but like I said before, I don't want to taint the information you might otherwise glean from your safaris into the nefarious night life to which so many people connected with this case seem to be attached."

"Father, are you going to tell us why you want us to meet you at the television station tomorrow morning?" asked Edward.

"Or why we won't be meeting this Thursday?" asked Jonathan. "The first meeting we'll have foregone in over six months?"

Father Baptist just smiled.

"He's being mysterious," said Arthur. "Let's humor him."

"So," said Father, downing his champagne and leaning back in his chair, "tell me what's been happening in the forgotten recesses of the soft white underbelly of our fair city."

"For one thing," said Jonathan, "we definitely believe Joel to be Tumblar material."

"He knows almost as many songs as Pierre," said Edward.

"And he can hold his alcohol," said Edward, patting him on the back, "so long as he doesn't mix his liquors."

"And he can defend the Faith on his feet," said Pierre respectfully, "even when he does blend his libations."

Joel looked uncomfortable, embarrassed, and a tiny bit proud.

"He had a close call, too," said Jonathan, "at 'The Hole in the Dike' last night."

"Yeah," said Arthur. "There he was, walking back from the bar with a couple of drinks in his hands—the rest of us were over by the piano having a most delightful argument with a couple of ex-Catholic neo-Freudian quasi-Marxists—and he bumped right into Sister Charlene Vickers."

"But she didn't recognize me," added Joel hastily.

"She didn't have time," laughed Pierre. "This fine young Tumblar-in-training purposely dumped his drinks down the front of her dress. Yes, I said dress. Not one of those drab housecoats nuns are so fond of these days. This was an evening gown. A rather fine evening gown, if I do say so."

"She was sputtering like a ruptured radiator," said Edward. "Joel had no problem slipping away."

"I knew she was that way," explained Joel. "Twice I saw her slip out of St. Philip's all decked out like a movie star."

"Peculiar behavior for a nun," said Arthur. He coughed twice. "What am I saying? These days, it's quite normal."

"You're sure she didn't recognize Joel," said Father.

"Positive," said Jonathan. "Edward and I hovered near her for a while afterwards to make sure. Seated at her table were Marsha Dukes, Stephanie Fury, that witch, Starfire, and a man we didn't recognize. She never mentioned Joel by name, just that clumsy bastard who had ruined her dress. Anyway, the way she squints, its a miracle any light reaches her retinas."

"With the beard gone," said Arthur, "Joel cuts a rather dashing figure, don't you think?"

"I propose," said Pierre, raising his glass, "that we set a date for his initiation."

"What kind of initiation?" asked Joel, eyes narrowing.

Pierre shrugged. "Haven't the slightest idea. We've never initiated anyone before. The four of us were, well, I guess we were just assumed."

"We must think of something," said Arthur.

"I'm sure you'll give it your best mental effort," said Father. "But for the moment, I suggest we stick to the subject at hand. Any idea who the man was at Sister Vickers' table?"

The Tumblars shook their heads.

"Martin," said Father, "do we still have that archdiocesan directory? There on the 'forearmed' shelf behind you."

I dug the volume from its niche amongst such classics in our "forewarned" collection as Waite's *The Book of Black Magic and of Pacts*, Cavendish's *The Black Arts*, and the new *Catechism of the Catholic Church*, and hobbled over to the desk with it. Archbishop Fulbright was on the cover in full color, his red robes flowing all around him like blood from a boil. His teeth looked bleached, and his precious amethyst ring had an airbrushed halo around it.

"Tell me, gentlemen," said Father, opening the book to the title page. There in glossy black and white was a photograph of the archbishop with his club of auxiliaries standing on some pretentious-looking steps. Jeremiah Ravenshorst was the only auxiliary left who had not met with premature extinction. "Do you see him here?"

"Hm no," said Arthur, taking the book into his hands. "That's not the man." He turned a couple of pages until he came to an assortment of smiling ecclesiocrats, the greasy cogs that keep the spinning wheels of the great archdiocesan machine lubricated and humming. "Here he is."

"Yes indeed," said Pierre, snatching the book from Arthur's hands. He studied the array of perky administrators carefully, then stabbed at one of them with his index finger. "Fellows, you agree?"

They gathered around him.

"That's him," said Edward. "That's the man."

"'Denzil Fedisck Goolgol,'" read Jonathan from the caption beneath the picture. "'Monsignor, theologian, and counselor.'"

"Really," said Father, eyebrows raised. "That does put a different spin on things. And you're sure the other woman at the table was Starfire?"

"Yes," said Arthur. "Her flyers are pinned up on every bulletin board and telephone pole in that part of town. Some of them have her picture on them. Come to think of it, I have one here in my pocket." He unfolded a piece of paper and handed it to Father.

"We are planning," said Pierre, "to attend her little talk at Popinjay's parish Wednesday evening. It should be good for a laugh."

"I intend to be there, too," said Father, looking up from the flyer in his hand, "now."

"Oh?" I asked. "I guess that means I'll be going."

"We must invite Sergeant Wickes and Lieutenant Taper as well."

"What for?'

Father just smiled, then folded up the paper and slipped it into the folds of his cassock.

"What fun," said Pierre, a fiendish look on his face. "We must be sure to bring lots of kindling, and a nice big pole to serve as a stake." He slapped Joel on the back, jiggling the worried expression on his face. Then he wrapped his arm around the young man's shoulders and added in a more serious tone, "Rest assured, dear chap, there is far greater likelihood of you or I being burned at the stake than a witch in this century."

The phone rang.

Not wanting to break the rhythm of the meeting, I ambled out of den and headed for the kitchen. I caught it on the seventh ring. "Ah, Lieutenant Taper. We were just talking about you."

"Can I speak with Jack?" He sounded exhausted.

"Well, he's tied up at the moment. Can I take a message?"

"Yeah, sure. Tell him that, at the time Bishop Mgumba and Madeline Sugarman were taking their last shower, Stephanie Fury, Marsha Dukes, Sister Charlene Vickers, and Monsignor Goolgol were having a meeting at the Chancery regarding the fate of 'Spotlight on Community.'"

"Ah yes. Mutual alibis. And, uh, Cheryl Farnsworth?"

"She was home alone."

"No alibi."

"Well, according to the others present, Sister Vickers called her several times on the phone during the aforementioned meeting to get her input."

"Oh. So she's covered, too."

"Yeah, so it would seem. I've gotta double-check the time frames, but I think they're all in the clear."

"Anything else?"

"No. You got something to add?"

"Well, Father Baptist said he wants to extend a special invitation to you and Sergeant Wickes to a Witchcraft Symposium Wednesday evening."

"Oh joy."

"That's the spirit."

41

"SO IT SUITS WELL THIS KNIGHT," Father Baptist was reading as I returned to the study. He was standing by the fireplace, *Sir Gawain and the Green Knight* balanced in one hand and his long-necked burl pipe smoldering in the other.

> ... and his unsullied arms;
> for ever faithful in five points, and five times under each,
> Gawain as good was acknowledged and as gold refinéd,
> devoid of every vice and with virtues adorned.
> So there
> the pentangle painted new
> he on shield and coat did wear
> as one of word most true
> and knight of bearing fair.

The Knights Tumblar were still seated in the study, listening intently.

"Why don't you read this next part, Pierre?" said Father, handing him the book. "From here to about there."

Pierre accepted the book with a ceremonious nod. He drew himself up before the fireplace, glass of champagne in hand, a far-off look in his eye, and a troubadour's lilt in his voice. As he read the words, I could almost imagine Arthur strumming a metal-strung harp in the background.

> First faultless was he found in his five senses,
> and next in his five fingers he failed at no time,
> and firmly on the Five Wounds all his faith was set
> that Christ received on the cross, as the Creed tells us;
> and wherever the brave man into battle was come,
> on this beyond all things was his earnest thought:
> that ever from the Five Joys all his valour he gained
> that to Heaven's courteous Queen once came from her Child.
> For which cause the knight had in comely wise
> on the inner side of his shield her image depainted,
> that when he cast his eyes thither his courage never failed.

"The Virgin Mary's image on the back of the shield, and a pentangle on the front?" said Edward. "Are you sure we're talking about a pentagram here?"

"It boggles the mind," nodded Father. "I know."

"But as I've often said," interrupted the gardener, "there's nothing like a good boggling to shake up the ol' gray matter."

"Of course," said Father, "the wiccans could easily turn this around and try to remake Mary into an image more to their liking—some kind of Earth Mother, I suppose—but the truth is that the pentagram was the Church's symbol long before they ever got their hands on it."

"Besides," said Pierre, "these references to the Five Wounds of Christ would be hard to get around."

"Unless," said Father, "they were circumvented by the fallacy of the 'Christ principle'—the insidious notion that there was no historical Jesus but just some sort of 'Christ essence' floating around in our collective memory. Once you accept drivel like that, you can convince yourself of anything you wish."

"That seems to be the main preoccupation of our day," said Arthur, rubbing his temples discouragingly.

"You're telling me," said Joel. "You should have been in my Foundational Christology class at the seminary. That's why I ended up on leave at St. Philip's."

"These are bleak times," said Arthur, filling his glass. "One wonders what our descendants will think, several centuries hence."

"I should think," said Father, "they will regard our century with astonishment. They will wonder at how the Church divested Herself of all that made Her precious and unique. They will marvel at the hedonism of our culture, and the resulting self-destruction of our society. And, I suspect, they will regard those of us who stand firm against the chaos with the same awe and fervor that we apply to, say, King Arthur."

Arthur stared at Father incredulously. "You're not serious."

"But of course I am," said Father. "Do you think King Arthur and his Knights of the Round Table had any idea that they would some day be the subject of legend?—that books, plays, and movies would be made about their adventures? Certainly not. They were just men of Good Will who saw a job that needed doing, who swore their allegiance to the Church first and their monarch second, and then went about doing what they could."

"But they were heroes," said Jonathan, "valiant soldiers, warriors."

"They were young men," said Father, "not a great deal different than you fine fellows. I suspect they decided to band together in a meeting just as informal—and yet somehow as formal—as the ones you hold here in my rectory. They wore breastplates, carried shields, and fought with swords, for that was the tenor of their day. You dress formally, study the doctrines of the Church, and fight with words, for that is the raw material you have to work with in your century."

The far-off look in Pierre's eyes grew even more distant.

"They lived in castles," continued Father, "because that was how rulers and soldiers fortified themselves. Drawbridges were as ordinary to them as parking meters are to you, as were messengers on horseback to your cellular phones. We look back on those times as fanciful and magical, fraught with life-threatening dangers against which a man's valor was tested. The time in which you live is infinitely more magical: look at the technical wonders at your disposal. Imagine Merlin's reaction to television, laser surgery, or just hot and cold running water. Consider that your time is just as fraught with life-threatening dangers—I speak, of course, of the evils that plague our society and imperil our immortal souls. Nothing could be more hideous than that which seeks to despoil our Eternity."

"You're exaggerating," said Joel. "You gotta be."

"Why do you think I keep this on my desk?" said Father, snatching DO WE WALK IN LEGENDS from between the hand-carved statues of St. Anthony and St. Thomas More. "J. R. R. Tolkien wasn't just writing fantasy, gentlemen. By his own admission, he was writing an allegory of the Church and the struggle of the faithful in times of heresy and spiritual upheaval."

"Wow," said Joel.

"'For not we but those who come after will make the legends of our time,'" quoted Arthur in a whisper.

"You gentlemen keep it up," said Father, "you keep on doing exactly what you're doing, and perhaps some day—"

"They'll exaggerate our deeds," said Edward.

"They'll misrepresent our exploits," said Jonathan.

"They'll misspell our names," said Pierre.

"And maybe you'll go unnoticed," said Father soberly, "forgotten in the jumble of history, lost in the shifting sands of time. But you will be remembered in the only book that matters."

"The Book of Life," said Arthur.

"The Apocalypse," added the gardener, "twenty-one twenty-seven."

We clinked our glasses and finished our drinks.

Tuesday, June Thirteenth

Feast Day of Saint Anthony of Padua, Doctor of the Church and "Hammer of Heretics" (1479 AD)

42

WHAT FATHER BAPTIST DID at the TV station the following morning, with the help of the Tumblars and yours truly, is best left for later. Since it all came out two days hence, there's no use telling the same story twice. I will mention, however, that during our lunch break, a long-haired guy in a tie-dyed shirt came strolling up to me. A string of discolored beads swayed around his neck, and he was so skinny that his ragged jeans didn't seem to move as he walked inside them. The sweet odor of strawberry incense wafted from his pancho, blending with the bittersweet tang of the ginseng cigarette between his lips.

"Hey, man," he said, a little bell jingling around his wrist as he made a peace sign. "My name's Martin."

Oh boy, I thought, another poor soul trapped in the sixties. "Hi. So's mine."

"Whoa, cool dude. Call me Marty. I knew we had somethin' in common, man. I was watchin' you and the padre from the control room. You're really somethin' else."

Ah, a critic with a favorable viewpoint, even if he was watching from the Pleiades Cluster. I smiled politely. "Thank-you."

"I really mean it, man. You and the padre, it's like, whoa, amazing. And the cane, is it, you know, like ... real?"

I squeezed the handle a little harder to be sure. "As far as I know."

"Cool."

"And what do you do around here, uh, Marty?" I asked.

"I'm the station archivist," he said, giving his tangled hair a fierce scratch. "They do an obit, or someone surfaces that everyone's forgotten about—you know, like some old movie star gets a 'lifetime achievement award'—they need a source tape, I dig it up in the video library."

"Really," I said. "You mean like if they do a story that involves, say, John F. Kennedy, you find some old footage on him."

"Yeah. Or if somebody mentions Jimi Hendrix, I got shots of him playing at the Los Angeles Forum—or better yet, the Monterey Pop Festival. Remember when he set his guitar on fire and then started prayin' to it? Whoa."

"Yes," I nodded. "No doubt one of the great telling moments in rock history."

"World history, man. World history."

I nodded again. "Tell me, you wouldn't happen to have anything on Bombing Fluid's last concert, would you?"

"Algernon Park?" squeaked my new friend, threatening to slip off this planet and pirouette to newsreel nirvana. "Jymmy Thinggob's last lead guitar solo? That's, like, one of my faves, you know? It was so, so ... *rad*. Like one, golden, blinding flash before, before, uh—"

"Before the lights went out."

"Yeah, heavy man. Deep. Before the lights went out."

"So do you?"

"Do my lights go out?"

"No, do you have any footage on Jymmy Thinggob's final performance?"

"Have I." He was so pleased with himself, he gave himself a magical mystery hug. "Tell you what. I'll run off a cart for you."

"A cart?"

"You know, a video cartridge, man. VHS okay?"

"I'm not sure. What's that?"

"You know, VHS for your VCR? Or do you want Beta or High-Res Eight?"

I shrugged. "We don't have a television at the rectory. I don't know what you're talking about."

"You don't have—?" His mouth fell open and his cigarette fell to the floor. "Man, I'm like, like, in total awe."

"I'm more of an Oz man, myself."

"Huh?"

"Make it VHR."

"VHS."

"Whatever. Thanks."

"Man," he said, shaking his head as he wandered away. "No television. Like, life without a TV screen. That's, like, beyond far out; all the way to ... *in front.*"

As I watched him disappear among the cameras, lights, reflectors, booms, dangling cables, and studio personnel, I took the liberty of crushing his cigarette butt under my shoe with a magical mystery twist. From beyond the technical thicket I heard his final comment, echoing among the hoists and dollies:

"Whoa."

43

"THAT WAS CERTAINLY A NEW EXPERIENCE," I grunted as we climbed into the Jeep outside the KROM building.

Pierre and Arthur waved as they zoomed by in the parking lot. In my rear view mirror I caught sight of Joel and Jonathan in the back seat of Edward's van as it lurched out another exit and merged with northbound traffic.

"Today is your day," said Father, "for new experiences."

"Uh-oh. Father, what's that I detect in your voice?"

"Amusement, perhaps. Or anticipation."

"At what?"

"At what lies ahead."

"And what is that?"

"The 'Shop of Shadows.'"

"And what is that?"

"Starfire's lair."

"And where is that?"

"Go right here, then a few blocks up, and left on Piedmont."

"And why are we going there?"

"Not we—you."

"Me?"

"Martin, my friend, I am going to ask of you something reminiscent of the kind of ploy Basil Rathbone would ask of Nigel Bruce in one of the old Sherlock Holmes movies."

"I'm cringing already."

"I want you to pay the wicca a visit in her little witchery shop. Just go in and ask questions."

"What kinds of questions?"

"Whatever comes to mind."

"What if nothing does?"

"Martin, I cannot in my wildest dreams imagine you at a loss for words."

"But what if she recognizes me?"

"That was twenty years ago."

"But what if?"

"Not to worry. I borrowed some items from the prop closet at the TV station that may be of help."

"Props?"

From within the folds of his cassock he produced a pair of glasses with lenses like Coke bottle bottoms, a bushy fake mustache, and a crumpled hat.

"I'm not wearing those," I huffed, punching the accelerator for emphasis. "I'll look foolish."

"All the better," he laughed. "The more you draw attention to yourself the better."

"Why? So you can sneak in the back door and ransack her files?"

"It's in the middle of the next block, there on the right. See that pink neon crescent moon in the window?"

"See that black cat running across the street right in front of us? Bad sign. I say we abort this mission."

"And there's a place for you to park, practically in front."

"Thank-you, St. Anthony," I hissed, pulling into a diagonal slot and jamming on the brakes.

"Fifteen minutes," said Father, hopping out of the car. "Just fifteen minutes is all I need."

I watched as he trotted down the block and, pumping his arms like a Keystone Kop, disappeared around the corner—at least, that's what he did in my fuming imagination. Actually, he strolled with the regal sacerdotal dignity fitting his office. He didn't pump his arms even once. As for me, using the rearview mirror for reference, I donned the infuriatingly stupid hat, the bristling mustache—it had a nasty little clip, like a clothes pin, that went inside my nostrils—and those abominable bug-eyed glasses.

"I don't remember praying for humility," I mumbled as I grasped the doorknob of the creepy little establishment. "But as Father always says, there ain't no humility without humiliation." A brass bell tinkled overhead as the door swung closed behind me. At least it was in tune with itself.

"Ah," said a female voice. "May I be of help?"

The owner of the voice approached from around the end of the counter, but all I could see through those infernal glasses was a rotund blur circumventing a larger rectangular one. I assumed the round, advancing splotch was the witch in question, and the stationary rectangular object was a display counter.

"Om I adrrrezzing Shdarrr-fire, de famuz vidge?" I said, trying to remember the rules of the accent I'd just made up in my head as I walked from the Jeep to the front door: T becomes D, W and V switch places, S becomes SH at the beginning of words and Z anywhere else, roll all R's, vowels are up for grabs.

"I am she," said the fuzzy blob. "Though I prefer the term 'wicca.' How can I help you?"

I pretended to look around, interested in her curious collection of wic-a-brac, but my eyes were beginning to water, irritated by the torturous sensation of focus-lack. "Werrry inderezding. Dell me, vot do you have in de vay of pendagles?"

"Pendagles?"

"Ah, my Inglish, id iz nod sho good. Pendagrrromz—izz dad de rrride vorrrd?"

"You mean pentagrams?"

"Yaw, dotz id. Pendagrrromz."

"Of course." She was very pleasant, but I began to detect a little fizz of impatience leaking between her syllables. "We have quite a wonderful assortment."

I felt her hand on my elbow, gently guiding me toward the blurry display case. If I hadn't reached up and rubbed my eyes, shifting the glasses so I could get a quick glance at my surroundings, I might have given myself entirely away by examining an assortment of Mesopotamian fertility symbols. Luckily, I managed to position myself in front of the medallion section, the majority of which were five-pointed intertwined stars.

"Ah," I nodded excitedly, tapping the glass with my fingernail. "Pendagrrromz."

"Are you interested in a ring or a pendant?" she asked helpfully. "I make them all myself. That way I can guarantee that they are infused with good spells. As you can see, I specialize in pewter."

"Yaw," I nodded enthusiastically. "Pendagrrromz."

<pre>
GARDENING TIPS: I could continue transcribing the

phonemic butchery in which I was engaged except

for three things. First, it's driving me crazy

trying to spell it all out. Second, it was driv-

ing me crazy then trying to remember all the al-

phabetical interchanges, hence my makeshift rules

kept mutating, so that within a few sentences my

D's had become T's and my TH's were dancing with

my CH's. And third ...

                                          --M.F.
</pre>

Our conversation was interrupted by the providential arrival of another customer.

"Excuse me," said the wiccan, relieved. "Yes, sir, may I help you?"

A tall, dark shadow approached from the direction of the decaying brass tinkle. "I am interested," said a soft but unmistakably masculine voice, "in purchasing a pentagram."

"Our most popular item today," she said, ushering the shape toward me. "They're over here."

My fake mustache itched.

"I see," he said, "you do have quite a collection. But I am a Satanist. I would like to procure one that is, um, inverted."

"Oh," she said, a little flustered, "I don't carry any of those. We only encourage white magic here."

"Excuse me," I interrupted, with all the appropriate mispronunciations. "As I understand it, sir, Satanists invert the Crucifix to denigrate Our Lord Jesus Christ." I placed my hand on my heart and bowed my head at the mention of His Name in spite of, or because of, the place in which I found myself.

"That," said the man, "is correct."

"Is that the same reason you invert the symbol of the pentagram?"

He hesitated. "Not exactly."

"Not at all," said the witch. "The pentagram symbolizes white magic. Turning it upside down invokes an evil intention. We wiccans are pagans. We don't believe in Satan, or Jesus Christ for that matter. Spirituality is a matter of internal forces, not the external entities personified by Christianity. Morality is self-realized, not imposed from some outside religious authority."

"I see," I said, "that you say that. But now I'm confused."

"How so?" asked the witch.

"Are you saying that Satan is not an intelligent, cognizant spiritual entity?"

"That's right."

"But you recognize the existence of evil."

"Yes, but as an innate force within us, not something from outside."

"You don't believe in external entities? But then who is this goddess you wiccans are always going on about?"

"Diana."

"So she made everything?"

"Well, there is also Cernunnos, her male counterpart."

"Okay, they made everything."

"In a sense, yes."

"But you just said they come from inside us, not us from them. Are you saying we made ourselves, and the earth, and everything?"

"Not exactly, but in a sense, yes."

Ah, now we were getting somewhere. The next trick was to find out where that was. "Your display case is brimming with icons of Egyptian deities. Are you saying they're not real, either?"

"They are reflections," she stammered.

"Reflections? You mean of the forces within us?"

"Yes."

"Then what you're really saying is that followers of your religion worship themselves."

"No, that's not what I'm saying at all." Even through the glasses, I could see her bristling. The sight made me more aware than ever of how itchy my fake mustache was becoming. "Diana, or Isis—she goes by many names—is the female force of the universe, the source of life, the wellspring of love, the fountain of peace."

"Ah," I said, flashing on my undiplomatic conversation with Stephanie Fury the previous Friday morning at St.

Philomena's. It made sense that they would use the same terms, seeing as how they frequented the same bars. That or déjà vu. "Then who are we?"

"We are her children. We are reflections of her creative energy."

"Then we are reflections of her."

"Yes."

"But if she's a reflection of us, and we're a reflection of her, then that's like holding a looking glass up to a mirror—some kind of mutual self-admiration feedback loop. So much for the nature of the universe. But now there is another thing I don't understand. How can there be any reflections in the first place without external light?"

Her face went through some kind of contortion, but I couldn't quite make it out. Just then I heard a momentary grinding sound, like one rough surface grating against another. I couldn't tell if it came from the back of the store or from her dentures, but, just in case, I had to press on to hold their attention.

"Just asking," I said innocently, wiggling my upper lip. The itch in my nostrils was really getting fierce, and my olfactory glands were beginning to secrete protective juices. Anxiety mounting, I turned to the man. "You say you're a Satanist. You intentionally pursue all that which is evil and vile."

"Yes," he said. "In the war between good and evil it is obvious that, on this planet at least, Master Satan has won. Does it not make more sense to cater to the victor than the loser?"

"Ah," I said. "Better to grovel in hell than submit in heaven. So you actually subscribe to the words of Jesus Christ: 'He that is not with me is against me.'"

"Why, yes, I guess I do."

"And also those of St. Paul: 'What shall we then say to these things? If God be for us, who is against us?'"

"Very true."

"You worship Satan, who is against Jesus Christ and also against His followers. So you invert the Crucifix to mock God and all His children."

"Yes."

"And you invert the pentagram to mock whom? ... or what? Witchcraft? According to the proprietor of this very establishment, she too is against Christ."

"I didn't say that," interjected the witch.

I spun around. "Then you're for Him."

"I didn't say that, either."

"Neither for nor against."

"Not in your terms."

"Ah," I said. "You contend that He is not real."

"Not exactly."

"He's another reflection, then."

"Yes."

"Of what?"

"Of the culturally dominant male ego."

"Ah," I said, turning back to the Satanist. "So, by her definition, what you're really against is a culturally dominant male ego."

"Not at all," he said.

"So you're for a culturally dominant male ego."

"I didn't say that, either."

"Come now, you can tell me."

"What?"

"You do believe in the reality of Christ, do you not?"

"Uh —"

"Well, you'd have to in order to worship His opposite."

"True."

"You'd have to, in order to desecrate Him in your Black Mass."

"Yes, that's right."

"In fact, in order to be a good Satanist — or should I say a bad Satanist? Funny, isn't it, where the limitations of language take you? Ahem, as I was saying, in order to be a practicing Satanist, you have to believe in what the Catholic Church teaches more than most Catholics do these days."

"I've never thought of it that way, but yes."

"Perhaps maybe you should consider to begin thinking of it that way."

Just then I heard something metallic shift against something soft and pliable. Either Starfire had drawn a knife from a sheath to cut my throat, or Father Baptist had nudged something in the back, thereby inadvertently instigating the same result.

"So," I said, clearing my throat loudly. "I hope you do not mind me asking you all these questions. My papa always told me it's the only way anyone learns anything."

"I don't mind," said the man, a hint of uncertain amusement in his voice.

"So," I continued, "Mr. Satanist, at the risk of pounding the point into the ground, you invert the pentagram to represent your opposition to witchcraft?"

"No," he answered. "I guess not."

"Yes," said the witch, simultaneously. "Well, not exactly."

"Hold it." I turned back to her. "A moment ago you said—"

"White magic has nothing to do with Satanism." Her voice was becoming rather shrill, my mustache was getting soggy from my ante-nasal drip, and my eyeballs were tingling like crazy. "They are complete and total opposites."

"But," I said, my upper lip twitching like a caterpillar on a hot plate, "unless I've missed something here—which I don't deny, being a simple man from an unpretentious village in an unpronounceable province of an unfamiliar foreign country—Satanism directly opposes Jesus Christ. You attempt to neutralize Him by denying His separate and distinct reality. As far as I can determine, you're both against Christ—you, sir, by active opposition, you, madam, by passive denial."

"Okay," she hissed. "Have it your way. We're both against Christ."

"Aha," I exclaimed. "Then you are on the same side. For the two of you, flipping the pentagram is just viewing two sides of the same coin. That's all I wanted to know."

She cursed abruptly, words I wouldn't care to repeat.

I turned to her and raised my right hand, pointing heavenward. "Madam, I would caution you against taking the name of the Lord your God, in whom you do not believe, in vain. There's an old saying where I come from: 'The fool who says there is no such thing as snow still dies in the avalanche.' I would also suggest that you take a stroll to the book store on the corner and procure a copy of *Sir Gawain and the Green Knight*. Stanzas twenty-seven and twenty-eight contain information that will be of enormous interest to you. You see, your confusion stems in part from the fact that you do not understand the true nature of your own symbols."

The Satanist's voice cracked as he said, "Who is this guy?"

"Someone," I answered loud enough for even someone in the back room to hear, "who is leaving."

At that point I really had to get out of there. My eyes were stinging, my nostrils were throbbing, my fake mustache was dripping, and I'd had enough of these people. Besides, I knew that such conversations served no useful purpose, other

than to provide amusement in the retelling.   As for Father
Baptist, as of that moment, he was on his own.

I turned in the general direction of the furry light I assumed
to be the front door, and shuffled toward it.   I was half-way
there when another thought occurred to me.

"By de vay, Mizz Shdarrr-fire," I said, slyly dropping a
Green Scapular into an umbrella stand by the door, "you
verrr vunz a Vroman Catolick, no?"

The temperature in the store fell by about ten degrees, but
there was no reply.

"Dat's vot I tot," I chuckled as the little bell tinkled above
my head.   "I con shpot a hex a mile avay."

45

"YOU'RE VERY QUIET, MARTIN," SAID FATHER BAPTIST,
his hair fluttering in the breeze as we roared down Seventh
Avenue.   The prop glasses were rattling on the dashboard, and
the fake mustache was clipped to the stem of the rearview mirror.

"I'm thinking," I said stiffly.

"What about?"

"The wording of my resignation."

"Resignation? From what?"

"From your service."

"I see."

"I think I'll move over to St. Francis of Assisi."

"Father Jay's parish."

"Uh-huh."

"It's a nice church, centrally located.   Novus Ordo, but
more on the conservative end of the scale than most.   Of
course, I can't imagine what you'd do there.   They have
automatic sprinklers. And they cemented over the garden last
year."

"Fewer hours.   There can't be less pay.   And as weird as
Father Jay is, he would never expect me to wear a disguise and
engage a witch and a Satanist in polite conversation while he
ransacked the back room—illegally, I might add."

"I'm not a policeman, Martin."

"It's still 'breaking and entering.'"

"The back door was unlocked, so I violated no locks or barricades. It was a business establishment, and I simply went in the rear door. There were no files to ransack, as you put it, but there certainly were items of interest. The trick will be dreaming up a 'probable cause' so Taper and Wickes can get a search warrant. I expect that they'll think of one tomorrow night."

"What's tomorrow night?"

"Starfire's talk at your new employer's parish."

I fished in my pocket for a tissue and wiped my pulsating nose for the umpteenth time. "And what did you find in the back of her store?"

"Nothing of interest to you, if you're really planning to leave."

"I haven't resigned yet."

"Nor have I accepted your resignation."

"So I guess we're still stuck with each other."

"For the time being. By the way, Martin, would you mind removing that horrid hat?"

"You don't like it? I've grown rather fond of it. Where to next?"

"Bishop Ravenshorst's residence. St. Barbara's Chapel."

"Down on Manchester?"

"That's right."

"Okay."

"Martin."

"Yes, Father."

"The hat."

"Yes, Father."

"You're still wearing it."

"Yes, Father."

46

ST. BARBARA'S CHAPEL, at first glance, aroused memories of saner times, when churches were made of brick and mortar, and stained-glass windows still depicted recognizable events instead of geometric heartburn.

The inside, of course, had been gutted. The original masonry had been painted over in flat gray. Everything ornate or hinting of artistic skill had been torn out and hauled off to pawn shops. Paintings had been replaced with felt banners. Devotional candles had given way to electric light sticks with digitally twitching flames. The nineteenth century marble altar had been demolished with pneumatic drills to make room for a stylized fresco of cubic children at play as a backdrop for the new picnic table. The rubble from the altar had been used to pave the walkway to the rectory behind the church. Waste not, want not.

For this reason I was hobbling along on the uneven ground alongside the walkway. By the end of my life I will have done many things that I'll regret, but one of them won't be treading upon the debris of a desecrated altar.

"Good morning, uh, Father," said a uniformed policeman stationed by the entrance to the rectory. "Sorry, Jack. It's hard thinking of you as, you know—" He rubbed his own blue collar.

"Ted Gorman," said Father, shaking the officer's hand. "Good to see you again. I know what you mean." He hooked his index finger over his Roman collar and gave his neck a thoughtful scratch. "I'm not used to it myself. This is my assistant, Martin."

Officer Gorman and I shook hands and exchanged appropriate grunts.

"So you're protecting Bishop Ravenshorst?" asked Father.

"Yeah, right. There's a pool, you know, down at the station. Most of the guys are betting he won't make it past Sunday."

"That long," commented Father. "What do you say?"

The policeman looked from side to side, though no one was around. "If I were a cold-blooded betting man, I'd lay odds he'll bite the dust Friday evening 'round eight."

"Really," said Father, folding his arms thoughtfully. "All the murders were committed in the evening, I'll grant you. But any particular reason for the date?"

"The pattern," said Officer Gorman. "If you mark a calendar, they're five days apart. Not when the bodies were discovered, mind you, but the days on which the murders happened."

Father froze. "Say that again."

"Easy," said the policeman. "Silverspur's body was discovered on Saturday, June tenth, but he was murdered on Thursday, June first. Brassorie was murdered in his chapel on Tuesday, June sixth. Mgumba took his last shower with that

Sugarman woman on Sunday, June eleventh. One plus five is six, six plus five is eleven—"

"Eleven plus five," said Father, "is this coming Friday, June the sixteenth. Congratulations, Ted. Have you shared this insight with anyone else? Chief Billowack, perhaps?"

"That old windbag? Hah! No, but I told Larry Taper because he's on the case, and he's one helluva guy."

"I agree. Thank-you. You've been most helpful. Shall we, Martin?"

"With odds like that," I said, pushing the doorbell, "I wonder how Bishop Ravenshorst's holding up."

"We are about to see," said Father as footsteps approached from within.

"Yes?" The last person I expected to answer the door did so. "Oh, hello."

"Miss Farnsworth," said Father.

"Father Baptist," she said, then looked at me a little puzzled. "Mr. Feeney."

Why the formality? Why that expression on her beautiful—?

The hat! That stupid hat was still on my head. Arrrgh. Bad enough that I'd been wearing it during our conversation with Officer Gorman, who naturally assessed me as a twit. But now her. My disobedience had been appropriately rewarded. There's an old saying where I come from: "If you behave like an adolescent, expect zits." Oh well, the damage was done. "Cheryl," I said, clumsily doffing the horrid thing.

She smiled politely and motioned us in. "I'm glad you're here. Stephanie and I were just about to leave, and he really shouldn't be alone."

I stiffened at the thought of another confrontation with a second witch in as many hours. This was certainly not my day. On the other hand, I should count my blessings. Ms. Fury could have answered the door instead of Cheryl Farnsworth. Zits either way.

"Yes," said Cheryl, leading us down a dark hallway, our feet thumping hollowly on the densely-waxed hardwood floor. "Stephanie's the liturgical coordinator, don't forget, and I'm helping her arrange the big funeral."

"Big funeral?" asked Father Baptist.

"You know," she said. "The police couldn't allow Bishop Brassorie to be buried last Saturday, since his grave had become a crime scene. And Bishop Silverspur's body, well, they had to do an autopsy. Now there's Bishop Mgumba and poor

Madeline. So we've decided to have a big funeral for all of them at once."

I was amazed that she could talk about such things and still come off bright and sweet as a summer flower. Me, I just wanted to crawl inside the hat and get hung on a hook somewhere.

"Really," said Father. "And where will this take place?"

"Here," said Cheryl. "Archbishop Fulbright has expressed his desire to concelebrate the funeral with Bishop Ravenshorst, but Jerry refuses to leave his residence, even with a police escort. So it was decided to hold the funeral Mass here at St. Barbara's this Saturday."

"The mountains come to Mohammed," I mumbled.

Cheryl either ignored or didn't hear my comment. "We'll have the Rosary Friday evening. It's a big church, and lots of people will be coming, not to mention the press. So actually it works out fine. The police, as you can see, are providing protection. Surely you'll be here."

"Of course," said Father.

"Later this afternoon I'm meeting with some television people to coordinate our activities. They're very schedule-conscious, you know. If we want the Rosary televised, for instance, we have to guarantee that the entrance procession begins promptly at eight-oh-one, and the whole thing must be wrapped up, sermon and all, by eight-twenty-seven, with a four-minute meditation precisely on the quarter hour. Commercials, we must make room for commercials."

"Well," said Father, "there is that. By the way, what is going to happen now to the 'Spotlight on Community' show?"

Cheryl took a deep breath. "The Rapture Channel is going to put together a couple of 'best of' broadcasts for this week, but after that I'm not sure. The crew had a meeting last Sunday evening, but nothing definite came of it. They're going to try once more sometime this coming weekend, so ask me again after that."

"In any case, you'll all be free this Thursday evening."

"I suppose so. Why?"

"I was going to phone you. I'm calling another meeting this Thursday evening, similar to the last two, but not at the Chancery this time. An old friend of mine, Alan Ross, owns Darby's on Sycamore Drive. You know the place?"

"I've never eaten there, but I've heard they've got great prime rib."

"That they have," said Father. "Everything there is superb. So you'll join us there for dinner, say seven?"

She hesitated a moment, thinking, then said, "Sure. It's archdiocesan business, isn't it?"

Throughout this conversation I was trying to come up with something intelligent to say to counteract the hat, which was now crammed into my coat pocket, but my synaptic network utterly failed me. Humility, I thought to myself, I don't remember praying for humility.

Twenty of Father Baptist's studies could have easily fit within the bishop's study's elegant boundaries and arched ceiling. The walls were lined with shelves of fine, polished wood, brimming with leather-bound books. There was a fireplace big enough for a basketball player to stand in, and a crystal chandelier that could have graced a ballroom. Dominating the room was a thirty-five foot mahogany table, dotted with stacks of books, manuscripts, musty scrolls, legal tablets, and writing utensils.

At the far end of the table sat Bishop Ravenshorst, head buried in his hands. Silently towering over him like a thunderhead preparing to drench the countryside was Ms. Stephanie Fury. They both looked up as we entered.

"Father Baptist," gasped the bishop, rising weakly. " I can't tell you how good it is to see you."

"I can't imagine why, My Lord," said Father. "I bring no good news."

"None?" The bishop didn't bother to shake hands. He just sank back into his seat with a dispossessed sigh and a skeletal rattle. "I was hoping you'd have caught the murderer by now."

"So was I," said Father, seating himself at right angles to the bishop.

"Father Baptist has come to invite us to a dinner," said Cheryl Farnsworth in a tone not unlike someone visiting a relative in the hospital who is about to undergo open heart surgery. "Thursday evening at Darby's."

"Really," said Stephanie Fury, slipping the strap of her black purse over her padded shoulder. She tossed me a nasty, questioning glance, as if to inquire whether I was included on the guest list.

On a descending roll, I just smiled stupidly, thinking perhaps now would be a good time to put the hat back on.

"That is not the whole reason I am here," said Father, "but yes, dinner will be at seven. Come hungry."

"I haven't eaten in days," moaned the bishop. "Or slept, or managed to get any work done." He gazed helplessly down the length of the table. "And I told the archbishop I'd have the research completed by Friday. Besides, I'm not going anywhere."

"Sure you are," said Father Baptist. "Martin and I will take you in our car, if you like. And I can arrange to have two policemen in the car with us."

"It won't help," the bishop whimpered. "Nothing will help against, against—"

"If you'll excuse us," said Ms. Fury rigidly, "Cheryl and I must get on with the preparations for Saturday's funeral."

"Yes," said Miss Farnsworth, snatching up her pocketbook from amidst the scholarly debris on the table. If she'd had a coat, I would have helped her on with it. If she'd had a puddle to step across, I would have cast mine down upon the murky waters. Yes, I'll admit it, I glanced around the room for some gnarly dragon to emerge from the shadows so I could demonstrate my flailing manhood to her. Funny the things that go through a humiliated mind. As it was, she was doing just fine without any assistance from me.

"Would you believe it?" she was saying. "The Old West Museum is going to loan us the Cordova Rosary for the service, and we're supervising the delivery this afternoon. We'll swing by later, Jerry. Maybe you'll want some dinner."

"I doubt it," sniveled the bishop. "But I don't want to be alone."

"Sure."

"What research, My Lord?" asked Father as the women turned to leave. My eyes were distracted by the sight of their receding fulcra. I doubt any studies have been done on the subject, but I'm convinced the muscles and contours of the hind side of a woman's knees are every bit as revealing as her palms—to one who knows how to read them. Of course, I make no claim to expertise—just amateur status. I returned my attention to the subject at hand.

"All this." The bishop waved his hands vaguely at the erudite detritus cluttering his landscape. "It all seemed so important last week. Now I could care less. The archbishop wants to dedicate the reconstructed Del Agua Mission a week from tomorrow. There's going to be a ceremony, long-winded speeches, and so on. As the official historian for the archdiocese, Archbishop Fulbright wants me to write a brief history of the mission and its founders, to be made into a booklet which will be distributed during the festivities."

If Bishop Silverspur was still around, I thought, he'd be organizing a picket line to protest the missionizing of the Indians in the first place. "Maybe that," I ventured lamely, "will take your mind off your problems."

"I doubt it," said the bishop wearily.

"So do I," said Father. "Martin, would you mind stepping outside? There is a matter I must discuss with His Lordship in private."

"Sure," I said, the weight of my sheer uselessness buckling my shoulders.

"What is it?" asked the bishop as I headed for the door.

"I would be less than honest with you," I heard Father say as I headed toward the door, "if I were to tell you that we'll get this murderer before he gets to you. I doubt very much that we will."

"Then what the devil do you want to talk about?" choked the bishop.

Father's stern but intensely compassionate voice reverberated down the hardwood hallway. "Your soul."

"Why should you care about that?"

"Somebody has to."

47

"YOU MUST BE ON GUARD," SAID FATHER BAPTIST through the confessional screen, "against such thoughts."

"I know, Father. I've really been slipping lately."

"Get a grip, Martin. These things, left unchecked, only get worse."

"I know."

"Anything else?"

"No, that's it."

"Very well. Say a Rosary—and at the end of each decade, call upon the Archangels for their vigilant assistance: 'St. Raphael, St. Michael, St. Gabriel, and St. Uriel; surround me, uphold me, and protect me.' Got that?"

"Yes, Father."

"And a Memorare said in honor of St. Philomena, Virgin and Martyr, might not be a bad idea, either."

"Anything you say, Father."

"Now make a good act of contrition."

Wednesday, June Fourteenth

Feast Day of Saints Eliseus, Prophet (Ninth Century BC), and Basil, Doctor of the Church (379 AD)

48

IT WAS THE FEAST OF ST. ELISEUS, the Old Testament prophet who received the cloak of his companion, St. Elias, as the latter was being taken up to heaven in a fiery chariot. The feast day was shared by St. Basil, one of the thirty-two Doctors of the Church, who once declared that he would not allow his soul to be turned aside from God by his love of any single earthly thing. We stand on the shoulders of giants.

At it was Millie's morning off, Father Baptist and I were on our own for breakfast. One meal of do-it-yourself corn flakes out of twenty-one ain't bad.

It was also the weekaversary of the morning I had excitedly hobbled up to Father in the garden with a newspaper under my arm, only to find that he already had been notified about Bishop Brassorie's murder. It was hard to believe that was only seven days ago.

With reporters hiding behind every bush and trash can, I hadn't ventured to the corner to fetch a newspaper for several days. However this morning, mumbling prayers to both Saints Eliseus and Basil, I braved the treacherous journey because I wanted to see Father's ad in the classified section. My prayer was answered; there didn't seem to be any reporters around.

As I slipped a quarter into the slot at the newsstand, I saw the words WHO ARE THEY? atop the right front column in tall bold letters. MYSTERIOUS MEN OBSERVED, it said below in smaller bold print, VISITING PRIEST-COP'S RECTORY. "Formally attired, they only come at night ..." began the story under the byline, JACCO BABS. Ziggie Svelte had provided a murky photo of unidentifiable blurred images. Considering Ziggie's talent and experience, the lack of focus had to have been intentional, fueling the flames of mystery. Nonetheless, the Knights Tumblar had been seen if not identified.

My next prayer was not answered. If it had been, some reporter—any reporter—would have accosted me along the way back to the rectory and received for his effort a crash course in physics: acceleration, collision, and the force of gravity. As it turned out, I encountered no inquiring minds all the way home. Reporters have Guardian Angels, too, I reminded myself.

Returning to the rectory, I turned the paper inside out and tossed it onto the desk as Father Baptist settled down in the study with his umpteenth cup of coffee. The "$100's" made elongated reflections on the four liquor bottles which still stood as silent sentinels around Father's work space.

"Responses to the ad should start trickling in this afternoon," said Father, sniffing his brew tentatively. Tact and the interests of camaraderie prevented him from drawing frank comparisons between Millie's exquisite Java and my bacheloric attempt at caffeine percolation. "We can swing by the post office on the way to St. Francis' tonight, or wait until sometime tomorrow. There's no rush."

"You'll want to read the front page," I said. "Mr. Babs spotted the Tumblars entering the rectory."

"Does he know their names?" he asked, rattling the pages noisily as he refolded them. "Did he follow them?"

"Doesn't say. Maybe he's saving it while the suspense builds. People love a mystery."

"It was inevitable, I suppose. I shall have to speak with them about it. Their usefulness may be at an end. Ah, Joel."

Our temporary boarder, so temporary that he was hardly ever there, came striding in with an air of purpose and determination far removed from the desperation of the bedraggled young man who had first approached me at the back of the church the previous Friday. "Father," he said, "Mr. Feeney."

"Joel," I acknowledged, handing him an empty cup and indicating the coffee pot resting on a pot holder under the discriminating nose of St. Thomas More. "Millie's out so we're on our own."

"I'm still full from last night," said Joel, puffing his cheeks and patting his stomach. He dribbled a little coffee for himself, then settled into one of the tired chairs.

"Big night?" asked Father.

"Very," said Joel. "There was a smoker at the lounge in the new Spritz-Terryton Hotel on Delmonico. The doorman assumed we were paying guests and, before we knew it, we were invited to sit at the head table. Pierre even gave a speech."

"Really," said Father, smiling broadly.

"You know Pierre," shrugged Joel. "He always says: 'If you act like you own the place, you'll end up doing so.'"

"What was his speech about?" I asked, adding more cream to the battery acid in my cup.

"What else?" laughed Joel. "The Faith. Oh, not directly at first. He began by comparing a good cigar to Noah's ark. Don't ask me how, but he did. Then he wove in the idea that only people with good taste go to fabulous smokers like the one we were attending, and only people with Good Will go to Heaven."

"Pierre does have a way with words," said Father. "But then—"

His thought was interrupted by the telephone ringing. Father Baptist scooped up the receiver from its cradle and said officiously, "St. Philomena's rectory. Oh, hello Albert. What's that? Yes, he's right here."

Father handed the receiver to Joel.

"Dad? Yeah, hi. What's up?"

Father Baptist and I exchanged glances as the little electronic voice buzzed in Joel's ear. We couldn't hear the words, but the rhythm was urgent and erratic.

"When did it happen?" Joel's face grew stern. "Really. Was your stuff insured? That's good. What do the cops—? That sounds like what they'd say. So what happens next? Yeah, I can catch a bus and be over there within an hour. Will do."

"What's wrong?" asked Father as Joel set down the receiver.

"Somebody stole Dad's truck last night. The truck isn't nearly as important as the tools and electrician's gear stored in the back. The cops figure he'll never recover that stuff. Luckily it was all insured. He says he wants me to meet him at the shop to help him do an inventory for the cops and the insurance company, but I think he's really just upset and needs someone to, you know, listen to him blow off some steam."

"You don't need to take a bus," I said. "I'll drive you over."

"That would be great," said Joel. "Thanks."

"You need anything while I'm out?" I asked Father.

No answer.

"Father?" I repeated.

He had just pulled a copy of *Saints to Remember* from the shelf and was riffling through the pages in search of some detail he wasn't about to divulge even if he had been conscious of us. I thought he mumbled something like "trick city" and "barbarous" but I couldn't be sure.

"Father?" said Joel. "Mr. Feeney, what's wrong with him?"

"Don't worry," I said as I grabbed my cane and struggled to my feet. "Something you just now said, or I said earlier, or someone said yesterday, or maybe last week, just got through to him, and he's checking it out. Probably means we're in for a doosie of a sermon this Sunday."

Joel watched as Father reached for another volume, oblivious to our concern. "Does he do this often?"

"I first noticed this behavior the day he arrived here at St. Philomena's. It's getting worse."

49

AFTER DROPPING JOEL OFF at his father's shop in Barkinbay Beach, I ran a few personal errands, like getting some typewriter ribbons for the Underwood and a new rubber foot for my cane. By the time I got home, Millie was back, and lunch was about to be served. Father was over his muttering spell.

The next bit of fun began that evening, just as it was getting dark. We met Lieutenant Taper and Sergeant Wickes on the steps in front of the St. Francis of Assisi parish hall.

"You did what?" Taper was gawking at me.

"I wore a fake mustache and thick glasses."

"And a hat," added Father.

"And a stupid hat," I nodded. "Meanwhile, Father here ransacked the back room."

"I did not ransack anything," said Father stiffly. "I, a potential customer, merely entered by the establishment's rear door, which was unlocked, and bore no signs indicating the proprietor's preference that the front door be used instead. I opened no drawers, went through no files. I simply looked around at what was plainly visible."

"And?" said Taper.

"I strongly advise you to go there yourselves," said Father. "If you've no basis for a search warrant, then go as I did, as customers. Or go as police investigators looking for information on witchcraft. Or better yet, after tonight, drop in as—Oh, Pierre! Arthur! Jonathan!"

"Good evening, Father," they said variously.

The three Tumblars were coming up the steps, formally clad, naturally. Pierre had added a new opera hat, tails, and a white-tipped walking stick to his wardrobe.

"Lieutenant Larry Taper," said Father, "Sergeant Wickes. I'd like you to meet three very interesting young men. This overdressed patron of the arts is Pierre Bontemps—"

"Properly dressed," said Pierre with a dashing bow. " A pleasure. Allow me to present my companions, Jonathan Clubb and Arthur von Derschmidt. Welcome to Popinjay's Palace. Of course, speaking personally, I would question the integrity of anyone attending this dubious little assembly. Just look around you."

"True," nodded Taper.

"Hmm," grimaced Jonathan, noting a couple of girls straggling by with ferns in their hair. They were sporting ponchos woven of some coarse, bark-like material. They were followed by a long-haired man all in black. A glass eye clutched in a skeletal pewter claw gawked at us from the chain around his neck. "On the other hand, some of the more bizarre people from Father Baptist's congregation are also here tonight."

"Oh?" asked Wickes, looking around curiously. "Who?"

"Why, us, of course," said Pierre, slapping both his companions on the back. Then he nudged Wickes with his elbow. "You, too, Sergeant."

"I'm not a member of Father Baptist's parish," protested Wickes.

"You can deny it all you want," said Jonathan sternly, wagging a condescending finger. "But you've been seen there. There are witnesses. Your affiliation with that radical reactionary group has already tarnished your reputation and bruised your credibility in the community at large."

"Shocking," scowled Arthur. "Simply shocking."

"Except with us," winked Pierre. "We find your reactionary tendencies most endearing. We'll make a monarchist of you yet. As for Madam Starfire—" Brandishing his walking stick, he pointed to a fluorescent orange poster tacked to the auditorium door. "—we find her brand of bogus metaphysics something more than humorous and less than funny."

"I don't follow you," said Wickes.

"Sure you do," said Pierre, hunching over and lurching awkwardly toward the door. "Inside, inside. This way. Walk this way."

"We'll be along in a minute," said Father.

"It's general admission," said Jonathan, lurching away after his companion.

Arthur followed suit. "We can't guarantee that we can save you any good seats."

"Don't bother," said the gardener. "With tonight's venue, there aren't any."

"Sir," huffed Pierre, drawing himself up in august indignation as the other two bumped into him. "Don't you dare cast dispersions upon such a time-honored institution as the circus."

With a hrmph and an ahem, Pierre and his two Tumblar companions straightened, adjusted their vests, then strode off toward the building whistling a three-ring calliope melody.

"As I was saying," said Father, watching them as they did a little jig before bounding inside, "you really should—"

"Excuse me," interrupted a young woman floating toward us in a flowing white tunic. Her long blonde hair was adorned with lilacs and grape leaves. She drifted up like an evening summer breeze, fingering a crystal pendant which dangled from her ivory neck on a silver chain. "Aren't you, you know, him—the priest who's tracking down the Holy Toast Murderer?"

"Is that what they're calling him?" smiled Father.

"A disk jockey on the radio this afternoon did," she said.

"Well in any case, yes, I'm he."

"Oh, I thought so. I could sense your emanations all the way from the parking lot."

"I told you not to have seconds of Millie's casserole," I whispered.

"What can I do for you?" asked Father, ignoring me.

She held up her pendant, a two-inch quartz shard entwined with a copper eel. "Would you, could you, you know, charge my crystal?"

"I don't know any blessings for crystals," said Father.

"No?" she frowned. Then she brightened. "Oh please. There must be something energizing you can say over it."

"Well, perhaps there is," said Father, taking the thing in his right hand and placing his left over it. He closed his eyes and muttered quickly but precisely, "Ave, Maria, gratia plena, Dominus tecum; benedicta tu in mulieribus, et benedictus fructus ventris tui, Jesus. Sancta Maria, Mater Dei, ora pro nobis peccatoribus, nunc et in hora mortis nostrae. Amen."

"There you go," he said, letting it slip from his fingers. "That's the most powerful prayer I know."

"Oh!" she squealed, clutching it in her grateful hand. " I can feel it! I can feel it!"

She wandered off toward the auditorium door, hugging the crystal to her cheek and crooning a dulcet, but somewhat disjointed melody to herself.

"As I was saying, Larry," said Father, shrugging off the interruption, "I strongly advise you and the sergeant to go to the 'Shop of Shadows' and check it out for yourselves, especially after tonight. I'm not sure what would constitute—"

"Well bless my soul," I interrupted in an unnecessarily loud voice. "It's Monsignor Goolgol."

Father blinked and turned to see.

GARDENING TIPS: For purposes of identification,

Sherlock Holmes studied such variant concepts as

the chemical components of cigarette ash and the

contours of the human ear. Fingerprints have kept

the FBI boys employed for decades. The typing of

blood, skin, and saliva has been considered admis-

sible in court for some years. The reliability of

DNA testing is still being scrutinized by specialists. They all have their methods. But I am

breaking ground in an entirely new field: <u>Adam's</u>

<u>apple</u> <u>oscillation</u>. For my money, there was only

one man on earth with a persnickety throat like

Monsignor Goolgol's. Though he was clad in non-

clerical attire--some sort of a silvery-blue cape

with a broad-rimmed velour hat pulled down over

his dark, darting eyes, and falconing a diaph-

anously clad woman on his left arm--I'd know that

flitting mass of laryngeal cartilage anywhere ...

                                        --M.F.

So did Father.

"Ulp," gulped the lizardly monsignor, unappreciative of public recognition.

The woman on his arm, upon closer inspection, turned out to be none other than Sister Charlene Vickers, former secretary to Bishop Brassorie and fourth tenor in the Altar Belles. She was harder to recognize, oddly enough, because there was so much of her to see. What gave her away was the pallor of her skin, the rhythm of her gate, and her unfortunate inability to do anything but squint. She didn't seem pleased, either, to be spotted as the monsignor's escort.

"Ah, Monsignor," said the gardener, still on the loud side. "And how long have you been fraternizing with nuns and witches?"

Perhaps the word should have been "sororityzing," but what the hey. The ethereal nun and the reptilian monsignor disentangled themselves and achieved arm's length apogee in a flash.

"I am a licensed theologian," explained Goolgol in a rather shrill gobble. "And in that capacity I am investigating the parallels between Christianity and witchcraft. In fact, I am

writing a book on the subject. Not—" Boy, did he emphasis
the not. "—that it's any of your business."

"It is," boomed Father, attracting the judgmental glances of
passersby, "insofar as murder is my business. Need I remind
you that I have a letter signed by Archbishop Fulbright, your
lawful superior, directing all Catholics in good standing to co-
operate with my investigation? I assume that includes you,
unless you tell me otherwise."

Ol' Goolgol's Apple was doing three-dimensional twirlies.

"As far as my business as a priest," continued Father, "it is
my responsibility to work for the salvation of souls, in part by
uprooting and disposing of error. In that capacity I admonish
you that there are no genuine parallels between Catholicism
and paganism."

"There are," countered the monsignor, eyeing Father's cassock and Roman collar with blatant contempt, "if you move
beyond your stilted preconceptions and allow higher understanding to permeate your consciousness."

A couple of sea nymphs and dogwood dryads applauded
nearby.

Encouraged, the monsignor continued. "There is no essential difference between believing in the Blessed Trinity and
the duality of Diana and Cernunnos, or the whole pantheon of
gods on Olympus for that matter."

I nudged Wickes in the ribs and whispered. "So much for
'Catholic in good standing.'" He gave me a "Shut up, I want
to listen!" look.

"When was the last time you recited the Athanasian
Creed?" asked Father.

"The what?" asked the monsignor.

"That long." Father Baptist seemed to have grown a few
inches in height—a trick of the light, of course. "Would God
have called Abram out of Ur if his monotheism did not set
him significantly apart from the polytheism of his coun-
trymen? Why was God's anger kindled when the Hebrews
built themselves a golden calf at Sinai? If, by your scholastic
trickery and linguistic gymnastics you cloud the issues which
divide truth from error, be warned: you will be held responsible for the souls who are lost in the process."

"It is clear," said Goolgol, lips and nostrils twitching spas-
modically, "that you are as narrow-minded as the reputation
which precedes you."

"The road to heaven is narrow," said Father. "The width
of my mind has nothing to do with it."

"Surely any thinking person knows," countered the monsignor, "that we need to understand the words of Christ in light of our present understanding."

Father took a step toward the monsignor, coming dangerously close to that maniacally bobbing Adam's apple. I considered yelling a warning, but I figured what the hey.

"Monsignor," said Father, "are you saying that Jesus Christ's understanding of His own mission was not as complete as yours?"

"Come on," said Sister Squint, grabbing her quivering companion's arm. "We don't need to listen to this."

"By the way," I mentioned to Sister Vickers, "I just love your habit, er, I mean nightie, uh, gown—"

The look she gave me. And I was just trying to pay her a compliment.

"And I do so look forward," I added, "to seeing you again tomorrow evening for dinner."

"Just wait until all this is over," hissed Goolgol as she tugged him away.

"Until all what is over?" asked Father Baptist.

"Just wait," squealed the monsignor as Sister Charlene yanked him inside the auditorium door.

"Feisty fellow," said Taper.

"Which one?" I asked.

"As I was saying," said Father, clearing his throat, "I'm not sure what will constitute 'probable cause,' but you must find an acceptable reason to visit the 'Shop of Shadows.' There are things there that will help clear up— Oh, here's Joel."

The youngest of the Tumblars was coming up the steps with Edward. Joel's poor-box vest had come undone and Edward's bow tie was crooked.

"Hi, Father," puffed Joel, running his fingers through his tousled hair. "I guess we just made it. Barely had time to change."

"How is your dad?" I asked.

"Pretty upset," said Joel. "His whole living was wrapped up in the back of that old truck. They found it, stripped and abandoned near the airport. All his tools were gone. Even with insurance it will take a few weeks—maybe months—for him to replace everything."

"I heard about that," said Lieutenant Taper. "The department computer kicked the report over to me, cross-referencing the last name. I spoke with Sergeant Martinez over in Barkinbay Division, and he said your dad's equipment will probably be percolating through the black market for weeks."

"Dad wanted me to take over his business eventually," said Joel sadly. "Don't get me wrong, he was genuinely happy when I told him I wanted to go into the seminary. But I was the only son who really 'had the spark,' as he put it, for electrical things. That's why he called me this morning. He knew I'd, you know, appreciate his loss."

"Sure," said Father. "I figured as much. I'll remember Albert at Mass in the morning. Martin, remind me to call him tomorrow."

"It looks like they just dimmed the lights," I said. "Maybe we should go inside."

"You still haven't told us why you wanted us here," said Sergeant Wickes as we walked into the lobby.

"You will see," said Father.

The auditorium was dark indeed. We stood at the back for a moment, waiting for our eyes to adjust. It was a five-hundred seater with a raised stage and heavy green curtains. Two conical beams of intense white light spanned the length of the auditorium, originating in a rear-wall control room, and colliding in a blinding ellipse at the podium at center stage.

Father "Popin" Jay, forehead glistening in the blue-edged spotlight, was making his supercilious introductions into a bulb-ended microphone mounted on a gooseneck stand. His over-enunciated P's, T's and S's exploded through the sound system like random canon fire in a Civil War reenactment: "Her re-PEW-TAY-SSSShun PREE-cedeZZZZ her ..."

As our vision cleared, we caught sight of Pierre waving his walking stick at us from front-row center. The white tip made wild patterns as it swirled in the beam of the spotlight over his head. Up on stage, it created an optical impression that Father Jay was appearing in an old, flickering movie.

"Author of seven books," ol' Popinjay was bellering, "on the theory and practice of modern witchcraft, its history dating back to pre-Christian times, and its practical relevance to the problems of our day."

"Hurry!" yelled Pierre, gesticulating frantically, oblivious to Father Jay. "It's about to start!"

"Yeah," called Jonathan, waving his arms wildly. "We shed blood saving these seats!"

Edward and Arthur were busy dusting off four folding chairs with their silk handkerchiefs, their backs to the podium.

The water nymphs and earth gonads in the second row looked at each other in astral horror.

"Almost done," shouted Edward at the top of his lungs.

"They're almost here!" cried Arthur, even louder.

"Oh brother," moaned Wickes, as we arrived at the front. "Let me out of here."

"Can't back out now," I said, grabbing his arm and keeping his forward momentum going.

"And here she is, uh, ahem, to enlighten us," continued Popinjay, flustered, "on the recently emerging practice of 'Pentoven Magick'—"

"Gentlemen," said Joel as we arrived at our chairs. They had saved us four seats, peppered between them. "So glad you could make it—"

"Shhhhhhhhhhhh!" hissed Pierre in enraged indignation. Then he cupped his hands around his mouth and shouted, "We're trying to hear up here! Do you hear me?" It hurt my throat just to listen to him. "We're trying to hear up here!"

"Yeah," yelled Arthur and Edward and Jonathan and Joel to each other, catching us new arrivals in the crossfire. "Shut up, will you? Yeah, you. Shut up!"

"Gentlemen," barked Father Baptist crossly. "In exceeding the bounds of propriety, you are embarrassing me and these fine men from the Police Department."

"And me," I said, rubbing my ear.

"Quite right," said Pierre, adjusting his tie. "Our sincere apology, Father, Officers."

"And me," I said.

"And you, Mr. Feeney. I'm afraid we got caught up in the emotion of the moment."

"Shhhhhhhhh!" they all agreed, melting sheepishly into their seats.

"—Starfire," announced Father Jay, mopping his brow as he stepped back from the podium.

From behind the curtain stepped a roundish sort of woman with shoulder-length gray-blonde hair. I finally got a look at the blur I had encountered in the "Shop of Shadows" the day before. Circumnavigating sixty-five or so, she was wearing a simple gown—sort of a black canvas tent—with a white rope around her wide middle. On her forehead was a gleaming crescent moon on a narrow band of silver. Every now and then it would send out a blinding flash of light as it caught the spotlight.

The applause from the audience was warm and inviting. A group of fern-frilled dryads somewhere behind us and to the right began chanting, "Starfire, Starfire, Starfire," to a hypnotic mixolydian aria. A contingent of straw-haired hags cackled and hummed in indecipherable wiccan glee off to the left. Real Halloween material. A cluster of warlocks several rows behind us were droning something reminiscent of a cross between "The Monster Mash" and "Blue Velvet"—yes, I know, it puzzled me at the time, too. The general hubbub around us went on for a minute or so, the banter rising and falling like boiling gruel in an iron cauldron. Finally, the cacophonous reception died down as Starfire cleared her throat.

"Fellow entities," she said sweetly into the microphone.

The clamorous racket rose and fell again.

"Welcome to planet earth."

You would have thought she'd just announced a three-for-one sale on anodized aluminum brooms. More applause.

"I don't believe it," said Sergeant Wickes.

"Me neither," said Lieutenant Taper.

They had landed on either side of Pierre, and so had the second best seats in the entire house.

"Can she see us?" asked Wickes.

"I don't think so," said Taper. "Not with those spotlights in her eyes."

"What's the problem?" I asked.

"Her," said Wickes.

"What's her problem?" I asked.

"Thanks for bringing us, Jack," said Taper.

"Don't mention it," said Father.

"Don't mention what?" I asked.

"How long did you know?" asked Taper.

"A couple of nights ago I came across a flyer with her face on it," said Father.

"Whose face?" I asked.

"Hers," said Father.

"Shhhhhhhhhhhh!" hissed Pierre, swishing his head around like a water hose gone wild. Then he jerked his head to attention and put his finger to his lips. "This is important stuff."

51

"I AM A SOLITARY WITCH," said the young woman. She was speaking into a microphone placed half-way up the right side aisle for questions from the audience. She was one of the girls disguised as trees who passed us in front of the auditorium. "I have been practicing 'the craft' on my own for almost ten years. Are you saying I should abandon my magical solitude in favor of this five-way power pact?"

"Not at all," said Starfire from the podium, her cheeks puffing with esoteric authority. "Nor am I suggesting that those of you who are in covens should break up your communities. All I'm trying to do is inform you that there is another branch of wiccan thought which centers around the number five. Five, like thirteen and one, is a powerful number—but unlike thirteen and one, its energies are triggered by sacrifice. When five hearts commit to such a pact, each one performing the profound act which we call 'immolation,' the cone of power thus generated is, to put it mildly, awesome. Do not forget that our wiccan ancestors have venerated the pentagram for untold generations. There is a reason why the pentagram has five sides and five angles."

"Surely, Madam Starfire" said another woman at the microphone in the opposite aisle, "you're not promoting blood sacrifices, you know, as in the killing of animals."

A murmur of fashionable revulsion rippled through the audience.

"That would violate our sacred dictum," said Starfire. "'An it harm none, so mote it be.' By 'sacrifice' I mean giving something to the goddess which is part of ourselves. When five people, be they women or men, give of themselves in this way, especially if channeled through a sixth person who acts as receiver, then the ramifications are nothing short of startling."

"But that would be six."

"That would be five plus one."

The audience responded with a subharmonic "Uh-hummmm."

"How did you come by this information?" asked a pepper-haired woman at the first microphone. "I've studied many grimoires in several languages and I've never heard of such a thing."

"Surprisingly," said Starfire, "one of my former students brought it to my attention. I'm sure she would want to remain anonymous, but she's been the receiver for my 'Pentoven' since last Imbolc, and I can tell you we've had spectacular results. My next book will be a journal based on our experiences. The information, I'm sure, you'll find invaluable."

"Ah," I heard Father Baptist say, "another book in progress."

"What's Imbolc?" asked Taper.

"The eve of February," said Father. "It's one of the four 'greater sabbats' of the wiccan calendar."

"There's a wiccan calendar?" asked Wickes.

"If you visit the 'Shop of Shadows,'" said Father, "you'll see a huge example on the wall in the back room."

"I guess what I'm asking," continued the pepper-haired woman, "is whether this approach is new, or whether it's a time-honored tradition."

"Let us say," said Starfire, "it is a new approach to a time-honored tradition."

"Nothing like a straight answer," said Joel beside me.

"You know that Sister Charlene is here," I whispered to him out of the side of my mouth. "What if she spots you?"

"She'll just think," he answered, "I'm that clumsy idiot from the bar. Even if she recognizes me, what can she say—one barfly to another?"

"If she sees you with Father Baptist, she might put two and two together."

"Around here, two plus two equals five."

"Huh?"

"I have a question," came a man's voice over the loudspeakers. Arthur had crept along the base of the stage, then trotted up the right aisle and seized the microphone.

"Why yes," said Starfire, holding up her hand to shield her eyes. "I can hardly see with these spotlights in my face. Is that a tuxedo you're wearing?"

"Why yes, it is."

"May I say you look dashing this evening, what little I can see of you."

"Why thank-you," said Arthur with a courteous bow. "And may I add that, though I have only recently become acquainted with your work, I am now your most ardent observer. My question, however, is this: isn't it true that the so-called wiccan rede—'An it harm none, so mote it be'—does not appear in any text anywhere at any time before the year 1930?"

"Certainly not," said Starfire, crinkling her forehead and thus tilting her flashing crescent hood ornament. "It is as ancient as the Carpathian Mountains."

"That's strange," said Arthur, rubbing his chin. "You see, I have it on good authority that Aleister Crowley thought it up. According to Frater Zarathustra's *A Brief History of Western Magick & the Modern Magical Lodge*, the wiccan motto is a distortion of Crowley's own Thelemic commandment: 'Do what thou wilt shall be the whole of the law.' He sold the modified line to Gerald Gardner for twenty pounds, roughly fifty American dollars at that time."

A negative growl rumbled through the auditorium.

"Arthur's been doing his homework," whispered Father Baptist across Jonathan's chest to Lieutenant Taper. "I'm pleased, but it may get him skewered. Uh-oh. Where's Pierre?"

"There," said Edward, pointing back up the left aisle to where Pierre had just snatched the microphone out of a startled wood nymph's hand.

"Nonsense," said Starfire.

"I quite agree, Miss Starfly," said Pierre, waving his opera hat in Arthur's direction. "The exchange rate was not that high in 1930."

"The name is Starfire," said the witch. "And—"

"Even so," said Arthur, "twenty pounds is twenty pounds."

"Sterling?" asked Pierre.

"I would assume so," answered Arthur.

"In any case, Miss Starfly," said Pierre. "I—"

"It's Starfire," said the witch sharply.

"I beg your pardon," nodded Pierre. "You said something a few minutes ago about the 'geometry of the pentagram.' Would you be so kind as to elucidate?"

"Certainly," she said uncertainly, peering through the glare uneasily at her questioner. "The properly-drawn pentagram can be viewed as an equilateral pentagon at the hub of five triangles. A pentagon is a figure defined as a polygon with five angles of 108 degrees. The triangles all have two base angles of 72 and the pinnacle angle of 36 degrees. All of these values have numerological significance."

"Yes, yes," said Pierre, hooking his thumbs behind his lapels. "But what does all this have to do with the Five Wounds of Christ?"

"I beg your pardon?" asked the witch.

"Miss Starfly," huffed Pierre, a mite condescendingly, "any scholar knows that the pentagram represents the Five Wounds of Christ."

"It does not," said the witch, stamping her foot.

"Oh, but it does," nodded Arthur, still at the other microphone. "As well as the Five Joys of Mary."

"I don't know what you're talking about," huffed Starfire, looking around the stage for non-existent bouncers.

"She didn't take my advice," I whispered to Wickes. " I told her where to look ... it ... up ..." Then I suddenly realized he wasn't in his seat.

"You see, Miss Starfly," said Pierre. "It's—"

"It's Star-FIRE," yelled the woman, jostling her crescent almost sideways on her head. "And you're disrupting these proceedings."

"I'm merely attempting to ask a question," said Pierre innocently.

"You haven't answered mine yet," pouted Arthur. "And I asked first."

"Rather volatile," said Pierre.

"And darned uncivil," added Arthur.

"I won't answer either of you," rasped Starfire.

"What about me?" A new voice entered the fray.

"Who's that?" asked the witch, peering through the blinding spotlights.

"I'd like to know," said Sergeant Wickes, who had taken the microphone from Pierre, "if you have ever offered your services to the police."

"What?" asked Starfire.

"As an expert on witchcraft," said Wickes, "to help solve a related crime?"

"Why, yes," said Starfire hesitantly, trying to place her new inquisitor's voice. "On occasion."

"And on those occasions did you go by the name Starfire?"

"I don't know what you mean."

"Come, Miss Smith—your name is Ambuliella Beryl Smith, isn't it?—don't be modest. Tell your fans how you've attempted to mislead the police in several matters relating to a string of recent murders in this city."

"Hold on there," yelled Arthur from across the auditorium. "Just because she lied to the police about her identity, and regularly fraternizes in local bars with several suspects in a current murder investigation—another detail she failed to mention to the authorities—is no reason to think she's anything other than a basically nice person. I ask you now, Miss Smith, for the record: are you a good witch, or are you a—hey! I say!"

Jonathan and Edward took hold of Arthur and dragged him bodily back up the aisle toward the rear of the auditorium, his heels making troughs in the carpeting all the way.

"I shall not go unanswered!" came his maniacal voice from the lobby and beyond. "Toto! Here Toto!"

I noticed that Father Baptist had covered his face with his hands. "I have to have a word with those fellows," he mumbled between his fingers.

"Miss Smith?" Sergeant Wickes' stern voice sounded awesome over the PA system. "Miss Smith?"

The stage was empty.

"Glad you came?" asked Father, fingers slipping from his face.

"You betcha," said Lieutenant Taper.

Thursday, June Fifteenth

Feast Day of Saints Vitus, Martyr and Holy Helper (303 AD) and Germaine Cousin (1601 AD)

52

MORNING MAIL.

Well, actually it was yesterday afternoon's crop. We'd swung by the post office on the way home from the fiasco at Popinjay's Palace the night before, but we were just getting around to opening it. Father Baptist and I were seated at the breakfast nook as Millie carried on her one-woman war against smooth metal surfaces.

"What's this, Thursday?" asked Father, opening the first envelope and removing its contents. "I placed the ad on Monday. So it's only been in print a day or two."

"Still," I said, scalding my lips on my first cup of coffee for the day, "you'd think, in a city this size, we'd have received more than three responses by now."

"'Dear FJB,'" read Father, "'In response to your ad in the *Times* regarding Miss Sugarman's final show, I didn't talk to Madeline that night, (though heaven knows I tried!). She has always been a dear, and such a big help with my problems (which have been numerous!). But the switchboard was jammed for that particular show. I tried and tried, but couldn't get through (I almost screamed!). It was as if we all had some sense that, well, you know what I mean. So my last conversation with her was really just a busy signal (how very sad!). I realize this won't earn me the reward you offered, but I thought you might like to know, (since obviously you loved her, too!).' It's signed, 'Sympathetically, Milwana Sanders.'"

"Obviously," snarled Millie.

"Maybe you should send her a holy card," I said, dabbing my throbbing lips with a napkin, "as a consolation prize. Do you know what she means?"

"About what?" asked Father.

"Whatever she said 'you know what I mean' about."

Father looked at me blankly.

"We're almost out of everything again," called Millie over her shoulder.

"I thought you went shopping yesterday," said Father.

"I went out yesterday," she growled, mercilessly bashing something flat in the skillet with a steel spatula. "I never said I went shopping. You can't buy anything without money."

"Still no check from the Chancery?" I asked, handing Father the second envelope.

He shrugged no. "The wheels of bureaucracy are inevitably slow."

"The squeaking wheel gets the grease," retorted Millie, slamming a glob of butter into the pan. "And this rectory's axles are as rusty as a cemetery gate."

"I'll see what I can do," said Father, tearing open the second envelope while I slit the third with a clean butter knife.

"This is interesting," he said, holding up a page of blue tissue that smelled of lilacs. "'Dear FJB, I didn't talk to Madeline the night about which you queried, but I'm still in direct communication with her, and if there's anything you'd like me to ask her for you, just let me know.' It's signed 'Into the light, Madame Veronya Ouspenszcky.'"

"Maybe she's Ambuliella's sister-in-law," I smiled, unfolding the final letter in my hand. The paper was thick, stiff, uneven in texture and color, sort of like handmade parchment, and it had a faint moldy smell about it. I eyed the handwriting. It was tall, flared, somewhat ornate, and executed in reddish-brown ink. "This one," I said, "takes the cake."

"Do tell," said Father, adding cream to his coffee.

"'My dear Father Baptist—'"

"Not FJB?" asked Father, halting his spoon mid-stir.

"That's what it says. Maybe I shouldn't read this. Perhaps it's personal."

"I've never given that box number to friends. I've taken great pains to keep my clerical name disassociated with it. That's why I used it for the ad."

"Somebody knows," I said, tapping the parchment for emphasis.

"Let's hear it," said Father, setting down his spoon.

I cleared my throat. "'I have been watching your exploits. I have no doubt that you will catch this insufferable murderer within the week. In fact, on my ancestors, I predict it. The time has come for you to meet a worthy adversary. Savor the moment. Expect me for Samhain.'"

"'Saw-win,'" corrected Father.

"S-A-M," I spelled it for him. "H-A-I-N."

"I know. It's pronounced 'Saw-win'—the old Celtic feast of the dead."

"'Sell-tick,'" I corrected him.

"No, it's pronounced 'Kell-tick.'"

"Whatever." What's with those Irish, anyway? "So when is 'Saw-win'?"

"The Eve of November, which makes 'Saw-win'—"

"Halloween."

"Right. And how does our ominous friend sign his name?"

"He doesn't. There's just a wax seal here. Some sort of crest. See?"

"Hmm. Where was it mailed?"

"Better and better," I said, gripping the envelope. "Would you believe Transylvania?"

"You're joking."

"No, it's right here on the postmark. 'Transylvania, HY'—that's got to be Hungary."

"Transylvania's not in Hungary, it's in Romania. Let me see that."

"Here."

Father eyed the envelope, brows furrowed. "That's not H-Y for Hungary. It's K-Y—Kentucky."

"Transylvania, Kentucky?"

"Of course. There's a university there."

I waved my hands. "Of course."

"No doubt some sort of prank," said Father.

"No doubt," I nodded. "Indubitably. Should I throw it out?"

"Never throw anything out until the file is closed, and even then it's a good idea to keep it a while longer. You never know what may have a bearing on the case, or where the fall-out may drift. For all I know, Larry Taper wrote this letter as a joke and sent it to one of his relatives in Kentucky to mail from that post office. But just in case, we'll hold on to it till we're sure."

"Sure of what?"
"Whatever."

53

"WHAT DO YOU MEAN, 'Billowack has other plans?'"

"He said the search warrant could wait," said Lieutenant Taper.

"Yeah," added Wickes. "Tomorrow's Rosary and Saturday's funeral rite take precedence."

"Tomorrow's funeral?" gawked Father Baptist. "What about yesterday's murders?"

"What can I say?" shrugged Taper. "We'll tackle Starfire's shop as soon as the party's over at St. Barbara's."

"Everyone's certain the fourth and last piece of the puzzle falls into place tomorrow night," said Wickes. "We're focusing our attention on that."

"Well," said Father, closing his eyes as if in pain. "Did you at least question this woman last night after the, uh—"

"Fiasco," suggested the gardener.

"Thank-you, Martin. After the fiasco?"

"No dice," said Taper. "She slipped away, and no one back stage saw her leave the building or knew where she was going."

"Poof," said Wickes. "Vanished into thin air."

"This," said Father, opening his eyes slowly, "is not—"

"Good evening, gentlemen," said the waitress. Her smile could have toppled city hall. "My name is Bonnie. Would any of you care for a cocktail?"

We were sitting in the bar at Darby's an hour before the others were scheduled to arrive. Bishop Ravenshorst was at the table with us: worried, pale, and very quiet. We had picked him up on the way—literally. Getting him to leave his bunker was no easy task. What he said next were his first words all evening.

"There is one wine I like very much. I even use it at Mass. But I can't imagine that you have it in stock."

"Try us," winked Bonnie.

"It's called Santa Barbara d'Umbria. It comes from a winery near Assisi in central Italy."

"I'll have to check on that," she said. "And for you sir?"

I respect a table server who can keep an order straight in her head without the use of a pad. It reminds me of the aproned proprietors in some of the Old World restaurants my dad used to take me to when I was a kid. "Ginger ale, please."

"Canada Dry or Schweppe's?"

I decided to present her with a challenge. "How about St. Thomas'?"

"Barbados or Key West?"

I eyed my worthy opponent. "Salisbury."

She didn't bat an eye. "I'll see what I can do, sir. Father Baptist?"

"Jack Daniels."

"Black label or private reserve?"

"Hmm." It wasn't often Father was offered choices like that.

She winked. "Mr. Ross said only the best for Father Jack."

"Private reserve then. When Alan—Mr. Ross—has a minute, will you ask him to swing by our table?"

"Certainly." Bonnie turned her attention to our policemen friends. "And you gentlemen?"

"Perrier," said Wickes. "I'm sort of on duty."

"Jägermeister," said Taper. "So am I."

"You're joking," said Father. "Bonnie, he's joking."

"No I'm not," said Taper. "Call it getting in touch with the murderer's mind."

"Call it drowning your sorrows in Vick's Formula 44," said the gardener.

"Believe it or not," said Taper, "I'm beginning to appreciate the stuff."

"But—" I began.

"I didn't say I like it yet," explained the lieutenant. "Just that I'm starting to tolerate it."

"You didn't say 'tolerate' the first time," I pointed out. "You said 'appreciate.' What's it good for besides sterilizing streptococcus strains in laboratories and dissolving clogs in drains?"

"If I can 'tolerate' your sense of humor," said Taper, " I can 'appreciate' a shot of Jägermeister. Make it a double, please."

"While I can 'appreciate' your sense of the absurd," I countered, "I can not 'tolerate' your choice in liquor."

"I'll be right back," smiled Bonnie, heading for the bar.

"Now," said Father, folding his hands on the table. "Sergeant Wickes, will you please continue?"

"With what? Oh," said the sergeant, "you mean about how everyone downtown knows the quilt gets completed tomorrow night? Sure. Obviously the murderer had four victims in mind. Four auxiliary bishops, as it turns out. That's why he or she cut the quilt into four parts, and also used the four hermetic symbols for earth, water, air, and as of tomorrow night, fire."

"What the d-d-devil are you talking about?" asked Bishop Ravenshorst. "What quilt? What symbols?"

"Things we managed to keep from the press," said Father. "And from everyone else, that is, until Monday. Your Lordship, I'm surprised none of this has percolated its way to you." He turned back to Wickes. "Anything else?"

"Well, this is a pet theory of my own, but the triangles carved into the victims—"

"What's this?" squeaked the bishop, turning an even whiter shade of pale. "Carved? You mean, l-l-l-like, with a knife?"

"Way to go," I said to Wickes.

He ignored me. "If you put three triangles together, along with the fourth one coming up—which will be no doubt be on the foot—you get a square. Right?"

"Come again?" I asked.

"Here." He pulled out his notebook and fancy gold pen. Turning to a blank page, he drew a simple square, then made two diagonals. "There. You see? Four triangles joined together make a square. When the murderer carves his fourth triangle, his scheme will be finished."

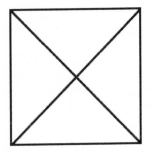

"Carves his fourth—?" Bishop Ravenshorst made a sound. Sort of an aural amalgam of a sob, a gulp, a gasp, a sigh, and a whimper. I wished I had a tape recorder.

"How do you know," I asked, "that the fourth triangle will be carved on the foot?"

"The left foot," said Wickes, precisely. "Stands to reason. The four human extremities will all be covered. Four seems to be the magic number in this series of murders."

"In any case," said Taper, "the police are going to be all over the place tomorrow night. That Farnsworth woman has been rehearsing the ceremony, even marking where everyone is supposed to stand with chalk."

"Yeah," nodded Wickes. "That way everyone—including the police and the TV cameramen—knows exactly where they're supposed to be and when. No surprises. They've even rehearsed with an 'extra' in case one of the principals gets stuck in traffic and can't make it."

"Oh?" I said. "Who?"

"Monsignor Havermeyer from St. Philip's."

"Billowack's so convinced fire will be involved," said Taper, "he's ordered two dozen fire extinguishers to be placed in readiness around the sanctuary, pins already pulled."

"I told him not to count on 'fire' in the sense of 'flames,'" said Father. "It's been bothering me that the Rosary and funeral will be taking place at St. Barbara's Chapel."

"Why?" asked Wickes.

"It's just that our murderer is consumed with symbolism," said Father.

"So?" said Wickes.

"Don't you know the story of St. Barbara?" asked Father.

"No doubt some sweet and gentle woman," ventured Wickes. "Probably a virgin." Somehow he made "probably" sound like "lethargically," and "virgin" rhyme with "ho-hum."

"You did go to Catholic school, didn't you?" asked Father.

"Yes," sighed Wickes, ever uncomfortable with the stigma.

"That explains it—your lack of useful knowledge, I mean," said Father. "After Vatican II, the nuns went, well, never mind."

"Loony," I offered.

"I said never mind," said Father. "St. Barbara lived in the city of Heliopolis in northern Egypt at the dawning of the third century. By all accounts she was a most beautiful girl, and her father was a pagan. Long story short, much to her father's ire, she was baptized a Catholic. When she proceeded to wreck all the idols in his house, he went into a rage. He had her tortured, and finally cut off her head with his own sword. Heaven responded accordingly—he was struck by lightning."

"So what?" said Wickes. Then he added sarcastically, "Does that make her the patron saint of lightning or something?"

"As a matter of fact, yes," said Father seriously. "Lightning, explosions, and artillery."

"Artillery."

"You may laugh, Sergeant, but can you guess the name of the city in which the California Divisional Artillery of the National Guard holds their annual ball?"

"Not Santa Barbara," injected Taper.

"Yes," said Father. "Of course, that's another case of following a form when the essence has been lost, but no matter. I'm concerned about tomorrow night because our killer, though dependent on symbols, or at least steering by them, is also rather loose in his interpretations. Bishop Brassorie was drowned, not by 'water,' but by liquor. Bishop Silverspur was suffocated—deprived of 'air'—but by being buried alive—from which the murderer derived the symbol 'earth.' Bishop Mgumba was killed by a 'fire,' but the focus of the murderer's attention was asphyxiation, not combustion, thus landing the incident in the 'air' category—in the murderer's mind, at least."

"So what you're saying," said Lieutenant Taper, "with respect to tomorrow night, is to expect anything."

"So that's what you were mumbling about yesterday, Father," I said. "You were prowling through *Saints to Remember*. It was 'electricity.' Right?"

He looked at me blankly.

"You know, when you were in that sniggertrance you sometimes go into?"

He continued to look at me blankly.

"Never mind," I said.

"I wouldn't worry, Your Excellency," said Sergeant Wickes to the quivering bishop. "All the other murders took place in isolation. The Rosary will be out in the open, with cops all over the church."

"That's what worries me," said Father. "How do you take out somebody in a public place, and your symbolism has you locked into a strict timetable, and your *modus operandi* has to involve fire?"

"Explosives?" said Taper.

"You mean a b-b-b-bomb?" shuddered Bishop Raven-shorst.

"Patron of the artillery," said Wickes. "So maybe a bullet? We should be on the lookout for a gunman?"

"Guh-guh-guh-gun?" gobbled Bishop Ravenshorst.

"How's anyone going to slip a gun past our metal detectors?" asked Wickes.

"How do you drown a bishop in his private chapel?" countered Father. "Or suffocate a man in his shower? This killer has imagination, a flare for the unexpected. Rest assured if shooting is his aim, he'll do it in stunning fashion, and in a way we'll least expect."

"Shooting?" gasped the bishop. "Shuh-shuh-shoot—?"

Before he had a chance to swoon, Bonnie arrived with a tray of drinks.

"Santa Barbara d'Umbria," she announced, placing a wine glass in front of our bereaved bishop. She presented him with a bottle wrapped in swaddling clothes. "I hope 1967 will do, My Lord."

"That was a very good year," I acknowledged, knowing as I do absolutely nothing about wine.

The bishop looked up at her with his mouth agape, his lips writhing like earthworms on hot pavement. The bottle uncorked, she poured a little of the precious fluid in his glass. I had to nudge his elbow to get him to lift it to his mouth. Another poke was needed to get him to nod his approval. The tasting ceremony completed, he managed to gurgle his blank appreciation as Bonnie filled the glass with the rich red wine.

The zombie having been served, she turned her attention to the living.

"Jack Daniel's PR for you, Father—or as Mr. Ross put it, 'P-R Jack for F-R Jack.' Hope you don't mind."

"Not at all. Just don't mention it to the press."

"Mr. Ross said he'd be by in a minute. Let's see. Here's St. Thomas' for you, sir—"

It was blue label. They had Salisbury. I was impressed.

She didn't notice my reaction, or seemed not to. What a pro. "—Perrier for you, sir; and Jägermeister for you. Will there be anything else?"

"Others will be joining us shortly," explained Father. "Alan said he could arrange for us to all sit here in the bar."

"So I understand," said Bonnie.

"I don't," said Lieutenant Taper. "Why call a meeting at a swanky restaurant like Darby's, then hold it back here in the bar?"

"Because," said Father, sniffing the pungent broth in his glass. "Ah," he sighed, closing his eyes, "this is grand." He took a sip, rolled the liquid around in his mouth, and then swallowed. "Sorry, I haven't tasted anything so fine in years. Because, Larry, there is a television in the bar." He indicated the wide-screen monster hanging from the ceiling in the corner.

"I don't get it," said Taper.

"You will," said Father. "Oh, gentlemen, here's my good friend, Alan Ross."

The flywheel-stomached proprietor came bounding up in his shirt-sleeves, a lick of his shiny black hair swinging like an oily scythe across his forehead. His cheeks were ruddy and his arms hairy. The ring on his left pinkie could have covered St. Philomena's utility bills for a year. And it had two fist-fulls of cousins. "Father Jack. Gentlemen. I trust everything is satisfactory."

"Of course," said Father Baptist. "Is our little—you know—ready to roll?"

"Steve Lambert just called from KROM," said Mr. Ross. "There's been a slight change of plans, but otherwise everything's all set."

"What do you mean?" asked Father.

"Nothing that will affect what's happening here," winked Mr. Ross.

"How does a change not affect what goes on here?"

"When is a change not a change?"

Ah, I thought to myself, Father Baptist has met his match in noncommunication.

"In any case," said Mr. Ross, looking over our heads, "it appears that the rest of your party is arriving early."

We turned to see Archbishop Fulbright standing in the arch between the main seating area and our semi-private cocktail lounge. At his right stood Monsignor Goolgol, googling like a pigeon at a statuary exhibition. At his left was Cheryl in an exquisite blue and green dress tastefully dotted with silver flowers. Behind them loomed the Altar Belles.

"Luis! Alfred!" Mr. Ross made a classic "maitre d' pop" by slapping his open mouth with the palm of his hand. "Quickly, move these tables together and fetch the place settings. Bonnie, another round of drinks for these gentlemen. Your Grace, my staff and resources are at your disposal."

"No," said the archbishop, glaring around the table. "Father John Baptist is in charge this evening. He's calling all the shots."

"But the archbishop," smiled Father Baptist, "is paying the bill."

The archbishop did not look pleased.

54

"SOLE ALMONDINE," SAID THE ARCHBISHOP, closing his menu with an air of mild triumph. He had been scouring the ten-page menu for some time, apparently in search of the inappropriate.

Don't get me wrong. Sole almondine can be very good. But in a restaurant where prime rib, filet mignon, and New York steak are legendary, why order fish? I was slavering voraciously at the thought of the chateaubriand Father Baptist and I were going to share.

"Another refill, Your Grace?" asked Bonnie, taking his menu. "Akavit?"

The archbishop swirled his almost empty glass and nodded.

"That's your fifth," whispered Monsignor Goolgol.

"And that's the third time this evening you've proved you can count," snarled the archbishop, his lips shiny with saliva.

Goolgol gulped. Then he took a big swig of his own club soda with a twist of lime.

GARDENING TIPS: More "minutes," i.e., visual aids:

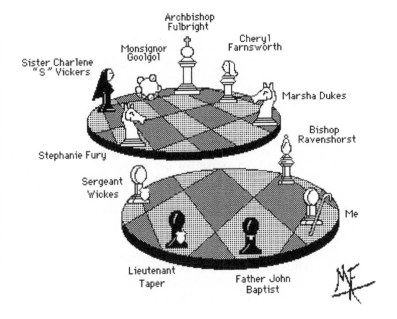

As you can see, the game was getting more com-

plicated, and the steaks more costly ("Boom

cheesh," reprise). At least our side of the

chessboard was a little less lonely.

                                        --M.F.

"What is Akavit, anyway?" asked Sister Vickers, dressed in a drab modern nuns' suit—nothing like the night before.

"Aqua vitae," said Marsha Dukes. "The water of life."

"Vodka," said the archbishop, downing his glass and then burping into it.

"You know," said Cheryl, reopening her menu. "That sole sounds good. Would you mind if I changed my order?"

"Not at all," smiled Bonnie. "You'd prefer the sole al-mondine to the rack of lamb?"

"Yes, I think so."

"Rice pilaf or—?"

"Potatoes au gratin."

"Very good." Bonnie—I mention this again simply be-cause I was so moved—did not write anything down, and still didn't notice that I noticed, which was all the more laudable.

Cheryl's change of appetite I'll leave for anyone's specula-tion.

"I'll be right back with your drinks," said Bonnie, "and the first course."

"I would like—" began Father Baptist, but he was inter-rupted by a shrill beep. Eyes turned to Sister Squint, who hastily dug around in her purse for her pager.

"Sorry," she said, silencing the rodent-like thing. "I meant to turn it off but I—"

Her sentence was interrupted by another shrill beep. This time it was Stephanie Fury's turn to hunt for a rat in her pocketbook. "Ulp," was all she said.

"We're going to add a new rule," said the archbishop, slamming down his glass. "The owner of the next pager that beeps at this table will pay for the whole damn meal."

That sent Goolgol fumbling frantically for mice in his pockets.

"I would like to propose a toast to all the women present," said Father Baptist, rising to his feet. "First to Our Lady, Queen of Heaven, Queen of All Hearts, and Empress of all the Americas."

"To Our Lady," said Lieutenant Taper and myself rather loudly as we rose to our feet. The rest mumbled their various levels of assent while remaining seated.

"And second," said Father, swinging his glass in a wide arc, "to the other ladies here present, in whose honor this feast is provided."

"What do you mean?" barked Ms. Fury, in the midst of the half-hearted clinks. "Our honor?"

Their honor, I thought. Yes, such a concept was rather shocking.

"You shall see," said Father. "Sometime nearer dessert."

Actually, his timing was a bit off. The evening came to a head while we were in the middle of the main course.

55

"TELEVISION?" SQUEAKED MONSIGNOR GOOLGOL. "You brought us here just to watch television?"

"I don't have one at my rectory," explained Father Baptist.

"There's one in the conference room at the Chancery," said Marsha Dukes.

"But alas," said Father Baptist, reluctantly downing his last Jack Daniel's of the evening, "the Chancery does not serve chateaubriand." He shot the archbishop a glance which seemed to say, blunt but piercingly, "Considering that you haven't yet sent me my check for services rendered, Your Grace, perhaps we should look at this costly repast as just wages."

But the archbishop ignored him, fascinated as he was with the inch of clear liquor in the bottom of his glass. What a mood he was in.

"Speaking of tuh-tuh-television," mumbled Bishop Ravenshorst, the wine wobbling dangerously in his glass as he clutched it for dear life with trembling hands. "Will the fuh-fuh-funeral be televised on Saturday?"

"Yes, Jerry," said Cheryl. "That's why we've been rehearsing, remember?" She glanced around the table. "Charlene, would you please pass me the black olives?"

Sister Vickers handed a small silver bowl to Monsignor Goolgol, who held it out to the archbishop, who didn't seem to notice. Winking, Cheryl reached across Morley's plate and took it from the monsignor's hand. "Thanks."

"And the Ro-ro-rosary tomorrow night?" twitched Ravenshorst.

"Yes," said Cheryl, nudging three olives onto her plate. "KROM, at least, is committed to live coverage. Other stations will most likely just present a few clips in their news reports."

"What about TCN?" asked the gardener.

"I doubt it," said Cheryl dryly.

"A 'totally Christian network,'" said Father Baptist dryly, "broadcasting a Catholic Rosary?"

"Don't count on it," grinned Lieutenant Taper. "Martin, could you shove the butter over here, please?"

"Ooooh." Bishop Ravenshorst held his head in his hands and moaned. "Why do I have to be involved?"

"Because you're my auxiliary," growled Archbishop Fulbright, still staring into the crystalline depths of his glass.
"You'll do what I—burp!—tell you to do."

"Don't worry, Jerry," said Cheryl soothingly. "You'll be
safe. We'll all be there. Archbishop Fulbright will be standing right beside you. So will Stephanie, Marsha, and
Charlene."

"W-w-what about you?" asked Bishop Ravenshorst.

"As I explained at rehearsal," said Cheryl patiently. "I'm
the director, choreographer, police liaison, and media coordinator. I'll be close by, but I'll be that blur you can't quite
see."

"You should see the Rosary they'll all be holding," said
Wickes to me. "It's huge, and all gold, with beads the size of
Christmas tree ornaments."

"And heavy," said Marsha Dukes. "It would take all of us
to carry it."

"The Cordova Rosary," I nodded. "I saw it once at the
Old West Museum."

"A remarkable artifact," said Father Baptist, "given jointly
by King Charles III of Spain and King Louis XVI of France
to the Del Agua Mission in 1787. You should all be honored
to carry such a weight."

"What about Monsignor Goolgol?" I asked. "Will he be
helping? Carrying the Rosary, I mean."

The monsignor glared in my direction, he who had made
quite a name for himself a year before when he tore a Rosary
to pieces in the pulpit and stamped the beads into crumbs.
"Liberation from superstitious nonsense," he had called his
little tantrum, and on the Feast of the Most Holy Rosary.
Gulping dryly, he turned his attention to the shaker out of his
reach beyond the archbishop's place setting. "Cheryl, the
salt?"

"Sure," she said, "if you'll pass me the pepper mill."

They exchanged condiments over Morely's half-eaten
helping of sole almondine.

"Is there any hollandaise left?" asked Stephanie Fury.

"Here," said Marsha Dukes, handing her a silver boat.
"We won't actually carry the Rosary. It will be resting on
posts."

"Already is," said Cheryl, peppering her potatoes. "I supervised as it was set in position this afternoon."

"So everything is ready," said Sister Vickers. "Could I
have that pepper when you're done?"

"Of course," said Cheryl, handing the grinder across to Monsignor Goolgol, who passed it on. Then Cheryl turned her head in our direction. "How about you, Father Baptist? Would you care to participate?"

"No," said Father. "I'll definitely be there, but like you, I'll be the blur in the background. My work will be with the police." He left out the part about not wanting to appear too chummy with this crowd in public, especially with the media present.

Just then, Alan Ross came striding up, the twinkle in his eyes reminiscent of Disney movies about Leprechauns. "It's almost time, Father," he said, checking his watch.

"Very well," said Father Baptist, tossing his napkin on the table. "Your Grace, Your Lordship, Monsignor, ladies and gentlemen, the point of the exercise is this: Bishop Silverspur was murdered on Thursday evening, June first. Bishop Brassorie was murdered the following Tuesday evening, June sixth. The following Sunday, June eleventh, Bishop Mgumba was killed in his shower, and Madeline Sugarman was somehow connected with it."

"So?" said Stephanie Fury.

"If Madeline Sugarman was connected with the third murder in the series, it stands to reason she was connected with the first two. However, all the ladies present at this table, with the notable exception of Cheryl Farnsworth, who says she was at home on stand-by, claim they were sequestered in the Chancery's television studio with Miss Sugarman when the first two murders were being committed."

"But we were," said Sister Vickers, eyes wide. "How else did poor Madeline's show go on the air?"

"How indeed," said Father. "There she was on TV screens all over the city, her signal transmitted from the Chancery building by microwave link to the Alleluia Christian Broadcasting Ministries building on Walnut Drive. From there it went out to the viewers, via cable, on the Rapture Channel—also known as TCN, the 'Totally Christian Network.'"

"Is there a point to this?" asked Monsignor Goolgol.

"Of course," said Father Baptist, tossing the vexatious monsignor a reassuring wink. "With very few exceptions, there is a point to all that I do."

"Then do get to it," said Ms. Fury, shifting uneasily in her chair.

Father looked up at the proprietor who was standing guard close by. "Is it time?"

Alan Ross consulted his watch. "Counting down." He did that mouth-pop sound, sending one of his staff trotting over to the controls of the wide-screen television.

The TCN logo came flickering into view, a flabby sort of cartoonish white dove with a suggestion of an olive branch in its beak against a bright red background. If you turned your head sideways it looked more like the silhouette of somebody's hand which had just had an unfortunate confrontation with a sledgehammer. "TCN," said a happy male voice as the ambiguous logo blurred into something suggesting a sunrise, "the Rapture Channel." The sunburst was underscored with the caption: CAUTION: THIS CHANNEL MAY BE SUDDENLY VIEWERLESS.

"Sergeant Wickes," said Father. "Is your phone handy?"

"My what?"

"Your cellular telephone. You do have it with you, don't you?"

Sergeant Wickes fished around in his jacket pocket. "Right here."

"I'll tell you when."

"When to what?"

"You'll see."

"Ladies and gentlemen," came a soothing masculine voice from the television speaker. "We at the Rapture Channel deeply regret the untimely death of Madeline Sugarman, who's celebrated show on issues concerning our Catholic brethren was normally aired at this time. Tonight we will be broadcasting the best of—"

There was a sharp snap, and the screen fluttered a couple of times.

"Tonight," cut in the unmistakable voice of Pierre Bontemps as the screen stabilized, "we are featuring something absolutely, positively, irrevocably, unmistakably, undeniably new! The colossal Archdiocese of Los Angeles, California, the most humungous bishopric in the whole uncivilized world, is proud to present—"

There was a blast of canned trumpets, followed by a splurge of jazz-fusion-rock-zydeco-something-or-other music that Marty, the archivist at KROM, had pieced together from themes scavenged from his vast record collection.

"—'The Catholic Controversy,' with your host, Father John Baptist—"

There was a burst of taped applause.

"—or, as we here at the Chancery affectionately call it, 'The Slap-Happy Bappy Latin Hour'!"

The applause reached a resounding crescendo, and there on the screen sat Father Baptist at a plush, television talk-show kind of desk. Behind him was a prop bookshelf lined with an impressive array of two-dimensional cardboard books, and a working electric fireplace. And of course, slouched more or less at right angles to him, was yours truly, Martin Feeney, gardenaire extraordinaire.

"Tonight," continued Pierre's voice-over as the applause went on and on. "Martin Feeney's rational reviews of local silly sermons—watch out Father Jay, your number is up—Millie's culinary suggestions for the up-coming Trad cook-off at St. Philomena's midsummer parish festival—she's got pointers that will make your tri-tips do the conga right across your barbecue grill—and our main feature, phone-in phantasms! And now, here he is, the cop-turned-priest-turned-cop-turned-talk-show-host ... Father Jooooooooooooohn BAPtist!"

While the canned audience roared, Monsignor Goolgol slammed his open hands on the table. Archbishop Fulbright belched rather loudly, but that didn't break his concentration on the clear fluid swirling around in the bottom of his glass. Stephanie Fury and Sister Vickers exchanged confused glances. Marsha Dukes muffled a terrified squeal in her napkin. Sergeant Wickes laughed openly, and Lieutenant Taper slapped Father Baptist on the back. All the while, Bishop Jeremiah Ravenshorst was curled up with his bottle of Santa Barbara d'Umbria, sniveling to himself like a platypus in a puma pen.

"Thank-you, thank-you," said the close-up of Father Baptist. I must say he looked stunning up there on the screen, all decked out in his regular old collar and cassock. Not exactly the next Fulton J. Sheen, but what the hey. The bright studio lights did call attention to the gold crown in the recesses of his mouth, but that just made him more endearing. "And how are you doing tonight, Martin?"

"Couldn't be better," said my own huge face as the applause died down. I cringed at the sound of my own voice, but rather liked the pensive set of my chin and the sagacious way I clutched my cane. "It's great to be here for your premier. And what a show you've got planned this evening."

"Yes, indeed," said Father Baptist to the front camera. "So let's get started."

Camera two on me. "We know there are many folks out there who are just dying to ask Father Baptist all sorts of annoying questions, so here's the number to call: one, eight hundred, nine-six-two-two-seven-seven-nine. That's one, eight hundred, YO BAPPY."

"Well I never—" Stephanie was furious.

"Now?" asked Sergeant Wickes, cellular phone poised.

"Now," said Father Baptist, resting his elbows on the dinner table.

The sergeant punched his buttons. I couldn't tell if he was thinking of numbers or YO BAPPY. He listened to the receiver, scowled, and tried again.

Up on the big screen, someone else had apparently gotten through.

"Hello?" squawked a tiny, electronically muted voice. "Hello?"

The images of Father Baptist and his sidekick looked up, as though the voice was coming from above their heads.

"Ah," said the close-up of Father Baptist. "Our first caller. We should have thought of some kind of a prize, Martin. No matter. Hello, you're on the air. And what is your name, sir?"

"Rollo," said Arthur's voice, pitched to a warbling falsetto. "How ya doin' Father?"

"Great. And what would you like to ask?"

"Well, I was at St. Philomena's two Sundays back, and I heard your sermon on the importance of reading the Bible every day."

"Yes."

"And you said the Douay-Rheims translation is the absolute best. Better than the New American, the New Jerusalem, or even the Living Bible which my wife just loves."

"That's correct, Rollo. The Douay is the only English translation faithful to the Latin Vulgate, which is the only truly official Bible in the world. All the others are derived from unauthorized sources—including, ironically, the so-called 'Authorized Bible' generally called the King James Version."

"That's what you said in your sermon, Father. That's exactly what you said. But here's my problem. I just can't handle all that formal language."

"What formal language do you mean?"

"You know, Father. All those thee's and thou's and thy's."

"That's a common complaint," commented Martin on the screen.

"Quite right," nodded Father's flashing crown. "All too common."

"Damn right," said Stephanie Fury across the table.

"Excuse me, Rollo," said Father on the screen, "do you speak any language other than English?"

"No, Father."

"I ask because, in most civilized tongues, there are what we call formal and familiar forms of 'you.' In French, for example, 'vous' is formal while 'tu' is familiar. Similarly, in German you would say 'Sie' or 'Ihnen' to your boss, but 'Du' to your companion. Following me so far?"

"Yes. I think so."

"In centuries past, English, which was principally derived from Germanic languages, also had formal and familiar pronouns. 'Thee' is the second-person familiar. It is the word you would use when addressing a close, personal friend. And you'll notice that in the Douay translation, second-person references to God are consistently familiar."

"Really."

"Yes. What you seem to be objecting to is not the formal language, but the informal language."

"I never knew that."

"Now you do. Thank-you for your call."

"Bless you, Father."

Taped applause erupted from the nonexistent studio audience.

"What's the point of this?" barked Monsignor Goolgol, his Adam's apple bobbing triple-time.

"Simply this," said Father calmly. "Sergeant Wickes. Any luck?"

"I just keep getting a busy signal," said the sergeant.

"Of course he can't get through," said Marsha Dukes. "You're not there. You're here. He's probably just calling a phone that's been left off the hook—" She caught herself.

"My point exactly," said Father Baptist. He nodded to Alan Ross, who popped his mouth at one of his underlings, who turned down the volume on the television. "Forgive the drama, but I wanted to prove a point. While I'm not actually at the TV station, I'm nonetheless on television. What you're seeing was videotaped at KROM two days ago and is at this moment being played back on one of their videotape machines. The signal is being fed via microwave link to one of the unused channels on the local cable network and is being decoded by the customized descrambler on the video monitor in this room. One of my parishioners happens to be a whiz at this sort of thing. It would not have been enough to just play the videotape on the VCR here. I had to demonstrate the possibility of broadcasting a pretaped talk show over cable from a television station."

"I'll be," said Lieutenant Taper.

"I grew suspicious of your alibi," continued Father, looking around the table, "when I encountered several of my parishioners who mentioned they had tried to call the show, but couldn't get through. I even ran an ad in two newspapers offering a hundred dollars to anyone who spoke with Madeline Sugarman on her last telecast. The results were nil. I realize this demonstration doesn't conclusively prove your alibi is phony, but it does raise considerable doubt—"

"Arrrrgh!" Archbishop Fulbright was clutching his stomach with one hand and the edge of the table with the other.

"Oh dear," gasped Marsha Dukes. "He's having a heart attack."

"No," grunted the archbishop. "Not heart—stomach. Arrrrgh!"

He slid from his chair, pulling the table cloth down with him. He hit the floor amidst the clatter and clash of dirty dishes and dancing silverware.

"Luis!" exclaimed Alan Ross. "Alfred! Somebody dial nine-one-one immediately."

"I'm not feeling so well, either," said Cheryl, gripping her abdomen and turning sideways in her chair. "Ooooooh."

"Maybe it's something they ate," said Stephanie Fury, rushing to help Cheryl.

"They both ordered the sole almondine," said Ms. Dukes as she knelt beside the archbishop, glaring up at Alan Ross accusingly.

"Food poisoning?" gawked Alan Ross. "From my kitchen? Never!"

"Arrrrgh!" groaned the archbishop on the floor.

"Ooooooh," moaned Cheryl, sinking in Ms. Fury's arms.

"Is anybody else feeling ill effects?" asked Father Baptist.

"Nothing another gallon of this stuff wouldn't cure," said Bishop Ravenshorst, slowly sliding down the side of his empty bottle. "Waitress? Waitress!" Would you believe it? He actually began to sing, "My Bonnie Lies Over the Ocean."

Sergeant Wickes was talking to somebody on his cellular phone. "Help is on the way," he announced. "Just hang on tight."

Within minutes we heard the sirens. Through the gasps and gawks of concerned restaurant patrons, a bunch of firemen came rushing into the lounge hefting big, clanking, unwieldy aluminum medical suitcases. The rest of us were directed toward the bar, where we were served complimentary cocktails while the paramedics went about their probing and prodding.

"This cannot be happening," said Alan Ross, wiping his dripping forehead with a silk handkerchief. "Not in my restaurant. Please, no."

"You and your bright ideas," smirked Monsignor Goolgol.

"Actually," countered Father Baptist, "I did prove my point. What's happening now has nothing to do with my demonstration."

"So what do you think?" I was asking Sergeant Wickes as the paramedics strapped Archbishop Fulbright and Cheryl Farnsworth to the gurneys and prepared to wheel them out. "Is this premature murder attempt number four, or something else entirely?"

"Beats me," he said, scratching his head. "Nothing about this seems to fit the murderer's *modus operandi*, except perhaps the preponderance of alcohol."

"There you go using Latin again. That's what overexposure to Trads can do to you."

"Make way," said a paramedic. "Coming through."

"Dush thish mean," warbled Bishop Ravenshorst, clutching a fresh bottle of Santa Barbara d'Umbria—compliments of Bonnie who would have done anything to keep him from singing another verse in her honor, "the Roshareesh's off?"

"Stop!"

The paramedics froze in their tracks.

Alan Ross gasped so hard he almost inhaled his handkerchief right out of his pocket.

Marsha Dukes squeaked one of her squeaks.

"Damn it." The archbishop had torn the oxygen mask from his face and was struggling unsuccessfully to get up on his elbows. "Ravenshorst," he coughed painfully. "Ravenshorst!"

"Yeshhhir," weaved Jeremiah.

The archbishop slapped away the paramedics and looked up at the only living auxiliary bishop in the Archdiocese of Los

Angeles. Ravenshorst's face was pale, and his lips were purple, but his eyes were burning like superheated coals.

"Jerry," gurgled his lawful superior, "do the damn Rosary tomorrow night or I'll shove that wine bottle down your chicken-livered little throat."

Friday, June Sixteenth

**Feast Day of Saint John Francis Regis,
Patron Saint of the Religious of the Cenacle,
Patron Saint of Kansas City, Missouri, and
Inspirer of the Curé d'Ars (1640 AD)**

∞ **Day of Abstinence** ∞

56

"MILLIE, WHAT'S WRONG?"

It was Friday, the morning after Archbishop Fulbright and Cheryl Farnsworth were rushed to the Good Samaritan Hospital to have their stomachs pumped.

Alan Ross, the proprietor of Darby's, was rushed to the same hospital after police analysts confirmed the presence of a compound of strychnine and atropine on the sole almondine they had eaten in his restaurant. He was released with a prescription for tranquilizers in one hand and a temporary closure notice from the Health Department in the other.

It was to become the morning of one of the most spectacular fireworks displays ever witnessed in greater Los Angeles.

For the moment, however, it was the morning that Millie hadn't banged a single skillet, slammed a single plate, or uttered a single word other than, "Mornin'," when Father and I came into the kitchen after Mass.

"Hmmm," she hummed, carefully cracking a third egg into a little metal bowl. She began whipping it delicately with a wire whisk. She deftly poured the yellow mixture into a frying pan and began nudging it around gently with a fork.

"This is spooky," I whispered.

"Millie," ventured Father, "are you going to tell us what's bothering you?"

"What could possibly be bothering me?" she asked sweetly over her shoulder.

"I don't know," said Father. "But something certainly is."

"Not at all," she said, sprinkling grated cheese on top of the simmering eggs.

"This may be serious," I whispered.

A moment later she approached, coffee pot in hand. "May I pour you a cup of coffee?" she asked me, pleasantly.

Paralyzed with fear, I said and did nothing.

Smiling affectionately, she poured some Java into my cup. A little bit slurped over the edge and slopped down into the saucer. She then turned her benevolent attention to my eating companion. "Father?"

When he didn't respond, she gingerly tilted the pot over his cup. A splosh ended up in his saucer, too. Silently, she went back to the stove.

"This is intolerable," shuddered Father to me. "She never spills a drop."

"Yes," I nodded. "Any second now Rod Serling's gonna step out of the pantry and say, 'Submitted for your approval—'"

"Shhh. Don't antagonize her."

My Rod Serling isn't very good anyway.

A few moments later she returned with a couple of plates, a cheese omelet steaming in each. These she set down, without comment, in front of us.

"Millie," said Father.

"Father," said Millie.

"If it's something I've done—"

"What could you possibly do, Father?"

"If it's something I've said—"

"What could you possibly say, Father?"

"All sorts of things, I guess, but in cases like this the imagination festers. Whatever it is, if you don't tell me, I can't do anything to rectify the situation."

"There's nothing to rectify."

"Okay," said Father, throwing up his hands, "when I've suffered enough, just let me know."

"Why Father, I've no idea what you're talking about."

"Millie, you're upset about something, that's all."

"Me? Upset?"

"I don't know what you're mad about, but—"

"Mad? I'm not mad, Father."

"Then what's gotten into you?"

"You might say," said Millie thoughtfully, wiping her hands on her apron, "I'm not sure how I feel, or what to feel."

Aha, I thought. One of those *woman things*.

"It's not that," said Millie to me, sharply.

Mind reader.

"It's just that—how do I put this?" She searched the ceiling for the right words. "I'm not sure what's worse: hearing my name used on television without my permission, or once it was, not being asked to appear after all."

"What on earth are you talking about?" asked Father.

"I was visiting the Cladusky's last night. Muriel invited me over for dinner. You've said enough times, Father, that neither the Catholic Church, nor any of Her holy Saints, have ever professed a 'rapture' at the end of the world—that that's a Fundamentalist invention."

"True," said Father, puzzled. "What's that got to do with—?"

"So of course I was a little unnerved when Muriel turned on her television and switched to the Rapture Channel. She said she wanted to see what they were going to use to replace 'Community Spotlight.' I'd never seen it, and I really didn't care, but the show that replaced it wasn't what I expected either, even though I didn't know what to expect."

Father remained silent, so I inserted a dutiful, "Yes, go on."

"There was this loud, brash, ridiculous music," continued Millie, her face scrunched up in remembered revulsion, "and an even more ridiculous announcer, and then there was this priest and his straight man sidekick—or was the priest the straight man? It was hard to say. Anyway, they were sitting there, acting like they knew everything about everything. And in the midst of it all, I heard my name."

Father looked at me.

I looked at Father.

We both looked at Millie.

She was still looking at the ceiling. "How did the announcer put it? Something about my pointers for making tri-tips dance the conga on a barbecue grill."

"You saw that?" I gasped.

"On TCN?" gawked Father.

"Like I said," said Millie, finally looking down at us. "I'm not sure what's worse, hearing my name on some strange TV show in the first place, or not being asked to appear to give those suggestions for the up-coming Trad cook-off in the second place. And since when are we having a midsummer parish festival?"

"Good heavens," said Father. "Are you telling us you saw that on television at Muriel Cladusky's house?"

"I certainly didn't dream it," said Millie.

Father sank back in his chair. "I don't know what to say. We videotaped that show last Tuesday as part of my plan to break an alibi. It was only supposed to be shown on the wide-screen television at Darby's."

"How did it go out on cable?" I asked. "It was supposed to be on a blank channel that no one uses."

Just then the doorbell rang.

We were about to find out.

57

"ISN'T IT FANTASTIC?" BEAMED STEVE LAMBERT as he strode into the kitchen with a newspaper under his arm.

"I'm not sure," said Father. "It depends on what you mean by 'it' and what you mean by 'fantastic.'"

"Haven't you seen this?" He slapped the *Times* down on the table. It was folded open to the entertainment section. There was a fuzzy picture of Father Baptist and myself, apparently photographed from a TV screen. COP-TURNS-PRIEST-TURNS-TV-HOST, said the headline. RAPTURE CHANNEL DECRIES UNSCHEDULED TALK SHOW.

"'This was not our doing,'" I read aloud from the article, "announced T. Thurston Muggermorton, associate producer of TCN, also known as 'the Rapture Channel,' at a midnight press conference. 'We never approved this broadcast. Imagine insinuating that the Authorized Bible, the King James itself, was translated from unauthorized sources.'"

"Uh-oh," said Father.

"'Or,'" I continued, "'suggesting that Martin Luther was anything but a saint, that he was a man driven by his passions, that had no moral right to found a new religion in his own image.'"

Father mouthed the words as I read them. He knew them all too well. He'd practiced them several times in the pulpit before he'd hit the big time.

"'And,'" I read on, "'to say that there are irreconcilable differences between Protestantism and the dogmatic traditions of the Catholic Church. The nerve. We would never have allowed such intolerant statements to go out on our Spirit-filled viewer-supported channel. We at the Rapture Channel all loved Madeline Sugarman and abhor the misinformation currently circulating in the press regarding the circumstances of her untimely death. She did such a great job of nullifying the differences between Protestants and Catholics. This priest is a lunatic.'"

"How big a lawsuit are they threatening?" asked Father wearily.

"Don't worry about it," said Steve. "The signal came from KROM. We'll testify you had nothing to do with the cable relay."

"And who did?" asked Father, an angry edge creeping into his voice.

Steve smiled broadly. "I told you you could be the next Fulton J. Sheen. It was no big thing to tap into their channel. I've got friends at the cable company and—"

"There's a big difference between Fulton J. Sheen's 'Catholic Hour' and 'The Slap-Happy Bappy Latin Hour,'" roared Father. "What we put together was just a ploy, a, a—"

"A hit," said Steve, pulling some sheets of paper from his sweater pocket. "Telegrams. I've also got a bud who works at TCN, and he FAXed me these. He said they were flooded with them the minute the show was over."

"You're kidding."

"Most were from Fundies who were—how should I put this?—"

"Yes, Steve, how will you put it?"

"Let's say, a bit peeved. Well, what did you expect? You hit a lot of nerves."

"I didn't expect anything. The show wasn't intended for broadcast, not on the Rapture Channel, and certainly not without laying some theological groundwork—"

"But you only said the kinds of things you've been saying from the pulpit at St. Philomena's."

"Right."

"And I told you you should take it to the air waves. Listen." He donned his glasses and read from the pages in his hand. "A Mr. Arnold Webster writes, 'I never knew that about the Douay Bible. I'm so glad I didn't throw mine away when the new-fangled ones came in. Thanks.' Here's another one from a woman named Esmerelda Schmidt: 'Haven't so enjoyed listening to a priest talk in twenty years.' And this: 'Where's St. Philomena's? My grown kids have often said they'd return to the Church if only they brought back the Latin Mass. We didn't know Pope John Paul II has given his okay. Even our pastor didn't know.'" He tossed the stack on top of the newspaper. "Read them for yourself. You think becoming the detective-priest got you some attention? Well, this show just put you on the map. In fact, I'd say you've just been handed the atlas."

"Well I'll be," said Millie, picking up the telegrams and sorting through them. "Amazing. Can I do a cooking spot on your show, Father?"

"I think KROM will insist on it," said Steve.

"Really," said Millie, giving her hair a gentle nudge with her open palm. There was no mistaking that gleam in her eye. She was working up the urge to go and bang some cookware around with a vengeance. I could see it all now: MILLIE THE RANCOROUS GOURMET, FEATURING CLANGING CUISINE.

"Yes," said Steve. "We've already been contacted by two of the local cable networks, and I wouldn't be surprised if the big boys will be buying us dinner this evening. Mo, our beloved producer at ROMedia News, is beside himself. He's been sniggering and snorting so hard all morning, he almost swallowed his sinuses."

"This," said Father, sinking back in his chair, "isn't happening."

"Romans," I said smartly, "eight—"

"—twenty-eight," snapped Father. "I know, Martin." He put his head wearily in his hands. "I know, I know."

58

"I DON'T KNOW WHAT YOU *THOUGHT* you were doing—" growled Archbishop Fulbright, shifting his bulk in the hospital bed. He was bleary-eyed, landslide-lipped, and generally in a fault-slipped temper. Nonetheless, he found the strength to say a few words to Father Baptist. "—but what you've *accomplished* is the undoing of twenty-five years of ecumenism."

"That was certainly not what I intended," said Father. "But I couldn't have planned it better."

"Father Baptist," sighed the archbishop, holding up his hand. "I have neither the strength nor inclination to argue with you. You will, of course, refuse to do any more such television shows."

"As long as my lawful superior so directs," nodded Father.

The archbishop eyed him suspiciously. "You do mean me."

"Of course, Your Grace."

"Why do I get the feeling you just speared a loophole?"

"I can't imagine, Your Grace. I fully agree that this matter got entirely out of hand."

"Hrmph. Well, in any case, I want you to make sure Bishop Ravenshorst goes through with the Rosary this evening as planned. The doc says I have to stay put, so someone will have to stand in for me."

"Already taken care of," said Father. "I understand they were rehearsing a replacement even before you took ill."

"You mean before someone tried to poison me."

"Correct, Your Grace. I believe Monsignor Havermeyer from St. Philips will be taking your place."

"That's right. Good."

"Will there be anything else, Your Grace?"

"Yes. I didn't get to see your entire debacle last evening, but Monsignor Goolgol has been bringing me telegrams. Bushels. Is it true what you said about the New American Bible being a mistranslation?"

"I wouldn't have said it if it were not so, Your Grace."

"But it's the version we've been using for the readings in the English Mass for twenty-five years. It's been approved by the National Conference of Bishops."

"That is unfortunately correct, Your Grace."

"But if you're right, then virtually everyone else is wrong."

"That, too, is unfortunately correct, Your Grace."

"And I suppose you think I should take some kind of stand in this regard."

"That would seem appropriate, Your Grace."

"Go away."

I blinked.

The archbishop stared at the ceiling and belched.

Without another word, Father turned and herded me out of the room. Standing just outside in the hallway were our pals from the police, Lieutenant Taper and Sergeant Wickes. They were both grinning from ear to ear, with pens poised as if begging for autographs. Each cradled a late edition newspaper folded to pages bearing photos of Father Baptist with his mouth open. FUNDAMENTALISTS FURIOUS, said one headline. A DARK STAR IS BORN, said the other.

"Not a word, Larry," said Father, holding up his hand like a traffic cop. "Not a single, solitary word."

"I didn't say anything," smiled Taper, pocketing his pen.

"You were about to," said Father. "The syllables had already formed in your mind. That goes for you, too, Sergeant."

Wickes shrugged impishly.

"Give an obscure priest a moment in the spotlight," I explained, "and it goes straight to his head. Now he thinks he's a mind reader—"

"Martin," said Father.

"—and for his next trick—"

"Martin."

"Excuse me, gentlemen, while I turn to stone."   Actually, I turned to look in room 316 as we passed, where I knew Cheryl Farnsworth was resting. The door was open but all I could see was the end of her bed and the peaks of her feet under the covers.

"In fact," said Taper, refolding his newspaper, "we don't want to talk about the—ahem—unauthorized broadcast, or even unauthorized Bibles. Really. As enjoyable as it would be to give you a hard time, we just dropped by to give you an update on last night's murder attempt, and to get some background info on this Cordova Rosary."

"All right," said Father, motioning them down the hall, away from the archbishop's open doorway.

"The docs say both Cheryl Farnsworth and the archbishop are going to be all right," said Wickes, "though they want them to stay in the hospital for a couple of days."

I noticed two uniformed policemen leaning against the wall, drinking rancid coffee from Styrofoam cups. "Are they here to keep our patients in or the Gideon's Bible people out?"

"Considering the nature of the case," said Wickes, "we thought it best to post guards."

"Good idea," said Father.

"Of course," said Taper, "with the rest of the hierarchy dead or disabled, Ravenshorst is on his own tonight."

"Unless," I noted, "he wants the archbishop to do a tonsillectomy on him with a wine bottle."

"Poor guy," said Taper. "In some ways your sweet Archbishop Fulbright reminds me of our dear Billowack."

"Same personality type," I agreed. "Both class-one active-aggressive Type A nasties, negative traits which, when properly understood in light of current psychological thinking, and when constructively channeled through empowered pathways and energy helixes, are a real pain in the neck to everyone within shouting distance."

"I thought you were going to turn to stone," said Father.

"Lode stone," I replied. "Loaded to capacity."

"Martin," said Father.

"Shhhh," I told myself. I must have had too much of Millie's Java. Or could it have been that, in spite of my generally smooth and even personality—Type Z-z-z-z—I was actually a wee bit nervous, what with poisoned seafood being served at the same table as my very own succulent chateaubriand? Or was it that I enjoyed the thought of my grinning face on televisions everywhere? Whatever the cause, my biorhythmic battery was swollen with a surplus of nervous energy.

"Anyway," said Wickes, "the kitchen at Darby's checked clean. No trace of the poison was found on any cooking implements, containers, aprons, anything. Everyone on the staff has been there for years—chefs, assistants, waitresses, servers, everyone—all trusted employees. There were no substitutes on duty last night."

"So we turned our attention to the half-eaten food still on the table," said Taper.

"And?" asked Father.

"The poison was sprinkled on the fish as a fine powder, definitely after the food was cooked. It didn't take much. A pinch was enough."

"Which means," said Father, "someone at the table applied it, right under our noses."

"Exactly," said Taper. "Someone could have done it while reaching for the salt or passing the Worcestershire sauce."

"Make a note, Martin," said Father, "to take better care who we invite out to dinner in the future."

"Make a note, Sergeant," said Larry, "to more carefully screen which dinner invitations we accept in the future."

"About this Cordova Rosary," said Wickes as we stepped into the elevator. "It's supposed to be all gold. What's the story?"

"It's a long one," said Father. "For that, you must take us out to lunch. I suggest Mexican—authentic Mexican."

"Can do," said Wickes, jabbing the button marked "G."

"Glad to see you still trust restaurant food," I said out of the side of my stone mouth.

"I trust you," said Father, "and these two gentlemen. But at this point, very few others."

59

"SURELY YOU REMEMBER THE CHAPEL HILL homestead incident," said Father Baptist, passing the stone bowl of innocent red to Sergeant Wickes and dipping his own tortilla chip in the treacherous salsa verde.

"Can't say that I do," said Lieutenant Taper, herding some beans and rice with his fork.

"It made headlines a few years ago," said Father. "Themolina Hubbard, heiress to the Roundhead Manhole Cover fortune, suffered a massive heart attack. In a fit of terrified—and, we pray, sincere—remorse, she summoned a priest to the hospital and received the Last Rites. Then, less than an hour before she succumbed, she called for her attorney, Cecil B. Wexlack—you will recall he was the chief council for Zachary Barclay—"

"The Barclay-Morgenstern case," said Taper. "I remember."

"Small world," said Father, devouring his dripping tortilla chip. The fumes from the salsa verde were almost visible. He chewed thoughtfully for a few moments and then continued. "Themolina changed one clause in her will, the one pertaining to the Cordova Homestead Estate on Chapel Hill."

"That wooded park downtown?" asked Taper. "Big as maybe two city blocks, surrounded by high-rises?"

"Larger than that," said Father. "And it's not really a park because it's not public property. The wall around it is quite high, and topped with wrought-iron spikes."

"There's a small lake at the south end," said Wickes. "Natural springs or something. Nobody takes care of it. It's kind of gone to seed. But there are swans, ducks, lilies, the works. All the top-floor restaurants overlook it."

"Prime real estate," said Father, "which is why poor Themolina's relatives tried to overturn the will when she left the land to the Church. They got a nasty Knights of Columbus talking-to in open court from the judge—O'Rourke, I think it was."

"Who happened," I interjected, "to be an old pal of Archbishop Fulbright."

"Yes," said Father, playing with the entrails of his crab enchilada. "The archbishop was, of course, delighted at the acquisition of two hundred and ten acres of tax-free land in the heart of the city, just minutes from the civic center and the Chancery."

"What does all this have to do with the Rosary?" asked Wickes.

"Everything," said Father. "Things got jumping when the archbishop brought in a bunch of county inspectors and surveyors to catalogue his new bauble. They discovered that the adobe ruin in the northwest corner, which everyone had assumed was just an abandoned hacienda, was actually the site of the Chapel of St. John the Baptist, which was the principle structure within the walls of the original Del Agua Mission—"

"I remember reading about that," said Wickes, retrieving a hot tortilla from the steamer in the center of the table. "The site had been forgotten for so long, some of the local historians were beginning to suggest it was a myth in the first place."

"But for the Cordova Rosary, they might have had a case," said Father.

"Hold it, hold it," said Taper. "I'm completely lost."

"Let me reconstruct it," said Father, "in chronological order. The Del Agua Mission, after which many streets and local sites are named, was founded by two lost missionaries, one Spanish and one French."

"Lost?" asked Taper.

"Padre Alonso Miranda," explained Father Baptist, "and Father Jean Pierre de Chantal had become separated from their respective companions almost three hundred miles east of here. They each wandered alone in the wilderness, lost, cold, but trained by their superiors in the techniques of survival in the wild, and maintained by their confidence in God. As it happened—as you surely know, in God there can be no coincidences—they met each other at a spring under the shade of an oak tree at the foot of what is now called Chapel Hill on

June 21, 1776. They did not speak the same language, and they belonged to different religious orders—"

"Another example," added the gardener, "where Latin came in handy."

"—but they had the same Faith and the same goal," said Father. "Within a year they had built up a sizable mission, where thousands of Indians were baptized, and around which agriculture and trade began to thrive. This was just a handful of years before Blessed Junipero Serra founded his own mission which became the hub of Los Angeles—the overwhelming fame of which all but obliterated the memory of its less-celebrated cousin, the Del Agua Mission."

"Just think," said Wickes, "while the United States was being born, the Spaniards were just making a foothold in the New World."

"You've got that backwards," said Father. "By the time the United States was founded, the Spanish presence in the New World was practically ancient. When the British pilgrims landed at Plymouth Rock, the City of the 'Holy Faith'—Santa Fe in what is now New Mexico—was already a thriving center of commerce, boasting forty-three Catholic churches servicing over thirty thousand baptized Indians. The California missions were admittedly a late activity of the Spanish involvement in the Americas, but the Catholic presence far predated the arrival of the English colonists."

"The Cordova Rosary," ahemed Lieutenant Taper.

Father Baptist nodded. "Because the Holy Ghost had guided the two lost missionaries to the spring at Chapel Hill just a few days before the Feast of the Nativity of St. John the Baptist, they named the church they built on the site, 'La Chapelle de Saint Jean Baptiste'—in French. The whole mission complex, which in its heyday included some eleven buildings, they named in Spanish after the waters John the Baptist had poured over the head of Christ Himself: 'La Misión del Agua de la Vida'—the Mission of the Water of Life. Such a unique undertaking caught the attention of King Charles III of Spain and King Louis XVI of France. In 1787 they jointly sent a remarkable gift, a huge Rosary made of brass and completely overlaid with gold."

"The Cordova Rosary," said Taper.

"The Cordova Rosary," nodded Father.

"Not pure gold," commented Wickes.

"No," said Father, "but gold enough. According to pioneer accounts, it was said to have been suspended by ropes above the main altar in La Chapelle de Saint Jean Baptiste. The beads were as large as softballs, and the loop over thirty feet in diameter. There it hung until the 1840's when control of California shifted from Mexico to the United States by force of arms. The mission was closed, 'temporarily' of course, by American troops as a 'precautionary measure.' Against what or whom was never made clear, though there were rumors that Mexican loyalists sometimes met there."

"Meaning," I interjected, "they went to Mass on Sundays."

"It was never reopened," said Father, "and fell into disuse. The sacred vessels and vestments were removed by the priests and recirculated through their orders to other missions. In time, as the city grew, the site became forgotten in the shuffle of trade and development. The Rosary, however, wound up in the hands of one Commander Arnold Gripweed Roundhead of the U. S. Military Forces. It is a matter of speculation whether he stole it outright, or attempted to preserve it from desecration. His family was Catholic, but who knows? Somehow, when one of the Roundheads passed on and his estate was assessed, the Rosary emerged as a 'family heirloom.' It was the one thing that proved that there had once been a Del Agua Mission, since each of the 'Our Father' beads was adorned with the royal crests of both Spain and France, along with the names of the two lost missionaries."

"Back around the turn of the century," I added, "oil was discovered on other lands owned by the Roundhead family. They needed a tax write-off or something, so they donated the Rosary to the Old West Museum."

"Archbishop Fulbright spent a bundle," said Father, "having the mission excavated, and then reconstructed. He has made strong suggestions in various public statements that the museum should seriously consider returning the Rosary to its rightful owner, the Church."

"Namely," I interjected, "Archbishop Fulbright."

"And it's a good probability that the act of loaning the artifact to the Church for the funeral service this evening is an indication that the museum is preparing to do so. That's probably why the archbishop is so adamant about the funeral going ahead on schedule. Any change of plans could tilt the applecart. Don't forget, the archbishop is planning a big dedication ceremony next week, sort of a grand re-opening of the Del Agua Mission to the public. It would be an opportune day for directors of the Old West Museum to make the transfer."

"So this Rosary," said Wickes, "has no—how should I put this?—funerary significance that you know of."

"None," said Father. "Its use tonight is purely political."

"Still," said Taper, "it's quite a tale."

"It was partly due to my reading of fragmented accounts about the mission," said Father, "that I chose John the Baptist for my religious name."

"Well then," said Taper, lifting his glass of ice water. "Here's to Fathers Miranda and Chantal."

"And to the Water of Life," said Father.

"The Water of Life," said we all—even Sergeant Wickes.

60

NOW WE GET TO WHAT HAPPENED THAT NIGHT, Friday, June sixteenth, at St. Barbara's Chapel. I'm reminded of the wisdom of Hijo Yahamata, former resident and survivor of Hiroshima. Dad hired him to tend the yard when I was five years old. He taught me everything I know about gardening. His words rustled like cherry blossoms when he used to say, "Hord on to your shover, reedle one."   Shovels ready? Okay, let's go.

As St. Barbara's Chapel was deceptively old-fashioned without and neo-mondo-minimalist within, this made all the complicated contraptions set up by the news media seem grossly out-of-place on the outside, but eerily at home on the inside. Sporting headsets with mouth-mikes, the various technicians looked like mutant insects as they flitted up and down the aisles, following the colony trail of black cables and power lines.

The pews were packed with curious archdiocesan dignitaries, notables, and self-inflated parish council leaders. Rumors had circulated that the Papal Nuncio was going to attend, but unless he was better disguised than Father Baptist, I didn't see him.

Yes, Father Baptist was indeed—how shall I put this?—nouveau-semblanced, camouflaged, sub rosa, under cover. His face having achieved prominence in the media, and with so many anti-defamation leagues threatening countermeasures, he had decided to alter his appearance. He wore the same thick glasses which had served me so well—though perched on the tip of his nose so he could see over them. His hair was slicked back with something akin to axle grease, which Millie had provided from a jar in the back cupboard—purpose unknown—and he wore an overcoat with the lapels turned up to hide his Roman collar. As a finishing touch he had assumed a bit of a stoop. In short, he looked more like a diocesan filing clerk than a controversial priest. As such, no one in the congregation questioned his presence as he glided here and there, inspecting the nave as well as the sanctuary. The policemen, of course, knew who he was and left him alone.

The police presence was pervasive, with uniformed officers stationed in every visible nook, cranny, archway, and aisle.

The fire department was also represented. Foam extinguishers were positioned at regular intervals all around the sanctuary. There was a contingent of fire fighters stationed at the right of the altar beside the alabaster cistern which served as a holding tank for some twenty gallons of Auxiliary Bishop Ravenshorst's favorite altar wine, Santa Barbara d'Umbria. Apparently he had it imported by the barrel. I questioned the propriety of such a cistern in the sanctuary until I noticed the newly-installed baptismal wading pool at the opposite side with heated jets and automatic chlorine dispenser, and decided what the hey.

The general feel and irreverent sound of the place was reminiscent of a high school auditorium just before a basketball game. Babble, prattle, rumble, grumble, chatter, blather, chit-chat, ripping wrappers. I sighed, remembering the days of my early youth, when a Catholic church was the most serenely silent place on earth no matter how many people were present or what the event.

I was relieved to see the Tumblars, decked out in their immaculate tuxedoes (except Joel in his black suit and vest), standing at attention along the wall near the side door. Their faces were stern and silent, exuding chivalric reverence amidst the profane clamor. Father Baptist, it seemed, had "had a word" with them. I took comfort in knowing that they were close at hand, a familiar oddity in a sea of absurdity.

All this I viewed from my niche near the front, a little alcove which had once housed a statue of St. Jude. A little brass plaque on the wrought-iron gate was all that remained. The statue was gone and the plaster pedestal on which it once stood was cracked and gouged from the violent removal of the Patron of Things Despaired Of. One can only wonder if he ended up in the same watery grave Bishop Brassorie had once intended for dear St. Rita, Patron of the Impossible. I was seated on a little stone devotional bench, absently fingering my own humble string of beads.

From that desecrated cubbyhole I could clearly see most of the church with its milling congregation, as well as the sanctuary. I even had a direct view of the open sacristy door just beyond the wading pool, through which I could see altar girls giggling as they brushed their hair and adjusted their gowns.

The caskets bearing the earthly remains of the deceased were set side by side before the picnic table. As a tribute to the funerary skills of the archdiocesan morticians, the coffins were open. Each of the occupants looked more charming than they ever had in life. The undertakers had gone to courageous pains to render Bishop Silverspur, who had spent the better part of a week in the ground before discovery, presentable to the eye and acceptable to the nostrils. Bishop Brassorie looked content, and Bishop Mgumba smiled in the complacent stupor of Oz. Madeline Sugarman looked, well, like Ms. Sugarman—cold, condescending, but peaceful, which is to say, finally silent. All four clutched silver Rosaries in their hands, folded in perpetual prayer. I'd overheard one of the video directors saying that the resulting sparkle of the metal beads under the bright lights, once electronically enhanced and vividly displayed on the nation's TV screens, would look "awesome."

Encircling the four caskets, draped over a dozen short posts, was the famous Cordova Rosary, polished to a dazzling golden frenzy for the occasion. In any other context, I would have called it "awesome," but here in this festival of media tinsel and saccharine grief, it seemed pathetically out of place.

Placed at strategic angles around this macabre scene were four video cameras, linked with coils of cables that slithered around the marble floor like wet licorice. Attempts to hide the cables with flowers had failed miserably. This was in addition to four or five hand-held camera operators who were roaming around the church for those oh-so-poignant close-up shots of mourners in the congregation blowing their oh-so-obstructed noses.

As painstakingly rehearsed, Bishop Ravenshorst would lead the procession of participants up the center aisle from the rear of the church to the sanctuary. He would take his place beside the Rosary's three-foot diamond-studded Crucifix which was propped up against the picnic table. Monsignor Havermeyer, Sister Charlene "Squint" Vickers, Marsha Dukes, and Sister Veronica Marie—AKA Ms. Stephanie Fury—and the unwillingly googling Monsignor Goolgol fanned out around him, taking their positions at each of the Our Father beads. They all knew exactly where to stand because Cheryl Farnsworth had marked their positions with chalk the afternoon before her unfortunate choice of sole almondine at Darby's.

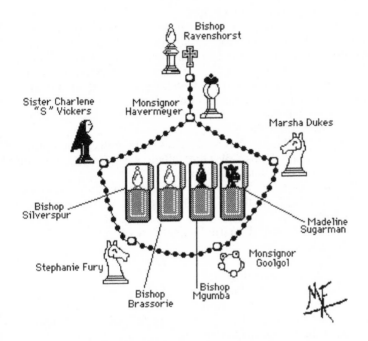

Needless to say, this arrangement held some sort of profound symbolic significance for those involved. From my vantage point in St. Jude's alcove, I couldn't help but recall old footage of Will Rogers roping a runaway horse.

Bishop Ravenshorst, according to the meticulous script prepared by the absent Cheryl, was going to bless the caskets with sand—ordinary dirt being deemed by the diocesan catechetical experts as "closer to the earth" than holy water—and then, with his left hand solemnly placed on the Crucifix, would make the Sign of the Cross with his right hand. The ceremony thus begun, he would lead the congregation in the Apostles' Creed, an Our Father, three Hail Mary's, and the Glory Be. Then each of his companions would take over for their respective decade. All of this had been meticulously worked out so as to fit within the twenty-seven minutes allotted for the event by the media.

I've explained all of what was supposed to happen so you'll appreciate what didn't.

Okay.

Five minutes to eight.

The show was about to begin.

There I was, fingering my beads, when a couple of silhouettes strolled to stop right in front of my lookout. Wouldn't you know, I'd been protecting my coveted spot for almost an hour and, just like at a parade, invariably two guys bigger than me come and plant themselves right in my line of sight, just as the festivities get under way.

"Psssst," I hissed.

They just stood there.

"Hey," I whispered fiercely—but reverently, since after all we were in the House of God, albeit a somewhat desecrated version thereof. "Outa the way."

"What was that?" asked one, rocking gingerly on his heels.

"I didn't hear anything," said the other, taking up his partner's lolling heel motion.

"Down in front," I snarled—again, reverently.

"There it is again," said the one.

"Yeah," said the other. "I heard it that time. Maybe this chapel is infested with rats."

"True," I rasped, "but that's not the point."

"Maybe it's a ghost," said the one.

"Yeah," said the other. "They say this place is haunted by the dead bell-ringer, Quasimarto."

"No," I snarled, not so reverently. "I'm a hired sniper, and you guys are in my line of fire."

"Is that you, Martin?" said Lieutenant Taper, turning to peer into the darkness of my niche.

"So this is how you treat your adoring public," said Sergeant Wickes as the two of them slipped in beside me. "Hiding in dark places."

"Couldn't handle the spotlight," I admitted. "Like I said before, no ambition. I was wondering where you guys were lurking."

"Cozy little nook you have here," said Taper.

"Yeah," said Wickes. "Real comfy."

"Well, sit down," I whispered.

They arranged themselves on either side of me on the stone bench designed for maybe two thin widows.

"Any minute now," said Taper.

"I can't stand the suspense," said Wickes.

"Like I said," said Taper after several long moments, "any minute now."

"Yup," said Wickes. "like you said—"

"Shhhhh," hissed the gardener, and then added, "Oh great," as two more silhouettes stepped into our line of vision. "Who now?"

"Is there someone in there?" asked Solomon Yung-sul Wong, the city coroner.

"Seems to be," said John Holtsclaw, the assistant coroner.

"Just us," said Taper.

"Come on in," said Wickes. "This is the best spot in the house."

"Was," I commented, struggling against that feeling we human beings get from time to time that we're losing control of a situation.

"Yes," said Mr. Wong, standing at the left side of the bench. "This is an excellent vantage point. You can see everything from here."

"Glad we found this spot," said John Holtsclaw, taking his position at the other end.

"Yes," I hissed. "We're all so glad. Now will you please—"

"Hey, man," said yet another silhouette, punctuated by the chitter of beads and the aroma of incense. "Anybody in there?"

"Who is it?" asked Wickes.

"Marty," said the shadow. "I'm the archivist at KROM. Hey, Cane Dude! All right. You don't mind if I sit here on the floor in front of you, do you man?"

"No," I groaned. "No, no, no ..."

61

PRECISELY ON TIME the festivities began. Cued by a director
in a headset, a couple of matrons in jeans and sweatshirts began strumming guitars and crooning into nearly-squeaking
microphones. "Greet the brand new day," they sang, "everything is fine ..."

The congregation hubbub gradually subsided, then died
abruptly as Auxiliary Bishop Ravenshorst entered the back of
the church, leading the procession of smiling clerics, nodding
nuns, and snickering altar servers down the center aisle.

"The night is done," sang the gals, "here comes the dawn,
the sun's gonna shine ..."

"Switch to camera two!" barked a producer somewhere.

There was a tense moment when Bishop Ravenshorst tripped
over a tangle of wires which the technicians had thoughtlessly
left sprawled across the center aisle. His mitre slid half-way
over his face as he struggled to keep his balance. Monsignor
Havermeyer, who was directly behind, reached out and stead-
ied him. I noticed that, under his snow-white funeral robes,
the monsignor was still wearing those tire-tread sandals I'd
seen in the atrium at St. Philip's.

I also noticed a movement along the aisle and glimpsed Joel
detaching himself from the Tumblars and going out the side
door in haste.

Suddenly there was a flash of light two feet in front of me.

"Marty," I hissed.

"Just lightin' a ciggie," he said. "Don't worry. It's legal.
Just a ginseng ciggie."

"Not in here," I said.

"It's just like incense."

"Not in here."

"C'mon, man. Be cool."

"Marty, put it out. Now."

"Oh," he sulked. "If it's gonna flip your pancake."

"It will. Syrup and all."

Bishop Ravenshorst took up his post beside the impressive
Crucifix. The others in the train spread out to their assigned
positions. Each placed their hands as reverently as could be
upon one of the large beads between the decades.

"We're all God's children, sitting in a ring," crooned the
musicians, and I use the term loosely. The station director was
making a swirling motion with his right hand as if to say,

"Make an end, you countermelodious hens." Obediently, they clucked to a halt. "Waiting for heaven. Sing, sing, siiii-iing."

Bishop Ravenshorst looked nervously at the director, who shook his head and pointed to the bishop's feet. Realizing he wasn't exactly on his mark, Ravenshorst inched over sheepishly and glanced back at the director who flashed him the okay sign.

"Ahem," said Ravenshorst. "Let us begin—"

The director was waving his hands frantically.

"Hm?—Oh," said the bishop, placing his left hand on the Crucifix. Getting another okay from the director, he proceeded. "In the name of the Father ..."

"And of the Son." About half the congregation joined in. The other half didn't feel so inclined.

"And of the Holy Spirit. Amen. I, uh, believe in God the Father Almighty ..."

I looked over toward the Tumblars. Joel was still gone. Then I looked around for the hunched figure of Father Baptist. I finally caught sight of him near one of the stationary cameras in the sanctuary. He was blending well into the shadows, and I wouldn't have noticed him if his slicked-down hair hadn't flashed a reflection.

There was a tiny, high-pitched squeak. One of the singer gals futzed with her microphone, checking for feedback.

"I believe in the Holy Spirit, the Holy Catholic Church ..."

Just then I thought I heard a metallic "bonk" from somewhere in the sanctuary, but saw nothing to indicate what it was.

"... the Communion of Saints, the forgiveness of sins ..."

Then a motion caught my eye. Something seemed to be moving, slithering along the ground. For a moment I thought it was a snake, gliding out from under the cistern of Santa Barbara d'Umbria at the right of the picnic table. It was dark, fluid, glistening menacingly in the bright spotlights as it careened across the marbled floor.

"What's that?" I whispered to Taper.

"What's what?" he asked.

"There, under the cistern. It's headed for Bishop Ravenshorst."

"Oh my God." Taper whipped a walkie-talkie out of his vest pocket. "Trouble," he whispered fiercely. "Something's moving on the ground near the bishop."

A policeman materialized out of the shadows near the picnic table, walkie-talkie in hand.   Frantically, he looked around then froze.

Whatever it was, it had just reached the bishop's shoes.   It seemed to pause at the encounter, thicken, then flow in graceful swirls around them.

"Get him out of there," barked Taper.   "Grab him—"

The sudden motion of the policeman caught the attention of the rest of the funeral party.   There was a startled gasp, but before anyone could think to move, there was a blinding—FLASH—and an explosion of sparks which blossomed like an erupting skyrocket.   Trails of discharging electricity careened in all directions, emanating from the jerking body of Bishop Ravenshorst.   His eyes bulged and his mouth gaped in a silent scream.

Then, before any of the others could think to react, there was another, brighter flash.   No, not one.   Several.   Each of the others—Monsignor Havermeyer, Sister Vickers, Stephanie Fury, and Marsha Dukes—were engulfed in the corona of an electrical storm.   Each of the "Our Father" beads had become a radiant fireball, with them attached.   They all writhed and squirmed, but couldn't free themselves.

All of them, that is, except Monsignor Goolgol who stood there, frozen with fear but apparently unharmed, while his companions screamed and burst into flames.

Teams of firemen, extinguishers in hand, stormed the sanctuary, white spray gushing in all directions.   Their efforts were useless, like moths batting a roaring campfire.

"Cut the power!" screamed the director.   "Cut it!   Cut it!"

Policemen were racing down the aisles, attempting to contain the congregation, which burst from the pews in terrified frenzy.

"Hey!   Watchit!"

Taper and Wickes stumbled over Marty as they dashed out of our nook.   As he started to get up he was knocked down again as Solomon Yung-sul Wong and John Holtsclaw snapped out of their daze and bolted into the chaos after them.

"Hey, man!" complained Marty.   "Hey!"

Suddenly the lights went out.   Someone had finally cut the power.   The sanctuary was plunged into a murky nightmare of puffing black smoke, crackling flames, and scurrying figures.

I strained to see Father Baptist amidst the zigzagging tumult, huddled beside the slumped form of Bishop Ravenshorst.   He seemed to be making the Sign of the Cross over the charred figure.

"I better get down there," I said, heaving myself to my feet.

"And you told me not to smoke," said Marty. "Ooof!"

I didn't mind stumbling over him. Actually, it felt good.

Somehow I managed to make my way to the sanctuary, buffeted and bumped this way and that by policemen and firemen running every which way. It was like groping through the pandemonium room in a fun house, strobe lights popping and rubber-masked demons screeching.

Suddenly I found myself face to face with the ashen face of Monsignor Goolgol. "Did I—?" he shrieked. "Did they—? Didn't you—?" Just as abruptly he was gone, re-absorbed into the nightmare.

I wandered on, jostled this way and that, making my vague way toward Father Baptist.

My feet bumped into something on the ground. I heard a pitiful groan. Instinctively, I bent down, then dropped to my knees, oblivious to the insolent protests of my straining spine.

I found myself cradling the head of Stephanie Fury. She looked up at me with glazed eyes. Her face was horribly blistered, skin recoiled in folds of blackened tissue. Madly dancing light from nearby flaming floral decorations played upon curls of smoke wafting from her singed hair.

"The power," she gasped. She clutched my arms as a spasm of pain rattled through her.

"Be sorry for your sins," I said lamely. "Sister, try to—"

"The power," she said again, and went limp in my arms.

I said earlier that Sister Veronica Marie and I had only had one conversation all these years. I shuddered to think that it had finally ended, and in this way.

62

"SHUT UP!" BELLOWED BILLOWACK.

"But I didn't do anything—"

"Officer, shut him up."

Joel looked at me, terrified. "Mr. Feeney!"

"And you shut up, too!" barked Billowack.

"Now see here, Officer," said Pierre and the other Tumblars variously.

"One more word out of anybody and I'll arrest all of you."

"On what charge?" asked Father. Even with his hair slicked down like a refugee from a black-and-white flick, he held an air of dignity, if not authority.

"Obstruction. Accessories after the fact. I'll think of something."

Here is where a horrifying evening got even worse. We were huddled on the lawn outside the church, about a half hour after the big flash. All around us, the minions of the fire and police departments were scurrying about, attempting to weave order out of the threads of chaos. The whole scene was made all the more bizarre by the continuous play of whirling, blinking lights from their vehicles. Even though it was summer, a damp chill had settled on the place.

Out of the corner of my eye I saw Jacco Babs and Ziggie, just beyond the police tape, chawing and chortling over the success of the evening. Where was a garden hose when you needed it?

"Whatcha got there, Sergeant?" barked Billowack.

Sadly, Sergeant Wickes held up a piece of cloth. "He had it in his hand."

"I can explain," said Joel.

"I'm sure you can," said Billowack, licking his chops. "Lemme see it."

"That's it," said Taper somberly. "The last piece to the puzzle."

"Triangle pointed up," nodded Wickes.

"Fire," said Father.

"You said it," said Billowack, towering over Joel. "And what a fire. Electrical fire. A virtual Colorado Rockies type thunderstorm. And you're an experienced electrician, aren't you, kid?"

"Y-yuh-yes," sputtered Joel. "But I didn't have anything to do with—"

"Sure you didn't. And I suppose this toolbox my men caught you with just outside the church is for fixing a stopped-up toilet."

"It's an electrician's toolbox, sir," stammered Wickes.

"I know it's an electrician's toolbox you idiot," snapped Billowack.

"I told you," stammered Joel. "I was standing near the side door just before the service began, and saw it sitting there on a bench. There was all kinds of other equipment out there, from the TV people and all, but it caught my eye. It's got my dad's name on the side. See? It was stolen from my dad's truck just a few days ago. I thought it looked familiar, so I went outside to be sure. I found that cloth in the toolbox." Joel's voice cracked. "It was wrapped around the soldering iron."

"That theft part does check out," said Taper. "Mr. Albert Maruppa did file a report—"

"Oh yeah?" coughed Billowack, towering over poor Joel. "I'm impressed. So impressed, I think I'm going to book you for suspicion of first degree murder." He did another canon count on his fingers. "Bishop Ravenshorst, Monsignor Havermeyer, Monsignor Glop-de-goop—"

"That's Goolgol, sir," said Wickes.

"I know it's Goolgol," roared Billowack. "Sister Vickers, Stephanie Fury, and Marsha Dukes."

"Not Havermeyer or Goolgol," interrupted Solomon Yung-sul Wong, arriving with John Holtsclaw, clipboards in hand.

"Huh?"

"Monsignor Havermeyer is not dead," explained Wong.

"Nor is Monsignor Goolgol," said Holtsclaw. "They're putting them in the ambulances now. Havermeyer's unconscious, in shock, and in bad shape, but he survived because he was wearing thick rubber-soled sandals."

"Goolgol's a nervous wreck," added Wong, "but otherwise fine."

"Why wasn't he electrocuted like the others?" asked Lieutenant Taper.

"Beats me," said Holtsclaw.

"Hrmph," scowled Billowack, sizing up the coroner and assistant coroner. He shook his hand to untangle his fingers. "What else you got?"

"This one's for the books," said Wong. "Someone did an amazing job of tapping into the video crew's current."

"Then it was boosted through a transformer," said Holtsclaw. "It'll take some time to determine the actual voltage, but it was enormous."

"The electrical details will take some figuring out," said Wong, scratching his head. "And it's not our field. The lab boys will have to deal with it. I heard one of them say that the wiring's all melted. The equipment the perpetrator used is fused solid from the heat."

"Whatever," said Billowack. "It's still open and shut."

"Except for one thing," said Father. "A motive."

"Don't be too sure," sneered Billowack. "While you've been sticking your nose everywhere it doesn't belong, I've been doing some real police work. I personally interrogated that Smoley kid just this morning, and I broke him down."

"I can imagine," said Father.

"Yeah," sniffed Billowack. "Didn't take long. You've lost your touch. I had him spilling the beans in no time."

"Beans?" I asked.

"It seems," said Billowack triumphantly, "that your protégé here didn't appreciate Bishop Brassorie's advances."

Joel gasped.

"And it doesn't take a rocket scientist," said Billowack, "to figure out that Brassorie threatened to make it impossible for him to get ordained if he refused."

"So you're pinning Brassorie's murder on him, too?" gawked Taper.

"Why not?" barked Billowack. "You've been saying all along these murders are all tied together. Whoever did one, did them all. I figure this kid had a gripe, a real bone to pick with the Church moguls, and he decided to do some housecleaning."

"You're crazy," moaned Joel. "Sure, Bishop Brassorie said—"

"Hold it, Joel," said Father sternly. "Don't say anything, not without an attorney present."

"But I didn't—" cried Joel.

"It doesn't matter," said Father. "Don't say another word."

"But—"
"Not another word."

Saturday, June Seventeenth

Feast Day of Saints Botolph (680 AD) and Ranier (1160 AD)

63

MILLIE MADE A VALIANT EFFORT to bang and batter her pans for our sake, but her heart wasn't in it. Father Baptist and I had retired to the rectory immediately after Mass, unable to endure the probing questions of the small, but outspoken Saturday morning congregation—except those of Mr. Turnbuckle, of course, who had stomped out when Father entered the sanctuary in black vestments yet again.

Father and I played with our food for the better part of a half hour, but all we'd succeeded in doing was rearranging everything on our plates.

"Well," I finally said, setting down my fork, "I guess it's over."

"What do you mean by 'it'?" asked Father, idly stirring his cold coffee. "And in what way is 'it' 'over'?"

I shrugged limply. "The casting quilt is complete. Earth, water, air, fire. The four auxiliary bishops are all dead, and several others besides. The murderer has succeeded in his mission."

"Not necessarily."

"What do you mean by 'necessarily'? And in what way is it 'not'?"

Father Baptist smiled wearily and summoned the strength to shake his head. "God bless you, Martin." He rubbed the back of his neck. "Yes, the quilt is complete, but we don't know if the mission, as you put it, has been achieved."

"We don't?"

"How can we know that the mission has been accomplished if we don't know what the mission is?"

"I don't follow you."

"We don't know whether the message of the quilt is a blueprint of the murders themselves, or if the murders are the means to another end entirely."

"I still don't follow you."

"Okay, let me use an illustration." Father crumpled his napkin and set it beside his plate. "Let's say you are an heir to wealth. There are four relatives between you and the family fortune. You get impatient and murder them one by one. What is your real goal, the murders or the money?"

"The money."

"Now do you follow me? The quilt is complete, but we don't know if the mission it represents is accomplished. There are many unanswered questions. For example, was the attempt to poison Archbishop Fulbright part of this plan? Was it something else entirely? Why were all these other people killed last night? Did they just get between the murderer and his target, or were they on the dart board as well? Why was Monsignor Goolgol spared? Our original mandate from the archbishop was to discover who killed Bishop Brassorie, and we've yet to do that."

"True," I nodded. "But somehow after last night, my heart just isn't in it anymore. Besides, except for some memorable adventures, we're just as much in the dark as when we began."

"Worse," he said.

"Most of our key suspects are toast."

Father grimaced at my poor taste in metaphors. "I was beginning to form a solid hunch about Stephanie Fury, but that is now history."

"And that poor lad Joel, rotting in jail," sighed Millie, approaching with the coffee pot. Seeing that our cups were still full, and getting cold, she shrugged and retreated to the stove. "I can't believe he had anything to do with this foul business."

"Nor can I," said Father. "Nor did he. I doubt if one night in jail is enough to decompose our Joel too much. He's made of sterner stuff than that. Nonetheless, we've got to get him out of there, and to do that we've got to discover the real fiend behind these murders. And to do that, we must discern the intent. Millie, Martin, our work is far from over."

Silence settled upon the kitchen for several minutes. I was just mustering the gumption to pick up my spoon and stir my cold coffee when there was a tap at the little stained-glass

French window next to Father's chair. With a start, and then a sigh, he reached over and undid the latch.

"You wasn't here last night, Faddah," came an accusing voice.

"I'm terribly sorry, Mrs. Magillicuddy. Please forgive me."

"But that's what I'm here for, Faddah," chided the dingy old woman, "but the other way 'round."

"So you are."

"I waited an' waited, an' me not feelin' well." She coughed a couple of times to prove her point.

"It grieves me to hear that."

"But anyways, now I'm here."

"Yes, you are."

"An' so's are you."

"So I am. Shall we proceed?"

"Bless me, Faddah, for I have sinned. It's been a week, y'know. Actually, a week an' goin' on fourteen or so hours, it has."

"Yes, my dear woman," he said solemnly. "It has."

"It's my Willum, Faddah. I try to be patient, but he hasn't come back, you see. He promised to love, honor, an' obey, but I can't help wonderin' where he's been keepin' his self."

"I can't imagine a more faithful soul," said Father sadly, "than William Magillicuddy."

"Nor can I, Faddah, nor can I. But I gets to wonderin', you know. An' if a wife don't trust her husband, then she's not a good helpmate. I know I done wrong to doubts him, I does. It's like I was thinkin' when I was watchin' the faeries the other night—oh, I almost forgot. You will give these here alyssiyums to your crotchety gardener, Mr. Feeney, won't you?" She handed him a bunch of dry weeds. "I should'a kept 'em in water, I knows, or they wouldn'a got so brittle, but as I said b'fores I've's been sickly."

"I'm sure he'll understand and appreciate the thought."

Crotchety? Me? Appreciate what thought?

"Last Sunday, a week ago it was," she continued. "That would makes it a whole week's ago t'morrow tonight. The faeries were a'dancin' an' a prancin' they was, 'rounds an' 'rounds they went arounds a fire they was. I knows the woods like the backs of me hand. Been a'goin' there ever since I was a wee thing, I was. 'Course, there wasn't any faeries back then."

"Mrs. Magillicuddy," said Father patiently.

"Well ya sees, Faddah, I knows it's a sin, it is, I knows it is, to watch faeries in their altogethers, if you gets me drift. Cover yer ears, Faddah."

Faeries? In their 'altogethers'?

"It's enough to plant impure thoughts, it is, even in a skull as thick as mine, even in a woman so old. An' that's why—if you must know, Faddah—why me mind keeps a'flittin', an' why I've been a'thinkin' so much about my good, gentle Willum: I misses him so.   An' that's why I needs your shriv'ness."

"I see," said Father. He thought a moment. "The Lord understands our struggles better than we do ourselves.   He yearns for our success, and knows only too well our tendency to fail. He doesn't just mark our failures, but carefully notes the effort we make to postpone them."

"Does He really? I means, does you really thinks so, Faddah?"

"I do. Remember: every time we say 'no' to a sin, even if it's just to put it off for another minute, every effort to do His Will instead of our own is noted."

"He really is, isn't He? Involved He is."

"With every detail of our lives. Count on it. And when we do fall, He expects us to admit our weakness, confess our sins, and try again. He knows that none of us is perfect, or free from sin, but He cherishes tenacity."

"'Ten-acidy?' 'Scuse a stupid ol' woman's lack of language, Faddah, but what's that?"

"Perseverance," smiled Father. "Stick-to-it-iveness."

"Spunks."

"That's it. 'Spunks.'   And also remember that, in His abundant love for us, He provides many opportunities through His Church to apply Graces to our spiritual wounds, and most of them are so easy that people dismiss them, refuse them, or just don't bother.   Just think, every time you bless yourself with holy water, your venial sins are washed away."

"You's so right, Faddah. You is ab'slutely so right."

"And your serious sins vanish in the confessional. Yet how many people refuse to avail themselves of its benefits?   Be grateful for your Faith, Mrs. Magillicuddy, and thank God for all the blessings He has showered upon you. And work on forgiving William for leaving, can you do that? It wasn't his choosing, you know."

"Yes, Faddah," she sobbed. "I knows it. I'm just bein' selfish, I is. I forgives him I do, an' I prays to God he forgives me, foolish woman that I am." She produced a gob of handkerchief, brittle from much use, and noisily used it some more. "That's all, Faddah."

"For your penance, say a decade of the Rosary for William, and one for yourself. Now, make a good act of contrition."

He rubbed his eyelids wearily while she expressed her sorrow in meandering Magillicuddyese. He muttered the Absolution in Latin, and made the Sign of the Cross over her bowed head. "Amen."

"Thanks ya, Faddah," she said at last. "An' do be sure Mr. Feeney gets the alyssiyums."

"I will," he nodded.

"The old crotch," she added.

"Yes," said Father. "Go in peace, dear woman."

Old crotch? Old crotch!

"And please see that St. Jude has a fresh supply of flowers." Father closed the window and turned the latch.

"I may be an old crotch," I said as he handed me Mrs. Magillicuddy's thoughtful gift. "But at least I know the difference between alyssum and hyssop."

"Really," said Father, giving the herbage in my hand a closer look. "You're right, this is hyssop. I wonder where she got it."

"The same place she got the 'periwinkies' which were really 'sage.' Probably Mr. Folkstone's herb garden."

"No doubt."

"She did go on a bit."

"Yes," he said, smiling thoughtfully. "As did I."

"And it's amazing to think that the next time we see her—"

"She'll be as lucid as you or me, or our dear Millie."

Without comment, she was removing our uneaten but thoroughly handled meals. She dumped them noisily in the sink and returned to take our coffee cups when the doorbell rang.

"I'll get it," said Millie, wiping her hands on her apron. " I need to do something useful."

64

A FEW MOMENTS LATER Lieutenant Taper and Sergeant Wickes trudged in. Millie had apparently gone to her room.

"How're we doing?" asked Wickes.

"Well," I said, slouching back in my chair. "Judging by the way I feel and the way you look, I'd say we're doing just awful."

"We just came from the morgue," explained Wickes.

"Ah," I said.

"Mind if I pour myself a cup of coffee?" asked Taper.

"Help yourself," said Father. "What's that under your arm?"

Taper tossed him a manila envelope. "Courtesy of Sybil Wexler."

"I must meet her one of these days," said Father, sliding the contents of the envelope onto the table. "Well, Martin, what do you think?"

 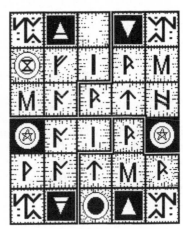

"I think," I said presently, "I'm going to be sick."

"What have the lab boys figured out," said Father, rubbing his chin thoughtfully, "about last night?"

"Well," said Taper, sitting down with his cup of steaming black coffee. "As far as they can tell, the Crucifix and the large beads of the Cordova Rosary were wired positive, like one end of an open switch. Each of the victims, when they stood at their designated places, was standing on a grounding plate—negative. When they laid their hands on the Rosary beads, they closed the circuit. When the murderer applied current—zap! An as yet undetermined amount of voltage went from the Rosary beads, through their bodies, direct to ground."

"And it had to be done remotely," said Wickes, lowering himself wearily into the remaining chair. "And it wasn't just one switch, because the Crucifix circuit was closed about two seconds before the others. One of the experts said something about 'remote solenoids.'"

"A solenoid, as I understand it," said Taper, suppressing a yawn, "is a switch that throws a switch. It's like those buttons on expensive stereos. You press 'play,' and that sends a command to an internal switch that engages the drive motor on the cassette player."

"I wouldn't know," said Father. "We don't have a stereo."

"No stereo?" mumbled Wickes.

"Anyway," continued Taper, "the murderer used some kind of remote control device. So what we have is a switch which remotely throws a switch that throws a switch. I'm getting a headache."

"Very technical," said Wickes.

"And where were all these switches," asked Father, "that respond to the remote control?"

"Right there in the sanctuary," said Wickes. "All the deadly wiring went to a little aluminum box hidden amidst all those cables on the floor. Switch central. Burkin, one of the new guys straight out of college, says he thinks one of the circuit boards was 'borrowed' from a 'sequencer.' Let me see if I got this right. A 'sequencer' is some kind of device that sends out 'on' and 'off' commands in some sort of pre-arranged order and at specific time intervals. Musicians use them to trigger all kinds of things on stage, from lighting effects to the playing of musical notes. But 'sequencers' aren't peculiar to the music biz. Apparently they're used in all kinds of things, from CB radio scanners to high-tech kitchen appliances. You really should talk to him if you want to know more."

"What about Monsignor Goolgol?" asked the gardener. "Why didn't he get zapped?"

"His bead wasn't wired," said Taper, "which, of course, looks very suspicious."

"And Monsignor Havermeyer was spared," said Wickes, "because he was wearing rubber-soled sandals. The current was high enough to penetrate, but not fatally."

"Which is also suspicious," said Taper.

"Hm," said Father.

"What was that thing moving on the floor?" I asked.

"What thing?" asked Father.

"I heard a 'squeak' and then a 'thonk'," I explained. "Then I saw something moving along the ground. Remember, Lieutenant? It's what made you spring into action. It came from under the cistern and went right for Bishop Ravenshorst."

"Oh yeah," said Taper. "Weird. There was a small charge set under the cistern. It was set off by the same solenoid method as everything else. It blew a hole in the bottom of the tank."

"You mean," I said, "what I saw was a stream of Santa Barbara d'Umbria?"

"Yes."

"It fits," I nodded. "Another murder, another liquor."

"I didn't see it from where I was standing," said Father. "But as you say, it fits. The murderer managed to connect the victim's favorite alcoholic beverage to the crime."

"Yes," said Taper.

"It also means," said Father solemnly, "that Archbishop Fulbright was poisoned the night before the Rosary to get him out of the way. Surely, as ranking prelate, he would have stood at the Crucifix. The murderer wasn't after him, he wanted Bishop Ravenshorst. By poisoning the archbishop at Darby's, he made sure that Ravenshorst would take his place, would be in the spot where the wine would flow."

"That makes sense," I nodded. "Better still: maybe the archbishop poisoned himself to bring about that very result."

"Then why would he also poison Cheryl Farnsworth?" asked Father. "As director, she wasn't going to be part of the Rosary ceremony anyway."

"It sure beats me," said Taper.

"Beats all," said Wickes.

"When was all that TV equipment set up?" asked Father.

"Some of it on Thursday afternoon," said Taper. "The rest some time Friday."

"And when was the Cordova Rosary set in place?"

"Thursday afternoon," I said. "Cheryl mentioned it at Darby's."

Wickes started to reach for his notebook, decided he was too tired to flip through its wrinkled pages, and relied on memory. "The museum arranged its delivery by armored car on Tuesday afternoon. It was locked in the sacristy for two nights.

Cheryl Farnsworth and Stephanie Fury supervised its placement on Thursday. And then everyone involved in the ceremony or the media production was there for rehearsals on Thursday and Friday." He closed his eyes and grimaced with the exertion of thought. "Except on Friday, when Archbishop Fulbright and Miss Farnsworth were in the hospital. I'm sorry, I'm having a hard time keeping all this straight."

"Plenty of time and opportunity for the murderer to set up his trap," said Taper. "Technicians, everyone, coming and going. But I'm too tired to think."

"We could all use some rest," agreed Father. "If only sleep were possible. What about Joel?"

"The lawyer you recommended has been to see him," said Wickes. "Drew de Montfort."

"I've dealt with him before," said Taper. "He's good."

"Has Joel made a statement?" asked Father.

"No," said Taper. "As I said, de Montfort is good. But ..."

"We've placed Joel at the chapel Friday afternoon," said Wickes. "Since he won't say why he was there, we can only guess. But he was definitely seen by several cameramen."

"Hm," said Father. "Billowack will run with that."

"Yes," said Taper. "He's convinced the Maruppa kid is our man."

"Are you?" asked Father. "Convinced?"

Taper ran his weary fingers through his hair. "I don't know what to think."

"So we've got fire and liquor," I said, also through waves of weariness. "What about a knife?"

"Oh yeah," said Wickes, shaking himself to partial alertness. "The knife."

"I thought there was a photo of it in the envelope," said Taper.

"So there is," said Father, shaking out another sheet. "Looks like the others."

"It was taped to the back of the Crucifix," said Taper. "But check out the serial number. CVIII. A hundred and eight."

"Thirty-six," said Father. "Seventy-two, seventy-two, and a hundred and eight. Where have I heard those numbers before, I mean, other than on the knives?"

"They do sound familiar," said Taper, rubbing his eyes. "Gosh, I need some shut-eye."

"Before you go to sleep," I said, "we've got fire, liquor, and the knife. What about hyssop?"

"Hell," said Taper, "I don't know. The boys'll be sifting through the debris for days. If there's any hyssop ashes there, they'll find them."

"Speaking of sifting," said Father, "last Monday your department did quite a bit: they searched here, the archbishop's office at the Chancery, St. Philip's, and the rest. What did all that invasion of privacy produce?"

"A pile of reports," moaned Taper, "this high. I haven't had time to read it all. I suppose you'd like copies."

"Indeed," said Father.

"I'll put Sybil Wexler on it," said Taper. "Billowack might not catch on if she puts in some major time at the photocopying machine. He's made it clear that he doesn't want Wickes and me feeding you any more police reports."

"A territorial animal," commented the gardener.

"Anything else?" asked Father.

"Yeah," said Wickes, shaking himself awake. "Here's the really spooky thing. I don't know why I didn't bring it up sooner. Bishop Ravenshorst's left foot—the fourth triangle."

"Someone carved a triangle on the bishop's left foot?" I gawked. "How?"

"Not carved," said Wickes. "It was burned."

"We just came from the morgue," said Taper, "which probably hasn't helped our disposition this morning. Those bodies laid out in a row. All those charred feet."

"What he means," said Wickes, "is that the soles of all the victims' feet, where the electricity went through them into the grounding plates—"

"Do you mean," said Father, "that Bishop Ravenshorst was standing on a triangular-shaped grounding plate?"

"Apex pointed toward the toes," nodded Wickes. "The voltage was high enough to burn an image right through the sole of his shoe."

"And the other victims," said Taper. "The others were all burned with five-pointed stars."

"Pentagrams?" said Father.

"Yes," said Taper. "Pentagrams in circles, like the ones on that damned casting quilt."

"Another deviation," said Father, his face in his hands, "without deviating."

65

"DO YOU KNOW WHO THAT WAS?"

His Grace, Archbishop Morley Psalmellus Fulbright, was pointing to the dark figure slinking out the hospital room as Father Baptist and I entered. Father shook his head.

"I've just had a visit from the Papal Nuncio," glared the archbishop. "'The Holy Father expresses his profound concern,'" he quoted, mimicking the Vatican ambassador's shrill, chirping voice, "'regarding the unfortunate turn of events within your jurisdiction.' They want my head, that's what they want."

I was about to remark what a fine trophy it would make over the papal mantelpiece when Father said, "Things are grim."

"Grim?" growled the archbishop. "Is that all you have to say? I hired—I ordered you to get to the bottom of this mess."

"It is a bigger mess than either of us dreamed at the time," said Father. "A plot more insidious than any I ever encountered when I was on the force."

"Don't patronize me."

"It wouldn't occur to me to do so. What we have here is a demonic scheme for murder of portentous proportions. It boggles the mind."

"Well my friend," spat Archbishop Morley, "you'd better get your mind unboggled. If I fall, there will be hell to pay."

"Well, there is that."

Considering that almost everyone close to the archbishop was now dead, you would have thought he would have been kinder to the few troops that were left.

Father Baptist took it all in stride. "When will Your Grace be getting out of here?"

"Tomorrow, they say."

"And the Del Agua Mission?"

"The Del Agua—?" The archbishop blinked. "Oh yes, the dedication on Wednesday. I hate to do it, but maybe I should consider canceling—"

"Oh no, Your Excellency!" A sweet feminine voice interrupted from the doorway. "You mustn't do that."

We turned to see Cheryl Farnsworth, nudging her way in through the doorway, seated in a wheelchair. Her hair was a bit unkempt, and the hospital gown didn't do her justice, but she still looked like a breeze on a summer morning.

"Good morning, Miss Farnsworth," said Father.

"And to you," she said brightly. She flashed me an ignoring glance.

My mouth opened. My mouth closed.

"Your Excellency," she said. "I've been on the phone all morning with the museum people. They're very upset, of course. There's no telling what damage the Rosary sustained last night—" Her features fell, her mind reeling. She had worked with the victims of last night's catastrophe. As far as I could tell, she had managed to keep a certain distance from them, socially. If they weren't her friends, they were at least close associates. And now they were dead. "—but they're still willing to negotiate. I think it would be a big mistake to postpone the dedication."

"She's right," said Father. "A show of courage after calamity is in order."

"And all the preparations are in progress," said Cheryl. "Poor Jerry's booklet will be delivered by the printers tomorrow, and everything's dated, and, and—" Perhaps her show of courage had a few holes in it. "—and, we simply must keep moving—"

"Of course," said the archbishop, a bit less gruffly. "Of course. We'll keep moving. The dedication ceremony will proceed as planned. It's going to be lonely up at the podium, but I'll manage."

"Good," said Cheryl. "We'll get some other speakers. There are many parish council leaders from all over the archdiocese who simply love to make speeches."

"Yes," said Father. "No doubt there are."

"I'd best be getting back to my room," said Cheryl, clumsily turning her wheelchair. It bumped the wall. "I hate this thing. Why they insist I use it and be a menace, I'll never know."

"Here," said Father. "Let me help you."

He spun her around easily and headed out the door.

I followed, nodding to the uniformed policeman who was posted just outside the archbishop's room. He looked at his watch, praying for his shift to end.

"I hear Monsignor Havermeyer is down the hall," said Cheryl, sadness again catching her breath. "They say he's regained consciousness."

"I'll pay him a quick visit," said Father, careening her into her room. There was another guard posted just outside her door.

"And the nurse told me Monsignor Goolgol's around here somewhere—oh."

Sergeant Wickes was standing at the foot of her bed, her medical chart in his hand. "Hello."

"Oh, it's you," said Cheryl, a bit warily. "Find anything interesting?"

Wickes put the chart back on its hook at the foot of her bed. "Just that you're scheduled to leave tomorrow. We're all glad you're feeling better."

"Thank-you," she said, a tinge of business creeping into her voice. "If you all don't mind, I have a number of calls to make."

"Sure," said Wickes, bumping his head on the wall-mounted television. "Uh, were you watching the ceremony last night?"

Cheryl swallowed audibly. "Yes. I saw the whole thing. It was awful."

"Yes, it was," said Wickes.

"And to think that Archbishop Fulbright and I would have ..." Her business tone slipped. "... been there, too, if not for ..."

"I think we should leave," said Father.

"Yes, of course," said Wickes. "Good-bye, Miss Farnsworth.

"Good-bye," she said, maneuvering herself toward the phone on the night stand. "Do keep me informed if I can help in any way."

Half-way down the corridor to Monsignor Havermeyer's room, Father stopped. "Sergeant, did you find something interesting?"

"Oh," said Wickes. "Not really. A hunch. I'll let you know."

"Hm. The guards were posted here all night, weren't they?"

"Yes. Billowack's orders."

"And we can assume that both Archbishop Fulbright and Cheryl Farnsworth didn't leave the premises?"

"I don't see how they could. I'll check with the guards, but I think it goes without saying."

"By the way, the hospital keeps records of all phone calls, don't they?"

"Sure. They keep track. The patients are billed for them."

"Do me a favor. Get me a list of all the calls Miss Farnsworth and Archbishop Fulbright made last night."

"Any reason why?"

"Not really. A hunch. I'll let you know."

"Touché."

A few feet away, Lieutenant Taper was leaning against the wall, wrapping up a call on a pay telephone. "Yeah, Chief. Sure. Be right over." He hung up the receiver and rolled his shoulders stiffly. "Hello again, Jack. How was your meeting with your lawful superior?"

"Not exactly edifying."

"Our superiors obviously emerged from the same mold." He turned to Wickes. "That was Billowack. Madder'n hell. We gotta get back to St. Barbara's."

"Something wrong?"

"Nothing specific. Just a lot of poking around to do. Bring soap."

"Speaking of poking around," said Father Baptist, "when are you fellows going to drop by the 'Shop of Shadows'?"

"One of these days," said Taper. "Why?"

"You'll know when you do. Now if you'll excuse me, I have a couple of other patients to visit."

66

"DID I—? DID THEY—? DIDN'T YOU—?"

Monsignor Goolgol was strapped down in his bed, rolling his head from side to side, whimpering the same perplexed litany as the previous night. His Adam's apple was oscillating in that persnickety way I've described before, except that his secret "erratic factor" switch seemed to be stuck on "yowza."

"Monsignor," said Father, standing beside the bed. "Monsignor?"

"Didn't they—?" gurgled Goolgol. "Did I—? Did they—?"

"Shows you," I said, "where sororityzing with nuns and witches will get you."

"Monsignor!" said Father, placing his palms on the edge of the bed and giving it a shake.

"Is this what he meant the other night," I mused, "at Popinjay's, you remember, when he spoke of moving beyond

your stilted preconceptions and allowing higher understanding to permeate your consciousness?"

"Not funny, Martin," said Father.

"It wasn't then," I said, "and it isn't now."

"What's your point?" said Father, straightening.

"I'll sum it up like this: so much for his theology, and all
the good it did him in a pinch."

"Theology divorced from God is not theology."

"That's what I mean. But then, he also said that you are as
narrow-minded as the reputation which precedes you."

Father shook his head slowly and turned toward the door.
"There's no reason for us to remain here."

"Of course," I said, following him, "I was recently described as 'dour.' Would you believe it? Me. 'Dour.' I've
got a pitcher full of 'periwinkies' and 'alyssiyums' to prove
it. So who am I to talk?"

"Martin, I admit that sometimes I wish you would—Oh,
Doctor Yomtov."

Father nearly collided with the puffy-faced Russian with a
humungouslav stethoscope around his neck.

"Ah, Fazzer Baptisk," said the doc, engulfing Father's hand
in his hearty paw. "I hear of you. You viziting Monzingyor
Goooooolgol."

"Yes," said Father.

"Waste of time, no? Dere'z not mutch vee can doo for him.
Maybe he znap out of it, maybe he don't. Who'z to zay?"

I wished this guy had been with me when I visited the
"Shop of Shadows." I like a Russian who enjoys being Russian. "I'm Martin Feeney," I said, extending my hand, "his
gardener."

"Dah," said Doctor Yomtov. "Dah. I zaw you on Tee
Vee."

"Tell me, Doctor," I said, "is it trauma?"

The doctor blinked. "I thot it vas comedy, no?"

"No, I mean Monsignor Goolgol. Would you say that his
doors of perception are—"

"Kaputsky," said the doc, whirling his finger like a rocket
spiraling out of orbit. "Beyond Sputnik."

"You never know," said Father. "Maybe a shock like this
will do him some good in the long run."

"Sure," I said. "Sure."

"I om Kotlick, you know," said Dr. Yomtov. "Russian
Rite, not one of doze infernal Orthodox."

"Really," said Father.

"Ond I plan to attent dedication uff your Del Agva Mission." He rubbed his hands together. "I unterstond dot wodka vill flow."

"I don't understand," said Father. "Wine, yes, that's an old California tradition. Or champagne. But vodka?"

"Dot'z vot I hear. I vouldn't miss it. Napoleon ant all his horses couldn't keep me avay."

"We'll look forward to seeing you there. But for now, we want to visit Monsignor Havermeyer. Do you know which room he's in?"

"Dah. Three tventy-zeven. On left."

We left the room and headed down the hallway. All the rooms we visited that morning were easy to find. We just looked for the guards posted outside.

"Ah," said Father. "Room 327. Good morning, Officer." The policeman nodded silently.

Monsignor Havermeyer was mummified in bandages. Only his eyes and mouth were visible. "Father Baptist," he rasped through the gauze, "Father Baptist. Thank-you for coming."

"What do you remember," asked Father, drawing up a chair beside the bed, "about last night?"

"Everything." The monsignor coughed violently, then cringed with pain. His hands were bulbs of surgical wrappings, useless. "Everything."

"If I believed in luck, I'd say you were a lucky man."

"If I believed in anything I'd be able to make sense of all this."

"Ah, now that is another matter entirely. Do you want to talk about it?"

"Yes." He swallowed dryly. "Oh yes."

"Martin," said Father. "Will you excuse us, please?"

"Sure," I said, grasping my cane and heading for the door. "Sure."

67

"FATHER BAPTIST? What brings you to Del Agua Mission?"

"I was just going to ask you the same question," said Father, shaking Roberto Guadalupe's hand.

After leaving the hospital, I had asked Father where he wanted to go next.

"I think I'd like to intrude on Father Nicanor," he answered as we got into the Jeep.

"Ah," I said, swerving out into traffic. "St. Basil's."

As usual, I spent the better part of an hour losing myself among the colonnades at the Maronite church while Father Baptist flensed his soul of unwanted flotsam and jetsam. He found me pondering a magnificent fresco of Our Mother of Perpetual Help in the archway facing the meticulously manicured flower garden.

"And now?" I asked as we boarded the Jeep again.

"I want to swing by Gerard's Winery," he said thoughtfully, "to pick up a bottle of wine."

"Altar wine?"

"No, Santa Barbara d'Umbria."

"Ah, for the liquor collection in the study."

"Yes."

I waited in the car for a quarter of an hour while Father purchased the wine and caught up on Mr. Gerard's family history.

"Next?" I said, firing up the ol' engine.

"I'd like to pay a visit to Chapel Hill."

"The Del Agua Mission?"

"Yes. I don't feel like going home just yet, and I thought I'd like to see the place that has been the underlying focus of attention amidst all these other distractions."

"Sure," I said, changing lanes. "Sure."

Presently we came to the tall stone wall that surrounded the Chapel Hill estate. I drove east along the north wall shaded with shaggy Eucalyptus trees, then south where the sidewalk along the wall was peppered with holly and juniper. As we whizzed along, we could see the tops of the virgin oak forest beyond the wall that was one of the estate's most striking features. Then I turned west along the south wall, which was crawling with ivy and other creepers. Occasionally a broad-winged bird flapped lazily over the lake which we could not see, but which we knew was on the other side of the stately wall. Then I turned northward along the west wall to the gated entrance.

A broad-shouldered guard waved us through, and we ground our way noisily up the gravel road toward the quaint but dilapidated structures of La Misión del Agua de la Vida—the Mission of the Water of Life. We stopped in the dirt parking lot under the shade of an ancient avocado tree, and trudged our way up a sandy path to what appeared to be the chapel on a hill dotted with juniper, oleander, and many fig trees.

Okay, that brings us to Roberto Guadalupe at the south wall of La Chapelle de Saint Jean Baptiste, wiping the sweat from his brow and leaning on his shovel.

From this spot, we could look out at the oak grove I mentioned before to the east, and off to the south the spring-fed lake, dotted with swans and other fowl. While Father Baptist and Roberto Guadalupe exchanged greetings I leaned on my cane, gulping the calm air and breathing in the mysterious vapors of history. Sergeant Wickes was right—it was unkempt and gone to seed—but it was more real somehow than all the high-rises and neon obelisks which peered down into its solitude from beyond the solemn stone wall which defined its sacred borders.

"What brings you to Del Agua Mission?" Roberto had just asked.

"I was just going to ask you the same question," Father Baptist was just answering.

"I got fired from the cemetery," said Roberto. "So now I work here."

"But I thought," said Father. "I mean, I distinctly—"

"Oh sí, Father. I know you put in a good word with the archbishop. It's this way. Mrs. Flores, the cemetery administrator, was so furious over that grave being dug a week early, she fired me. She just wouldn't listen. So I called the Chancery—that same number I'd called before—and spoke to the man himself, the archbishop, again. He said you'd put in a good word, and offered me this position." He drew himself up a few inches. "Superintendent of Landscaping."

"You're content?"

"It beats digging graves, and this is a job that will take years. I am happy."

"Then I am pleased."

"Roberto," called another familiar face, coming around the corner of the building.

"And I brought my own staff," beamed Roberto. "The men who worked with me at the cemetery. Duggo, you remember Father Baptist."

"Sí, of course," said Duggo, bowing his head respectfully.

"And where is Spade?" asked Roberto.

"He's on the phone, still trying to get through to the dis-patcher at B&B's."

"Liquor distributor," explained Roberto to Father. "Somehow overseeing supplies for the dedication fell to me, too. B&B delivered a truckload of booze, but they got the quantities all wrong."

"Can there ever be too much champagne at a dedication ceremony?" asked Father.

"No," said Roberto. "But unless you're the Russian Army, fifty cases of vodka is out of line."

"That might be overdoing it," agreed Father.

"Roberto," said Duggo, "I came to tell you that the truck from the lumber yard has arrived."

"Ah," said Roberto, letting his shovel fall to the ground. "For the speakers' platform. You are here about the dedica-tion, Father. No?"

"Partly," said Father. "And partly just to visit the mis-sion."

"Well, come and see."

I followed Father Baptist, Roberto, and Duggo around the southeast corner of the building where some men were unty-ing a stack of two-by-fours on a flatbed truck. The vehicle had been backed into a sort of bare-earth square with a cov-ered well in the middle.

One of the lumber men looked at a paper fluttering on his clipboard. "Are you Guadalupe?"

"Sí."

"Where ya want 'em?"

"There," said Roberto, pointing to the ground next to what looked like a brick platform. "Miss Farnsworth said the plat-form was to be built over the old oil press."

"An odd choice of location," noted Father.

"Well," said Roberto, "it does face the garden, or what's going to be a garden when I'm done with it. I guess right now it's more of a courtyard. The ground is fairly level, so the folding chairs can go there. We'll throw down some car-pets to keep the dust down. As for the oil press, it is deep, but we can build right over it. Excuse me a moment—Hey! Any luck?"

Roberto's other man from the cemetery, Spade, was stand-ing at a strikingly out-of-place telephone booth which the phone company had elected to build in the far corner of the dirt courtyard. He waved a yellow receipt in one hand while gripping the receiver in the other. "Not yet, Roberto," he called. "The dispatcher, he's out of the office. I'm trying to get through to the dock foreman."

"Keep at it," said Roberto, shaking his head.

GARDENING TIPS: There was a time when telephone booths were a colorful part of contemporary cultural art. The Brits had their bright red bread boxes, the Hilton Hotels had plush rosewood cubicles with valet dialing, and American common sense produced steel-and-glass death traps with folding doors that pinched you going in and coming out. All these approaches to the concept of a public pay phone shared three things in common:

1) privacy--you could close the door whether it bit you or not;

2) shelter from wind and rain (and in the case of the Hilton lobbies, a place in which to hide from the hotel manager after the party); and

3) creativity--you'd never know what you were going to find wedged into the coin slots, or what budding artist had spray-painted the walls two minutes before your arrival, or whether a receiver would be hanging at the end of the chord or just bare wires.

I mention this because somewhere along the line the telephone folks decided to melt down all the metal and glass it would normally take to make traditional phone booths and mold the results into those modern contraptions where the phone resides in what looks like half an egg shell on an aluminum post. No privacy, no shelter, no vandalism. But also no style.

It was just this sort of "space-egg" pay phone that had been planted in the otherwise ancient earthen square of the mission. No attempt had been made to blend the thing into its surroundings. No little thatched roof overhead, no half moons cut into bar-room type swinging doors. Instead it stood there like an alien explorer in a silver jumpsuit inspecting a quiet Mexican village where running water hasn't even been considered yet.

This did not bode well for the future ambiance of the mission.

                                        --M.F.

Meanwhile, I hobbled over to the brick platform. It was about three feet high and flat on top, and in the center was the gaping hole of the ancient olive press. It was about six feet in diameter. I could only see a few feet down into it from that angle.

"The foreman says I gotta speak with the dispatcher," called Spade from the pay phone. "Dios mio."

"Patience," yelled back Roberto.

Noticing a crumbled stairway to the right, and curious about this primitive technology which had supported the ancient mission, I lurched my way up. Carefully, since some of the stones were wobbly, I inched closer to the hole.

A large round steel grate was mounted inside, about two feet below the rim. The raised words "Roundhead Manhole Covers" encircled the open mesh pattern in the middle. I smiled at the incongruity of this brazen stamp of the Roundhead family, of which Themolina Hubbard was the tragic heiress. Marveling at the impulse that had caused her to donate this estate to the church, I crept a bit closer. Ten feet further down I could see dark, murky water. There was no way to tell how deep it was. No doubt it collected there during the winter rains.

"Careful, Señor," barked Duggo.

I jerked up straight. If he hadn't startled me, I wouldn't have done so. And if I hadn't done so, my cane would not have caught in a crack between the stones. And if my cane had not wedged itself so, the loose stone by the rim would not have dislodged, teetered, and slid into the hole.

"Ayi!" cried Duggo.

There was a sharp metallic clang as the stone struck the metal grate. I thought I was seeing things, because the grate seemed to sink. No, not sink. Tilt. It was hinged on one side, and the weight of the stone caused it to swing open—downward. The thing made an awful groan, like some ghastly damned creature in a monster movie. It shook the ground on which I was standing. The fallen stone scraped and tumbled along the steepening slope of the grate, wobbled on the brink, and finally slipped off the edge. Frozen, I watched as the stone plunged down the chute and broke the surface of the dark water with a hollow kerthunk.

A few heartbeats later, the grate groaned back to its level position. The dragon belched in satisfaction.

"I, uh, what the—?"

"Get back." Duggo had dashed up the steps and was clutching my arm. "What falls in," he said sternly, "it stays in."

"What kind of a contraption is this?" I said.

"I don't know, Señor. But it is best that we keep away, no?"

"It's best that we keep away, sí."

Snickering something in Spanish, Duggo helped me back down the steps, into the freezing gaze of Father Baptist. He held me there until icicles started forming on my chin, and then he turned to Roberto.

"As I said, an odd place to put a speakers' platform."

"Not really," shrugged Roberto. "We will build a strong platform, this on my honor. But just to be sure, Duggo, get some wire and fasten that grate."

"Sure thing," said Duggo, strutting off.

"I heard a kid fell in there once," said the lumber man with the clipboard. "Then his friend fell in trying to get him out. They spent two lonely nights down there until the cops found them."

"Years ago," said one of his companions, "a little girl died in there, back when this was called the Roundhead Estate."

"Ah," said another, "the cops have been chasing people out of this park for years. If you ask me, it's a good thing that it's finally going to be put to use. Did I hear them call you 'Father'?"

"Yes," said Father Baptist. "I'm a priest."

"Say, you're the one who caused all that ruckus on TV."

"I admit it," sighed Father.

"My wife said you're nuts, but I thought you made sense. You gonna be on again this week?"

"No. It was a one-shot deal."

"That's a shame."

"Well," huffed Roberto. "While you guys unload the truck, I'm going to show the Padre around."

"Sure thing."

I watched as Roberto led Father around the far corner of the chapel.

"Look out," said the man who thought Father made sense.

Three pine boards thumped to the ground where I had been standing.

Enough was enough.

"I'm going for a walk," I said to nobody in particular, and started down a path that seemed to meander in the general direction of the oak grove.

In a few minutes, I forgot the icicles on my chin. In fact, I forgot just about everything including my name. The brittle oak leaves crunching under my feet, the smell of dense undergrowth, the comical flutter of butterflies trying to stay in one place as the breeze gently swept them between the hoary trunks of the ancient trees, all combined to give me a sense of unexpected peace. This was a marvelous place, something out of a storybook. Something deep within me, something hungry for a moment of serenity, drank deeply at the well of solitude.

I wandered aimlessly through the forest, no dread of losing my way. After all, there was a city around me. Surely the missionaries who founded this mission had sought solace in this very grove, a place where time took a permanent siesta, where the words "Be still and know that I am God" made impeccable sense.

Somehow I knew when I'd reached the heart of the forest. There was nothing else it could be. The trees parted and revealed a circular meadow of lazily bobbing grass. As in a dream, I walked toward the center, leaving my spinal arthritis behind in the shadows of the stately trees.

There was a wide, flat stump, black as granite, in the very middle of the meadow, just the right height for one Martin Feeney to rest his bones upon. From all ages, I thought, God knew that I would be passing this way, and though this tree had served many a different purpose, it was comforting to realize that one of its designs was to provide a resting place for me.

"Dear Lord," I whispered, "thank-you for ... everything."

GARDENING TIPS: Sergeant Wickes told me the above description was a not-so-veiled attempt at poetic insight, and was a "gross departure from my usual desultory banter"--again, words I did not know he knew. Well, what the hey. I'll leave it in. It was--how shall I put this?--what it was.

--M.F.

I don't know how long I sat there, perhaps a half hour. Wishing I could remain, but deciding that it was time to leave, I heaved myself up with the help of my cane and discovered

that my spinal arthritis had ventured out of the woods and returned home.

"Well," I grimaced. "There is that."

As I turned around to get my bearings, I noticed something
interesting. About fifteen feet from the stump, and going all
around it in a perfect circle, was a trampled path. I guess I
had been too taken with the magic of the place to see it before. Someone had definitely been walking in circles around
this stump, walking enough so that in places the grass was
completely worn down to the bare dirt.

Then I noticed my hand. It was black with soot.

Examining the stump, I realized that it was charred,
scorched, blackened by fire. Someone had obviously built a
roaring campfire upon it, and recently. How could I have not
noticed the acrid smell?

The lumber man had said that the police had been chasing
people out of this park for years. Luckily, they hadn't left
any beer cans behind.

Swatting the seat of my pants, I started back across the
meadow.

I stopped again.

That smell. That unmistakable smell. I turned and looked
at the plants I had just crushed with my feet. I stooped down
to be certain, oblivious to the pain in my back. My vertebrae
snapping, I straightened and proceeded to wander about the
meadow, zigzagging this way and that. At a clump of curled,
dry fronds, I drew to a halt.

"Yes," I said out loud. "Yes. It's all coming together
now."

My suspicions confirmed, I lurched off in the direction of
the mission.

68

"YOU'RE SURE," SAID FATHER as we roared out the gates
and out into traffic. "You're absolutely sure."

"If you weren't in such a hurry," I huffed, "you could
have seen for yourself."

"I have to get back for confessions."

"I know, I know."

"But if you're right—"

"I   am."

"—then we must speak with Mrs. Magillicuddy as soon as possible. Do you know where she lives?"

"I can check the parish records."

"Do that.   While I'm hearing confessions, you do that."

69

"I DID THAT," I ASSURED HIM.

"You're sure."

I sighed.   "I'm sure."

He scratched his temple, thinking.   "What about address corrections from the fund drive?   We requested that on the mailing."

"Been there," I said.   "The envelope sent to Mrs. Magillicuddy came back stamped, 'Undeliverable as addressed, unable to forward.'   That was marked down in the parish address book."

"But I've been to her house, back when William took ill.   It was a little shack up on Peppertree Court—"

"Which is now a twenty-four hour laundromat.   I strolled up there while you were kneeling in front of the Blessed Sacrament after confessions—if you can call what I do 'strolling.'   Progress, Father, progress."

"Hm.   I'm surprised that Muriel—"

"I called her when I got back.   Mrs. Cladusky, in spite of being the alleged pilferer of Mrs. Magillicuddy's intentions, is not privy to her current address."

"And what about—"

"I called police headquarters about an hour ago.   Lieutenant Taper was indisposed, but Sergeant Wickes ran a computer search.   Nothing."

"She must live somewhere."

"Yes, but at present it's her secret."

"Sorry to interrupt," said Pierre Bontemps, refilling his flute with champagne, "but we did come here on business."

"I apologize," said Father, leaning back in his chair.   " I have been ignoring you gentlemen."

"We understand, Father," said Edward, tugging his vest. "You're immersed in this murder case."

"And so is Joel," said Arthur.

"But since our fellow Tumblar is in the stockade," said Jonathan, "and his keeper, Billowack, won't let us see him, we thought we'd better come to you."

"I don't know that there's anything I can do about that," said Father. "De Montfort is—"

"Yes, yes, yes," said Pierre. "He's a good man. But there must be something we can do. Have they charged him yet?"

"No," said the gardener.

"So, how long can they hold him?" asked Arthur.

"Seventy-two hours," said a voice from the doorway. Wickes and Taper strutted in as Millie fluttered toward the kitchen muttering something about putting the kettle on. If these two detectives had looked tired in the morning, they looked dead this evening. "Then we have to formally charge him or set him free."

"Ah, the gentlemen from the police," acknowledged Pierre, rising to his feet. The other Tumblars followed suit.

Taper dumped a pile of files on Father's desk, which was already overflowing with debris. "Courtesy of Sybil Wexler."

"Fine," said Father, rubbing his hands thoughtfully. He opened the top file and began scanning the contents.

"Before you get absorbed," said Wickes, "Billowack's hot to wrap this case up, and he's been fuming about loose ends. Taper and I plan to do another search of the homes of all the deceased in this case on Monday. We'll throw the 'Shop of Shadows' into the tour at no extra charge. You interested?"

"Hm," said Father, eyebrows furrowed, eyes scanning right, darting left, scanning, darting. "Hm."

"Too late," said Taper, "he's engrossed. I've seen it before, years ago. The only man I knew who actually enjoyed reading police reports."

"Sniggertrance," I observed. "We have ceased to exist. In any case, officers, Father Baptist accepts your invitation. Why not start the tour with breakfast here?"

"Sure," said Taper. "I'll bring some treats from the wife's garden."

"And I'll bring some fresh-ground coffee," said Wickes.

"And I'll try to snap Father Baptist out of it by then," I said.

"Hm," said Father, turning a page.

"Hm," said Taper, finding some wall space to lean against.

"Hm," said Wickes, doing likewise.

As the Tumblars settled back into their seats, silence settled in the room, broken every minute or so by the scrape of paper as Father turned a page.

The bottles of liquor stood like ominous sentinels at the four corners of Father's desk. The now-discarded bottle of Evian water had been moved next to the hand-carved statues of St. Anthony of Padua and St. Thomas More, who were huddled off to the side, taking notes and making profound comments between themselves. DO WE WALK IN LEGENDS teetered on the brink, threatening to fall into the over-flowing waste paper basket. Every inch of the top of the desk was buried in a mesh of photographs, lab reports, and hastily-scribbled notes in Father's haphazard shorthand.

"Lieutenant Taper," said Pierre presently, after clearing his throat and wetting his whistle with a sip of champagne. "It seems to us that our comrade, Joel, is being treated most unfairly."

"He is being held for questioning," said Wickes with an apparent lack of enthusiasm. He was scratching his head in slow motion. "And since he hasn't answered to our satisfaction—"

"He hasn't answered anything at all," interjected Taper, rubbing his beard stubble in the same, dull, slow-motion mode as his partner.

"—we have no choice for the moment. On Monday he'll either be charged or released. That's up to the DA."

"Perhaps if we could see him," said Jonathan, "maybe we could find something out."

"No doubt," said Taper. "And you'd report anything he had to say directly to us? Even if it implicated him further in the crimes?"

"Well—"

"Besides," said Wickes, "Billowack's in charge. If he says no visitors, that's final."

"Billowack," said Arthur disgustedly. "He's the one I gave my statement to. I told him that Joel had spent the previous two nights at my place because we stayed out so late. Joel saw an article in the newspaper about the big-deal Rosary and funeral. It was an interview with Cheryl Farnsworth. She was going on and on about what a high-tech state-of-the-art production it was going to be. Joel, he knows wiring, and he was interested in seeing it. I dropped him by St. Barbara's Chapel that afternoon and went on to do some shopping. I picked him up two hours later."

"Did he have any tools with him when you dropped him off?" asked Taper. "Or any kind of electronic parts?"

"No," said Arthur decisively. "Absolutely not. When I came by to pick him up, he was a bit disappointed because the technicians had caught him poking around and chased him off."

"Three times," said Wickes, still demonstrating the slow-motion scratch.

"So he's persistent," said Arthur. "But he didn't have time or opportunity to do what they're accusing him of."

"Were you with him last Sunday?" asked Taper.

"We were out late," said Jonathan.

"All of us together," said Arthur.

"We were Tumbling," said Pierre.

"And the Tuesday before that?" asked Wickes.

"We didn't know Joel on the Tuesday before that," said Jonathan.

"We first met him on the Saturday after the Tuesday before the Sunday you just asked about," said Pierre.

"Skip it," said Wickes, his hand dropping to his side. "Like we said, it's out of our hands."

"Then what can we do?" asked Edward.

"Wait," said Taper.

"Father Baptist," said Arthur, setting down his flute glass. "Surely there is something we can do."

Father's attention seemed riveted to a small sheet of blue paper which he was holding under the desk lamp. From where I sat it looked like some sort of print-out.

"Father Baptist," insisted Pierre.

"Hm?" said Father, looking up, though his attention was obviously still on the page in his hand. "You've all given your statements to the police?"

"Yes," they nodded severally.

"And you're still faithfully making a novena to St. Anthony of Padua?"

"Yes," they nodded again.

"Then I suggest you finish your champagne."

They did so, but not with their usual flourish.

Sunday, June Eighteenth

Feast Day of Saints Mark and Marcellian, Martyrs (3rd century)

70

TERROR GRIPS ARCHDIOCESE, read the Sunday headlines for those living in igloos or anyone who hadn't been keeping up with the dailies. ARCHBISHOP HOSPITALIZED, FOUR BISHOPS MURDERED, FOUR LAY PERSONS DEAD, continued the scandalous scoreboard in increasingly smaller type, bottoming out with, TWO MONSIGNORS SERIOUSLY INJURED.

Immediately after Mass, at Father Baptist's request, I had slipped out of the sacristy door and shot—if you can call my laborious lurching 'shooting'—down to the corner. I had two objectives. First, to get a copy of the morning newspaper. Second, to circumvent the gaggle of huffing, puffing parishioners who were no doubt gathering in front of the church to ambush Father Baptist. It didn't occur to me that I was a decoy.

Third, and this was a spur-of-the-moment kind of thing, I bought a copy of *The Weekly Ecto*, not so much because I felt plasmic, but because Starfire's photo figured prominently above the feature article: FIVE ELIXIRS THAT WILL MAKE A MAN LOVE YOU NO MATTER HOW LIBERATED YOU ARE. This was not a rag I had ever read before, nor would I ever again, but police work is police work.

Tucking the *Ecto* within the thick folds of the *Times*, the entirety of which was devoted to the "scandalous and ominous tragedies which have traumatized the Catholic community in our city." There were column-wide photos of Bishops Silverspur, Brassorie, Mgumba, and Ravenshorst. Beneath their saccharine faces were the slightly colder mugs of Sister Charlene Vickers, Stephanie Fury, the "celebrated" Madeline

Sugarman, and the apparently not-so-celebrated Marsha Dukes. Off to the sides were smaller photos of Monsignors Goolgol and Havermeyer "recuperating from their electrically-related injuries." The page was dotted with the beginnings of stories about each, with "continued on page ..." instructions for more serious researchers. In the lower left corner was a picture of Archbishop Fulbright looking grim. It had been taken at Bishop Brassorie's funeral—the first one—just before the release of the ill-fated bird. There was even a shot of Father Baptist in the lower right corner. COP-TURNED-PRIEST-TURNED COP STUMPED, announced the caption over Jacco Bab's byline.

"Aha, there you are," a blustering voice burst upon the shores of my reverie.

"Oh," I said, "Mr. Turnbuckle. "How are you this morn—"

"I wondered where you slipped off to. And where is Father Baptist? He disappeared after Mass."

"Beats me," I shrugged. "He must be around here somewhere."

Mr. Thurgood T. Turnbuckle smacked the newspaper in my hand. "This is what he gets for sticking his nose where it doesn't belong."

"Now Mr. Turnbuckle—"

"Such a shame," squealed Irma Dypczyk, grabbing my cane arm, which was akin to kicking the stilts out from under a house built on the edge of a precipice. "What will we do?" she cheeped. "What's becoming of our Church?"

"I don't know, Mrs. Dypczyk. It seems to me—"

"It don't get no worse than this," said Patrick Railsback.

"No it doesn't Mr. Railsback, but you never know—"

"Yes, I do."

I shook them off, veering left to avoid Steve Lambert, the cameraman and career-splicer from KROM. Then, my confidence swelling, I executed a magnificent swoop to the right, shot without comment between Jacco Babs and his talking flash bulb, Ziggie, ricocheted off the effulgent aura of Pierre Bontemps, only to be brought up short by a cavernous maw lined with two rows of glaciated teeth.

"Tell Father I'm rootin' for him," chawed Freddie Furkin, the fellow from the Chancery motor pool.

"I will, Mr. Furkin. I certainly will."

"Gracious me," said a kinder, gentler voice.

"Yes you are, Henry," I said to Mr. Folkstone, patting him on the shoulder as I squeezed by.

Seeing a clear space between the opposite-facing backsides of Mrs. Supplewhite and her daughter, Clarice, I made a burst for freedom. But it was a trap.

"Mr. Feeney," screamed a female voice, even though the mouth of origin was only inches from my face.

"Oh," I blinked. "Mrs. Cladusky."

I found myself cornered by a kind-hearted but fierce-lunged dirigible of a woman, whose culinary fame and predilection for garlic preceded her.

"Mr. Feeney, have you seen dear Mrs. Magillicuddy?"

"That's exactly what I was going to ask you."

"She must be here. She never misses Mass on Sunday."

"I should hope not. If you do bump into her—"

"I'll tell her you're looking for her. And you tell Father I'll be making my Bennie stuffed cabbages Thursday night, and he's welcome to come for dinner."

"I'll be sure to—"

"I had no idea our Father Baptist was so important," exclaimed Mrs. Theodora Turpin. For a moment I thought she had a megaphone pressed against my other ear. "Isn't it just amazing?"

"Yes, Dear," nodded her husband, Tanner. "I think it is."

"Hogwash," said Mrs. Patricia Earheart, jabbing her finger menacingly at Mr. Gregory Holman's stomach. "How can you say such a thing?"

"Because it's true," he said.

"But it can't be," she countered.

"But it is."

I steered around them, right into a ray of sunshine who goes under the name of Danielle Parks, our "in lieu of" choir director. She was accompanied by a buoyant puff of patchouli known as Wanda Hemmingway.

"Martin," they squeaked together. "We just heard about Cheryl Farnsworth. Poisoned. Have you seen her? Do you know if she's all right?"

"As far as I know, she's being released from the hospital today."

"I was digging through my scrapbook," said Wanda, "and I found some clippings from the Algernon Park disaster. I thought you might be, you know, interested. Here, I made some photocopies."

"Right," I nodded as she wedged a manila envelope under my cane arm, "Jymmy Thinggob's last lead guitar solo."

"He remembers," said Danielle.

"I told you he would," said Wanda.

"Oh hey," I said, snapping my fingers. "Just call me—"

"Mr. Feeney," another mouth blared in my face.

"What? Oh, it's you again, Mr. Turnbuckle."

Trads—you gotta love 'em. I managed to shoulder my way through the stampeding herd, avoiding their horns where possible, sustaining flesh wounds where it wasn't. By and by, the crowd thinned and I was able to make some progress upstream. Somehow I broke through into the open space of the shaded garden between the church and the rectory, and immediately tripped and stumbled headlong into the hunched-over haunches of Mrs. Magillicuddy, who was preening the flowers along the edge of the mossy brick path. It was a bit like running into a glutenous pillow. She let out a high-pitched "Eeek!" as she flopped over unceremoniously into the ivy. I lost my footing and, arms flailing, landed beside her.

"Mr. Feeney!" she sputtered, thrashing around in the greenery. "What on earth—?"

"Oh," was all I could think to say as I scurried to help the old woman to her feet. "Oh."

"Is that's any ways to treats a lady?" she said, adjusting her adipose folds and swatting leaves from her thick wool sweater.

"Oh," I stammered, attempting to help her in her huffing recombobulation. "Oh."

"What's this poor old world coming to?" she puffed.

"The end," I finally muttered. "No doubt about it. I'm terribly sorry, Ma'm. And I'm also very, very glad to bump into you—I mean, to find you."

"Well, that you have, young man. It's a good thing for you that my Willum isn't about, or he'd saves me honor, he woulds."

"And rightly so, Ma'm. Do forgive me."

"An' look at you," she said, picking a couple of leaves off my jacket. Then she disentangled a sprig of ivy from my hair. She began to smile in spite of herself. "Well, no harm done, I guesses."

"I certainly hope not," I oomphed, stooping to retrieve my cane. "And I am glad to see you. I wanted to thank you for your kind gifts. The periwinkies and alyssiyums."

"Ah," she said, eyes twinkling. "You likes'd 'em."

"Very much."

"They was a bit on the dry side, they was."

"Yes, but I put them in water and they're doing fine."

"Oh good," she beamed. "Thirsty they was."

"Also, Father Baptist has been looking for you, but we don't have your address. You must have moved, and—"

"Lookin' for me, he is? What on this earth would the good Faddah want with the likes of me?"

"It's kind of a long story," I grunted, groping for the newspapers which I'd dropped during our collision. Wanda's envelope has sustained a footprint from yours truly. "I'm sure he could explain it better than I could."

"Here, Mr. Feeney," she chuckled, bending over and scooping up the two newspapers. "Let's me help you with that. Men an' their backs. When ol' Adam fell in the Garden, he bruised his spine, he did, an' men have been moanin' and achin' ever since. Every time I needs somethin' done, my Willum starts a'rubbin' his lumbago. We women folks were cursed with child a'bearin', but hell made a home in the weak backs of our men, it did. Here's your newsin'papers, young man, as if we didn't already knows the news was bad—" She froze, mid scoop. "Mother of Mercy."

I was still hunched over, trying to get a grip on Wanda's manila envelope. Grunting, I straightened up. "What is it, Mrs. Magillicuddy?"

She was examining the faces on the front page of the *Times.* "Me faeries."

"You know these people?"

"These here ladies," she said, tracing their newsprint features with her fingers. Marsha Dukes, Stephanie Fury, Sister Vickers, Madeline Sugarman. "Yes, I've seen 'em in the woods, I have. They comes reg'lar as clockwork, they does. Ev'ry fifth night they comes to do their dancin', they does. An' lookie here."

"What is it?"

"Them." Her finger had migrated to the faces of the four murdered bishops. She scrunched up her face, concentrating, mouthing the names around missing teeth. She looked up at me with puzzled eyes. "Can faeries be bishops?"

"A profound question, Mrs. Magillicuddy. You recognize them?"

"All buts this one here." She indicated Monsignor Havermeyer. "He's not their kind. I can see he's not, I can. But all these others, I've seen 'em many a'time. Not all at once, minds you. Faeries has their own ways, they has. At least the ones I've seen. So go on, tells me I don't's know what I'm a'talkin' about."

"I wouldn't dream of it," I said. Not that I was really following anyway.

"One male faerie at a time it seems must be, it does," she said, touching her finger to her chin. "The women faeries has their funs—oh dear, I mustn't say, I mustn't." She clapped her hand to her mouth, suppressing a giggle. "No, me stars, or I'll be confessin' me heart's evil thoughts till the sun shines, for sure I wills."

I fidgeted with my cane while she hedged and hawed in her embarrassment. Something in my heart softened for this complicated, confused, fascinating, and incredibly lonely old woman.

"There was once, there was," she finally continued, maneuvering her mind around an occasion of sin. "Not so long ago. Days go by, they does. But I remembers the night, even if I forgets the day, I does."

"Something happened?"

"This one here." She was pointing to the picture of Bishop Brassorie. "He broke the rules, he did. He should a'known better, not with faeries, he shouldn't'a. Another man he brought along, he did, all draped in black, he was, an' his face in shadow."

"A man," I said.

"A man faerie, or a man man, I don't knows. But the women folks was upset. They covered their heads, they did, when they saws 'em a'comin'. They cursed the one who brought him, they did. They didn't approve, they didn't. No sirs, they broke up before their dancin' was done, they did. But I digresses, I does. All in alls, faeries have their ways, if you knows where to finds them."

"Where have you seen them?"

"Why, in the woods."

"The woods."

"The woods is like home to me, it is," she said wistfully. "Me Willum showed me how to get in, years an' years ago. Oh, the signs say, 'Keeps out,' but that never stopped me Willum, no it didn't. He found a hole in the wall behind the eucalyptuses, he did. Our secret, it was. We used to go there at night, ways back then when we was a'courtin'. The old stump." She hugged herself at the memory. "He proposed

to me there, he did. Of courses, that was long before the faeries came."

"It must have been very romantic."

"That it was, that it was. I still goes there when the mood
a'takes me. Such lovely flowers as you'll never find anywhere else. The woods. Willum's an' mine's."

My heart was racing. I, Martin Feeney, had been right about
my hunch. A new chapter in the annals of criminology was
being written as we spoke. "Woods, you say."

"You know," she said slyly, "near the ol' church. Not this
ol' church, the other ol' church."

"Is it a long way from here?"

"I likes to walk, I do. An' no place is as far as you thinks
once you start a'puttin' one foot's in front of the other'n."

"And do you know the name of the old church?"

"St. Della Gwer's, me thinks I heard someone calls it, I did.
Me Willum an' me, we just a'called it 'our's place.'"

"Oh, Mrs. Magillicuddy. You must tell this to Father Baptist."

"Oh him," she smiled. "He knows all my sins, he does."

"But what I mean is—"

"They dances, you know. Arounds a fire they dances."

"That must be a sight to see."

"It is, young man, it is." She paused for a moment. "Of
course, you bein' young an' manly an' full of vinegar, it
would put ideas in your head."

"You think so?"

She looked at me sternly. "I knows so."

"Hm," I hedged, not knowing what to say to that. "Are
they friendly?"

"Friendly?" she scoffed. "Faeries, friendly?"

"I mean, do you ever speak to them?"

"Young man, don't's you knows anything?"

I shrugged. "Not much, I'll admit."

"Then let's me tells you something," she said, tapping the
Times stiffly with her brittle fist. "Nobody with an ounce of
sense talks to faeries when they're a'dancin'. They're beautiful, they is, an' graceful, too, under the stars an' all. An'
them in their altogethers—ahem. But they don't cater to us
humans, they don't. If they catches you watchin' them,
they'll turns you into a toad or something worse, they will."

"So how—?" I was thinking of the size of the meadow.
"So how do you get close enough to see them?"

"'Noculars," she said, smiling broadly. "My Willum was in the war, he was, an' he brought back a pair of 'noculars. He used 'em to watch birds an' things, he did."

"Oh," I said. "Binoculars."

"I watch through Willum's 'noculars from the edge of the wood, you see. I doesn't want to spend me days turned into an old tree stump or a block of salt."

"Very wise of you. Mrs. Magillicuddy, you really should come into the rectory with me. Father Baptist would be most interested—"

"An' this one!" She had turned her attention to the face of Starfire on the front page of the *Ecto*. "She's one of 'em, too."

"Pay dirt," I exclaimed. "You're sure."

"Of course I'm sure. She's the one's what stands there with a big wand or something in her hand, she does. Kind of fat, she is, an' sings like an old crow, all shrill an' warbly, like scratchin' a slate with your fingernail. It's enough to give you— Oh!"

Suddenly, the papers slipped from the old woman's gnarled hands. Her eyes fluttered and the muscles in her sagging cheeks quivered furiously.

"Mrs. Magillicuddy?" I whispered, alarmed. I took her hand and patted it gently. "Are you all right?"

Just as suddenly, her face relaxed. Blinking, she looked around as if snapping out of a dream. She yanked her hand away from me. "Mr. Feeney?"

"Yes, Ma'm."

"Oh, it is you, isn't it? What was I thinkin'?" She scratched her forehead thoughtfully, then snapped her twiglike fingers. "Oh yes, I was thinking that these here flowers need tendin', they does. An' you callin' yourself a gardener. You should be ashamed."

"I am," I admitted. "More than you know."

"Well," she said, turning away. "I must be on about me businesses."

"Mrs. Magillicuddy," I oophed, scooping up the papers which had slipped to the ground again. I scampered up behind her. "You were saying about these pictures."

She turned and looked at the newspapers in my hand without recognition.

"You were telling me about the faeries," I said.

"Faeries?" She was genuinely puzzled.

"In the woods."

"I don't knows what yer talkin' abouts," she said.

"I don't either," I said, marveling at how easily the wheels in her head could slip gears. Perhaps that chapter in criminology would have to wait.

"I may be an old woman," she huffed, "but I isn't bonkers."

"No," I said, my heart sinking, "certainly not." Not knowing what to do, and not wanting to alarm her, I tried to resume a calming attitude. "As I was saying, Father Baptist and I were concerned because we don't have your current address."

"Oh that," she said. "I moved out. Too many memories, there was, in that little house."

"Where did you move to?"

"I just goes where I goes."

"You mean you don't have a home?"

"The whole world is me home," she said calmly. "Until the Good Lord, hopefully, invites me into His, to be, hopefully, again with me Willum."

"I see," I nodded sadly. My chance for greatness as a sleuth had come and gone, for the moment anyway.

I suppose I should have pursued the matter further, or invited her inside for coffee, or fetched Father Baptist, or run three times around the block, or something useful. But more than ever, my heart just wasn't in it.

"Good day, Mrs. Magillicuddy."

"An' you cheer up, Mr. Feeney. You've no cause to go 'round so grim all the time."

Ah, I thought, at the moment I do.

71

"SHE'LL BE ALL RIGHT," said Father Baptist. He was laying on the bed in the stark, bare cubicle he called his bedroom. The shades were drawn, and the only light came from a votive candle which bobbed beneath a small, chipped statue of Our Lady of Fatima on the night stand.

I rarely entered his little room, and only when invited. In this case, though I had entered with permission, I felt unwelcome.

The moment I'd entered the kitchen after my discussion
with Mrs. Magillicuddy, Millie had been all over me.

"Didn't want any breakfast," she had hrumphed. "Hasn't
eaten in two days. He's sick, that's what he is. You'd better
check on him, Mr. Feeney, or there's going to be another
body to be accounted for."

"His?" I had asked.

"Yours," she barked, snatching an empty frying pan from
the stove, "if you don't do something straight away."

"Right," I said, backing into the hallway.

First I looked in the study. It looked much like it had the
night before. There were the four sentry bottles standing
guard over the chaos of files and reports, and Sts. Anthony
and Thomas More arguing theology beside the waters of
Evian, but no Father Baptist.

Then I checked the spare room where Joel had slept.
Nothing there. The bathroom being likewise empty, I headed
for his bedroom down the hall. The door was closed, so I
knocked.

"I'm not hungry, Millie," came his voice.

"It's me, Father. Martin. It's important."

There was a sigh followed by the clunk of a telephone in its
cradle. Then came the creek of bedsprings. "Very well," he
said finally. "Come in."

And there he was on the bed in the dark, his left arm over
his eyes, a blue paper in his right hand at his side.

"Say your peace," he said.

Unnerved by the situation, I gave him a brief outline of my
conversation with Mrs. Magillicuddy. "And then she just sort
of snapped out of it," I concluded, "back to tending the
flowers, as if we'd never spoken of faeries in the woods."

"She'll be all right," he said. "Mrs. Magillicuddy's
Guardian Angel will see to that. He gets combat pay, I assure
you. Sometimes I think she was assigned St. Gabriel himself."

I just hung my head.

"Martin, you confirmed our suspicions in the woods near
the mission. That's the important thing. Besides, as you say,
she snapped out of the misty past and into the stark present. I
doubt there's more she can tell us until the mood overtakes
her again. If she's living in the woods at Chapel Hill, as I
think she hinted, she'll be easy to find. Let it be."

I looked around the room. It didn't take long, since there
was little to see. The bed, a chair, a tiny writing desk. The

statue of Our Lady of Fatima. "So what are your plans for today? You want to go back to the Del Agua mission, check out the woods?"

"No."

"Then what?"

"This is Sunday. I intend to rest."

"So you won't be needing me?"

"Why? Do you have something to do?"

"I could think of something, sure."

"Then do it. Be home for dinner."

"If there is any."

"Meaning?"

"Millie's very upset that you're not eating. I wouldn't be surprised if she ups and leaves. You know how she gets about men who don't stuff themselves with the results of her labors."

"Please assure her that I will be fine by this evening. I just need to rest. Heavens, I just ... need ... to rest ..."

"I'll try. Do you mind if I take a couple of things from your desk in the study? I have an idea—"

I suddenly realized he was asleep, his breathing slow and on the verge of a profound, sacerdotal snore.

"God bless you, Father," I said, closing the door.

Well, I did have an idea.

I ducked into the study and searched through the papers on the desk. A few fell to the floor, but I left them. God would know His own. Finding what I wanted, I slipped the sheets into the same manila envelope that Wanda had given me earlier, tucked the envelope into the folds of the *Weekly Ecto*, cuffed that within the *Times*, and headed for the kitchen.

"Well?" said Millie, hands on hips.

"Father gives his word that he'll be hungry for dinner," I said as confidently as I could. "He just needs some rest."

"We shall see," she huffed, hefting a fourteen-inch skillet. "And what about you?"

"I'm going out," I said, bracing myself for a dent in the skull. It didn't come. She turned to the sink, disgusted. "I know we don't pay you enough for this," I ventured.

"You don't pay me anything," she scowled. "Well, be off with you. But see that you come home hungry, or there'll be Hell to pay."

"Too high a price," I said, grabbing the door knob. "I'll be famished. On my word, I'll personally consume a horse."

"That, at least, is meat we can afford.

72

I KNEW I COULD FIND IT. And I did.

WIDE EYE DO DAT? asked the crooked sign over the warped doorway.

"Here goes nothing," I said as I turned the rusty knob, still unclear as to how fortunes could be untold.

That insufferable bell tinkled its non-note as I entered. Everything seemed the same in Willie 'Skull' Kapps' curious establishment. All the twisted, gnarled, ghastly things that had been dead before remained, thankfully, dead.

"Courage, Martin," I whispered, creeping slowly through the store. I paused beneath the bizarre collection of casting quilts. Their patterns played havoc with my retinas, and their mysterious purpose did worse to my itching imagination.

"As I understand it," Father's voice seemed to echo in the space between my ears, "the blank space is the focus of the entire pattern, the locus of intention. Everything else on the casting cloth somehow points to it."

"Well," I mused under my breath as I gazed at the quilts, the blank spaces in their patterns shouting out—for what? Vengeance? Promotion? Love? "I don't know what your makers were bargaining for, but I suspect they got what they deserved."

A chill rippled down my spine as something in one of the cabinets wiggled its tentacles at me. When I turned in that direction, it became still.

"Hrmph," I mumbled. "Dead. I knew it. I knew it all the time."

Deciding first of all that a rousing show of courage was in order, and secondly that if I didn't do something I'd go bonkers, I took action.

"Hello," I called. "Anybody here?"

"I'm closed," came a wiry voice from the room behind the beaded curtain.

"But the door wasn't locked."

"Then I guess I'm open, mon."

While the proprietor bumped and thumped in the room beyond, making himself presentable, I amused myself with furtive glances at the shriveled things in one of the glass cases.

"Hey Martin Mon," said Willie finally, materializing through the beaded curtain. "Wot brings you to the House of

Guillaume du Crane Cristal?" He looked around. "And no Jack the Black? He no come back?"

"Just me," I said, wondering if the admission was wise.

"Whud chu want wid me, mon? Ah—" He gave me a knowing wink. "Dah Voudou is ripe for dah soul, mon. You come back to learn more, eh? And widdout Jack." He licked his lips. "Ah, I understand."

"Er, not exactly. I was hoping you could help me with something. Actually, a few things."

"Dah Voudou will help with every ting, mon."

"Well, yes," I said, spreading the front page of the *Ecto* on the counter. It looked fitting, somehow, with all those mummified thingamabobs under the glass. "Do you know this woman?"

"Oh, detecting you are," he said, leaning over and examining Starfire's photograph. He straightened, the bones and twigs and other paraphernalia in his steel wool dreadlocks rattling up a storm. "I know dis witch."

"You do."

"She's bad mojo. Whachoo wanna know about her?"

"Anything you can tell me."

"She's been around a long time, mon. Long, long, time. And she has many names. Starfire she calls herself, and writes books of nonsense." He snickered. "And she snows the police, I hear. Ambu—, Ambullabum—"

"Ambuliella Beryl Smith."

"That's it." He slapped his skeletal knee. "Where'd she dig that one up?"

"You said she has many names."

"Yes I did, mon. Eight years, ten years ago she was working as Esther of Ether, in addition to her regular gig. I pulled a prank or two with her, but bowed out. She was wicked."

"How so?"

"Would you like some mweemuck root tea?"

"No thanks," I said, remembering the rancid brew from the last time.

"No trouble," he said. "It'll only take a minute."

"No, really. Please go on."

"Well," he said, tapping her picture thoughtfully. "She knew things about electricity, mon. White man's demon. I think she took some night classes or something. Or got it from books. However she come by it, she knew it well, and how to use it. She had a little seance room over on 3rd Street. It was wired every which way. She had these buttons at her feet, and she could turn off lights and make ghosts appear like nobody's business. She even wired up the seats, so her clients could get a mild zap when things started appearing. Not enough to hurt them, just to get make them real nervous, fidgety like. One time an old widow woman knocked a glass of water over on her lap and almost got electrocuted. Scary stuff."

"So?"

"I quit, mon. Like your Father Jack says, I can be as phony as a seven-dollar bill. But there are rules, mon. There are definitely rules. I prefer the old ways."

"On that point, at least," I nodded, "I'm with you."

"Brothers," he smiled. "I knew it the first time you came in here with Jack the Black."

"I've got a few more things to show you."

"Sure you don't want some tea?"

"Well—"

"I'll make it weaker this time, just for you, mon."

"You got any Lipton?"

He laughed loud and wide. "Sure, mon. Come into duh back, and we'll pretend we're British."

"Lipton isn't British."

"Neither am I, mon."

"True," I said as he parted the beaded curtain.

73

I THOUGHT I COULD FIND IT. And I did. In fact, I found several things at Chapel Hill, some of which I wasn't even looking for.

It was about one o'clock when I parked the Jeep under the avocado tree in the dirt parking lot beneath the mission chapel. Cane in hand, I trudged up the sandy path and made my way around the crumbling building.

In the dirt square with the covered well and that dreaded olive press, I saw Roberto Guadalupe and another man arguing. The other fellow was obviously a geek. The plastic pocket protector in his short-sleeve shirt said, B&B'S FINE LIQUORS: QUALITY AND QUANTITY. It was the quantity that was in dispute.

"Look, Mr. Guadalupe," the nerd was saying, pointing to a piece of paper in his hand. "Fifty cases is fifty cases."

"The archbishop," countered Roberto, "he likes his vodka. Sure. Fine. Marsha Dukes, the archbishop's secretary, she proposes that it would be a nice touch to have a fountain of vodka next to the fountain of champagne. Fine. Cheryl Farnsworth, the planning director, agrees. Fine. She orders five cases? Again, fine. Ten? Too much, but okay, fine. But fifty? She's a smart lady. She not gonna order fifty cases when half that would be twice what we need. Señor, what are we going to do with fifty cases of vodka?"

Ah, I thought. So that's what Dr. Yomtov was talking about at the hospital. Anyone can have a fountain of gushing champagne at a posh affair, but in the Archdiocese of Los Angeles "the wodka vill flow." What the hey, or as Dr. Yomtov would say, "Vot dah hay."

"That's your affair," the dweeb was squeaking, waving his precious piece of paper. "The purchase order says fifty, and we delivered fifty. It was special-order stuff. What am I gonna do with it?"

"I'll tell you what you can do with it—" Just then Roberto noticed me. "Oh, Señor Feeney. Can I help you?"

"Just looking around," I said nonchalantly. "Don't mind me."

As I wandered past the space-egg pay phone and on into the wilderness, the two men continued to disagree to agree. My destination: the north wall of the estate.

I passed through a dense grove of figs on the far side of the chapel and found a path that veered off to the left, worn more by weather than human feet. That brought me to the west wall. I turned right and followed the ancient adobe barrier until I reached the northwest corner of the estate.

Success: the north wall. Mrs. Magillicuddy had said that her husband had once found a secret hole there behind the eucalyptus trees. The trees, of course, were on the outside of the wall, and the inside was a steep slope crawling with junipers, holly, wild roses, bougainvillaea, kumquats, a plethora of California cactuses, and a tangle of what grapevines become when not tended for two hundred years. So, rather than try to find a crack hidden behind all that prickly shrubbery, I started at the northwest corner of the enclosure and simply meandered eastward, thirty or so feet from the wall, scanning the ground for any sign of an occasionally-used footpath.

About halfway across the estate, I found it.

I almost walked right by it, crossing as it did my heading at such an oblique angle that I at first mistook it for my own footsteps in the grass.

Once I knew what to look for in terms of width and weight of stride, I retraced the footpath back to the wall and determined that it emerged from a leafy thicket between two pomegranate trees. Beyond the wall I could see the entangled tops of three enormous eucalyptuses. Though there were dozens more along the wall, I thought I could recognize their shape if I needed to find them again.

Having found the source of the path, I proceeded to follow it southward, swerving this way and that around fig trees, apple trees, natural boulders and dazzling clusters of birds of paradise. After a while the landscape became dotted, then increasingly cluttered, with oak trees. I found myself trudging over a crunchy blanket of accumulated leaves. Soon the branches closed in above my head. About a hundred yards into the forest, by a trick of unexpected shade and the proliferation of dank woodsy undergrowth, I lost the path.

From that point on, it was a "needle in a haystack" kind of thing.

But I did not give up.

I had something better than a homing beacon. I had something better than a divining rod tuned to "Magillicuddy." I had something better than a road map, a CB radio, or an encounter with a local who knew the way.

I had St. Anthony of Padua.

So, having stilled myself and made the Sign of the Cross, I offered an Our Father, three Hail Mary's, and a Glory Be to the saint with the famous tongue. No sooner had I crossed myself in conclusion and pulled out a handkerchief with which to blow my nose, than a gust of warm wind puffed toward me out of the south and buffeted my face. Fluttering in that breeze was an orange butterfly with brown spots and highlights of fluorescent turquoise. Despite all its efforts to pump its way elsewhere, it came directly at my face. This wouldn't have been a big deal, except the sudden motion startled me. In my alarm, I threw up my hands to protect my eyes, forgetting that I was still clutching my cane. The handle conked me on the forehead, stunning me for a moment. It didn't help my self-confidence quotient one bit. At the same time, the cane's tip smacked a low-hanging branch, loosening a tiny clump of bright green lichen, which was instantly picked up by the same breeze that had delivered the butterfly.

The impression I got was of a brightly colored, multi-legged spider hurling right at me.

I freaked, lost my balance, stumbled backwards over a protruding root, performed several inspirational airborne dance routines which demonstrated the principle of gravity in a sylvan setting, and alighted on my posterior. The ground on which I landed was sloped, and the blanket of dead leaves draped upon it broke my fall. But it also gave way under my weight.

Somewhat perplexed, I rolled over and over in an avalanche of tumbling leaves, whirling twigs, damp mulch, decayed plant matter, dirt, and whatever settles on or lives on whatever settles on the floor of an oak forest. After a few thrilling heartbeats of this stirring activity, I came to a belly-flop stop between the splayed roots of a huge tree.

Unhurt, except for my pride and my persnickety spine, I managed to get to my feet with the help of my cane and the use of many readily available and conveniently located handholds on the roots and trunk of the tree. My handkerchief miraculously still in my hand, I proceeded to wipe biological debris from my face. Somehow, as I was dabbing the hollows of my eyes, the same breeze which instigated these events snatched the cloth out of my hand and whisked it around to the other side of the tree trunk. Irked, I climbed over the formidable roots in search of it. I found the handkerchief snagged on a clothes hanger which was dangling from a branch of this same tree. It was one of several hangers, some empty, some bearing skirts and blouses and sweaters and the like.

"Thank-you, St. Anthony," I said aloud, surveying Mrs. Magillicuddy's current address. She wasn't there, and considering the distance from St. Philomena's to this place, I didn't expect otherwise. The point was to establish where we could find her if we needed her.

It was actually a marvelous, though penitentially simple, abode. Aside from the shelter of the dense branches overhead, the bole of the tree was hollowed out on that side, no doubt by a fire which had occurred centuries ago—perhaps before the arrival of Padre Alonso Miranda and Father Jean Pierre de Chantal. This provided protection from wind and rain. I was careful not to disturb anything in the camp, but I could see bedding and blankets stored inside the hollow. A few feet from the tree, a couple of adobe bricks, no doubt from the mission ruins, served as the sides of a crude stove.

Black and gray ashes, cold but recent, lay between. A hubcap laid on top served as a grill, and nearby was a kettle, saucepan, and skillet, all hanging by their handles from the tender branches of an oak sapling.

No doubt about it, this was the Casa de Cuddy.

That settled, I looked around to get my bearings. The way I figured it, the faerie meadow was due west, between me and the mission chapel. Brushing dry oak leaves from my arms and shoulders, I trudged off in that direction.

A short while later, the trees parted and I was standing on the edge of the sanctuary that had imparted such feelings of profound peace the day before. Unfortunately, serenity was not to be mine this time around. I found the meadow curiously unsettling, and that in itself was ominous, considering the basic beauty of the place. Convinced as I was that unholy ceremonies had been celebrated around the ancient stump, the gently waving grasses took on a vicious, sinister air. There was no way I could rest in such a place, wondering if someone was watching, and not necessarily Mrs. Magillicuddy.

My chest tight with suspicion, I skirted the edge of the meadow, looking for signs of another footpath. On the western side I came to a place where the meadow grass gave way to sage and chaparral. Here was the likely source of Mrs. Magillicuddy's 'periwinkies.' I found a place where the flora was somewhat flattened, no doubt by the less-than-weightless feet of flagitious faeries. With a shiver, I elected to follow that very footpath in the direction of La Chapelle de Saint Jean Baptiste, vowing to sprinkle my shoes with holy water when I got back to St. Philomena's.

As I approached the rear of the crumbling chapel, I saw what appeared to be part of an abandoned stable. It was there that I found the next interesting thing. I never would have imagined, nor would it have ever occurred to me to imagine, what fifty cases of vodka looked like, piled up in a make-shift storage area. PRODUCT OF SCANDINAVIA, proclaimed the side of each carton. Curious, I pried up one of the cardboard lids and hefted one of the bottles, amazed. These cartons did not contain hand-sized wino flasks, nor were they the sort of bottles found on the mirrored shelves in bars. No, these were great, big bottles—the kind a ladder-climbing nephew buys his rich uncle to impress him with his gratitude, largesse, and bravura.

"Dr. Yomtov," was all I could think to say, "must've prayed very hard for this."

A few feet from this giant mountain of imported vodka squatted a mole hill of local champagne. I counted two dozen cases. Between the cubic mounts lay two multi-tiered stainless steel boy-we're-gonna-impress-your-socks-flat-off liquor fountains. Three days hence, these would be the center of attention at the dedication ceremony—at least, for some of the people in attendance. I had to admit that Marsha and Cheryl had a delightful flair for the grandiose. The archbishop would be pleased. Dr. Yomtov would be even more pleased. For now, the silent fountains were just big, empty kitchen utensils.

Behind the fountains, and between the mounds of liquor, I caught sight of more boxes back in the shadows. I might not have noticed them, except they were mostly red, and much more oblong than all the other cartons. The words LIZARD KING PYROTECHNICAL SUPPLIES and CAUTION: EXTREMELY FLAMMABLE were emblazoned in yellow letters on every side, along with the redundant message: KEEP AWAY FROM FIRE.

"Fireworks?" I said aloud. I didn't know the dedication ceremony would go that late. Nor did it seem wise to set off skyrockets so near those dry, untended woods. Perhaps the plan was to shoot them off over the lake—now that would make for some nice photographs. Surely Cheryl was bright enough to have figured that out.

I waved my hand in mute wonderment and continued my Jeep-ward trek.

When I rounded the building and crossed the dirt square where Roberto Guadalupe and the dweeb from B&B's had been arguing, I found the altercation concluded. The geek was nowhere in sight. Roberto waved from the telephone booth as I walked by. He still looked angry.

"I will not be held responsible for this," he barked into the receiver. "No, it is not my doing."

"Nonetheless," I said a few minutes later as I climbed into the Jeep. "Thanks again, St. Anthony."

74

"YOU HAVE BEEN BUSY," said Father Baptist, his cheeks bulging with Millie's Irish stew. In his effort to please our dear housekeeper, his words came out more like, "You huff bim bibby," but what the hey. He's a priest, so I'll clean up his act.

"Yes, I have," I said. It came out more like, "Yesh aw hob." Men talk.

"There's more," bellowed Millie in true form, ladling out another portion for each of us. At long last, she was on top of things again. "It's amazing how a man can get hungry just sleeping, but God works in mysterious ways."

"That He does," nodded Father, tearing off a chunk from a home-baked loaf of sour dough. "So let's have it, Martin."

Meekly, I looked up at Millie for the "go ahead." The important things being settled to her satisfaction, she nodded graciously and headed back through her domain.

"The pepper please, Father. Before visiting the woods on Chapel Hill, I had an interesting chat with your friend Guillaume."

"Willie? Whatever about?"

I pointed at the copy of the *Weekly Ecto* at my elbow. " I wanted to see if he knew anything about our dear Starfire."

"Did he?"

"Yes, indeed. He worked with her for a brief time when she called herself Esther of Ether. Phony seances. And get this: in addition to all her other talents, she's an electronics wizard, or kilowatt sorceress, or whatever."

"The butter, please, Martin. Indeed. How so?"

"She had her seance room wired with buttons at her toes, mood lights, holographic ghosts, the whole shebang. She even wired her clients' chairs so they'd get a mild jolt when the shenanigans began. Just enough to get them jittery. You follow me?"

"The salt, Martin. So what do you conclude from all this?"

"Isn't it obvious?"

"You tell me."

"She knows how to hook up wiring, switches, you name it. Surely she could have arranged the deadly display at St. Barbara's."

"More bread?"

"Father, aren't you listening?"

"I'm all ears. Well, mostly mouth at the moment, but whatever part of me isn't chewing or swallowing is at your disposal."

"You don't sound impressed."

"Oh I am, Martin. I am."

"And this, added to the fact that we now know that Bishops Silverspur, Ravenshorst, Mgumba, and Brassorie were in the habit of frolicking in the 'altogether' with Marsha Dukes, Madeline Sugarman, Sister Vickers, and Stephanie Fury—*and* Ambuliella Beryl Smith, also known as Starfire, waving her magic wand—not to mention that hyssop grows wild there; and all of the above had a habit of tracking it all over the place. Well, there you have it."

"Hm. There is all that."

"Yes, there is."

"I wonder who Bishop Brassorie brought to the dance—the man in black. Mrs. Magillicuddy said the women stopped their dance?"

"Don't know," I shrugged.

"Another mystery. Ah well, what's one more?" He scratched his temple thoughtfully. "What else did you show Willie?"

I drew a photograph out of the envelope. "The completed witching quilt."

"And what light did he shed on that?"

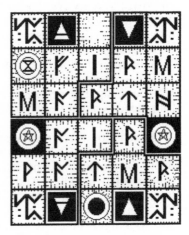

"Much, and not so much. He indicated that, in the quilting tradition as he understands it, the empty space is the focus, but we already knew that. The pentagrams go without saying, but you've got a different slant on them, too. The black dot in a circle at the bottom center he called 'very bod mojo, mon.' The dot is 'dah eye of dah serpent,' the lens through which the witch guides his intention. The circle around it, he called 'muy mucho bod mojo.' Apparently some witches consider a circle around a symbol to be an omen of sacrifice. But what kind of sacrifice, and how extreme, without knowing the particular witch, he couldn't say."

"And the double-circled X in the upper left?" asked Father. "Everything else on the quilt is either centered or balanced, but that X is off to the side without counterpart. It breaks the symmetry of the entire quilt."

"That, he didn't know. Roman numeral for 'ten.' Maybe it's a stylized hourglass, the sand of fate dribbling away and all that. Maybe it's just filler—the word 'fire' is the only word that's made up of an even number of letters, so it's offset on the quilt."

"No," said Father, setting down his fork. "I don't think so. Our murderer is a fiend for details. That X means something, something significant. And there's something else that doesn't add up."

"What's that?"

"The numbers on the knives, remember? Thirty-six, seventy-two, seventy-two and a hundred and eight. Those numbers hold a key to something, and it's almost on the tip of my tongue, but it just doesn't come."

"Anything else?"

"Yes, the other numbers are wrong."

"What other numbers?"

"Count up the people involved. Four dead bishops plus four dead women plus Starfire. That's nine. Covens always consist of thirteen."

"Monsignor Havermeyer should have been one."

"Except the murderer, who knows so much about everyone's movements and habits, probably knew he'd be wearing rubber-soled sandals. And Mrs. Magillicuddy didn't identify him, did she? And though Monsignor Goolgol also met with the 'faeries,' he wasn't part of the plan, apparently. No, we're still looking at nine. Nine intended, nine dead."

"Didn't Starfire say something about 'Pentoven Magick'? Five?"

"Where are the fives in this quilt? Four elements. Four men, four women. Plus the odd witch. There's still something missing."

"I see what you mean, though I don't see what you mean."

"So do I, and neither do I."

"That's what I like," I said, wiping my mouth with my napkin. "Clarity."

"What else have you got in that envelope?"

"Oh," I said, starting to spill the rest of the contents, "just some newspaper clippings Wanda Hemmingway gave me earlier from an old rock concert. Jymmy Thinggob's last guitar solo. Apparently, he—"

"Dessert," announced Millie.

I shoved the clippings back in the envelope and snatched up my spoon.

Father grabbed his.

"Ready," we said together.

Monday, June Nineteenth

Feast Day of Saints Gervase and Protase, Martyrs (165 AD), and Saint Juliana Falconieri, Virgin (1340 AD)

75

"READY," EXCLAIMED LIEUTENANT TAPER, gulping down his third cup of coffee with gusto. "Wits restored, warrants in pocket, we're off."

"A magnificent breakfast," said Father, tossing his napkin on the table.

"Thanks to Mrs. Taper," smiled Millie, "and her kind generosity."

"And thank-you, Sergeant," I said, grabbing my cane, "for the excellent Java. Isn't that what the classic movie detectives called it?"

"A generic term for everything hot, dark, and caffeinated," beamed Wickes, brimming with knowledge, draining his cup. "This was actually 'Kona.'"

"Whatever it was," said Father, "I'm ready for anything."

And anything it was.

First we paid a visit to Bishop Brassorie's plush residence at St. Philip's. Nothing new to report there. The place still reeked of Jägermeister.

But back down the stairs, through the botanical gardens, and down a long hallway awaited the private quarters of Sister Charlene Vickers, recently deceased.

"Who or what is that supposed to be?" asked Taper, pausing at a large oil painting over the electric fireplace.

"Diana 'knowing' Cernunnos," said Father, shaking his head.

"No wonder the woman developed that perpetual squint," remarked the gardener. "Looking at that every night would give anyone Goolgol eyes."

"Probably did," said Wickes, examining a horn-shaped cigarette lighter on an end table. He nudged it with the top of his gold pen. "This thing's engraved. You know anyone else named Denzil Fedisck Goolgol? I'll check the report from last week and see if the lab boys lifted any prints from it."

"Shoes," said Father. "I want to see her shoes."

He made for the bedroom and rummaged around in the closet, Taper looking over his shoulder.

"Anything?" asked the lieutenant.

"Yes," said Father, producing several pairs of shoes. "Hyssop for sure on this pair. And there's a bit of clay on this one. Only a chemical analysis can tell us if it's from the infamous grave."

"Remember the sample you found last week?" asked Wickes, nudging a wood-carved statue of a buxom nymph on the night stand. "At the front door?"

"I do," considered Father.

"That places her at the scene of Silverspur's murder," said the gardener.

"Not necessarily," said Wickes. "She and a lot of others were at the grave site for Bishop Brassorie's funeral. Remember we also found clay in Archbishop Fulbright's office."

"But Father Baptist found the clay near the doorstep here at St. Philip's two days before that," countered the gardener. "So I repeat, she was at the scene of Silverspur's murder."

"But Silverspur was murdered," Taper paused to calculate, "seven days before that. She had a whole week in which to get that stuff on her heel."

"Yes," said Father, thoughtfully rubbing a bit of clay between thumb and forefinger. "There is that. The trail is growing cold."

"Right," said Wickes, opening a drawer with his handkerchief. "Hello, what's this?" With his pen, he scooped up something dangling on the end of a stainless steel chain. It was a pendant of some sort, silvery and shiny. The beveled edges caught the light in a peculiar way, hinting at colors that weren't really there.

"A 'P'?" suggested Taper.

"Or a broken 'A'?" suggested the gardener.

"The style is familiar," said Father Baptist. He looked at me. "Where have we seen something like this before?"

"Cheryl wears something like it," I said, perhaps a bit reluctantly. "Different design but same technique. But hers is made of gold. This looks like silver, or maybe pewter."

"But made by the same hand, you think?" said Father.

"I'm no expert," I said. "But I'd say the ladies shopped at the same tinsmith's."

"Or had a mutual friend who did," said Father.

"We'd better shove off," said Taper. "We've got a lot more stops to make."

76

AND A LOT MORE STOPS WE MADE. By late afternoon we had explored many a closet and sifted through numerous underwear drawers.

At three-thirty we stopped for coffee injections and napkin analysis at a little slop-stop called "Goober's." By "napkin analysis" I mean we were huddled around one of those little wobbly tables, listing our findings on recycled paper napkins. Mine looked something like this:

Subject	Hyssop	Clay	Pendant
Bishop Brassorie	√	√ (at front door of residence, not in personal rooms)	
Bishop Silverspur	√		
Bishop Mgumba	√		
Bishop Ravenshorst	√		
Sister "S" Vickers	√	√	√
Madeline Sugarman	√	√	√
Stephanie Fury	√	√	√
Marsha Dukes	√	√	√

"Looks to me," said Wickes, "like everyone on this list visited that meadow on Chapel Hill."

"And," said Taper, "that the four women all visited Bishop Brassorie's grave. But whether that was from the funeral on June tenth, or the murder of Bishop Silverspur on June first, we've no way of knowing."

"Except for Sister Vickers," said Father Baptist. "She tracked clay into St. Philip's several days before Bishop Brassorie's first funeral. Don't forget that."

"It would also seem," said Taper, "that the four ladies wore, or were in possession, of similar pendants."

"If they were followers of Starfire," said Father, "then the pendants might be the magical symbol of their coven, or 'Pentoven.' I told you gentlemen last week that you must see the back room of Starfire's 'Shop of Shadows.'"

"Let's call it a day for now," said Taper. "The Sergeant and I have to log in all this information at the station, and then cross-reference it with the lab reports. We'll explore 'The Shop' tomorrow."

"'Tomorrow and tomorrow and tomorrow,'" quoth the gardener.

"I don't suppose Chief Billowack is losing any sleep," said Father, "over the fact that Starfire is still at large."

"We've got bulletins out on her," said Taper. "She'll turn up."

"At least," said Wickes, doodling on a fresh napkin, "we can slow down for a while. The string of murders is over."

"You're sure of that," said Father.

"It's like I said," beamed Wickes, admiring his handiwork. "Four triangles make a square."

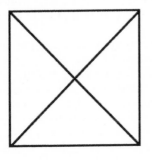

"May I take this?" asked Father.

"What for?"

"Just to keep my file complete. Perhaps you'd like to sign and date it?"

"Some day," said the gardener, "it may hang in the Museum of Unsolvable Murders and the Sleuths that Solved Them. I think it's in London."

"Go on," smiled Wickes.

Father folded the impressive napkin and tucked it into one of the folds in his cassock. "You never know."

77

"JOEL," SAID FATHER BAPTIST SOLEMNLY, "you must gather all your courage."

"Sure," said the lad, seated at the institutional table, shoulders slumped and hands fidgeting. He hadn't shaved in several days and his beard was struggling to reclaim his face. "Sure thing, Father."

Father was seated at the table, facing Joel. I was sitting at the end, watching them both.

"I haven't much time," said Father. "It took all my powers of persuasion, and calling in a few favors, to get in to see you. Chief Billowack—"

Joel grimaced.

"—only let us in here on three conditions. First, that we be brief. Second, that I persuade the Tumblars to cease their vigil on the front steps."

"They're out there?" asked Joel, brightening. It wasn't much of a glimmer, but in this gray place it was almost brilliant.

"Didn't you know they'd rally around their captured comrade?" frowned Father.

"I guess I should have known," admitted Joel.

"They've been hounding the authorities for days, demanding the chance to see you. So take heart. You have friends. Third, I have promised to persuade the Tumblars to stop giving statements to Jacco Babs, a stipulation with which I fully concur. But as to the first point, I must press on. I have some questions."

"Shoot," said Joel, squaring his shoulders bravely.

"I need to know why you had Arthur drop you off at St. Barbara's Chapel the other afternoon."

"Oh that. I was just curious. Electronics, technology. I read about it in the paper. I wanted to see how they did it."

"That's what Arthur said."

"That's the truth. I may be a seminarian—or not, I'm not sure anymore—but wiring and lighting, that I know. I was just looking around."

"You got a good look at everything?"

"Until the technicians shooed me away, like I was gonna break something."

"Good." Father produced a glossy from some hidden pocket in the folds of his cassock. "Lieutenant Taper, God bless him, provided me with this photograph. Do you recognize it?"

From where I sat, it looked like a picture of a cigar box that had been smoked, stogies and all.

Joel rippled his forehead in concentration. "Yes, I think so. What is it?"

"You tell me."

"Hell if—I mean, I don't know. If it's what I think it is, I saw it in the sanctuary near the big golden Crucifix. It was on the floor amidst all kinds of cables. There were all these wires going into it."

"There were lots of boxes on the floor," said Father. "Transformers, relays, junction boxes. What's so special about this one?"

Joel swallowed. "See this smaller box mounted the side? It has some push buttons on it. They were illuminated at the time. They're all melted together in this picture, but they struck me as funny."

"Why?"

"Well, it was obviously a pager, though considerably modified. This one has a little readout at the top that displays the number of the person that just called you. It's all melted and twisted here, but I saw it clearly in the chapel under those high-intensity video camera lamps. I was wondering why there was a pager bolted onto this larger box in the middle of all that other stuff."

"Could it have been part of some kind of communications system for the technicians?" asked the gardener.

"Then what was it doing on the floor?" asked Joel. "Half-buried in all those wires, and mounted on this box?"

"You're sure it's a pager," said Father.

"I was thinking of buying one for my dad's birthday next month and was checking them out at the stores. This is one of the more expensive models. I think I left a brochure in my room at St. Philomena's."

Father picked up the photo, eyed it carefully, and slipped it back inside his cassock. "We have to go, Joel. But before we do, I must tell you that I think Chief Billowack has convinced the DA to press charges."

"No," said Joel, his shoulders slipping. "This can't be happening."

"But it is," said Father. "You must be strong. I saw your father outside and I'm going to tell him what a brave man you are."

"My father?" Joel gasped. "He's here? I don't want him to see me, not like this."

"He knows that, and I doubt they'll let him in anyway." Father reached into his cassock and produced a small holy card. "This is St. George, Patron Saint of Chivalry. He spent time in worse prisons than this, and with less hope of release. Commit yourself to his protection."

"Sure," said Joel weakly, accepting the card with quivering fingers. "Sure. I'll do that." He didn't sound convinced.

"I also must tell you that it concerns me greatly that the murderer knows you."

"Me?"

"Or at least enough about you to steal your father's truck and place his toolbox in plain sight so that you would investigate and be implicated."

"This is getting too weird," sighed Joel. "If the murderer knows me, then I know the murderer."

"Perhaps," said Father. "Perhaps not. Certainly not in the same way. There are many mysteries in this conundrum, and I've yet to sort them all out."

"Too weird," mumbled Joel.

"I swear to you," said Father, "on my honor as a priest, that you will not be in this place for long. I will clear your good name and reputation, and soon. For the moment, your incarceration might serve to make the murderer confident in his strategy. In any case, I will not rest until I bring him to justice."

Sensing the meeting was over, I began to rise.

"You go ahead, Martin," said Father, producing a stole from one of his many pockets, unraveling it, and hanging it around his neck. "Joel and I need a couple more minutes in private."

"Sure thing," I said, knocking on the door for the guard outside to let me pass. "I'll go see if the Tumblars have ceased and desisted yet."

78

"WHAT'S THAT YOU'RE READING?" asked Father Baptist, holding a wooden match to the bowl of his pipe and sucking deeply.

"St. Thomas More," I said, showing him the cover. *"The Sadness of Christ."*

It was eleven-thirty that night. Tired as we were, we couldn't summon the energy to seek out our rooms. So we compromised with weariness by reading in the study, me in my usual chair and Father behind his desk.

"You know what gets me about St. Thomas?" I said. "If I were locked away in the Tower of London, waiting for my head to be chopped off, I'd be writing volumes on what a scoundrel King Henry VIII was."

"I doubt Thomas Cromwell would have permitted you the use of your typewriter," mused Father.

"Then I'd've written it with charcoal," I declared, "on the very wall. 'HARRY IS A FINK!' in three-foot letters. But what does Sir Thomas write? Listen to this."

I wish that sometime we would make a special effort, right after finishing our prayers, to run over in our minds the whole sequence of time we spent praying. What follies will we see there? How much absurdity and sometimes even foulness will we catch sight of? Indeed, we will be amazed that it was at all possible for our minds to dissipate themselves in such a short time among so many places at such great distance from each other, among so many different affairs, such various, such manifold, such idle pursuits. For if someone, just as an experiment, should make a determined effort to make his mind touch upon as many and as diverse objects as possible, I hardly think that in such a short time he could run through such disparate and numerous topics as the mind, left to its own devices, ranges through while the mouth negligently mumbles through the hours of the office and other much-used prayers.

I closed the book. "See what I mean? His time's running out, the executioner is sharpening his ax, and Thomas More is concerned with his inability to concentrate when he prays."

"He did have his priorities," noted Father. "Besides, Martin, don't forget that he had probably come to terms with his fate. I suspect that if you were in the same position—let us hope not, but these things have a way of 'just happening' in the scheme of things—but were you to find yourself similarly disposed, I have a hunch that you would concern yourself with the Four Last Things rather than waste your time slinging insults at your enemies."

"Don't be too sure."

"Don't you be, either."

"I wonder what Joel's thinking as we speak, now that he's been formally charged with murder."

"I doubt the terror in his mind has coalesced into anything as solid as rational thought just yet. But he'll get through it. He's a Maruppa."

"And I an honorary Tumblar," I added, shifting uncomfortably in my chair. "They told me so in front of the police station. So what are you reading?"

"Oh this," said Father, showing me the cover. "The *Malleus Maleficarum* by Heinrich Kramer and James Sprenger."

"Neither of us seems to go for best sellers."

"This was quite the rage in the 15th century," said Father, blowing a perfect smoke ring. "'The Witches' Hammer,' it was called by its detractors."

"As in 'witches hammering' or 'hammering witches'?"

"It was written at the direction of Pope Innocent VIII. Kramer and Sprenger detailed the evils perpetrated by witches, and exposed as heresy the disbelief in witchcraft."

"You mean that Catholics are required to believe in it?"

Father smiled. "Most Catholics today don't believe in much of anything, I'll grant you. But they certainly did in 1484."

"Hm. Sounds interesting. Maybe when you're through with it—"

The phone rang.

Father Baptist scooped up the receiver. "St. Philomena's. Oh, yes Lieutenant. No, Martin and I are just sitting here reviewing books. What's on your—?"

His face fell.

"When?"

He set down his pipe.

"How?"

"The Witches Hammer" fell to the floor with a thump.

"I see. Thanks for letting me know. You'll keep me aprised of developments. Good night."

He set the receiver down.

"What is it?" asked the gardener.

"Another complication. Monsignor Goolgol is missing."

"Missing."

"A nurse found his bed empty about an hour ago."

"He was strapped down. How did he get loose? Chew through the restraints with his teeth?"

"No," said Father grimly. "The straps were cut, as though with surgical scissors or a very sharp knife."

Tuesday, June Twentieth

Feast Day of Saint Silverius,
60th Pope and Martyr (165 AD), and
Saint Florentina, Abbess (636 AD)

79

"AFTER ALL YOUR POKING AND PRODDING," said Lieutenant Taper as he jimmied the lock, "this had better be worth it."

"It will be," said Father. "I assure you."

The little brass bell, so in tune it was practically hugging itself, tinkled its lively unison as we entered "The Shop of Shadows."

"Oh," I said, looking around at the display cases. Unlike Guillaume du Crane Cristal's sinister fortune untelling salon, Ambuliella Beryl Smith's little shadow shop wasn't shadowy at all. In fact, it was rather cheery, not to mention pristine. Morning sunlight streaming in through the window gave the place a safe, hobby-store kind of ambiance. The crescent moon-shaped neon sign in the window, although turned off and not radiating its usual brilliance in the pink spectrum, nonetheless managed to cast a happy smile shadow on the hardwood floor. I smiled in harmony with it. "So this is what it looks like."

"I thought you said you came in here last week," said Wickes.

"Yes, but I was wearing a disguise at the time." My nostrils itched at the memory. "Glasses this thick. I had such a headache. My job was to amuse Starfire and her Satanist customer over here at the 'pendagrrromz' counter, while Father Baptist ransacked the back room. You remember don't you, Father?"

"I remember your hat," he said, ignoring the display cases and heading for a door behind the cash register. "Gentlemen, this way."

I didn't know exactly what to expect, as Father had been unclear all week about what he had found back there. And as a lot can change in a week, Father did not exactly expect not to find what wasn't back there.

Yes, there was a lot not to find in that back room at "The Shop of Shadows." The pane of frosted glass was no longer in the back door—well, a few shards remained around the edges, but the overall effect was one of absence. The rows of whatever had been on the shelves over the work table were gone, and whatever had been on the work table itself along with them. The drawers yawned in various degrees of openness, all of them empty. There were a couple of small wooden boxes set against the wall, but they were filled with nothing.

Something that wasn't not there, and which therefore caught my attention, was a heap of fine sand in the corner, maybe eight inches high and several feet around.

"Whoops," said Wickes, surveying the lack of evidence with his hands on his hips. "Nobody touch anything. We'll get a crew here to dust for fingerprints."

"Sorry, Jack," said Taper, nudging one of the empty wooden boxes with his toe. "You told us how many days ago—"

"That doesn't matter now," said Father, stooping to examine that sand in the corner. "What wasn't done, wasn't done. Now you only have my word for it."

"What can I say?" said Taper.

"Nothing," said Father. "This sand was in those wooden boxes. There were tanks of propane over there, and a small smelter on the table, ingots of various metals on this shelf, jeweler's tools and modeling clay on that one."

"Molds?" asked Taper, examining the wooden boxes. "These are molds?"

"So Starfire makes her own jewelry," said Wickes. "So?"

"And 'pendagrrromz,'" said the gardener. "Don't forget her 'pendagrrromz.'"

"I repeat: so?"

"And knives," said Father.

"You mean—!?" said the cops and myself together, sort of like a Greek chorus.

"No," said Father, "I saw no exact replicas of the little scimitars our murderer is so fond of, but there is this matter of

style we've been grappling with, which becomes highly sub-
jective. I couldn't prove, just by describing the items I saw
here last week, that Starfire made the scimitars that have been
found at the crime scenes. Nor could I swear that the pendants found among the effects of the deceased women are all
Starfire's handiwork. The lab boys might have been able to
match alloy formulae, or find some kind of microscopic
similarity between them—'sculpture ballistics,' I don't know.
But now, all we have is my opinion, based on memory."

"Anything else that you wanted us to see?" asked Taper
meekly—well, "cop" meekly, which isn't all that meek.

"Several items," said Father. "Nothing conclusive. All of
it now rendered hearsay. I'd say we may as well forget it, unless your lab boys find something interesting."

"Kind of an odd burglary, isn't it?" I asked, eyeing the
broken glass on the floor near the back door. "The thief
took some tools, equipment, and supplies for making metal
ornaments. He apparently took some of those ornaments
from this back room. But as far as I could tell, nothing was
disturbed in the front room."

"No," said Taper, "I don't think anything was."

"Then it would seem," said Father, "that this burglary was
not so much a matter of loot, as a matter of cleaning out this
room."

"Of knives and such," said Wickes.

"And who knows what else," said Father. "I suggest you
step up your efforts to find Starfire, Lieutenant. Perhaps
there's someone, one of the local shopkeepers, perhaps, who
can tell us more about what was back here."

"Perhaps we should drop in on Cheryl Farnsworth," said
Taper, "and see how she's getting along, now that she's out
of the hospital."

"Yeah," said Wickes. "Maybe she can shed some light on
these pendants."

"Miss Farnsworth's pendant is made of gold," I reminded
them. "Pewter was Starfire's specialty. Just look in the display cases out front. There's no gold anywhere."

"The style, Martin," said Father, "the style."

"What's this?" Taper was dislodging something from a
protruding nail on the edge of the work table. "Part of a
strap."

"Looks familiar," said Father. "Martin?"

"I don't know."

"Remember when we last saw Monsignor Goolgol?" asked Father. "Yes, see here along the edge. 'G-S-H.' Good Samaritan Hospital."

"You think Monsignor Goolgol did this?" asked Wickes.

"Perhaps," said Father. "Though it would seem strange that he would still have his restraints with him."

"This strap is clearly from the hospital he escaped from last night," said Wickes. "How else would it have gotten here?"

"Good question," said Father.

"Hey," I said, looking behind the door through which we had entered the room. There was something rolled up and leaning in the corner. "What's this? Some sort of map?"

"Don't touch it," said Taper. "Fingerprints."

"Sure," I said, hands in the air. "Be my guests. You guys are the experts."

I marveled at the way they handled the roll without touching it. They must take special classes or something. Anyway, a minute later, we were all looking at the flattened print, about six feet square.

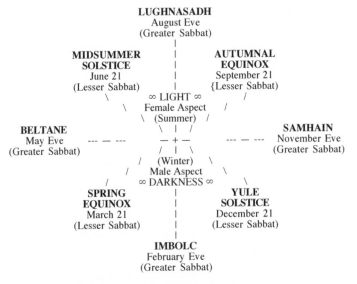

∞∞∞ **THE WICCAN CALENDAR** ∞∞∞

LUGHNASADH
August Eve
(Greater Sabbat)

MIDSUMMER SOLSTICE	**AUTUMNAL EQUINOX**
June 21	September 21
(Lesser Sabbat)	{Lesser Sabbat)

∞ LIGHT ∞
Female Aspect
(Summer)

BELTANE	**SAMHAIN**
May Eve	November Eve
(Greater Sabbat)	(Greater Sabbat)

(Winter)
Male Aspect
∞ DARKNESS ∞

SPRING EQUINOX	**YULE SOLSTICE**
March 21	December 21
(Lesser Sabbat)	(Lesser Sabbat)

IMBOLC
February Eve
(Greater Sabbat)

∞ ∞

"This," noted Father, "was on that wall over there."

"Very interesting," said Taper.

"What's a 'sabbat'?" asked Wickes.

"A distortion of the Hebrew word, 'shabat,' which we like-wise distort in English into 'Sabbath.' Witches call their feast days 'sabbats.'"

"Sort of like Sundays?"

"More like Holy Days of Obligation."

"Hm," said Wickes, "Samhain seems to be their name for our Halloween."

"That's 'Saw-win,'" I corrected him, with an air of patient authority.

"S-A-M," he spelled it out for me. "H-A-I-N."

"I know," I assured him, clasping my hands behind my back and rocking professorially on my heels. "Nonetheless, it is pronounced 'Saw-win'—the old Celtic feast of the dead."

"'Sell-tick,'" he corrected me. "As in Boston Selltics, and like being blessed with a Selltick Cross."

"What do you expect from football players and clergy? It's pronounced 'Kell-tick,' as in 'Celtic harp,' and 'quelling the storm'"

"'Quelling'? Where do you get 'quelling'?"

"It's from the Old English word 'cwellan'—C-W-E-L-L-A-N—notice the hard 'c'—which means 'to kill.' That is, 'cwellan' meant 'to kill,' whereas 'quelling' means 'to allay or subdue.'" I must have been doing some reading in my spare time.

"Okay Bigbrain," said Wickes, pointing to the word "Lughnasadh" at the top of the wiccan calendar. "Pronounce that."

"Easy," I said. "But I'd just be showing off."

80

"IT JUST DOESN'T ADD UP," said Father, seated at his desk in the study. "Why would Monsignor Goolgol break into Starfire's shop? And even if he did, how did he cart off all that heavy equipment? He didn't have a car when he left the hospital. According to the police, his is still parked in the lot at St. Barbara's chapel. He certainly didn't hire a cab and have it wait in the alley while he burglarized the shop."

"How did he cut his straps at the hospital?" I asked. "Maybe he had help."

"But whose?"

"Starfire's?"

"Hmm. Possibly, but why?"

"Maybe she needed help carrying the heavy stuff. We know he was at least on familiar terms with her, uh, 'Pen-oven.'"

"But he wasn't in any condition to help anyone, Martin. You saw him yourself."

"Unless he was faking lunacy, which in his case, wouldn't have been that hard."

Absently, Father reached over the heap of files on his desk for the plaque next to St. Anthony of Padua and St. Thomas More. DO WE WALK IN LEGENDS was teetering on the edge of the desk and threatening to fall.

Just then the phone rang.

As he turned to answer it, he bumped St. Anthony, who knocked into St. Thomas More, who began to topple as well. I lunged from my chair and caught the statue, just as it slipped off the edge of the desk.

"I'll be glad when this is all over," said Father, hand on the receiver as the phone rang a second time. "It will be nice to see the top of my desk again. Hello, St. Philomena's."

I was cradling St. Thomas More, examining him to see if the collision with St. Anthony had left a mark.

"Yes, Your Grace," said Father. "I can be there in, say, a half an hour. May I ask why?"

Having determined that St. Thomas' head had sustained no damage—this time around—I was attempting to return him to his place.

"I see," Father was saying. "Excuse me, Your Grace." He cupped his hand over the mouthpiece. "Martin, what's that?"

"What's what?"

"Those papers—right where you're putting St. Thomas."

"What? Oh, these are just some photostats from some old *Rolling Stone* articles. I put them here over a week ago. The Jymmy Thinggob incident."

"Let me see." I handed them across the desk. He eyed them for a moment and then returned to the phone. "Oh yes, Your Grace, I'm still here."

I could hear the tiny voice of the archbishop buzzing in
Father's ear as he shuffled through the pages. "Yes, I understand—Martin, isn't this a picture of Miss Farnsworth?"

I nodded. Indeed it was. A much younger Cheryl, her red
hair long and straight with a terricloth sweatband around her
forehead. "It was terrible," said the caption. "Poor Jymmy
Thinggob. His best solo ever, and his last."

"Yes, Your Grace, I'll be there. Good-bye."

Father returned the receiver to its cradle, then he looked at
the pages in his hand. "Is this what Wanda Hemmingway was
talking about?"

"Yes," I said. "She was singing in a band called Salvador
Dolly, and Cheryl was the stage manager of Thinggob's
group, Bombing Fluid. It was at a big concert at Algernon
Park, years ago. Something apparently shorted in the wiring.
A similar thing happened to Brian Jones when he was playing
with the Rolling Stones once, though Jones only got knocked
out. Apparently, when Jymmy Thinggob stomped on his
wah-wah pedal— Let's see, Wanda gave me a manila envelope
with some more clippings about it from some other magazines. It's here somewhere."

"Hm," said Father, gingerly setting the pages on the northern side of the slanting chaos on his desk. "I'll have to get
back to it. Right now, I need the use of your typewriter, and
then we have to get to the Chancery Office pronto. Archbishop Fulbright has something important to say."

"About what?"

"We'll know that within the hour."

81

"YOUR GRACE," said Father Baptist as he took his seat at
that huge table in the archbishop's conference room.

"Father Baptist," nodded His Graciousness.

"And Miss Farnsworth," said Father. "You're looking
well, but perhaps a little tired."

"Thank-you," said Cheryl. "I'm still a bit off kilter. The
doctors said I might feel a bit queasy for a few days. Hello,
Mr. Feeney."

I nodded and kept silent.

"When I last spoke with Lieutenant Taper and Sergeant Wickes," said Father, "they were on their way to your apartment. They had some questions to ask you."

"I've been here all morning," she said.

"They'll no doubt catch up with you," said Father.

"Ahem," grunted Archbishop Fulbright. "You remember Mr. Shlomo Brennan and Mr. Guilio Gerezanno, co-counsels for the archdiocese."

"Of course," said Father.

Ah, I thought, the rats have been persuaded to report to the maze for today's experiment. Something's up.

There were a lot of empty chairs. It was unnerving to think that less than two weeks ago they had been filled. But the room seemed anything but empty. Was this to be a conference of ghosts?

"There have been a great many developments since we last met in this room," said the archbishop, rubbing his ring. " I find myself without any auxiliary bishops, and practically no personal staff."

"Indeed," said Father.

"And I must admit that I'm most disappointed in your performance, Father Baptist. I hired you to find Bishop Brassorie's killer. Then things got out of hand, mushrooming into wholesale carnage. And now I have been informed that the police have arrested a young man who you were protecting under your very roof. What do you have to say about that?"

"Much," said Father Baptist, "but I get the distinct impression that first Your Grace has more to say."

"Indeed I do. I had hoped that in procuring your services we could ferret out the culprit while keeping scandal to a minimum. Instead, we find you harboring the murderer at St. Philomena's while attracting undo and unsavory publicity upon yourself, not to mention inflicting immeasurable damage to the ecumenical policies of this archdiocese. My advisors and I find the present situation untenable."

"Your advisors being Mr. Brennan and Mr. Gerezanno."

"And Miss Farnsworth," growled the archbishop. "Not to mention the Papal Nuncio. Oh yes, your activities have aroused the attention of Rome."

Sounds to me, I thought sadly, like what they used to call in Old Testament times "casting lots to select the emissary goat." Leviticus sixteen, most of the chapter.

"I see," said Father evenly. "I discern that what I have to say will not allay the decision that you and your esteemed advisors have obviously already made."

"There is no excuse," barked the archbishop. "You may give your explanation, but there can be no excuse."

"I agree," said Father. "Excuses are futile. As for explanations, I can see that they would fall on on deaf ears."

"You watch your tone," said Mr. Brennan. "We are looking at some heavy liabilities here."

"We were against hiring you in the first place," sniffed Mr. Gerezanno. "The police were perfectly capable of handling the situation without your interference."

"That is why," said Father, "their expert consultant on matters of the occult, one Ambuliella Beryl Smith, recently revealed as the popular witch Starfire, is now one of their principle suspects. But we wouldn't want to clutter the landscape with facts."

"Now see here," snorted the archbishop.

"Nor would we want to consider that one of the deceased auxiliary bishops, Eugene Brassorie by name, was a pedophile, and this fact was known to the archbishop before making the appointment."

"Father Baptist!" barked the archbishop.

"And then, knowing this, the archbishop promised him the post of coadjutor."

"Father!"

"And that all four auxiliary bishops—Silverspur, Brassorie, Mgumba, and Ravenshorst—were fraternizing with witches and attending their covens. And that the ranking theologian of the archdiocese, one Monsignor Denzil Fedisck Goolgol, was likewise involved. And that four women intimately involved in the affairs of these men and the administration of the archdiocese—Madeline Sugarman, Marsha Dukes, Stephanie Fury, and Sister Vickers—were numbered among those same witches.'"

"Father Baptist!!"

"Nor would it enter into your august deliberations," continued Father without skipping a beat, "to consider that the reigning archbishop of Los Angeles has visited the same coven, not far from where we are now sitting."

"How would you know that?" roared Archbishop Fulbright.

"There was a witness," said Father.

I made a sound, something between a cough, a choke, and a gasp. It hurt.

Father Baptist turned and looked at me with those unnerving eyes that seemed to whisper, humble but magnificently, "Considering that I'm about to be driven out into the wilderness, Martin, allow me the opportunity of playing a wild card, a bluff, just to see if my hunch is right." But all he said was, "Are you all right, Martin?"

"Yes," I wheezed. "I'm okay. Thank-you, Father."

"Enough," bellowed the archbishop, jowls quivering ferociously. "Father Baptist, Chief Billowack has informed me that the quilt puzzle left by the murderer is now complete. The string of murders is at an end. The murderer is now in custody and has been duly charged. You are hereby relieved of any and all investigating activities with respect to the matter at hand."

"I am fired?"

"Yes, damn you! To put it bluntly: you—are—fired!!" He pounded the desk three times for emphasis. It was overkill, in this gardener's opinion, but hey, it was his conference room.

"Well," said Father, taking out an envelope from the folds of his cassock. "There is this."

"That photograph will not help you now," hissed His Graciousness. "That incident on the bridge happened long ago, and too much else has gone awry for that to matter any more."

"Oh no," said Father matter-of-factly. "You misunderstand. This is my bill for services rendered to date. I took the liberty of drawing it up when I got your order to come at once. If you check your records you'll see that I have yet to be paid, and our agreement clearly stated that—"

"Out!" hollered Archbishop Fulbright, grabbing the envelope from Father's hand and tearing it up into jagged little bits. "Get out of my sight, and don't ever approach me, not on any pretext, ever again. Do you hear me? Out! Out!! Out!!!"

I gave Cheryl a long, searching look as I followed Father Baptist out of the room, but she was busy examining her palms.

"Well," I said, huffing along side Father as we wound our way down the stairs of power. "That's that."

Father seemed lost in thought.

"The nerve," I mumbled. "Who do they think they are?"

"What's that, Martin?"

"I said, 'Who do they think they are?'"

"Archbishop Fulbright is the Prince of the Church in this archdiocese," said Father. "That's who he is, and long may he reign. As for the others, they may think as they may."

"It's unfair. You did your job, and you did it well."

"Too well," said Father. He swallowed painfully and loud. "That's the problem. Yet, I saw this coming from day one."

"I guess we'll have to return the Jeep to the motor pool."

"I don't see why," said Father. "Martin, if the archbishop's rude actions teach you nothing else, they will serve as a reminder to open envelopes and read the contents before tearing them up."

"I don't understand."

"In addition to my bill, the archbishop destroyed the loan instructions from the motor pool. We've no way of telling when it's to be returned."

"Surely the motor pool will have copies."

"Then we'll simply have to rely on Freddie Furkin, who is now a member of our parish, and whose wife is an active member of the 'Ever-Twangin' Mostly-Saggin' Steel-Pluckers,' to tell us when to bring back the car."

"Ah," I said.

At last we reached the lobby.

"Are you all right, Father?" I asked as we pushed through the big glass doors to the world beyond.

"What do you think?" he sighed.

It was then that I noticed tears in his eyes.

We rode back to St. Philomena's in silence.

82

"I SHOULD THINK," SAID MILLIE spooning enormous helpings of stuffed cabbages onto our plates, "that being fired by the likes of Archbishop Fulbright would give any self-respecting priest a hearty appetite."

"It does," said Father, obediently scooping the stuff into his mouth. "Believe me, I'm famished."

"Me too," I assured her.

"Mrs. Cladusky gave me her recipe," smiled Millie, "in exchange for my 'Surprise des Anges.'"

Father looked at me.

I looked at Father.

"Hmmmm," we intoned together.

We kept shoveling it in, but it tasted like cardboard.

83

T WAS ALMOST MIDNIGHT WHEN, after another futile evening of sleeplessness, I roused myself and went to the study to
read. Finding it vacant, I crept through the rectory until I was
certain that Father Baptist wasn't there. Puzzled, I stole outside, crossed the garden to the church, and tried the sacristy
door. It was open.

The only light inside the building came from the bobbing
flames of votive candles in their racks before statues of the
Blessed Virgin, St. Joseph Her most chaste Spouse, St.
Philomena, St. Rita Patron Saint of the Impossible, St.
Jude—and of course the large candle in the red Sanctuary
Lamp which assured us of Christ's presence in the Tabernacle.

It was by that combination of dim lights that I saw Father
Baptist. For one chilling moment I thought he was
dead—murdered—right there, as he knelt at the Communion
rail before the Blessed Sacrament. But upon creeping closer, I
could hear his slow, regular breathing.

He had slumped down on his haunches, asleep. His cheek
was nesting in the crook of his right elbow and his left hand
was cradled in the valley of a book which lay open on the rail
just inches from his face. It was *Sir Gawain:*

> Now these five series, in sooth, were fastened on this knight,
> and each was knit with another and had no ending,
> but were fixed at five points that failed not at all,
> coincided in no line nor sundered either,
> not ending in any angle anywhere, as I discover,
> wherever the process was put in play or passed to an end.
> Therefore on his shining shield was shaped now this knot,
> royally with red gules upon red gold set:
> this is the pure pentangle as people of learning have taught.

"By the Five Wounds of Christ," Father mumbled in his dreams. "The Five Wounds ..."

As silently as I could—you know how your feet squeak on polished marble when you're trying to be quiet—I went over to the rack of votive candles in front of the Blessed Virgin Mary. Taking a fresh candle, I lit it off of a burning one, and made for the front pew. I set my little reading light on the edge of the seat and pulled my bent copy of St. Thomas More's *The Sadness of Christ* from my hip pocket and began my vigil.

A MEDITATION ON DETACHMENT
While a prisoner in the Tower of London, 1534

Give me the grace, good Lord,
To set the world at nought;
To set my mind upon thee,
And not to hang upon the blast of men's mouths;
To be content to be solitary,
Not to long for worldly company;
Little by little utterly to cast off the world,
And rid my mind of all the business thereof ...

I looked up from the page and pondered the slumped figure of Father Baptist. "Yes Lord," I whispered, "give me the grace. Give *him* the Grace."

To think my greatest enemies my best friends;
    For the brethren of Joseph could never have done him
        so much good with their love and favor
            as they did him with their malice and hatred.

These attitudes are more to be desired of every man
    than all the treasure of all the princes and kings,
        Christian and heathen,
            were it gathered and laid together all upon
                one heap.

Thus I fell asleep, a few feet away from the man who had followed orders, had done his heroic best, and had been cast outside to be devoured by wolves.

Wednesday, June Twenty-first

Feast Day of Saint Terence (1st Century), and Saint Aloysius Gonzaga (1591 AD)

∞ Midsummer Solstice ∞

84

"MILLIE, WHAT'S WRONG?"

I had just come in from tidying up the church after morning Mass.

Earlier, Father had shaken me awake just minutes before the early-bird parishioners began arriving for their daily wee-hours Rosary. My reading candle had melted into a formless blob and expired on the end of the pew. It would take a chisel to pry it loose.

"'Five,'" he had hissed in my face.

"Huh?" I said, trying to dig my tongue out from between my lips and my gums. "Ib's fibe o'clog?"

"No, it's six-fifteen. But it's not 'four.'"

"Nob pore?" I yommed—or rather, yawned, wiping drool from my chin onto my sleeve.

"No, Martin. Not 'four.' 'Five.' *'Five.'*"

"Gotcha," I said, groping for *The Sadness of Christ* which had slipped down beneath the kneeler. "It's definitely 'five,' not 'four,' even though it's six-fifteen."

"Sixteen," corrected Father, glancing at his wristwatch. "Hurry. We have to get ready for Mass."

"At six-thirty," I nodded.

"Right."

I didn't know what we had been talking about.

But I did then and do now know one thing: no matter what's pressing on Father Baptist's mind, you'd never know it from his first "In nomine Patris" to his final "Ite missa est."

When he says Mass—be it four, five, six-fifteen, or six-thirty—nothing exists but himself and the Blessed Trinity. And sometimes I'm not so sure about himself.

Afterwards, Father Baptist preceded me to the rectory while I stayed behind in the church for a few minutes to tidy up. My duties completed, and that candle dislodged from its perch, I headed across the garden and opened the kitchen door.

I knew there was something wrong the moment the sole of my shoe touched the linoleum floor. Some detail was off center, out of place, or subtlely haywire. Perhaps it was the frost on the windows in the middle of summer; or the way all the clocks, timers, and even the hourglass in the rectory were stopped at precisely seven-seventeen; or maybe it was the row of cockroaches that exited hurriedly between my feet toting their luggage in tiny wheelbarrows. Whatever it was, it aroused in my entrails that rarely-awakened primeval inkling known among experts of the genre as the "Uh-oh Response."

Well, I told myself as I planted my other foot on the linoleum and pulled the door closed behind me, whenever anything's amiss I consult Father Baptist to find out what to do about it. But before that, if I want to get a grasp of what's really wrong in the first place, on the universal level, I go to the top woman in the field, the grand dragoness of all that can go wrong, the femme de foreboding:

"Millie," I asked with complete confidence in her abilities in this regard, "what's wrong?"

"He's done it again," she said disgustedly. She stuffed her hands so far down into the pockets of her apron that her fingers broke the seams. "'No time for breakfast,' he says, as if I have nothing better to do than wait around for whenever he thinks it *is* time."

"I'm sure he has his reasons, Millie."

"I'm sure they're not good enough," she said.

"But isn't this your morning off anyway? I should think you'd be glad—"

"Glad? That I'm not needed? I'm a woman, after all. I've got a right to change my mind once in a while. Once in a very great while. But him?"

"Millie, I don't see—" I stopped in my tracks. Aha, I thought. One of those *woman things.*

"It's not that," said Millie to me, sharply. "And I do wish you'd stop thinking such things."

Mind reader.

"And that too."

I opened my mouth. I thought better of it. I closed my mouth.

She pulled her hands out of her stretched-out pockets. "One day he's up, the next he's down. That's it. I give up. I quit."

"Don't do that, Millie. It's just a temporary situation. Let me talk to him."

"You do that," she said, wiping her hands on the shreds of her apron. Then she reached behind her back and untied it. "I'll be around somewhere. Now that I'm unemployed, maybe I'll catch up on some reading. He's in the study. There's coffee on the stove if either of you comes to your senses."

With a feeling of deep foreboding, I entered the study.

Father was seated behind his desk. The four liquor bottles maintained their silent watch over the evidential debris while St. Anthony of Padua and St. Thomas More argued the finer metaphysical points of chaos.

"Martin, I think my switch has finally flipped." He motioned me to a chair.

"Come again?" I said, lowering myself into the indicated sitting vessel.

"I'm sure I've mentioned my old mentor, Chief Mercer. He was my predecessor, my teacher, and my friend. This was way back, when I first transferred into Homicide. He used to describe our work as—"

"'Vacuum cleaner mode,'" I interrupted. "Yes, I remember you talking about him recently. You just keep sucking up clues and storing them in your pouch."

"Until the moment of turnaround," said Father, "when you suddenly realize that you have enough facts to put it all together."

"'Exhaust mode.'"

"That's right. 'Exhaust mode.' My switch is officially flipped."

I sat forward in my chair. "So you're saying you've got it all figured out?"

"Not entirely, but enough to take action. First, I want to see if I can verbalize what's been coalescing in my brain for the past several days. If I can't explain it to you, then I'll never get it past Chief Billowack."

"This should be interesting," I said, sinking back to my original slumped posture. "And to think, me a litmus test for Bulldog Billowack."

"Martin, just this once, try to maintain."

"Maintain what?"

"Just maintain."

"Hm. Okay, it's done. Please proceed."

He ran his fingers through his hair, adjusted his collar, and
iggled around in his squeaky chair for a moment, just to
1ake sure everything was properly settled.

"From the onset," he began, "I have found this to be a
1ost confusing case. I've been involved with serial killers
efore, and I've dealt with a number of murderers who inten-
onally left clues behind, whether out of sheer egomania or
1e desire to be stopped. But this case—" He waved his
ands over the sea of papers. "—involves a mind so twisted,
nd yet so undeniably focused, I am at a loss for words."

I smiled when he said this, not because it was funny, but be-
ause it wasn't really true—not because Father was dishonest,
ut because we all have limits when assessing our own talents.
.s his unofficial chronicler, I knew full well that the one thing
ot lost to him was the grasp of words. I had watched some of
1em emerge from the carriage of my typewriter during the
ree hours, like the morning after Bishop Mgumba was mur-
ered:

```
    "Air," he answered.   "Just a hunch.   Everything

about this killer is perplexing.  His patterns are

explicit and daring, yet convoluted and volatile.

He boldly leaves a blueprint, yet there's an un-

dercurrent of unpredictability in the way he car-

ries out the plan.  There's an underlying flavor

to it all, but it's like a taste on the tongue I

can't quite place ...
```

"Where to begin?" asked Father. "When looking at a
nagnificent tapestry, how can one determine where the first
titch was hooked?"

"I can't imagine."

"Neither can I. So I'll just start—" He snatched up a piec of paper, a napkin in fact, at random. "—with this. Sergean Wickes has expressed his opinion more than once—this is hi drawing in my hand—that if you take the four triangles tha were either carved or burned on the extremities of the dea bishops, you could construct, or rather reconstruct, a square.'

"Four murders," I nodded. "Four triangles, four sides to square. It fits."

"Yes it does," said Father, "if we're talking right triangle Specifically isosceles right triangles."

"It's been a while since I studied geometry, Father. Refres my memory on the myth of the handsome Isosceles and th poisoned pomegranate of his mother, Triangula's, reflec tion."

"Martin."

"I'm maintaining, I'm maintaining."

"An 'isosceles' triangle has two equal sides," explaine Father, "and a 'right' triangle has one angle of 90 degree If you put them both together, you get a triangle with the tw equal sides adjacent to the 90 degree angle. In other word exactly what you get four of if you criss-cross a perfec square."

"As in Sergeant Wickes' diagram."

"Yes." He flipped over the napkin and doodled somethin on the other side, switching between the sharp and dull edge of a "number 2" pencil for the thin and broad strokes. "I he's right, then the murderer's symbolism should run lik this:

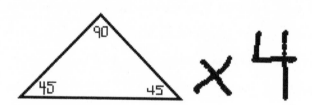

"'90 degrees plus 45 plus 45' all times 4. Follow me s far?"

I looked at it hard. It was hard to maintain and concentrat at the same time. "I think so."

"If we duplicate this '90 plus 45 plus 45' triangle until there are four of them, and we arrange them so that their apexes are touching, we get this." He flipped the napkin over again to reveal the first drawing, to which he added the numbers:

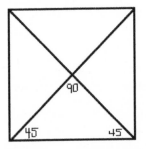

"Right," I said. "Wickes' square made of four triangles."

"Yes," he said, continuing to scribble in numbers, "we do indeed find ourselves with a square, and this supports the conclusion that our murderer's symbolism is based on 'four.' If you add up all the angles you get—" He jotted a column of numbers along the edge of the napkin. "—720. The murderer's final tally of symbolic angles is 720. If that is tenable and true, if 720 has been achieved, then the series of murders is at an end. We still have a murderer to catch, but at least the bloodshed is over."

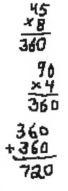

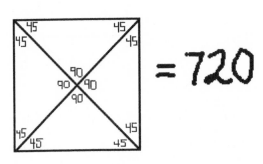

"Tah-dah," I said, sitting back in my chair and folding my arms. "Like I said before, it fits."

"No, it doesn't."

I leaned forward again. "'Scuse me?"

"Look at these photographs from the police files Taper left here the other night. I know, I know, they're ghastly to look at, be we must set our nausea aside for the greater good. Do you see anything consistent with these triangles?"

"They're all triangles."

"Astute."

"The triangles?"

"No, you Martin. Look more closely. The apexes of these triangles are all pointed toward the fingers or toes, out toward the digits."

"You mean the murderer doesn't mean to point them inward to make a square?"

"Give the man a ginger ale. In each case, the apex points out from the body, not inward towards it. If our murderer is one tenth as consistent as I think, then we're not dealing with a square."

"Sure we are," I said, snatching the pencil out of his hand. I scribbled furiously. "Look:

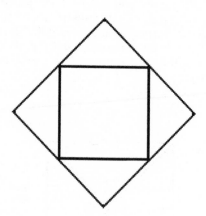

"Four triangles facing out," I said triumphantly, "still make a square."

"Hold the fizz," said Father. "There's a problem."

"Now what?"

"The angles, Martin, the angles. Look at the photographs again. Are the triangles left behind by the murderer right triangles? Do you see any 90 degree angles anywhere?"

Swallowing my rising bile, I examined the photos. "I guess not."

"I know not." He pulled the desk drawer open and began to rummage through the clutter within. After rearranging the contents two or three times, he finally came up with a clear plastic protractor—a semicircular ruler for measuring angles by degrees. This he slammed down on the top photograph and began shoving it this way and that. "I knew it. I knew it."

"You knew what?"

Hastily, he snatched a photocopy of some lab report and turned it over. On this he set the protractor and began drawing another triangle, punctuating it with numbers. Examining his handiwork, he spun it around for me to see. "Wouldn't you say that a more accurate depiction of each of these grisly triangles would look something like this?"

"Hmm," I hmmed. "36 plus 72 plus 72."

"Yes," said Father. "Those are the numbers the murderer had in mind."

I opened my mouth wide. "The knives."

"The knives," nodded Father. "And with them in mind, we've also got to deal with the number 108." Whipping the paper around again, he added that number to his drawing, and then extended one of the descending lines of the triangle. "Now, speculate with me. Use your imagination. Suppose, just suppose that our murderer is not focusing on the number four but on the number five.

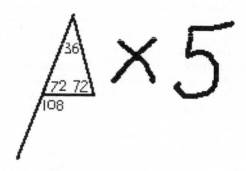

My mouth was still open. "Excuse me, Father. What you've drawn there looks like —"

"The pendants we found among the effects of the deceased women. Yes, Martin."

My mind was spinning. "Where do you get five?"

"How many extremities does the human body have?"

"Let me see," I said, grabbing a sheet of blue paper. It was the computer readout Father had been holding the other night in his room. I started to read it—a short list of telephone numbers—but saw that he was looking at me sternly, so I turned it over and doodled on the back side. "Two arms," I counted as I drew, "two legs, and a head. Five."

"Give the man another ginger ale," said Father.

"I don't see where this is going."

He snatched up the pencil and began extending the lines on his drawing. "Five is the key, Martin. Five times 108 makes a pentagon, a five-sided polygon with five angles of 108 degrees. Five times 36 plus 72 plus 72 gives us five triangles around the pentagon. Now do you see? We're not dealing with a square, we're dealing with—"

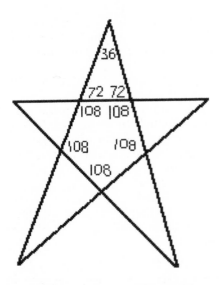

"A pentagram," I whispered, which was hard to do because my mouth was still wide open.

"Bingo," said Father, hastily filling in the numbers. Then e set my stick-figure beside his drawing. "A pentagram."

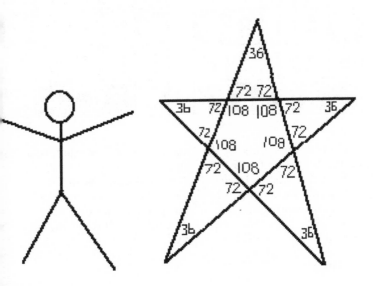

"More numbers to add up," I said, doing some franti
math on the back side of another lab report. "Um, ul
1,440—I think." I double-checked my math. "Yes, 1,440
is."

"Keep that number in mind," said Father. "It may be use
ful later."

"Done," I said, writing it in the palm of my left hand
"And now I remember where we've heard these numbers be
fore. Starfire's lecture. I could swear she talked about th
pentagram as a pentagon surrounded by five triangles, and sh
gave these same degrees."

"Very good, Martin."

"Starfire."

"And now we turn to these," he said, producing the photo
graphs of the completed casting quilt and Sybil Wexler'
computer translation.

"Everything points to the empty square," he said, reaching
for the blue sheet. "Everything."

"We know that," I said, "but what does it mean?"

"I think we can dismiss the notion that our murderer is a
wistful romantic, caught up in popular notions of wicca
spirituality. He—or she—is extremely intelligent, well-in
formed, and incredibly cunning."

"Yes. Er, Father."

"Hm?"

"I notice you've been inserting the feminine pronoun, 'or she,' into your vocabulary again. Are you beginning to suspect someone of the softer sex?"

"I am willing," said Father pensively, "to accept the possibility that a mystery as convoluted as this one may well have sprung from a feminine mind."

"Such as Starfire's."

"Perhaps."

"'Not that random,'" I said.

"What's that?"

"I was thinking of an interchange I had with Ms. Sister Stephanie Veronica Marie Fury out in the garden two weeks ago. It was Archie Goodwin's response to Nero Wolfe's line: 'Women are random clusters of vagaries.'"

"Hm," said Father thoughtfully. "Well, Mr. Wolfe's misogyny aside, and whether our murderer is male or female, we'll dispense with new age drivel. If our murderer doesn't partake of it, neither should we."

"In other words, let us eat meat."

"Precisely."

"If that's the case, I need some coffee. Millie left some on the stove, just before she gave notice. You want some?"

"No," said Father. "But tell Millie, on my honor, I'll be ravenous for dinner."

"I'll tell her," I said over my shoulder. "But no promises."

When I got to the kitchen, I got a whiff of something I'd never smelled there before. Something burning.

"Oh, it's you," said Millie.

I turned and promptly swallowed my tongue.

Millie was seated in the dining nook, cigarette in one hand, a glass of port in the other, and a book between her elbows. "What're you looking at?"

"Oh, nothing, nothing." I went to the cupboard and fumbled for a mug. Wouldn't you know, the first one I grabbed had the words LIFE'S A BITCH AND THEN YOU DIE on the side? I wondered where it had come from as I slipped my hand into a pot holder. "Is this coffee still hot?"

"Is the flame still on under it?"

"Yes."

"Then if it hasn't steamed away, it's hot. If it has, then it's very hot."

I hefted the pot. A thin layer of dangerously concentrated sludge slurped around at the bottom.

"Ah," I said with forced enthusiasm. "There's a tad left."

"It was full when I set it there," growled Millie. "Oh well, it's your stomach."

"Any cream?" I asked.

"No."

"Well, sugar then?"

"Help yourself."

"Thank-you, I will. Er, spoon?"

"Top drawer on the right."

"Ah yes. Here we go." I shoveled in a couple of snowy white mounds and stirred. Then I watched in horror as my spoon dissolved.

Millie crushed her cigarette in a small soup bowl which had been conscripted into service as an ashtray. The butt lay there in a crumpled heap beside two lifeless companions.

"Uh, what're you reading?" I asked, as nonchalantly as I could, which wasn't convincing, but under the circs, what the hey?

"Just something I picked up in the study," said Millie, stuffing another ciggie into her mouth. "Father's taken to just leaving things on the floor for any old housecleaning lady to pick up."

I looked at the header on the open page. *Malleus Malefi- carum.* "Pretty wicked reading, Millie."

"No more wicked," she paused for a light, "than what's been going on around here lately."

I waited for the puff of sinewy smoke to caress my face. "Uh, Father Baptist said to tell you that he swears he'll be hungry for dinner."

"Will he," she sneered, sipping her wine. "And I hope you'll enjoy cooking it for him."

"Now Millie—"

"'The devil cannot create new species of things,'" she read aloud in rigid tones, "'therefore when natural butter suddenly came out of the water, the devil did not do this by changing the water into milk, but by taking butter from some place where it was kept and bringing it to the man's hand ...'"

I left the room, duly mortified, and thoroughly impressed by her determination to enhance her mind. Her voice drifted down the hallway as I returned to the study. It sounded spooky.

"'... Or else he took natural milk from a natural cow and suddenly churned it into natural butter; for while the art of women takes a little time to make butter, the devil could do it in the shortest space of time ..."

85

"DID YOU TELL HER?" ASKED FATHER as I sat down in my chair.

"I told her," I answered, cradling the coffee mug in my hands.

"And what did she say?"

"Something about the devil not being able to turn water into butter directly, but rather by stealing milk from a cow and churning it up in a flash."

"Come again?"

I shook my head. "I'm not sure I can explain."

"I'm not sure I want you to."

One sip from the mug and I knew experientially what had happened to my spoon. I set it down on the floor next to my chair and rubbed my hands together. "Okay," I coughed, "please continue."

"I've been reviewing some occult books," began Father, indicating several volumes scattered on the floor near his feet. "Eliphas Levi, Israel Regardie, Montague Summers. I believe I've found the answer there."

"Do tell."

"They have a lot to say about the symbolism of numbers. Let us start with the triangle." Taking up another sheet of paper, he drew the figure.

"The number three," I commented.

"Denoting the Holy Trinity," nodded Father. "The Father, the Son, and the Holy Ghost. We'll dispense with a study of that Mystery of Mysteries for the moment. For reasons wonderful and glorious, God made the material universe, which is represented in occult literature by the square." He drew this below the triangle. "And from this occultists derive the four hermetic elements of which everything tangible is composed."

"Earth, air, fire, and water."

"Right. And then, in an awesome moment of Love, God created Man. Man is a curious amalgam. He stands with one foot in the tangible universe, and the other in the intangible.

Tell me, Martin, what is it that God placed in Man that differ-
entiates him from all other corporeal creatures?"

I shrugged.   "Aside from a sense of humor, I'd say a
soul."

"Don't let all this ginger ale go to your head, but yes. God
gave Man a 'living soul,' as we're told in Genesis.   Into the
mix of earth, air, fire, and water, God infused—"

"Spirit," I said.

"Exactly. Earth, air, fire, water, and spirit. The number of
Man, then, is—?"

"Five."

"So in occult metaphor, the symbol for Man is—?"

"The   pentagram?"

"The pentagram. Now, with that in mind, take another look
at our casting quilt. Fire, earth, air, water. Look at how they
are lined up, and remember that our murderer is a fiend for
complexity of detail."

   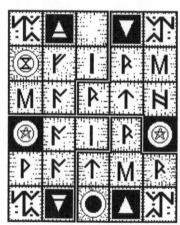

I propped my elbows on the edge of the desk and leaned
over the photographs, oblivious to several dislodged papers
which drifted to the floor.   I scanned the rows from left to
right, over and over.   "What am I looking for?"

"Start with the blank square, the focus of intent, and go
down the column to 'dah eye of dah serpent,' as Willie calls
it."

"I-R-I-T," I read aloud.   "I-R-I-T."

"Now consider the joined letters in the four corners."

"P-S, or S-P," I muttered.   "P-S, or ... S-P-I-R-I-T.
pirit."

"Bravo," said Father. "The focus of our murderer, the
pex to which he or she climbed by means of four murders, is
Spirit.' The essence of life, of the power of being, of the
oul itself."

"Earth, air, water, fire," I gasped, "and spirit running down
rough them all."

"Ingenious, isn't it?" said Father.

"A fifth element." I slumped back in my chair. "So the
urders are not over yet."

"Not yet," said Father. "Now it becomes clear why the
iller dished out the pieces of the casting quilt to us one by
ne: so we'd assume that with the fourth and last segment, the
eries would be at an end. But in actuality, the fifth murder
as woven into the fabric of the quilt from the very be-
inning. The fifth murder was the primary target all along."

I gulped. I gulped again. "But who?   Who is number
ve?"

Father set the blue sheet —stick figure side up—in the mid-
le of the desk. - "Let's go through the murders, one by one.
he first—"

"Bishop Silverspur."

"—was killed by the element 'earth.'"   He reached for the
urgundy bottle and placed it near one corner of the paper. It
etered on the uneven layers of files underneath, but stayed
pright. "Silverspur's favorite liquor was, for want of a better
ame, 'Blood turn fire, brain turn ash.'"   Taking up his pen,
e jotted this information beside the right foot of my stick
gure, along with the hermetic symbol for 'earth.'"

"Okay," I said, enjoying the coalescence Father had prom-
sed.   "Next?"

Father grabbed the Jägermeister and set it down at the next
orner. "Bishop Brassorie, late of this parish, was killed by
rowning in this awful stuff. In the murderer's mind, it stood
or 'water.'"

"May he and his poor taste rest in peace."   Okay, so I
lipped in the maintaining department. I immediately recov-
red my wits.

Father added the information beside my drawing's right
and. "And then perished Bishop Mgumba."

"Asphyxiation in a shower," I said. "'Air' sign. Had a
redilection for white rum."

The bottle was set in place and the info added to the draw
ing.

"Bishop Ravenshorst," said Father.

"Fire," I said. "And what a fire it was. Santa Barbar
d'Umbria."

Bottle placed and so indicated.

"Four bishops," said Father, dotting the "i" in "Umbria.
"Four bishops. What comes to mind when you think of aux
iliary bishops?"

"Pedophilia."

"Try again."

Oh, so we were back to "Martin maintaining." I grimace
with the effort.

"In the hierarchical order of things," said Father, "author
ity flows downward from above. From whom did these fou
bishops derive their power?"

"Uh, um, from the *arch* -bishop?"

"Bingo," he said, doodling further. "And what is our i
lustrious archbishop's favorite liquor?"

"Vodka," I said, visualizing fifty cases in the stable behin
La Chapelle de Saint Jean Baptiste, awaiting Archbishop Ful
bright's gleeful consumption. "Specifically, Akavit."

"Which means?"

"'The Water of Life.'"

"And incidentally, where will he be speaking today?"

"La Misión del Agua de la Vida."

"Which means?"

"'The Mission of the Water of Life.'"

"This will have to do." Father snatched the Evian wate
bottle from the vicinity of St. Anthony of Padua and St. Tho
mas More, who nodded their sagacious approval. He placed
at the top of the page near the head of the drawing. "An
one more incidental footnote. What day is today?"

"Wednesday, June twenty-first."

"Hint: think wiccan."

I visualized the calendar at the "Shop of Shadows." "Th
Summer Solstice," I gasped. "A 'Lesser Sabbat.'"

"Exactly. Oh, and another thing."

"Another thing?"

"I know, Martin, this case never seems to run short of then
Consider this: it has been noted before that the killings tak
place at five-day intervals."

"There's that number five again."

"And, if we count five days forward from last Friday's disaster, we arrive at—"

I counted on my fingers. "Today."

"Yes, today. The series of murders culminates, according to
intricate plan, on the Summer Solstice."

"Do you know what this means?" I asked, grabbing my
cane and struggled to my feet.

"It means we'd better get moving," said Father, who was already half-way to the door.

On impulse, I picked up the blue sheet. "I'm right behind
you, Father."

We were buffeted by louder and louder echoes of Millie's
voice as we approached the kitchen. She was still reading
aloud from the *Malleus Maleficarum.*

"'... But because in these times this perfidy is more often
found in women than in men, as we learn by actual experience, if anyone is curious as to the reasons, we may add to
what has already been said the following: that since they are
feebler both in mind and body, it is not surprising that they
should come more under the spell of witchcraft—'"

"Millie," I said, "Father Baptist has solved the case!"

"Oh he has, has he?" she growled, taking a puff on her
tenth cigarette. "Well, you couldn't prove it by me. You see?
It says right here: 'For as regards intellect, or the understanding of spiritual things, they—' Meaning women,
meaning me. '—they seem to be of a different nature than
men.'"

"Millie—?"

"Being of a different nature than you two, and being more
prone to witching ways, I'd say you're talking to the wrong
customer."

"Martin," said Father, hand on the kitchen doorknob. "We
must hurry."

"You do that," said Millie. "You hurry off. You've
solved the crime, after all."

"Not entirely," said Father. "But—"

"What's that in your hand?" she coughed at me.

"This?" I stammered. "Oh, it's sort of the blueprint of
how Father figured out what the murderer is up to."

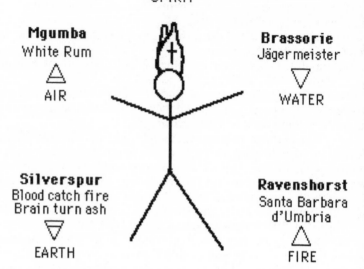

Fulbright
Akavit—"The Water of Life"
SPIRIT

Mgumba
White Rum
AIR

Brassorie
Jägermeister
WATER

Silverspur
Blood catch fire
Brain turn ash
EARTH

Ravenshorst
Santa Barbara
d'Umbria
FIRE

"Hrmph," she puffed, glaring at the blue page with one eye shut but the other open enough for both.

"Martin," harumphed Father Baptist, pulling the door open.

"Haaaaarumph," trumpeted Millie, gulping her wine.

Completely flustered, I shyly folded the page and stuffed it in my pocket. "Coming Father. See you for dinner, Millie."

"Phooey," said our former housecleaner.

86

"WE WERE JUST COMING TO SEE YOU," said Pierre and the Tumblars as we ran right into them just outside the door.

"Gentlemen," said Father, "we're in a terrific hurry. We have to stop the dedication ceremony at Chapel Hill."

"You won't get in," said Jonathan.

"We just came from there," said Edward.

"Billowack has a pack of guards at the entrance," said Pierre. "Would you believe it? They had specific orders to bar us from the premises."

"What's Billowack got to do with security at a church function?" asked the gardener. "He's in Homicide, not Crowd Control."

"Ah," said Pierre, "the chief's fingers seem to be in many pies."

"He charges Joel with the murders," said Jonathan, "but guards the archbishop like a hawk, just in case."

"And so you drove all the way here to tell me?" said Father.

"What else were we to do?" asked Jonathan. "Scale the walls?"

"Besides," said Edward, "one of the worst-mannered and least-bathed of the lot specifically told us to tell you, Father Baptist, to stay away."

"That sounds more like the archbishop's style than Billowack's," said Father. "The chief can't crow about solving the murder if I'm not there to gloat over."

"Fulbright, on the other hand," I noted, "has his dishonor to protect. Father Baptist's insight is a mirror he'd rather avoid."

"No matter whose ego gets bruised," said Father, "we must stop the ceremony."

"Then stop it we shall," said Pierre. "Comrades, to the van."

"To the van," they all cheered, falling in behind Father.

"You and Mr. Feeney come with us, Father," suggested Edward. "I parked in back."

"I feel a Crusade coming on," said Pierre.

"One moment," said Father, halting abruptly. He eyed Edward up and down, then Pierre, then Arthur. "I have an idea."

"What?" asked Jonathan.

Without a word, Father turned and headed back toward the rectory. We watched him open the kitchen door and step inside. We could almost hear him saying something to Millie, and Millie snarling something back. A few seconds later the door opened again, and he came huffing toward us on the brick path, something black and shapeless tucked under his arm.

"What's that?" asked Arthur.

"Not another disguise," grimaced the gardener.

"We must hurry," said Father, squeezing through us on the way to the rear parking lot.

Within minutes we were all in Edward's van. Father Baptist told me to ride "shotgun" since the front seat was the easiest for me to haul myself in and out of.

"To victory," announced Pierre.

"Victory," rallied the others.

"Gentlemen," said Father sternly. "This is not a game, and yet it is a most deadly game. I am certain that Archbishop Fulbright's life hangs in the balance. We might be met with considerable resistance, but he must be prevented from giving his speech on the speaker's platform at all costs."

"Resistance?" asked Arthur.

"You mean we might get ourselves arrested?" asked Edward, gunning he accelerator as he shot out into traffic.

"Possibly," said Father, sinking deep into his seat.

"To share in the predicament," said Pierre loftily, "of our fallen comrade, Joel."

We were jerked crazily this way and that as Edward steered the vehicle that way and this. The scenery whizzing by the windows changed rapidly. Less wood and more cement. The same with shrubbery and billboards.

"That is the least of our worries," said Father, hanging on as Edward fired his boosters and transcended gravity up the freeway on-ramp. "You all saw what happened the other night at St. Barbara's chapel. Our lives may well be at risk."

"To save a pig," sniffed Jonathan.

"To save a pig," agreed Father, "who is a Prince of the Church."

"For the honor of Holy Mother Church then," shouted Pierre.

"For Holy Mother Church," roared them all.

"Uh, Father," I ventured, or rather half-shouted over the roar of the engine. It was a struggle to turn sideways in my seat. The shoulder strap was a hindrance, not to mention the G-forces. "Two things bother me, aside from the fact that we could get ourselves killed."

"Yes, Martin?"

"Well, you surmised that the fifth element is 'spirit.'"

"That I did," nodded Father—not because he was agreeing but because Edward had just tapped the brakes to avoid rear-ending a cement truck.

"Signified by the 'water of life,'" I added as my cane
ipped away and landed in the crawl space between the two
ont seats.

"The what?" called Father.

I made a megaphone with my hands. "I said: 'Spirit' is
gnified by the 'water of life.'"

"Yes," shouted Father.

"Here's my pro—ulp!—blem." My voice cracked as Ed-
ard saw an opening around the cement truck and took it.
ly cane rolled to and fro on the floor between the front seats.
'Earth' I can picture in my mind. Likewise, I can conceptu-
lize 'air,' 'fire,' and 'water.' But I don't have any reference
>r this 'water of life.'"

"Holy water?" yelped Jonathan.

"No." Father clutched his shoulder strap as Edward darted
iagonally across two lanes to avoid a school bus. "It's
>mething entirely different. How much do you know about
\e medieval alchemists?"

"They wore pointed hats," said Pierre. "A bit more stylish
\an the bishops of today."

"They attached themselves to royal courts," said Arthur,
and claimed to be able to turn lead into gold."

"Not just lead," said Father. "Iron, copper, and other base
\etals."

"You really think they did that?" called Edward over his
houlder as he executed another swerving surprise. The
ansmission growled ominously.

"Gentlemen," said Father, digging his heels into the mat to
emain in his seat, "consider this: these men prayed before
>nducting their experiments. Don't you think their chances
>r success were greatly enhanced when compared to the
hemist of today who merely dumps his compounds into a
eaker to see what happens?"

"They prayed?" gulped Arthur, astonished. "Who to?"

"To the Angels," yelled Father, gritting his teeth against
nother surge of acceleration. "Those who govern the pattern
nd substance of the universe."

"You mean like demons?" called Jonathan.

"No," shouted Father, "I mean the Angels, the messengers
f God who guide the stars through the heavens, the planets in
\eir orbits, and electrons around their protons. I can see that
ou gents haven't yet been exposed to the Church's teachings
n such things."

"I have," said Pierre, hand on heart. "I have a particula
devotion to the Angels who agitate bubbles in champagne."

"But," stammered Jonathan, "I thought alchemy was in th
same camp as witchcraft. You know: evil, like astrology."

"Only if you're a Fundamentalist," countered Fathe
"They find evil in the darndest places, and nail the drawe
shut so no one else will see what they've hidden. Then the
manage—"

"Drat," spat Edward, hitting the brakes. The whole va
tipped forward, as did everyone inside.

"—to convince everyone else—"

"Aha!" barked Edward, stomping on the accelerator. Eve
ryone spilled backwards.

"—not to look there, either," said Father, struggling to a
upright position. "These are the same people, don't forge
who outlawed Christmas in colonial times."

"And Shakespeare," said Pierre. "Can you believe it
They actually banned the Bard."

"Hamlet spoke to his father's ghost," said Father.

"And since Prods don't believe in Purgatory—" added P
erre.

"Shakespeare was expendable," said Arthur.

"Let me put it this way," said Father, steadying himself a
the van seemed to teeter on its two right wheels. "Jonathar
the danger of these medieval practices is not in the magic;
system itself, but in the tendency of the uninformed and inte
ligence-challenged to fall into the trap of denying Free Wil
'The stars do not compel, they impel.'"

"St. Thomas Aquinas," said Pierre, both hands on heart.

"Correct," said Father. "Free Will is basic to all th
Church's teachings. But to say—"

"Whoops," spat Edward. Three horns blasted, one on eac
side of the van and one in front. I closed my eyes, not wan
ing to know.

"—that the study of the relationship of nature to man is ev
is as absurd as denying the force of gravity. To say that a
chemists cavorted with demons is like saying that I do th
same at Mass."

"Fundies do say that," yelled Edward, gripping the steerin
wheel maniacally.

With the next lurch, the black bundle slipped from unde
Father's arm and landed on the floor. It rolled toward me
unraveling as it came.

"Isn't that—?" I asked, recognizing the garment.

"Yes," nodded Father.

"Whoa!" barked Edward. "Hold on!"

The next thing I knew, my back was slammed up against the glove compartment and my left sleeve was caught on the passenger door's window crank. I was, in other words, turned completely around.

"Was this flip necessary?" I rasped in Edward's direction, clawing my way back to my perch.

He didn't hear me, yelling as he was: "Comin' through! God will know His own!"

"So astrology and alchemy aren't evil," Jonathan was grimacing, shaking his head.

"If they were," answered Father, "then St. Thomas Aquinas and his mentor St. Albert Magnus could not have been canonized."

"And they were both Doctors of the Church," ahemed Pierre. "Don't forget that."

"To the midievals and ancients," yelled Father over the metallic din of shuddering side-panels and grinding gears, "these topics were regarded as fields of lifelong research, not ha'penny solutions for lonely hearts and feeble minds. Today they have become watered down to a degree of dilution beyond uselessness. But many Saints studied them within their proper contexts, with the guidance of holy teachers, and suffered no ill effects."

"But," mumbled Jonathan, "so many religious people say—"

"The same thing about the pentagram," interrupted Pierre. "Remember? No matter what some people think, in truth it's a holy symbol."

"Astrology," said Father, "is simply the study of the relationship between the macrocosm of the universe and the microcosm of our lives. It stands to reason that there is a relationship, since God created the heavens as a setting for the diamond of His efforts: Man."

"You mean we're like jewelry?" asked Edward over his shoulder.

"No," said Father, "but Adam and Eve were."

"Before the Flaw," added Pierre.

Darkness momentarily filled the van, then exploded back into daylight as we soared under a bridge. A row of concrete pillars went flickering by, then the steel skeleton of an overpass under construction. A splatter of welder's sparks streaked across the edge of my peripheral vision.

"Father," I coughed. "About the 'water of life.'"

He was gathering up the black bundle which had fallen onto the floor. "I'm getting to that."

"Right. Sure."

"Perhaps it is better called the 'elixir of life.' It was a substance much sought after by the alchemists."

"That's what turned lead into gold?" asked Arthur.

"No," said Father, tucking the thing back under his arm. "The whole lead-into-gold business is blown entirely out of proportion. The real goal of the alchemists was the discovery of the 'elixir of life,' often referred to as the 'philosopher's stone'—a substance which could produce eternal health and life."

"Did they ever discover it?" asked Edward over his shoulder.

"Perhaps," said Father. "It depends how you define 'discover.'"

"And, I suppose, how you define 'eternal,'" said Arthur.

"And 'ever,'" said Pierre. "Don't forget 'ever.'"

"Before you get too metaphysical," I interrupted, "can we please get back to my point? What kind of a murder weapon is an 'elixir'?"

"Good question," said Father. "How do you kill someone with 'spirit'? I don't have a clue. What we do know is that Archbishop Fulbright's favorite liquor is that Scandinavian vodka, Akavit, which also means 'the water of life.'"

"And I saw fifty cases of the stuff," I said, "piled up behind the mission. Not to mention a considerable pile of fireworks. And, I almost took a joyride in the olive press, which is now directly under the platform where the archbishop'll be giving his speech."

"This is getting very complicated," said Jonathan.

"And dangerous," said Father. "There, Edward. Edward! Get off at the next off-ramp."

"Gotcha," said Edward, maneuvering with abandon. "But as we said before, they won't let us in."

"Martin knows a way," said Father.

"I do?" It took me a second to rattle the ol' moth balls. Then I exclaimed, "The hole in the north wall!"

"Bravo," said Father. "Mrs. Magillicuddy told Martin that there's a way into the estate behind one of the eucalyptus trees. He's seen it."

I felt my heart settle back down my esophagus as Edward descellerated to an appropriate velocity beneath the speed of sound.

"But only from the inside," I countered.

"It shouldn't be too hard to find," said Jonathan.

87

"HERE WE ARE," SAID EDWARD.

"There are the front gates," said Father, pointing. "Don't bother slowing down. The guards are still there and the gates are closed. Just go north and turn right."

"A lot of cars parked along the street," observed the gardener.

"Quite a crowd," said Jonathan. "Look, they go all the way down the block, and around the corner."

"They're making everyone walk through the checkpoint at the front gate," said Father. "Billowack's not smart, but he's not stupid."

"The cars thin off up ahead," said Edward.

"And there are our signposts," said Father. "The eucalyptus trees."

Indeed they were. About twenty of them, towering in irregularly-spaced clusters along the outside of the wall. They had grown so big over the years that the sidewalk was warped and buckled.

Screeching the van to a halt, Edward yanked up on the parking brake. We all tumbled out onto the sidewalk. Our footsteps were accentuated by the crackle of eucalyptus leaves which blanketed the ground.

"It was near a group of three trees," I said. "And roughly midway along the wall."

"It must be here somewhere," said Father. "Fan out, everyone. Remember, groups of three."

This was made all the more difficult because of some prickly old bushes with thorns as old as the mission that were clustered between the trunks of the stately trees and the impenetrable wall.

"Maybe we'll have to resort to hefting each other over," said Pierre, wiping his forehead with a hand scratched and streaked with blood.

"No," said Father, shifting the bundle under his arm. "The spikes along the top are dangerous. Keep looking."

"Listen," I said.

An amplified voice came from somewhere beyond the wall. As booming as it was, the words were indecipherable. It was vaguely masculine, which meant it could have been otherwise.

"Noon on the dot," I said, glancing at my watch. "The first speech."

"Hurry," said Father. "The ceremony has begun."

"How many speakers do they have lined up?" I asked. "The archbishop's probably last."

"I don't know," said Father. "Most of those slated for speeches are now dead. It might be a very brief ceremony indeed."

"But they've been replaced by parish counsel leaders," I said. "It may be dark before the archbishop goes on."

"Hallooo!" cried Pierre. "Over here. I've found the tunnel."

We all raced for the spot where he was standing. He was using his body to restrain a particularly nasty-looking branch. In the shadows behind was a diagonal cleft in the wall, a place where the adobe had been undermined by a rainstorm many decades ago. The hole was dark, low, jagged, and damp, but it was the only way in.

"Take courage, men," said Pierre. "The only way in is through."

One by one we stooped and squeezed our way through the crevice. It wasn't hard for the young lads, or for Father Baptist, being seasoned yet supple, but for Martin Feeney, the arthritic gardener with a tangled clothes hanger for a spine, it was an ordeal. I tried not to groan.

"If Mrs. Magillicuddy can do this," I reasoned, "so can I." And so I did, but it cost me. It was only a few feet of tunnel, but it was excruciating. My eyes were shut through most of it.

I knew we were through when the echoing, booming sound of the speech in progress suddenly became louder, echoier, and boomier. Unfortunately it didn't get any clearer, so I still couldn't tell if the speaker was a man or a woman. Maybe it was a nun.

We emerged through the criss-crossed branches of the two pomegranate trees I noted before, but from the other side. Pushing through this last prickly barrier, we halted on a patch of thick green grass which overlooked the estates of Chapel

ill. From there we could study the lay of the land and make
decisions about which path to take.

The most obvious course was the path which began at our
very feet and wandered ever leftward in wide, lazy arcs, even-
ally disappearing in the shade of the great oak forest. It was
e most even, level, obstruction-free, gardener-friendly
ourse. Unfortunately, it did not go in the direction of the
ission, which was off to the right.

The quickest way there seemed to be an unmarked trek
own a rocky ravine which was choked with the gnarled
keletons of ancient, withered grapevines—vestiges of the mis-
on's heyday. Beyond this, the land rose in uneven leaps and
urges, sprinkled with holly, bougainvillaea, cactuses, wild
ses, and kumquats. The missionaries must have had a thing
or plants that fight back. This rise culminated in the steep
ll upon which Padre Alonso Miranda and Father Jean Pierre
e Chantal, so far from their homes but so close to God, had
ecided to build La Chapelle de Saint Jean Baptiste. The
eremony we had come to interrupt was on the other side of
at building.

"Martin," asked Father at my side. "You've been up at
is end of the estate before. What's the quickest way to the
hapel?"

"Your guess is as good as mine," I answered, scratching my
calp. "I came up along the west wall to our right, and re-
urned through the woods off to the left. But I was stopping a
t, exploring, and making detours."

"I say we go west," said Arthur. "Then follow the west
all south until we're even with the mission, and cut over
astward through that grove of fig trees."

"We might just as well take the path through the woods," I
aid, pointing toward the enchanted land of faeries and Magil-
cuddy's. "I know how to get to the meadow, and the chapel
due west from there."

"But the only way in is through," said Pierre, his finger
riggling at the end of his rigid lance of an arm. Our eyes
olled down his arm and dropped into the rocky ravine below
ith its inviting barbs and thorns.

"Right, left, or straight," pondered Jonathan.

"Listen," said the gardener.

The tone of the booming voice had changed. It had
ropped by at least an octave. Either the present voice was a
an and the former a woman, or the former was a modernist
riest and the present was a liberal nun.

"Decisions," said Arthur.

"We must split up," said Father. "It is likely that securi
has been informed of our banishment from the proceeding
They'll be on the lookout. If we approach in several sma
groups, we increase our chances for success."

"Or multiply our opportunities for arrest," mumbled th
gardener under his breath.

"Divide and conquer," said Pierre. "I shall lead the par
that takes the straight path."

"Straight as the crow flies, maybe," said the gardener, fo
lowing the contours of the terrain with his finger, "b
crooked as a crumpled paper bag as the cockroach crawls."

"Pierre, you may have it," said Father. "Jonathan, Edwar
you go with him. Arthur, you come with me along the wes
ern wall. And Martin—"

"I'll only slow you down whichever way I go," said th
gardener, dejected. "I cannot run, and you'd have to help m
climb, and I'd have to take rests along the way."

"Martin," said Father, giving my shoulder an encouragir
squeeze.

"I'll take the path through the woods," I said. "I probab
won't get to the mission until it's all over, but you nev
know. Maybe I'll cut off the killer's retreat."

"We all do our part," said Father, relaxing his gri
"Who's to say? Yours might turn out to be the decisiv
course. In any case, gentlemen, all of you remember: Arc
bishop Fulbright must not set foot on that platform. Also, t
on the lookout for Starfire. You all know what she looks lik
And, be particularly wary of anyone with a cellular phone o
walkie-talkie. The events at St. Barbara's were set off with
call to a phone-activated device. Let us say a Hail Mary as w
depart."

"Gentlemen," quoted Pierre, right arm raised as if holdin
a spear. "'Do we walk in legends or on the green earth in th
daytime?'"

"Hail Mary," said Father, and they all joined in as the
went their various ways.

"Right," said the gardener, watching them depart with th
energy and endurance of youth. Pierre, Jonathan, and Edwar
skidded their way down into the treacherous ravine, dust bi
lowing around them. Father Baptist and Arthur grew small
and smaller as they hiked westerward along the wall. I gath
ered up my cane and headed for the woods, rubbing my low

back thoughtfully as I went. "Now and at the hour of our death. Amen."

All the while the animated voice blathered away over the amplification system. As the branches of the oak trees closed over my head, the sound became more muffled and indistinct, but surprisingly no less loud.

I don't know exactly how many minutes it took me to find Mrs. Magillicuddy's camp. This time I didn't need St. Anthony's refresher course in freeform somersaulting. The place was much the same as it had been the other day, except the air was heavy with the smell of coffee. The pot was still cooling on the hubcap grill.

I considered tossing a couple of crumpled dollars into the hollow of the tree, but stayed my hand. What would delight this strange old woman more, I asked myself: a few dollars, or the sense that her privacy had not been violated in her absence?

Sometimes charity requires another currency than cash.

From there I headed for the meadow of the dancing witches—or faeries, in Mrs. M's metaphysical world view. The meadow also looked much the same. The eerie stillness of my previous visits was demolished by the disruptive, intrusive amplified voice which came pouring into the meadow over the treetops like water into a flushing toilet. I thought I perceived a new voice. This one squeaky and perky, but still a gender puzzle.

Having come this far, I knew I had to head west.

The question was should I go around the meadow, or through it? Should I stick to the safety of shadows, or wander in the light of day? I was alone, don't forget.

Around or through?

Then it occurred to me that my preferences were not a priority. I had wasted time resting and pretending to think. The moment required courage, not self-indulgence. Time was of the essence, and the quickest way was indeed through.

"Place on thy heart one drop of the Precious Blood of Jesus," I could almost hear Father Baptist say, *"and fear nothing."*

Imagining the first part was easy, but mustering the second was another thing. *"But,"* I knew Father would say if he was standing beside me, *"the former, if prayed in earnest, will produce the latter ... eventually."* Grateful for the thought, and having no time for eventuallies, I made the Sign of the Cross, and stomped as bravely as I could across the meadow.

In hindsight, it was fortuitous that I did so—though also
frightening, as it turned out. For in my haste to get through
and beyond the place, my attention wandered from the immediate. By that I mean that if I had been paying attention to
my feet I wouldn't have tripped over something in the thick
grass.

Falling headlong into a clump of green, aromatic sage brush
wouldn't have bothered a younger man, but to a man with an
inflamed spine, impacts of this sort are borderline traumatic.
But neither youth nor stamina would have insulated me from
the terror that rippled up through my guts and gripped my
heart as I realized that what I had tripped over was a human
foot.

As I scrambled to my feet, I saw that the sandaled foot was
attached to a leg. That, at least, was to be expected. And the
leg had a companion, but it was bent at an excruciating angle.
The body was clothed in some sort of brown tunic with a
crimson sash. The tunic had a hood with black lining which
fanned out above the shoulders. Cradled in the hood was the
head, with open eyes staring glassily toward the sky. And the
smile—it was the most bizarre smile I had ever encountered
not because the facial muscles were frozen in a macabre par-
ody of hilarious rapture, but because the face wasn't involved.

The smile was a gash cut deeply into the tissues of the throat
gaping widely from ear to ear.

Resting on the victim's chest was the knife that had made
these gruesome lips where none should be. I shuddered to
think of a mind so icily brazen, so utterly cold and bold, that
having committed so brutal a crime, it would think to set the
bloody weapon gently and obviously upon the breathless
bosom of the unfortunate victim, as if to coo, "There there
there there."

As horrified as I was, a wave of fascination surged up from
within and overwhelmed me. After the complicated numerological discussion with Father Baptist that morning, I simply
had to know. I had to see for myself.

Enduring the agony of another stoop, I hunched down and
examined the little scimitar. I didn't have to fish for a twig
with which to turn it over. The murderer was a braggart, after
all. There was the number, glistening in coarse pewter lines in
the noon sun:

MCDXL

"One thousand four hundred and forty," I whispered, gazing into the upturned face with its condescending, sightless eyes. The ground around the neck and shoulders was saturated with blood. The heart had continued beating after the wound was inflicted, pushing blood out through the gash in rhythmic gushes until, deflated, the vessels had collapsed.

The expression on the face and the glaring eyes suggested that the victim had been thoroughly aware of what was happening.

It occurred to me that it might be proper to close the eyes, but that was asking too much. Turning away, I became protractedly sick. The volume, not the fact, came as a surprise because I had skipped breakfast along with Father Baptist.

The coffee. A whole pot of coffee steamed away into one cup of hazardous mud.

That nasty business concluded, I snatched up my cane and headed in the direction of the mission, wishing more than at any other time that I had Father Baptist for company. By that time, I imagined, he was groping his way through the grove of fig trees around the chapel walls. Pierre and his companions, I guessed, were huffing and puffing at the summit of their climb, the ordeal of the pricklies behind them.

Why, I asked myself, was I sent on alone? Pierre had Jonathan and Edward. Father had Arthur. I had ... me. Three, two, one. Numbers again. Why the uneven division?

It was hard to think with that infernal, ceaseless, gobbling orator yacking away over the loudspeakers.

"That's right," I said aloud as my thoughts congealed. " I would have held them up. It's better this way."

I walked a few paces and stopped. "Better for whom?"

I walked and halted again. "For the quest," I realized. "Archbishop Fulbright's ass, and don't you forget it. It *is* better this way."

Nonetheless—and made all the less unacceptable by the ceaseless banter echoing through the trees—it was not a pleasant afternoon for finding oneself deep in the woods, alone, beyond all earshot, and only a few receding yards from a corpse.

"Gotta save the archbishop," I huffed as I worked up to a pretty good pace, considering I was limping worse than usual,

"'cause he's a prince of the Church. Gotta save the archbishop—"

I stopped short again.

"From whom? With Starfire dead back there in the
meadow, who's left? Who else could have committed these
crimes?"

Then it dawned on me that her savage murder had occurred
quite recently—uncomfortably so. Perhaps within a half
hour. The blood had still been glistening wet. I was probably
using the same footpath as the killer.

I was alone in these mysterious woods, and the shadows between the trees had just become unbearably menacing.

Making a sound I can only shamefully describe as a whine, I
broke into a run. Even for me, it was a run.

88

FEAR IS A POWERFUL STIMULANT. Adrenaline can make
your muscles perform activities you never suspected they
could accomplish. But the body has its limitations. Mine had
been exceeded within a couple of minutes as I lurched crazily
through the woods in the direction of the chapel.

The amplified voice seemed to have taken on almost certain
masculine characteristics. It was getting gradually louder, and
a few parts of actual words were beginning to poke through
the aural clutter. "Blah blah once made a comment about
blah blah after a blah-blah in the blah-blah-blah."

I finally collapsed against a lumpy old oak tree. The wave
of adrenaline had subsided, leaving me weak and shaking.
Even if the murderer had leapt out from behind the trunk,
brandishing a fiendish implement of impending doom, and
glared at me with blood-lusting eyes, I wouldn't have had the
ability to say anything more courageous than, "Hang
on—(gasp!)—I'll be with you—(wheeze!)—in just
a—(squeak!)—a minute—(rattle!)."

And of course, the realization that I was indeed just that
helpless, that my fate was completely, totally, and irrevocably
out of my hands, induced the sense within me of utter calm,
much like the serenity I had experienced in the meadow a few
days before.

'How silly of me," I whispered between gasps, "to regard profound revelation something that is in reality the Norm." Indeed, when are we ever in control of our lives? of our dies? of our existence? We who did not decide to be born? e who try with furious frenzy to assemble the details of our ily existence, only to see them unravel at every turn, disas- mbled by the Hand that truly holds us in its awesome lm—that Palm through which a nail was once driven in def- ence to the Almighty Father's awesome Will, pierced that we ight be saved from the futility that is ourselves.

How silly of me to think otherwise. How foolish, how arro- nt, how proud—

"How're ya doin', Mr. Feeney?"

I blinked and looked around.

"What brings yer to this neck of the woods I'd likes to ow, I woulds."

Pushing away from the tree and swaying on rubbery legs, I zed in the direction of the chapel. The roof rose through e trees. I had come farther than I'd thought.

"Are you deafs as well as blinds, are you?"

"Mrs. Magillicuddy?" I called. "Where—?"

"Up here I is," she cackled. "Best view in the house, even ough's it's rightly outsides, but nevertheless, here we is."

And there she was, sitting on top of a knoll to my left, bin- ulars cradled in her lap, balancing a cup of coffee on her ny knee. She looked like she was ready for the parade.

"C'mon, Mr. Feeney," she beckoned. "A view this good ould be shared, it should."

Not for the life of me having a better idea, I lumbered up to here she was seated, slipping every other step on the slick een grass.

"My word," I panted as I reached the summit.

"Yours an' mine's," she agreed.

From where Mrs. Magillicuddy sat she could look right over e stable roof directly down into the courtyard and see the ily clad people seated in their folding chairs, pretending to joy the pretentious festivities set before them. There must ve been three or four hundred in attendance. I didn't ther to strain to see if I recognized anyone. Most of the ople I knew would not have been invited, nor would have me if they had been.

Most of the women were wearing those breezy summer hats, e kind made of finely-woven straw, with rims three feet in ameter so they were constantly nudging and scraping each

other when they turned their heads to gab. From this ang
they looked like a patch of agitated mushrooms.

Since this was Southern California, and summer to bo
men were not expected to wear suits and ties. The mode
standard required shorts, Hawaiian shirts, sunglasses, and sa
dals. This was, after all, a semi-formal occasion. Sunglass
were not optional.

"You can see it all from here," I declared.

"Yes I cans," she nodded with toothless enthusiasm.

"There's the speakers' platform," I pointed. "And the l
tle covered well in the middle of the courtyard, and the fou
tains of champagne up front, and well, everything."

"That they are," she agreed merrily, "an' is."

An unsettling thought occurred to me. "Uh, Mrs. Ma
illicuddy, you didn't happen to pass through the meadow o
your way here, did you?"

"Me?" she squeaked. "In broad daylight? You are a
imbecile when it comes to faeries, you is. You nevers, b
nevers, set foots on the grass where faeries dance at night u
der the light of the sun, you don't's. You'll turns into
block of salt for sure if you does, you will. An' in this he;
you'd crumble into a pile or granu'ls in minutes. Fit f
shakin' on somebody's lunch, you'd be."

I patted myself to make sure, but the symptoms she d
scribed had not yet manifested themselves.

Just then there was a burst of applause and an electron
crackle as another speaker stepped up to the microphon
"I'll try to keep this short," said the voice, echoing in i
regular delays from each end of the mission complex.

It was Cheryl Farnsworth.

A shiver ran through me. She was standing on the platfor
inches above that hungry metal jaw over the deep pit below.

But again, there was nothing I could do from here. Matte
were in another Hand.

Crinkling her brow, Mrs. Magillicuddy lifted the heavy bi
oculars to her bird-like eyes. "My word," she gaspe
"There she is."

"Miss Farnsworth?" I asked.

"I don't knows her name, you ninny. But that's he
Her!"

"Who?"

"Look for yourself," she insisted, thrusting the binocula
into my inept hands. "There at the mikey-phone, she is."

Hefting the binoculars, I swung the beast this way and that until I found the blur that resembled a platform. Mrs. Magillicuddy's eyesight must have been very poor indeed. It took me a minute to adjust the focus.

"Sees her, do you?" squawked the old woman. "Do you sees her?"

"Yes," I said, eyeing Cheryl. "You mean the woman in the purple dress?"

"Yessirs," she laughed. "All sequins an' sparkles. An' a pretty blue scarf. She must be boilin' in that outfit."

"She's quite a sight," I agreed.

"What's did I tells you, I did?"

"I don't understand, Mrs. Magillicuddy. What about her?"

"She's the queen."

"The queen?" Well, sure, to an old crone's addled mind a woman in a stunning dress making a speech on that platform all decorated with flowers and crepe paper loops might seem rather regal—and to me, perhaps a bit enchanting—but—

"That's what I's been trying to tells you, Mr. Feeney. Has all that gardening you neglect put roots through your brains? That's the queen, I tells you."

"The queen."

"Of the faeries," she cackled. "How many times has hey's been a'coming to the meadow in me and Willum's woods? How many times' I's been a'crouchin' in the thickets, a'watchin' an' a'wishin' I could be young an' beautiful agains? She's an enchantress, she is. The fairest of the faeries, she is."

"In the midst of unspeakable troubles of which I needn't speak today," Cheryl was saying, "he has been a rock of resolution to those of us who work for him." Her words came drifting up through the trees which parted for her voice in the breeze. "So rather than bore you with the extensive text I had prepared by way of introduction, and considering the midday heat, I say let's get on with it. I give you Archbishop Morley Fulbright."

The audience clapped appreciatively as His Graciousness stepped up to the microphone.

"Thank-you Miss Farnsworth," said the archbishop magnanimously.

Cheryl backed away, smiling and clapping. She turned to the audience, encouraging them to take up the acclamation. Dutifully, the people were rising to their feet, giving the last living bishop in Los Angeles a roaring round of applause.

"Thank-you, thank-you," said Morley in tones that said "Sit down," but with gestures that said, "Oh, do keep it up."

"The queen," I whispered, stunned.

"Give me a turn at them 'noculars," chortled Mrs. Magillicuddy.

Dumbfounded, I handed them over.

"Whahoozie," said Mrs. Magillicuddy, struggling with the focus knob. "You must be blinder than a bat, you must. Mr Feeney, I thinks you should go see a— Mr. Feeney?"

It was rude of me I know, but I was half-way down the hill tumbling and thrashing like the blind bat that I apparently was.

"Oh my God," I was saying as I regained the trail and proceeded toward the ceremony. I felt a Hand prodding me all the way. "Oh my God oh my God oh my God ..."

89

"THIS IS INDEED A MOMENTOUS OCCASION," Archbishop Fulbright was bellowing into the microphone, distorting the hell out the speakers. The audience had finally settled back into their seats. "An event of monumental consequence for myself as archbishop, for those here today, for our community of and within Los Angeles, and of course, for the world at large. Dare I say it? For history herself." He almost gave himself a hernia of the tongue, twisting the poor thing into an impressive "fleur de lis" as he overemphasized "his" and "her" in that last phrase. "After so many years buried under the desultory dust of lugubrious neglect, the Del Agua Mission rises again as a resplendent beacon of sanguine hope in these dark and troubled times. To think that the commendable—yet in the light of modern insight we might add 'naive'—dream of two wandering missionaries ..."

I had just rounded the corner of the stable and was entering the square when a voice bleated at me from the right.

"Hey you."

I turned to see an alligator-faced guard strutting toward me, his jiggling paunch sagging menacingly over his holster belt. He was a city cop: badge, personality, and all.

"Where did you come from?" he barked. "And where do you think you're going?" Notice the philosophical depth of this compound question which reflects the inner turmoil in us all.

<u>GARDENING</u> <u>TIPS</u>: When finding oneself in a potentially confrontational situation, the first and most expedient course is honesty. Most people respond positively to simple sincerity, brief and uncluttered with superfluous details. If that doesn't work, attempts at courtesy and humor should be made. But if all else fails, remember that the stick is always mightier than the toe.

--Ancient saying, loosely distilled

from the wisdom of Hijo Yahamata.

As quoted by yours truly,

--M.F.

"From there," I said, hooking my thumb over my shoulder. Then I pointed forward. "To there."

"Oh, a wise guy."

From where I stood, which was about three feet from the space-egg pay phone, I had a side view of the speakers' platform. Morley had taken command. The other people who had already spoken—parish leaders, supposedly, but by the looks of them, I'd say they were unwilling file clerks and conscripted floral arrangers—were seated behind him, fanning themselves and swatting flies with their programs. Cheryl, who was easy to spot in that shimmering purple dress, had maneuvered herself to the far end of the stage and was easing herself backwards down the steps.

"You listening to me?" growled the policeman.

"I'm sorry, Officer," I mewed, trying the polite approach. "I meant no offense. I need to have a word with the woman who just spoke. Miss Farnsworth."

"You and everyone's uncle. You a hobo or something? What were you doing in the woods? And how did you get in there in the first place?"

Courtesy having failed—me, a hobo?—I tried humor.

"The cracks," I said.

"What cracks?"

"The cracks of perception. I slipped through. Don't you read Blake?"

"Now look here, Bub. I don't got all day. State your dab gum name and your dern gub business or I'll have to arrest you."

Words failed. For one thing, "dab gum" and "dern gub" were imprecations with which I was completely unfamiliar. I didn't know if I'd been praised or insulted, or if my name and business had just been cast into that eternally eschatological realm where all inanimate objects go when they've been damned by the living. For another thing, time was a'wasting.

I turned and looked him in the eye. "Officer, there are times when a man's gotta do what he's gotta do." With that, I gripped my cane as hard as I could and slammed the tip down on his right foot.

"Yeow," he cried, arms flailing, dancing on the other foot.

I didn't wait for him to recover his wits. My only chance was to force my way between two sharply dressed men who were standing a few feet away, facing the ceremony, their backs toward me. Just beyond them, gaggles of people were drifting to and fro in the wide aisle around the seated area. If I could push between those men and lunge into the stream of slowly swirling bystanders, I stood a fair chance of losing myself in their midst.

This was my plan.

Clutching my cane, I turned away from the dancing guard, and made for the gap between the Pillars of Hercules.

"Grab him," called the cop, hopping mad.

"Got him," answered one of the sharply dressed men.

"Done," announced the other.

"Lieutenant Taper," I gasped as two sets of hands suddenly pinned my arms uselessly at my sides. Instantly I knew what it's like to have your blood pressure tested in stereo. "Sergeant Wickes?"

So much for ancient sayings, origin unknown.

"Cool it, Martin," hissed Taper in my ear. "Let me handle is."

I stopped struggling and stretched my neck to get a look at e platform again. Cheryl was gone.

"Let me have him," the cop was growling, limping up from hind, stork-like. "That bastard broke my toe."

"With a rubber-tipped cane?" I said innocently.

"We'll take care of him, Officer," said Taper with a note of thority. "We've dealt with this guy before. Right Mar- n?"

"Oh yeah," I nodded. "Them and me, Officer. Ooooh ah."

"He's a bit, you know," said Wickes, freeing one hand for a oment to tap my forehead.

Since I was facing the opposite way, I couldn't see the ard's face. I could, however, hear the buttons on his shirt rniating against the expanse of his gut. And I could feel the at of his stare on the back of my skull, withering my neck irs.

"He's mine," I heard him say.

"No, Officer," said Taper firmly, but not as firmly as he as gripping my arm. My fingers were tingling from lack of rculation. "This man is involved in a murder investigation. e's mine."

"But —"

"Officer, return to your post."

The guard's buttons moaned pitifully as he took a deep eath, and then sighed merrily as he let it out slowly. eah," he said disgustedly. "Sure. Whatever you say."

"Okay, Lieutenant," I said as the sulking scrapes of the ard's footsteps retreated in the direction of his post. I was isting my head this way and that, trying to catch a glimpse that purple dress. "Sergeant, if you'll just let me go—"

"Shhhh," shushed Lieutenant Taper close to my ear. What're you doing here, Martin? Didn't you get Bil- wack's order?"

"He'll kill you if he sees you," whispered Wickes in my her ear.

"Luckily," I hissed back out of both sides of my mouth—it as quite a trick, "reality does not begin and end within the ay goop between Montgomery Billowack's wax factories." then announced more in Sergeant Wickes' direction than eutenant Taper's: "Father Baptist has broken the code."

"What code?" asked Wickes.

"Whadduya mean, 'what code'?" I gawked. "What's bee driving you bonkers for the last two weeks?"

"You mean besides you and Father Baptist," chortle Wickes.

"Keep your voices down," shushed Taper.

"I don't have time for this," I huffed, squirming, but the tightened their torque on my arms. "Let me go."

"Martin," said Taper sharply. "What code?"

"The casting quilt," I whispered angrily. "What oth mind-boggling, son-of-a-mom code is there?"

Wickes was chuckling softly. "But we already figured th out days ago."

"No," I retorted, "you did not." That came out of m mouth as the whispered equivalent of a yell. Several b standers turned to see what kind of steam pipe had broken gasket behind them.

"Keep it down," whisper-barked Taper.

"Sure, sure." I shook my head. "While you guys wor about disturbing the sublime serenity of these elegant ladi and gentlemen, not to mention Chief Billowack's lopside conception of reality, the archbishop is about to die."

"Die?" asked Wickes.

"Die," I said. "Expire, pass on, perish, cash in his chip kick the collection plate, succumb."

"How?" asked Taper.

"I don't know exactly. But I can tell you this: As we spea His Gracefulness is standing on a platform built over a dee pit with a flip-top lid. I know. I almost fell into it myself th other day."

"It's wired shut," said Wickes, shaking is head. "I checke it myself."

"When?"

"Sometime late Monday while they were building th stage."

"And it hasn't been checked since?"

"Not that I know of."

I whirled on Taper, if you can call a sixteenth of a turn "whirl." "Lieutenant, you worked with Father Baptist fo years. You probably know him even better than I do. D you really value Chief Billowack's powers of deduction abov his?"

"No, of course not."

"Or Sergeant Wickes'?"

Taper glanced at his junior partner. "Well—"

"Hey," said Wickes.

"Shush," I shushed. "Then you can do one of two things. You can stand here exercising your lips and grips while waiting for the archbishop to die some horrible, unspeakable death, or you can go push him off the speaker's platform before that happens. I'd do it myself, but I doubt that I'm strong or coordinated enough."

"Yeah, right," said Wickes. "Billowack would have our necks for dinner and our badges for dessert if we pulled something like that."

"Hey," I shrugged. "It's your necks or the archbishop's. Speaking of necks, there's one torn open from ear to ear back in the woods over there."

"What's that you say?" asked Taper. "Whose?"

"Starfire the witch."

"You mean she's dead?"

"Really most sincerely. And I've since found out something even Father Baptist doesn't know."

"Is he here?" asked Wickes. "If Billowack catches him, he'll wring his neck. He issued orders to lynch anything in a cassock."

"Necks are in demand today, I'll grant you. Now if you will excuse me, gentlemen, I must try to find the one attached to Cheryl Farnsworth."

"She just gave a speech," said Wickes.

"And just as soon as she turned the podium over to Archbishop Fulbright," I said, "she slipped away."

"You're right," said Taper, looking toward the platform. "She's not there."

"Which brings us back to my two things," I said. "But now there's more. You can hold me here, beating yourselves silly with your lips, or you can prevent another murder. If tossing the archbishop off the stage is beneath you, then learn to delegate authority. Tell some rookie to do it. Meanwhile, go check out Starfire's corpse in the woods. You might even decide to come back and arrest me, since my footprints are all around the body. I'll take that risk. I'm so stupid I even tripped over it. You'll look even more stupid when it comes out that I reported a crime and you didn't act, and that was after I told you how to prevent a murder and you chose not to. Frankly, at this point, I don't care what you do."

Sensing that their grip had loosened during this part of the discussion, no doubt due to sheer boredom from listening to

two dull speeches simultaneously, I struggled free. Withou
another moment's hesitation, I followed my original plan an
waded into a backwash of people who were lolling along th
outer edge of the courtyard, sipping champagne and gos
siping. I drifted away, as it were, on the tide.

"Hey," I heard Wickes whisper-shout behind me.

"Never mind him," said Taper. "We've got to do some
thing—"

The rest of the lieutenant's words were drowned by a fresh
flourish of animated sound waves emanating in amplifie
splendor from the speakers' platform.

"... and now for some truly exciting, remarkably exhila
rating, and enticingly unexpected news," Archbishop Ful
bright was blathering in earnest. A more compelling reason
for a ban on thesaurus-based speeches could not be imagined
"As you know," he said, back of right hand pressed to hi
forehead in adjudicatious dismay, "I've been proposing th
construction of a new cathedral for years, but certain specia
interest groups, which I need not name, have consistentl
hampered my plans to tear down one of our oldest, aestheti
cally outmoded, and architecturally medieval churches an
replace it with a splendid, utilitarian, synergetic modern struc
ture. I've never understood the selfish mentality of those who
oppose change, who cling to the familiar old at the expense o
the refreshing new ..."

I was slowly zigzagging through the bystanders, working m
way around the crowded rim of the courtyard. There seeme
to be more people milling and mixing than sitting and listen
ing. Well, what did the archbishop expect? The people wer
acting no different than they did at his Masses.

" ...We live in a time of great change," continued the arch
bishop, turning a page with a flourish, "in which change fo
the sake of change has become the recognized and expecte
mode of operation of the power of the supreme transcenden
spirit of our age, which is to say ..."

A page later I was nearing the steps by which Cheryl had so
recently made her furtive exit from the speakers' platform.
had come all the way around the courtyard without so much
as a glimpse of her.

From this new angle I could see the two stainless steel foun
tains, one happily spurting champagne and the other blithely
gushing vodka, right in front of the platform, both within easy
spitting distance of the archbishop himself. Folks were stroll

ing by right in front of His Highness, helping themselves while he spoke.

Sitting in the front row of folding chairs, with the best view of the archbishop and the shortest distance to the tinkling rivulets of Akavit, was Dr. Yomtov from the Good Samaritan Medical Center.

Beside him sat Jacco Babs, the master of the twisted quote, and his photographer and T-shirt valet, Ziggie Svelte. Jacco looked bored. His notebook sat scribble-less on his knee. Ziggie, on the other hand, seemed to be enjoying himself, taking picture after picture of the Catholic social elite as they meandered by their choice of fountains, filling their plastic crystal glasses with happy juices.

"... In an age," droned Archbishop Morley Psalmellus Fulbright in a tone usually reserved for eulogies, "when all the computers in the world are merging into one huge artificially intelligent super-brain through the miracle of fiber-optic telephone communications ..."

At the amplified mention of the word "telephone," I glanced back toward the space-egg at the opposite corner of the square and spotted the shimmering purple dress, and inside it the woman who had introduced Archbishop Fulbright as a "rock of resolution" a few minutes before. She was inserting a coin in the slot and lifting the receiver to her left ear.

And then it hit me.

"... *be particularly wary of anyone with a cellular phone or walkie-talkie. The events at St. Barbara's were set off with a call to a phone-activated device ...*"

But Father Baptist hadn't thought of the pay phone—perhaps he hadn't noticed it when he had visited the mission on Saturday—but the logic was the same:

    —If there was some kind of explosive device rigged under the
       platform;
    —And if it was set to be triggered by a telephone call;
    —And if I saw Cheryl Farnsworth making a call at this very
       moment, albeit from a pay phone;
    —And if ...

Suddenly I remembered the blue sheet of paper on which Father and I had doodled that morning, the one I had showed

to Millie on our way out. "The blueprint of how Father figured out what the murderer is up to," I had called it.

I fumbled in my pocket, pulled it out, and unfolded it in
such haste I tore one of the seams. Flipping it over, I scanned
the other side, the side I'd only glimpsed earlier. GOOD
SAMARITAN MEDICAL CENTER said the logo in the upper
left corner. It was a computer printout of telephone calls
made from Room 316 on June sixteenth. There were five
phone numbers, none of which I recognized. I didn't have to.
Something else was becoming apparent:

> — If June sixteenth was the Friday on which Bishop Raven-
>   shorst and three women had been electrocuted at St. Bar-
>   bara's Chapel ... a quick finger-count proved this to be the
>   case;
> — And, if 316 had been the room where Cheryl Farnsworth re-
>   cuperated after having been poisoned at Darby's ... if
>   memory served me, it was;
> — And if this printout was correct ... and there was no reason
>   to believe otherwise;
> — And if she made a call at the precise time of the electrical
>   explosion at St. Barbara's ... yes, there was a call placed
>   at 8:07 pm;
> — And if that call had been made to the pager connected to the
>   switching device discovered by the police ... yes, here was
>   the number: "555-0202 mobile";
> — And if "mobile" meant "not bolted down" as in "a pager" ...
>   which I was pretty sure it did;
> — Then ...

"Wow," I said aloud, my head spinning. A switch had
definitely just flipped to "exhaust mode" in my head.

Without taking the time to fold it, I jammed the blue sheet
back into my pocket. With renewed vigor, I started elbowing
my way towards the space-egg phone booth, some hundred or
so feet away.

"Miss Farnsworth," I called. "Cheryl. Don't do it!"

She didn't seem to notice. Her attention was divided between looking at Archbishop Fulbright up there on the platform, and listening for a dial tone.

Satisfied on both counts, she raised her right hand with the
distinction of a faerie queen, extended her index finger toward

buttons, and made an elegant jabbing motion with her
ist.

90

DOESN'T TAKE LONG to punch in a telephone number on
ouch-tone phone, yet the events I'm going to describe in
s chapter all occurred within just that length of time. Ob-
ve:

PUNCH. The first number of seven.
I wish I could say something dramatic like, "I sprang into
tion." If I didn't have spinal arthritis, and if I hadn't in-
med it via numerous jarring activities within the last half
ur, and if I were thirty years younger, and perhaps if I'd
rtaken at the stainless steel fountains, and of course if pigs
d wings and rain was beer, I might have done just that. As it
is, and as I am, I did my best. I'll leave it to my Maker to
cide if it was good enough.
Seeing Cheryl jab the first number, "I lumbered into ac-
n," pitching this way and that in the general direction of
e phone booth at the other end of the courtyard.
"... On the event of the dedication of this mission built in
nturies past," the archbishop was hollering, "I'm an-
uncing the construction of a new cathedral only a stone's
ow away on land which is clearly the property of the arch-
cese, on land that is not the concern of special interest
oups who would stand in the way of multilateral advance-
nt, on land that has been entrusted into our humble care for
e greater glory of progress. I mean, of course, that shabby
igle of unkempt trees over to my left."
"The woods?" gasped a gruff old beetle of a man as I el-
wed past. The gray and white hairs in his ears, like those
otruding from his nostrils, bristled with insect fury. "Does
 mean the woods?"
"That's virgin forest," exclaimed the equally gruff old she-
etle at his side, probably his wife. "Oak trees older than
is city."
"He wouldn't dare," snarled a similarly gruff young she-
etle at his other side, probably their progeny.

"Outrageous," sniffed the gruff old bug.

"The insufferable windbag," snorted his gruff old wi
bug.

"There'll be hell to pay for this," huffed their teen-b
offspring, secure in her lessons.

Just then there was a scream. A man's scream. It ca
from the direction of the stable.

"Did I—? Did they—? Didn't you—?"

"Where'd that guy come from?" barked the same gua
who had met with civil resistance from my trusty cane.

"Get him," yelled Lieutenant Taper's voice. Ah, at least
was finally making himself useful. "He escaped from t
hospital two nights ago."

"Escaped?" gulped the guard, who had perhaps h
enough for one day. "You mean he's nuts?"

"Completely," said Wickes, breaking into a run. "Wor
than the other guy with the cane."

"Yikes," winced the cop, limping into action.

Between the twitching antennae of the gruff old bugs w
were so displeased with Archbishop Fulbright's plans for t
woods, I saw Taper, Wickes, and the staggering guard desce
on Denzil Fedisck Goolgol's quivering Adam's apple l
than ten feet from where Cheryl Farnsworth was standir
Two plumpish blondes in matching strapless dresses squeak
as they were bumped aside by the constabulary convergenc
but most of the people in the immediate area didn't seem
notice. The monsignor's pale arms flailed crazily in the a
the remnants of hospital restraints still trailing from his bo
wrists. He was wearing one of those tied-behind hospi
gowns—a momento, no doubt, of his recent escape. Lucki
he was also wearing loose blue hospital pants, the kind wo
by male nurses and surgeons, so his behind behind the tie
behind need not be described here.

For a moment, four men coalesced into one rolling, rockir
bouncing ball of human turbulence. But Goolgol squirm
free and flopped out onto the ground several feet away like
greased trout.

"Did I—?" he continued to scream as he groped toward t
speakers' platform on all four flippers. "Did they—? Didr
you—?"

"Grab him," yelled Taper.

Basically, the scenario repeated itself ten feet or so closer
the stage.

"Forget that," barked Jacco Babs to his strobe-popping
dekick, Ziggie, who was focusing his camera on a buxom
ocialite's décolletage as she leaned to hold her champagne
lass under the bubbly flow in the fountain. Jacco was wig-
ling his scoop-sniffing finger in the direction of the Goolgol
quad. "Get a load of this."
Without skipping an F-stop, Ziggie obliged.
Seeing I wasn't going to get any help from Taper and
Vickes, I didn't bother to try to catch their attention. Instead,
continued my struggle in the general direction of the phone
ooth. Most of the people in my path were like the oaks in
he old forest, except less gracious.
"'Scuse me," I huffed, trying to nudge my way between
vo deep-rooted sycamores. They wouldn't budge. I tried to
o around but blundered into three more immovable trunks.
'Scuse me. 'Scuse me."
With a sinking heart, I saw Cheryl's finger dart again at the
uttons.

PUNCH. The second number of seven.
"Hey you! Stop!"
"It's him!"
"Nail the bastard."
I hadn't moved more than ten feet when another commo-
on erupted at the foot of the steps I had just moved away
rom.
Out of the corner of my eye I saw a black cassock being
ackled from three directions at once by uniformed police-
en.
Naturally, this was enough to divert my attention from
heryl. I spun around. "Father Baptist?" I called, peering
round wiggling antennae, between chawing mandibles, and
hrough jewelry dangling from twitching forelegs. The bug
amily had brought their relatives. I backed up and bumped
nto the immovable sycamores. If I'd had claustrophobia, I'd
ave been sweating.
"Way-dah-go, men," yelled the unmistakable voice of
Bulldog Billowack from somewhere in the bushes behind and
o the left of the speakers' platform. What he was doing back
here I'll never know. "Hang on. I'm coming."
Snarling like attack dogs, the three cops rose to their full
eight, dragging the figure in black to his feet. Though
vinded, there was still fight in him.

"Aaaagh!" howled one of the officers as a black-sleeve
fist made contact with his protruding stomach.

"I'll show you, Padre," growled his partner, followe
abruptly by his own, "Aaaagh!"

"You son of a—" said the third officer, swinging his pa
with all his might. If he'd been a discus thrower, and his han
was detachable, it would have sailed right over the chapel roo
"Yeow. What kind of a priest are you?"

The first officer was attempting to apply a hammer loc
"You know how we take care of troublemakers like you?"

" ... bulldozers," announced Archbishop Fulbright, wh
either didn't hear or didn't care about the minor skirmishe
springing up all around him. He was in full form, undaunte
and triumphant. "Yes, the bulldozers will commence the
holy labors on the first of next month. Within a few week
my friends, the woods will be no more ..."

"Mrs. Magillicuddy must be having a cow at this very mc
ment," I mumbled.

"Forget that," barked Jacco Babs, elbowing Ziggie, who wa
still absorbed in the Goolgol conundrum. Jacco's snoopin
finger was wiggling in the opposite direction toward the cas
sock-punching event. "Get a load of this."

"... the ground will be cleared and leveled," dreamed th
archbishop, "ready for the next phase to begin ..."

"Ooof!" said the three cops as the black cassock erupted i
renewed frenzy.

"Gotcha," said Ziggie, shutters fluttering, as the cop
obliged.

Realizing there wasn't a thing I could possibly do to alle
viate the situation, I turned my attention back to the space-eg
phone booth.

There stood Cheryl, cool as a proverbial cucumber, castin
the most unnerving smile toward the archbishop as he wave
his wings, preened his feathers, and expounded on his ne
nesting plans.

"'Scuse me, please," I said, renewing my pointless driv
across the back of the courtyard. "Sorry about that. 'Scus
me. 'Scuse me."

Still smiling, Cheryl raised her button-poking finger again.

PUNCH. The third number of seven.

"To the fray!" cried a familiar voice. "Now me lads, mak
lively!"

"Now what?" hollered another guard near the platform.

"To victory," yelled the same voice, which of course belonged to Pierre Bontemps. "Charge!"

"To victory," answered Jonathan and Edward. "Eeeeaaaaggghhh!"

The three Tumblars burst out of the thicket to the right and behind the platform, slashing through floral arrangements and hanging decorations as they went. Flower petals and crepe paper ribbons streamed from their arms as they approached the rear of the stage. Their clothes were frayed and torn from their trek "through rather than around." Suddenly, several mountain-sized police guards materialized between these valiant Tumblars and the back of the stage. Undaunted, the Tumblars spun on their heels, rushed around the side of the platform, and dashed to the front. There they stood their ground, arms folded, between the two stainless steel liquor fountains, less than six feet from the archbishop's feet.

"Your Grace, hear us," said Pierre, in tones as close to a yell as one can get without showing off their wisdom teeth. "Your life is in grave danger. We've come to offer our—oof!"

Pierre was knocked off his feet by a uniformed policeman, formerly a first-string tackle at Ogre State.

"Right on," cheered Jacco Babs, nudging Ziggie, who dutifully changed focus for this unexpected development which had landed right at their feet. "Bravo, bravo."

Jonathan and Edward struggled to pull the officer off their comrade, only to find themselves knocked down by two more.

"Your Grace!" they all cried. "Hear us!"

"... It will be a bright new day for the brand new Church," the archbishop was saying, his tone growing loftier by the syllable. "Picture it if you can, my friends: brilliant towers of steel and glass, glistening in the morning sun, digitized bells proclaiming the joyous message: Come to me my sacred sycophants, and I will give you ..."

"Arrest them," roared another all-too-familiar voice. Chief Billowack had emerged, his jowls rippling like the glossy fur of a marauding grizzly bear. "Do you hear me? Bloody arrest the whole lot of them. No, not the spectators, you imbecile. Father Baptist and his gang of merry men."

"What the hell kind of a priest are you?" roared one of the officers who was still at the far end of the platform, wrestling with the cassock.

"That's what I've been trying to tell you—ooof!"

Either those cops never went to church, or they didn't read the newspapers. They obviously didn't know their department's history. "Lynch anything in a cassock," had been Chief Billowack's orders. And so they were about to.

Except the man they were about to string up was not Father Baptist. It was Arthur—Arthur wearing Father Baptist's spare cassock and Roman collar. That's what Father had fetched from the kitchen before we left the rectory. Arthur must have donned it in the fig grove. A good idea, as it turned out, except for poor Arthur, who, in spite of a heroic effort, was no match for three over-stuffed policemen. He had agility, poise, stamina, and speed. But the cops had sheer weight on their side. All they had to do was sit on him and it was all over.

"Yield," cried Arthur.

"Who're you calling a 'yield'?" snorted one of them.

"It means 'surrender,' Mitch," said his partner.

"Who? Me?"

"No, Mitch. Him. Father Baptist."

"I'm not Father Baptist," gasped Arthur, fighting for breath.

"Sure you're not."

"I'm what's known as a diversion," winced Arthur cooperatively.

"Sure you are, Father. Sure you are."

PUNCH. The fourth number of seven.

I was still some twenty feet away from the phone booth.

"Free!" called Pierre, throwing off his assailants and dashing to the foot of the speakers' platform. "Rally around me, lads. The day is not yet done."

"The Tumblars!" called the others, twisting out of the clutches of the officers who were trying to slap handcuffs on their wrists. "The Tumblars! Hurrah!"

"Did I—?" screamed Monsignor Goolgol. I couldn't see him, but his warble drifted high above the heads of the crowd. "Did they—? Didn't you—? Didn't somebody—? Didn't anybody—?"

"Arrest them," roared Billowack, flames spouting from every orifice above his neck. "I don't care who gets hurt."

"Hey you! Stop!"

Another commotion erupted at the far side of the platform. Father Baptist—the real one this time—was half way up the steps, trying to shake a policeman loose who had grabbed his leg.

"... towers of crystal, towers of hope ..."

"You've no business here," huffed the policeman grappling with Father Baptist. "You were told to stay away."

"More than you think," said Father through gritted teeth. "Business, I mean."

"Listen to him," pleaded Fake-Father Arthur, similarly imposed. "He's trying to help."

"Whud thuh hell's goin' on?" bellowed Billowack, stomping toward both cassocks.

PUNCH. The fifth number of seven.

"Yeow!" yelled the officer who was grappling with Father Baptist.

"You forget I've had the same training," said Father Baptist. "Better, actually." Executing an amazing kick-spin-flip, I leapt off the steps and shot for the guys who were manhandling Arthur. "And as for you—"

The cassock-eating trolls went flying.

Whirling around, Father dashed for the steps again. Arthur was at his heels.

Several prominent ladies who were seated behind Archbishop Fulbright on the stage squealed like piglets at the sight of two marauding priests charging up the stairs. They shrieked even more when Father barked, "Everyone off this stage!"

"Just who do you think you are?" drawled one lady who was fat enough for two.

"The Face of Death," said Father, "if you don't get out of here."

"I'll have you know—"

"Now! Arthur?"

In some respects it might not have seemed proper for a priest and a pseudo-priest, who looked enough like a priest to have been mistaken for one twice, to knock a few double-wide ladies hard enough to send them backwards-somersaulting off the rear edge of the platform and into a patch of low-growing junipers. Their short but dramatic flight was punctuated by a screech not heard on this planet since Rodan sat on a volcano.

"... towers of faith," the archbishop was chanting, "towers of progress, towers of love ..."

"Hey, man," said a face with which I had just collided.

I'd recognize the aroma of the archivist from KROM anywhere. "Marty? What brings you here?"

"Whoa, Cane Dude," he said, rattling his beads with gl
"Didn't I tell you? I'm a Cath'lic from waaaaaaay back."

"Really," I said, "I could tell."

He blinked. "Whooooooa, man. Like, how did y
know?"

"Later," I said conspiratorially. "But first, for a real thr
keep your eyes on that speakers' platform."

"Hey, man. Like, why?"

"Trust me," I winked, patting his shoulder as I lurched
by.

"Sure, Cane Man. Sure. Where ever you go, firewo
fly."

"... towers of joy, towers of ..."

"Your Grace!" yelled Pierre, taking a stand again betwe
the fountains.

"Hear us!" yelled the other Tumblars who had managed
get to his side.

"Oooooo," cooed some nearby ladies. "Lookie the
They're so cyoooooooot."

"Keep it up," cackled Jacco Babs, slapping his and Ziggi
knee in stereo. "I can't believe it. Another front pager."

"Almost there," I was huffing. "Almost there, alm
there."

PUNCH. The sixth number of seven.

Ten feet to go.

"Martin," said Solomon Yung-sul Wong, the city coroner

"Yeah, Martin," said John Holtsclaw, his assistant.

"Yo," I waved as I hobbled past them, only to be broug
up short by a couple of snorting social peccaries. These m
have been distant cousins of the squealing piglets who had j
been pushed off the stage.

"Your Grace," said Father Baptist, approaching his law
superior at the microphone.

"... peace," the archbishop was saying, "towers of tra
quillity, towers of security ..."

"Did I—?" wailed Monsignor Goolgol who had just cla
ored up onto the rear of the platform. Somehow he had ma
aged to elude Lieutenant Taper, Sergeant Wickes, the bi
bellied guard, and a flock of screeching, back-flipping, paris
leader ladies. He was waving his hands, the straps of the hc
pital restraints dangling from his wrists like thin, white ma
ples.

His eyes were glassy tide pools, smooth and glistening on
e surface, but teeming with mysterious multi-tentacled life
ithin. "Did they—? Didn't you—?"

"Morley," said Father Baptist sternly. "Listen to me.
ou've got to—"

"... towers lifting the hearts of mankind and womankind
."

"She didn't," giggled one of the social hens in my path.

"She did," clucked her friend.

"Eeeeeeek!" they both shrieked, bending backwards in a
asm of shared hilarity.

It was like the opening of a drawbridge. Suddenly, a course
esented itself. With all my might—which admittedly wasn't
uch by then—I burst through the narrow, jiggling channel
d dove for the phone booth.

"Cheryl," I yelled, "don't!"

For the first time in all this ruckus, she pivoted her head to-
ards me, her golden pendant swinging into sight as she did
). There was a flash of purple sequins as her body shifted
ithin the dress. I can't begin to imagine the thoughts that
ickered behind those chilling, glacial eyes, or the kind of
ind that tugged the muscles of her face into such an alluring
nile.

Alluring? Yes, if you have a thing for serpents.

I thought I'd outgrown my reptilian period when I entered
y twenties, but ... surprise, surprise.

"Why Martin," she said softly, paralyzing me with her
enetrating stare. "How in the world?"

I gulped as her finger went for the last button.

PUNCH. The seventh number. Too late.

Close as I was, I could hear the click of circuits. A tiny
lectronic chirp came from the tiny speaker in the receiver.
imultaneously, a louder warbling sound came from the di-
ction of the speakers' platform. The connection had been
ade.

Her smile broadened.

I lunged anyway, knocking her backwards. The receiver
ipped from her hand and thonked me in the forehead. Her
ead made a dull sound as it collided with the edge of the im-
ervious space-egg dome. Her legs buckled and she toppled
) the ground, grabbing for me as she fell. I sprawled on top
f her, the blue scarf snagging in my open mouth and my left

hand entangled in the chain around her neck. A most aw
ward moment.

Something snapped.

A moment later I was shaking the stars out of my eyes as
forest of human legs gathered around us.

"Did you see that?" said a voice somewhere up in th
branches. "This guy's nuts."

"Kick him if he tries to get up," said another voice.

"But he's dangerous, Dear," said the first.

"Police," cried yet another voice.

Through blurring eyes, I looked down at something in m
hand. It was the pendant which I'd seen so many times dan
gling from Cheryl Farnsworth's elfin neck. Funny, but :
slow as time had become, it downshifted again into an arduou
crawl. Amidst the encumbering shadows of yammering spe
tators and their condescending knees, I knelt there staring
the golden amulet resting in my palm.

In my mind's eye I envisioned another pendant, this on
made of pewter. It was the one we found in Sister Charle
Vickers' room. It was so real, I could have reached out an
touched it, but I was too absorbed in the progress of m
thoughts to think to do so.

Suddenly another memory flooded swiftly in and pushe
both pendants aside. This new intrusive image was scrawled i
Father Baptist's peculiar hand, a drawing he had made only
few hours before:

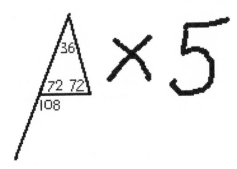

Then, as if huffing in indignation, the two metal pendants came drifting back, this time superimposing themselves on Father's scribblings.

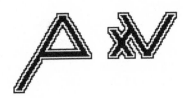

And then I saw the connection.

The number of the pendant on the left was 36 + 72 + 72 + 108, equaling 288. The meaning of the pendant on the right suddenly became obvious.

xV.

Times five.

288 times 5 equals ... 1440.

"Keep that number in mind," said Father's voice, just as I'd heard it that morning. *"It may be useful later."*

I blinked and stared at my open palm. There it was, just as I'd jotted it back at the rectory:

1440.

"Yes, Father," I whispered, "it has proved useful."

With the same hand, I turned the pendant over. Tiny Roman numerals glistened yet another equation:

MCDXL x II = X = ∞

1440 times 2 equals ... X?

The enigmatic X in the casting quilt. The symbol for which Willie Kapps could find no purpose. An hourglass? No. Merely something to fill a space? No.

X was the Roman numeral for 10.

The 10 was in a circle.

What had someone said about circles?—circles on casting quilts?

" *... some witches,*" echoed the voice of Guillaume du Crane Cristal, also known as Willie "Skull" Kapps, sipping his mweemuck root tea, *"consider a circle around a symbol to be an omen of sacrifice."*

Sacrifice.

The wheels were spinning faster as the clock slowed down:

- —A pentagram is composed of 5 triangles;
- —5 triangles represent 5 people;
- —5 people, according to Starfire's brand of fru-fru, make a "Pentoven";
- —The total number of degrees in a pentagram is 1440;
- —1440, therefore, also represents 5 people;
- —"1440 times 2" equals "5 people times 2";
- —1440 times 2, therefore, equals 10 people;
- —10, on the casting quilt, was in a circle of sacrifice;
- —Therefore ...

Ten was the number of people who had to die.

For what?

What was the goal represented by the blank space in the
sting quilt?

Spirit."

The symbol for infinity. Cheryl Farnsworth had sought the
mber of the "elixir of life" and found it in "infinity."
And as all these things flickered through my reeling brain,
d all within the blink of an eye, mind you, the next se-
ence of events set in motion by Cheryl's phone call com-
nced.

t began with a shrill, warbling sound.
t came from the speakers' platform.
Against all desire to the contrary, I turned to look at what
s happening.

"Whoooooah," groaned Marty a few feet away, dropping
ciggie in trippy ecstasy.

91

. TO THE LOFTY DIVINE PINNACLES," Archbishop Ful-
ght was moaning, his eyes uplifted and his fingers em-
cing the sun, "of the interpersonal interpretational god-
od."

He had finally come to a period.

That's when the phone rang. It was one of those intrusive
ctronic sounds that was more of a shrill two-toned trill than
esounding old-fashioned ring. Not a welcome conclusion
such a long release of warm episcopal wind. It was also a
incongruous, coming from somewhere under the platform,
neath the spot where the archbishop was standing.

"Huh?" blinked the archbishop.

"Huh?" gasped the gardener as he was caught under the
npits by a pair of steel claws. His shoulders were suddenly

rubbing his ears, and his elbows went out at bizarre angles.
found himself being hoisted onto his feet.

"Okay, Bub," growled a voice inches from my right e
"I'm takin' you to see the chief."

The big-bellied guard, having abandoned the attempt
capture Monsignor Goolgol in favor of less slippery pr
tightened his grip on my knotted arms and pushed me in
direction of the platform.

"But Officer," I protested.

"But nuthin'," he answered, giving me an angry shal
"Get movin'."

The phone rang again. Fulbright's eyes darted defensiv
this way and that. His gaze fell upon the pair of approachi
cassocks. "Father Baptist?!?! What in heaven's name—?"

"Indeed," said Father Baptist, "in Heaven's name."

"Stop your dab gum struggling," ordered the gua
bringing his knee up into the small of my back and propelli
me savagely.

"Awrk." I tripped over something—my own feet
his—and teetered forward, stumbling to my knees near t
cascade of gaily gurgling vodka.

"Mr. Feeney," yelped Edward who, along with Pierre a
Jonathan were attempting to stand their ground between t
liquor fountains as three policemen climbed all over ea
other to tear them limb from limb.

"Get up," barked the guard, yanking me to my feet in su
a way that my elbows met over my head. Then he threw
against the front of the speakers' platform. "I'll bre
your—"

"Dern gub it!" I groaned as my chest collided with t
edge. My ribs rattled audibly. Wincing, I looked up as l
Graciousness, Morley Fulbright, fists on hips, turned to fa
Father Baptist.

"How dare you—?"

"Forgive me, Your Grace," said Father. "I know precis
what I'm doing."

With that, Father curled into a running crouch. Arthur f
in beside him. The two of them ran right into Archbish
Fulbright at a wild, improvisational angle.

"Father BaaaAAAAAAHHHHHHHH!!!" brayed the arc
bishop at the moment of impact. He kept on bellowing as t
three of them flew off the front of the stage. I ducked as th
soared right over my head.

This primitive attempt at triple-manned space-flight had no
~ance of achieving orbit. The weight and speed vs. thrust
~d gravity were all wrong. Predictably, the doomed space-
~aft achieved its brief apogee and then fell, breaking apart as
~ plummeted to earth.

Father Baptist landed in the midst of the Tumblars, who
~shioned his fall without breakage of limb or bone.

Arthur, cassock flapping, came down sideways on the edge
~ the champagne fountain. The thing jerked, teetered and
~ueaked as it twisted off its polished metal stand and toppled
~ the ground. This was an appropriate end to Arthur's career
~ an astronaut and a cleric. He sat there on the ground, jaws
~pen, as a stream of the bubbly poured from the top of the
~ckeyed fountain into his gaping mouth.

As for Archbishop Fulbright, he bellowed all the way
~own—"AAAAAAHHHHH!"—crashing right on top of
~iggie Svelte as the camera's strobe made one final punctu-
~ing flash.

In the midst of all those descending bodies, somebody's
~nee, foot, or fist must have caught my own pot-bellied captor
~n the temple, because he ended up face-up on the ground,
~ars and tweeting birds circling above his forehead.

As for me, it was all I could do to hold on to the edge of the
~age while my vertebrae clanged like a windchime in a gale.
~hatever repercussions we were going to have to face, at least
~rchbishop Fulbright was safe.

"What the bloody hell is goin' on?" roared Chief Bil-
~wack, thrashing around somewhere in the chaos like God-
~illa being attacked by submarines.

With all the clash and clatter, only yours truly heard the
~icking of switches underneath the stage. Cheryl's phone call
~as being answered. One by one, electrical pathways opened,
~lowing a stampede of cascading currents to bolt for their
~estructive destinations.

A millisecond later, Monsignor Goolgol was standing at the
~xact spot vacated by Archbishop Fulbright. He clutched the
~icrophone stand with both hands, knuckles white with confu-
~on.

"Did I—?" his plaintive voice went out over the public ad-
~ress system. "Did they—? Didn't you—? Didn't—"

And that's when the flash came.

All those cases of fireworks I'd seen in the stable went off at
~nce. They had been cunningly hidden in the flower pots and

planters that dotted the stage. They were all of the white vari
ety. No snazzy colors, just pure white.

It was so bright that everyone covered their eyes.

Everyone but me. My reflexes being substandard, and m
hands already occupied in clutching the edge of the platform
and mostly because I was captivated by the whole business, m
eyes were wide open.

Mesmerized, I looked on as the platform blew apart, e
plosive charges erupting underneath the planks. As th
boards and studs scattered, I watched Monsignor Goolgol fa
arms and straps flailing.

"—I?" was his last uttered word as he landed on the gra
two feet below, belly-flop style. It turned into an agonizin
scream as he realized that something was burning his face.
raised, red-hot heating element had been bolted to a strateg
spot on the metal platter. It was burning its image into h
flesh, scorching his nose, blistering his cheeks, searing h
eyes. He tried to heave himself off the thing, but the surfac
of the grate was slippery, smeared with oil. His arms and le
kept sliding out from under him, slamming his head again
the searing metal triangle. The apex pointed up, scalding i
treacherous angle into his bony forehead.

Whatever wire had been used to secure the swiveling lid,
was no longer there. The grate tipped, groaning menacingl
Monsignor Goolgol's body shifted accordingly. He sighe
convulsively, relieved to be free of that bizarre branding iro
But his elation was momentary. It vaporized as he began t
realize his blind peril. The angle of the tilting grate wa
growing steeper and steeper. He scrambled to find a finge
hold on the oily surface without success. Whimpering pathet
cally, he slipped closer and closer to the descending edge
With a final yelp, he slid off into the swirling froth below.

Gallons and gallons of Akavit engulfed him, every drop siz
zling with countless thousands of volts of deadly electricit
For a man who preferred club soda, it was a horrible way t
die.

"Pickled instantly," would be the comment of Solomo
Yung-sul Wong within the hour.

"Sort of the distilled version of electro-plating," Joh
Holtsclaw would add, consulting his clipboard. "Flash i
corruption. You could bury his body directly in raw dirt an
leave it there for a year. When you dug him up, he'd still b
perfectly preserved."

"The funeral boys will have a field day with this," concluded Solomon Yung-sul Wong with a knowing look.

Meanwhile, as all the monsignor's recent questions were answered while his body was electro-marinated, the grate returned to its original flat position with a resounding metallic burp. With that, five cardboard bundles attached to the bottom of the lid burst open, dumping blocks of dry ice into the mixture. Gushers of white mist shot up through the grate, up through the gaping hole in the platform, and billowed outward, pouring off the stage like a river of thick, sweet, fudge-like clouds.

I shivered as the fog surged past me. Swallowing a wave of nausea, I released my hold on the platform and turned around.

"Whoooooah," groaned a hippie in the back of the stunned audience. "Awesome, dude."

"Oh my word," sniveled the archbishop as the fog rolled by, clawing his way free of the tangle of arms and legs that was Jacco Babs and Ziggie Svelte. Shaken, he sprawled back on the ground, looking up through the white mist toward the incandescent orb of the noonday sun. Surely it had to be one of the eeriest things he'd ever seen in his life.

Or perhaps, I mused, the most beatific.

Strange noises began intruding on the confusion: the sputter of dying fireworks, the cries of terrified people running every which way, the slurp and gurgle of the ominous cocktail under the platform, and finally the easing see-saw of my heaving lungs.

I watched through swirls of frosty mist as Archbishop Fulbright looked up toward the sun through the churning haze, tears streaming from his eyes. A shadow fell across his face. "Oh, gracious me," he said, smiling magnanimously and extending his hand. "Oh my dear woman, please help me up."

"Your worships," said the silhouette, curtseying as best as her crickety old legs would allow. "Here's what's an old lady who calls them woods over yonder 'home' thinks of your highness'es crystal cathedral, she does."

"Huh?"

With that, Mrs. Magillicuddy conked him on the head with her beloved William's sturdy, war-time-issue binoculars. They survived the shock intact. The archbishop survived, too, but wasn't aware of that fact for almost an hour.

92

"PENTAGRAMS?" ROARED CHIEF BILLOWACK. "One thousand four hundred and forty degrees? That's a lot of crap, Jack."

"Then explain to me," answered Father dryly, "how I knew that Archbishop Fulbright's life was in danger on that platform."

The archbishop, massaging the huge bump on his forehead, grunted.

All parties concerned had been transported to police headquarters for questions, statements, arguments, reprimands, and general confusion.

"You were told to keep out, Lombard," said Billowack, jabbing Father Baptist in the chest with a flick-wrist gesture reminiscent of Cheryl Farnsworth's final button-jab, but with a lot more punch.

"And if I had stayed away," answered Father, "Archbishop Fulbright would be dead."

"Even so," slavered Billowack, "I should arrest the whole lot of you."

"Sure," nodded Father, looking over at the Tumblars. "Sure. You do that, and just imagine what would happen in your jail tonight."

"To Joel," cried Pierre, raising a paper cup full of machine-dispensed coffee, "our released comrade."

"To Joel," cheered them all. Since paper cups don't make proper toasting sounds, the Tumblars improvised. "Clink," they laughed as they bumped cups together. "Clink, clink clink-clink, clink."

"To Father John Baptist," saluted Arthur. "Long may he sleuth."

"Long may he sleuth," they agreed. "Clink-clink, clink clink-clink."

I was sitting on Lieutenant Taper's desk, two aisles removed from the excitement, licking my right thumb and using it to rub away the ink in my left palm.

1440 ...

"Keep that number in mind ..."

I doubted I'd ever forget it as long as I lived.

Just then Ziggie Svelte came strolling by, humming merrily, kissing an eight-by-ten glossy photograph. "Mr. Feeney," he winked, "word has already come back."

"Word?"

"From the news service. I sent this picture out over the
res less than a half hour ago. Already nominations are
oding in. It's all unofficial, you understand, but the indi-
tors are good."

"Nominations?"

"For a Strobie."

"Is that anything like a Grammy?"

"Yeah, but for newspaper photographers. And this honey is
ticket to the big leagues."

"I thought Jacco Babs already is in the big leagues."

"He is, but I'm just his photo-gopher."

"You walk in his shadow."

"Right, but no more."

"May I see it?"

"Sure. By year's end, everyone within walking distance of
ewspaper stand in the western world is going to recognize
You wait and see."

At first I wasn't sure what it was. Sort of a Stonehengey
d of assortment of stubby rocks arranged in a semicircle.
, there were two such semicircles, one swinging up, the
er down. Between was a cavern of some sort, with some
t of blurred, rubbery, bloated mass in the middle. And
spended above that was something glistening and bulbous,
t of like a wet punching bag.

"Is that a uvula?" I asked, pointing to the hangy-down
ng.

"It is," beamed Ziggie.

"So this here is a tongue, and these are teeth."

"Yup."

"So this is a picture of a mouth."

"A wide open mouth."

"Right. I've never seen one quite so wide. One, two, three
d crowns. And the owner of this mouth is, uh, scream-
g?"

"Uh-huh."

"And the identity of the owner of this mouth is ...?"

He hesitated, reveling in the moment. His cheeks puffed out
if containing an explosion. The detonation finally burst
ween his lips. "That's His Excellency, Morley Psalmellus
lbright, Archbishop of Los Angeles as seen from the per-
ective of the photographer who broke his fall from the
eakers' platform at the Del Agua Mission."

"You don't say." I examined it with fresh appreciatio
"And this picture—"

"Will be on the front page of every newspaper tomorro
morning, the lead story on every TV newscast this evenin
and on the covers of at least three major magazines t
month."

"Flattering." I handed it back to him. "Somehow I do
think the archbishop will be pleased."

"Here," he said, "you can keep it. Let me autograph it f
you. Trust me, in ten years it will really be worth somethin
A genuine Svelte, signed on the day of exposure."

"Sure. Why not?"

He scribbled something illegible in the lower right corner.

"Thanks." I waved the photo.

"You bet." He snapped his fingers.

As Ziggie strolled off, I slid off the desk and moseyed off
no particular direction, room to room, cubicle to cubicle. Th
was my second sojourn inside this police station in three da
and both visits were on this floor. I didn't think I'd ever wa
to work in a rat's maze like this.

Gardening at St. Philomena's was so much more rewardin

A few minutes later I happened to pass a large pane of gla
On the other side was the industrial gray room in which Fath
Baptist and I had spoken with Joel a few days before.

I froze.

She was sitting alone, chin nestled in her hands, elbows re
ing on the edge of the table. The purple sequined dress,
ravishing in broad daylight, now seemed startlingly out
place, as did the sky blue scarf, which hung like a brok
horseshoe around her neck. Her red hair was disheveled, a
there was a nasty crimson line around her throat where I h
inadvertently torn the chain and pendant from her as we fe
She did not seem sad so much as lost in thought, her eyes f
cused somewhere beyond the walls.

Without a second thought, I turned the doorknob and
myself into the room, knowing there was no handle on t
other side. Until someone came along, I'd be locked in w
her.

Somehow, I didn't mind. And if you ask me to explain t
thoughts and feelings that were whirling around in my sk
and chest, I'll just shrug. Gardener, deroot thyself.

Her eyes turned in my direction as I entered, but no oth
muscle moved.

"How's your head?" I asked, sitting down across from he

"I'll live," she said, not exactly coldly, but without dis-
cernible emotion.

"I'm really sorry about that," I stammered. "I mean,
about knocking you down."

Her shoulders heaved a fraction of an inch. "Just damaged
my pride a little." I almost thought I perceived a ghost of a
smile around the edges of her lips, sort of like the things that
seemed to move in Willie's shop. When I blinked it was gone.

"How are you?" she asked.

"Me?" Like I said, I had no way of explaining.

"You."

"Puzzled, I guess." How many times had I opened my
mouth to say something, anything, even some mundane or
stupid thing to this woman and nothing came out? And now
that something significant certainly needed to be said, how
dare I think I'd fare any better?

"You're not puzzled," she said, again with the hint of a
smile that wasn't really there. She interlocked her fingers and
rolled her shoulders in a feline stretch. "My life is an open
book."

"Or a casting quilt."

"Or a casting quilt," she nodded. There, a smile. The
muscles at the edges of her mouth actually tightened a wee bit.
The rest of her face remained inert. "What is it you want to
ask me, Martin?"

Martin. Not Mr. Feeney. Not just nothing. But Martin.

"I guess I'm trying to understand," I finally said.

"What's to understand?" she said. "Don't you remember
me?"

"Remember you?"

My mind flashed on her asking the same question two Sundays back. *"You don't remember me, do you?"* had been her
exact words on the front steps of St. Philomena's.

"I don't know what you mean," I finally said.

"Until you do," she blinked, "you won't know how it
started. But I can tell you where it ended."

"Infinity," I whispered.

Her eyebrows did a little hiccup. "What about infinity?"

"1440 times 2," I said, trying ever so hard not to sound like
a clever fellow being brilliant, "equals 10, within the rules of
your logic. Once ten people had been sacrificed, you got
your heart's desire: the blank space on the casting quilt. The
final symbol in the equation on the back of your pendant is
infinity.'"

"Very good," she smiled even more. "Did you figure [a]
this out, or was it your friend Father Baptist?"

"He laid the groundwork. The last bit was my own d[e]
duction, but I'm sure when he and I compare notes he w[ill]
have already reached the same conclusion."

"He picks his friends well."

"I wish I could say the same for you."

She tugged her right ear thoughtfully. "You know, befo[re]
he came along—Father Baptist, I mean—when I was planni[ng]
this whole thing, I really thought I would achieve my go[al]
without interference, without anyone figuring it out until I w[as]
finished. When he started nosing around, that possibility b[e]
gan to fade. But I knew from the beginning, deep down, I'[d]
spend the rest of my days behind bars."

"Then why did you go ahead with your plan?"

She let her ear go with a dull snap. "Because I deemed t[he]
goal worth it, obviously."

"And what is that goal?"

"As you said, Martin, 'infinity.'"

"Which means?"

"Oh come now, Martin." She folded her hands on the t[a]
ble and leaned forward on her elbows, not a gesture of e[n]
thusiasm but rather cool concentration. "What does everyo[ne]
truly want? Money? Perhaps. But money's no good if yo[u]
health fails. Long life? The longer you live, the more mise[ry]
you experience. Love? Sure, everyone wants to fall in lov[e]
but only a miserable few want to stick it out once it gets bo[r]
ing. And the sad thing about love is that it invariably does g[et]
old all too fast."

"You have a dim view of life."

"So do you. Still, I sensed you were interested—"

A blush exploded on my face.

"—and for a brief moment, there on the steps of S[t.]
Philomena's, I considered changing my mind. Perhaps, [I]
thought, this man could keep it interesting. But you know, t[he]
ladies in the choir were right: I'm not your type. And you'[re]
not mine."

"I don't know what to say."

"Then don't say anything." Again with her half-smil[e.]
"Just promise me one thing."

"What's that?"

"Wear that stupid hat at my trial."

My blush must have worsened. No man could have so much blood rushing to his head without either rupturing or blushing.

"It will make me laugh," she said, reaching out and touching my hand. Her skin felt cold.

I didn't feel like making her laugh, not with my throat so tight.

"It'll be a short trial," she said. "You won't have to wear it for long."

I swallowed. My ears popped. I swallowed again.

"But you know what?" she continued, tugging her ear again. "It was already too late. The magick was already working. The casting quilt, I mean. I couldn't stop the spell any more than you could abandon your friend the priest. You love him far more than you could ever love me or any woman."

I swallowed again, stalling as I chose the right words to explain that camaraderie between men was an entirely different thing; that male fellowship has nothing whatsoever to do with … But of course, I said nothing.

"So where was I?" she said. "Money, love, what else? Health? The philosopher's stone? The elixir of life?"

"Akavit," I said. "'The water of life.'"

"Even the alchemists didn't get that far."

"Eternal youth? Is that what you wanted?"

She shook her head.

I tilted mine. "Then what?"

She bore into me with those glacial eyes. "Power."

"Power?"

"I wanted power. Spiritual power. For that, I was willing to assemble a group of angry, disenchanted, gullible women. Marsha Dukes thought she was made for better things than secretarial work, even if she couldn't spell. Madeline Sugarman sought the limelight, but wasn't good enough to compete in the 'real world.' She settled for a lame religious talk show on a dubious network. Stephanie Fury you knew about: a former nun who had been oppressed by a male-dominated religion. I could tell you things about her, things that would curdle your blood, but not now. And then there was Sister Vickers: a nun oppressed by the same religion—afraid to leave, gritting her teeth every moment she stayed."

I opened my mouth to say something, but suppressed the impulse.

"Naturally," she continued, tapping the table with her long fingernails for emphasis, "all these women knew nothing of classical metaphysics. They didn't understand that, as women, they could never be what they wanted to be because they simply weren't men. Not because men pull the strings, but because higher forces do."

I found my tongue. It had slipped into my shirt pocket. "I'm surprised to hear you say that."

"Not all sorceresses are frustrated feminists," she said, the closest thing yet to animation in her voice. "Like your Father Baptist, I have read the grimoires—the truly old scrolls. I've no use for the wishful thinking of retentive misanthropic shrews. Facts are facts. Men and women have different destinies. Only fools mess with destinies."

"What do you call ending peoples' lives?" I pressed my palms down flat on the table. It felt sticky. "Isn't that messing with destinies?"

"Perhaps I am a fool," she said matter-of-factly. "Not as bad as Starfire, but a fool just the same. She didn't hate men. She just liked cash. She was a con-artist and a charlatan."

"For that she deserved to die?"

"No, not for that."

"Then for what?"

"Not now, Martin."

That stopped me cold. I rubbed my fingers with my thumbs, trying to roll away whatever I'd picked up from the table top. "And why the bishops? Do you hate the Catholic Faith that much?"

"Not at all. At least, not the way you think."

"Then why?"

She began to toy with her scarf. "Later, Martin."

"Hm." I tried wiping my palms against my pant legs as nonchalantly as possible. "Is there anything you can tell me now?"

"Do you really want to know?"

No help for it. My hands remained tacky. "Yes. I'll admit I have, uh, feelings about you. I haven't felt this kind of attraction for, well, a long time. I admit I'm not used to it." I tried rubbing my palms together. "Or comfortable about it. As for love, I don't know. Attraction isn't love." I gave up and balled my hands into sticky fists. "But if there wasn't even a chance, I'd like to know why."

She sighed long and hard. "What difference does it make?"

"None," I shrugged. "You asked, so I asked."

She folded her arms and leaned back in her chair. "Find [th]e women who have no love. They didn't just lose it, or [co]me to distrust it; they pulverized it. By a sheer act of will, [the]y have forsaken their destiny as women. Convince them [tha]t they can conquer the men who pull the strings in their [liv]es, or in each other's lives, and they'll do anything. Add to [the] mix five men who have lost their faith. As I said, men [do]n't really pull the strings. If strings are meant to be pulled [at] all, they are meant to be pulled by women. The pattern [tur]ns upon itself."

"Like the pentagram."

"Yes, like the pentagram."

"Is this that envy Sigmund Freud was talking about?"

"In a magical sense, yes."

"And by manipulating these pathetic people with promises [of] what—happiness? empowerment?—you engineered all [the]se murders?"

"I pulled the strings. It was my destiny. First I titillated [the]ir imaginations. I promised the opening of doors of in-[cre]dible ascendancy in their lives. Then, when they thought [the] ideas were their own, we drew in the parallel catalyst. For [me]n with withered faith, it doesn't take much to instill coun-feit hope. Their hunger betrays them. One by one, we [lur]ed the bishops to the meadow with assurances of magical [wo]nders."

"Except once, when Bishop Brassorie brought the arch-[bi]shop."

"Ah yes, you know about that." She leaned forward and [res]ted her elbows on the table. Apparently stickiness didn't [bo]ther her. "I wasn't prepared to let him know who I was, so [I h]id. I don't know if he suspected. It doesn't matter now. It [wo]uld have been better if he had been the one to die, but [M]onsignor Goolgol filled in for him. That was his destiny. [Th]e pattern is complete."

[I] shrugged. "So now you have this 'power'?"

She shrugged back. "I do."

"And what good is it behind bars?"

"You don't understand the real nature of power. We are all [pri]soners in these vessels of flesh. And the flesh is weak, and [vu]lnerable. A virus is so small that a million of them swim-[mi]ng in a drop of water may never meet, yet such a tiny thing [ca]n dismantle any of us. You've had the flu. You know what [I] mean."

"I admit we're helpless before God. He made us out
nothing, and that is ultimately what we are."

"True, if you believe in God."

I wrinkled my eyebrows. "Don't you?"

"I don't know. Nor am I happy with terms like 'g
force' and 'universal mind.' What I do know is that a
power worth having is only in the mind." She tapped
forehead. "In here, each of us is an eternal universe. Thi
of the enormity of your thoughts and dreams, how deep is
ocean of our consciousness. In here, each of us is infinite.'

"Infinity." There was a bit of sand in my tone, but she
ther didn't notice or didn't mind.

"But the great joke," she said, a tiny spark flickering acr
her irises, "is that this infinity is trapped in these coarse fles
forms. We get ill, we grow old, we die. But the mind, surely
survives."

"You mean the soul."

"Whatever you want to call it, I can't believe it ends
death. But even if it does, it is the only power worth having
the here and now. With it, I can transcend this fleshy se
ulchre. There is nothing that I cannot do in here."

"And what of good and evil?" I asked.

"What of them?" she said, the spark in her eyes abrup
blinking out. "They are relative discontinuities, inventions
men who think they pull the strings. There is no good or e
there is only purpose."

"I begin to understand what you mean when you say tl
there is nothing you cannot do in there."

The spark flickered again on the dullness of her eyes.

I cleared my throat. "And for this, uh, 'power,' you kill
ten people?"

"Ten people who were wasting their life force."

"You set yourself up as quite a powerful judge."

"That is the nature of power. Those with it judge tho
without."

"And so now that you have this power, you'll enjoy it
jail."

"Again, Martin, you don't understand the true nature
power. Without it, I could live in a palace and still be a sla
within my body. But with it, even if I am in jail, I am tro
free. I am free within myself."

"Sounds like the definition of Hell to me."

"Perhaps. But better to rule there than serve in yo
Heaven."

"I can't disagree with you more."

"You wouldn't be you if you didn't."

That seemed to be a compliment, but I wasn't sure. I de-
ded to change course. "So why the pendant? 'Times 5.'
nd the other ones your women had in their possession?"

"You've read Tolkien? *The Lord of the Rings.*"

"Many times."

"'One ring to rule them all ...'"

"'...and in the darkness bind them.' You got them to con-
nt to something like that?"

"Exactly."

"I remember now. At Starfire's lecture she mentioned 'five
us one.' You organized a 'Pentoven', and you were the
lus one.'"

"Yes. I was the high priestess, the 'receiver.' I was outside
e 'Pentoven', but I was in control. I taught them that sacri-
ce is the key to 'Pentoven Magick,' and the highest sacrifice
, of course, human. So as a 'Pentoven plus one' we lured
ich apostate bishop to the meadow with promises of pleasure
nd magical secrets. Afterwards, one woman—a different one
ich time—was to accompany me to apply the appropriate
eath."

"Pleasure before business," I said. "Dance before death.
hat explains the hyssop at every murder scene. You and
ich woman tracked it there on your shoes."

"An obvious clue," she nodded. "I never thought anyone
ould ever connect it to the meadow at Chapel Hill. How did
ou do it? Father Sherlock again?"

I almost laughed, but my throat and heart were still too tight.
No. Chalk it up to an old woman's bad eyesight. She pre-
nted me with a bouquet of what she thought was 'allysi-
ums,' but as an altar boy from way back, I knew it was hys-
op."

"No kidding. You don't mean that kindly old woman who
ves in the woods?"

"You know about her then?"

"Sure. No waste of life force there. I didn't know that she
as aware of us. I stayed as far away from her as I could. She
eemed harmless."

"She is, except with binoculars. Then she's lethal. But you
ere saying that for each murder a different woman would
ccompany you to commit the crime."

"Yes. Bishop Silverspur was first. After receiving what we
alled 'the Pentoven's favor' in the meadow, Sister Vickers

and I took him to the graveyard with promises to reveal secr
of Indian magic. He wanted to be 'close to the earth.'"

"So you killed him with earth."

"That's right."

"And you left a paper trail to implicate Archbishop Fu
bright. Why?"

"I arranged for Marsha Dukes to pass him the memo in
stack of papers. He didn't know he was signing an order
dig a grave. I'll come back to why in a moment."

"Sure. It's your story. Of course, you realize I'll repo
everything you say to the police."

"Good," she said. "You can double-check my confessic
before I sign it. Make sure I don't leave anything out." S
leaned forward slightly. "Don't worry. It will be a short tri
I fully intend to plead guilty."

Was that another reference to that stupid hat? Not sure,
simply repeated, "So you killed Bishop Silverspur wi
earth."

"Yes. Likes attract."

"And Sister Charlene tracked clay on her shoes from th
grave to the clerical residence at St. Philip's."

"That was not intentional. I hope it proved confusing."

"Very."

"Good."

"And the liquor?"

"Oh, you mean—"

"'Blood catch fire, brain turn ash,'" we said in unison.

"In some of the ancient grimoires," said Cheryl, rubbir
her knuckles pensively, "great emphasis was placed on th
drinking of 'soma.' It was probably some kind of narcoti
or combination of distilled spirits, but no authentic formu
has ever been found. I decided that, as a show of proper i
tention, each man would die with his favorite liquor. It ma
not be impeccable magick, but it seemed fitting."

"I suppose," I shrugged.

"What do you mean, 'suppose'? Surely, as a teetotaler yo
would understand."

I stiffened. "What do you mean, 'teetotaler'?"

"You disdain alcoholic beverages, do you not? Why Ma
tin, I thought that, at least, would be one part of my plot tha
you would approve."

"Disdain? I cherish them. I'm afraid you don't unde
stand the true nature of 'abstinence.'"

"Perhaps I don't."

"I know you don't. But we digress. Please continue."

Her shoulders gave a wee shrug. "Five days later—Father Baptist saw through the alibi of the TV show. Yes, it was pre-taped. While 'Spotlight on Community' was going out on the Rapture Channel, Bishop Brassorie, like Silverspur before him, was also 'favored by the Pentoven.'" Her tone of voice remained even, but the massage she was giving her knuckles grew a bit agitated. "Afterwards Marsha Dukes helped me to drown him in his own chapel."

"With Jägermeister," I grimaced.

"Somehow," she grimaced back, "in Bishop Brassorie's case, it seemed the most fitting of all."

"Why is that?"

"Not now, Martin."

"Again with the 'Not now, Martin,'" I shrugged. "Okay, so each woman helped murder another woman's string-pulling man. Clever. So why did you purposely set Bishop Silverspur's liquor bottle in such a way that Roberto Guadalupe, the cemetery foreman, would be sure to find it when they lowered Bishop Brassorie's coffin into the open grave?"

"It was important to reveal the piece of the casting quilt that was buried with Bishop Silverspur. That's part of the magick."

"And the triangles carved in the hands and feet?"

She paused, considering her reply. "The Bible says, 'An eye for an eye, a tooth for a tooth.'"

"So?"

A moment passed.

"Not now, Martin," we said in unison.

"Meanwhile," she continued, "Madeline Sugarman the 'cable star' was getting edgy. It seemed my brand of witchcraft was becoming a bit too severe for her. When confronted with the immediacy of the act in Bishop Mgumba's shower, she threatened to balk. So I had to kill her prematurely. I ignited the fumes of the white rum with my lighter, and held the shower door shut. It wasn't a pretty sight. I told the others it was an accident."

"And they bought it?"

"If they'd bought this much, why not that? But then your priest friend started getting close, so I had to improvise."

"You planted the knife in Fulbright's office."

"Marsha Dukes did that. It was easiest for her, since she worked there."

"But why implicate the archbishop?"

"Just to get him out of the way, temporarily. It had been part of my plan from the start."

"His signature on the order to dig the grave."

"Right. But with Father Baptist's intrusion, I had to make sure."

"So you had Marsha Dukes plant the knife."

She nodded. "The police never could have held him for long. It was necessary that he not be at St. Barbara's for the Rosary. That death was for Bishop Ravenshorst—fire."

"But Father Baptist interfered."

"Yes. He convinced that buffoon, Billowack, not to act."

"So you resorted to poison at the restaurant."

"A pinch of white powder sprinkled on his fish as I reached for the salt."

"And since you had already wired the Rosary at St. Barbara's, you poisoned yourself to secure your alibi. From the hospital, you phoned your own pager which was wired as the trigger. It started the sequencer, and you knew about such things because you used to be involved in rock music. That's probably how you killed Jymmy Thinggob on stage."

"Jymmy Thinggob was another matter, but yes. I killed him, too. The swine. But I don't want talk about—"

"I know: Not now, Martin." I took a deep breath. "I suppose you told the others that they'd be perfectly safe if they stood on your chalk marks."

"Trust, I'll admit, is hard to come by these days."

"And getting harder all the time. Meanwhile, you had already stolen Mr. Maruppa's truck and electrician's gear, just to implicate Joel at St. Barbara's."

"As I said, I was forced to improvise. I had to confuse the police."

"So you spared Monsignor Goolgol. His was the only Rosary bead that wasn't wired. And then you helped him escape from the hospital for the same reason. To keep us guessing."

"Right. He thought himself an innovative theologian, but not even my gullible girls took the boob seriously—except Sister Charlene. She felt a bit sorry for the jerk. He was a man in a position of power, or close to power, and his strings were ripe for pulling. He was probably the most interested in witchcraft of all the men, but I never planned to kill him. He went bonkers anyway. I cut his restraints and let him go. I planted a piece of his strap at the 'Shop of Shadows' just to add another bit of confusion to the trail. By the time of the dedication ceremony at Chapel Hill, Billowack didn't know

ich end was up. But he got cocky because he had Joel Ma-
ppa behind bars."

"Another diversion which you arranged by putting the
urth piece of the casting quilt in the toolbox."

"Yes."

"So it was you who broke into Starfire's shop."

"I thought it best to dispose of the evidence regarding the
ndants I had designed and she had made in the back room.
ie police will find all that stuff in Bishop Silverspur's car.
I give them the address of the parking garage where it's
rked."

"And then, I guess, the last two evenings were busy times
r you."

"The wee hours of the morning, actually. I learned a lot
out pyrotechnics and special effects when I was the stage
anager for Bombing Fluid."

"The death you planned for Archbishop Fulbright was
ite impressive," I said around a cube of cold butter which
d somehow formed in my mouth. "Special effects."

"I thought the finale should be spectacular."

"It was."

"Thank-you, Martin." She hugged herself with cold satis-
ction. "Security had become lax, since Billowack thought
: had his man. No one was around to interfere when I wired
e platform for the last sacrifice."

"Pickled in Akavit, the 'water of life.'"

"It seemed fitting."

"So why the quilt?"

"It's part of the Magick. And, by designing it to appear
at 'four' was my goal, I hoped to allay suspicion for the
ial blow."

"Archbishop Fulbright."

"The real source of power for them all; and everything
me together on Midsummer Solstice, the best of all possible
nes."

"But Monsignor Goolgol got it instead."

She shrugged. "Their destinies crossed. But as I said, the
rpose of the quilt was still fulfilled."

"So you created two 'Pentovens.' Five women, five men.
ou were the 'plus one' for both of them. And then you sac-
iced them all for the sake of your 'infinity.'"

"Yes."

"Surely you knew that eventually the casting quilt would
deciphered, and sooner or later it would be traced back
you."

"At which point the sacrifice would be complete. Ten pl
one: me."

"You. And here you sit with your power."

"Yes, here I sit."

"I feel sorry for you."

"Not nearly as sorry as you're gonna feel for yourself
crackled a voice through a speaker in the wall next to t
door. "Feeney, what the hell are you doin' in there?"

Startled, I turned and saw Chief Billowack, Lieutenant Tap
Sergeant Wickes, and Father Baptist looking at us through t
window.

"Oh nothing, nothing," I said as I rose from the tab
"How long have you been listening?"

"Long enough," snapped Billowack. "I should let you r
in there with your girlfriend."

Blood rushed to my cheeks again. I looked at Taper, th
Wickes, and finally Father. They stared back, but said not
ing.

I turned to say good-bye to Cheryl. The words of Ecc
siastes chapter seven, verse twenty-seven came to mind — "A
I have found a woman more bitter than death" — but what
said was, "Is there anything I can do for you?"

"I can't imagine what."

"No, neither can I."

93

THE DRIVE HOME WAS PERHAPS THE WORST PART of t
day, for in the end, the foundation upon which daily life
built remains securely in the realm of practicalities.

"I think you're wrong."

"She wouldn't dream of —"

"Yes she would. She's been wanting to do it for years."

"But just because —"

"You bet, 'because.'"

Father Baptist and I were in the Jeep Cherokee heading f
St. Philomena's on the longest day of the year.

I doesn't matter who said what.

Whatever her decision, we would survive.
Somehow.
I gunned the accelerator.
"Maybe we should just, you know, keep on going. Perhaps drive up to Mendocino, the wine country? There's still ome daylight left ...?"
"Maybe we should be reciting a Rosary."
"Right. Pass the Beads."
"Here."
"Thank-you. You lead."
"Be my guest."
"No, you."

94

BUT WHAT ABOUT CARBON FOURTEEN?" asked Sergeant Vickes.
"One test," said Father Baptist, "out of so many. And ince when has carbon fourteen been considered reliable? I vas reading only the other day in *Science Review* that a test vas run on the shell of a living mollusk, and the result indi- ated the poor creature had been dead for twelve hundred ears."
"You read a lot, Jack," said Lieutenant Taper.
"Yes, I do, Larry."
"Anyone for dessert?" asked Millie, intimidating hands on nmitigating hips.
"After all that?" asked Taper, pushing his plate away and atting his stomach. "I don't see how—" He looked up into er sizzling eyes. "But, uh, of course, I can always shake a eg to make more room."
"That's a dear," said Millie, scooping up the dinner dishes. 'I made something special, just for the occasion."
I looked at Father. He looked at me.
We smiled.
Everything was back to normal at St. Philomena's.
"So you really believe the Shroud of Turin is genuine?" sked Wickes incredulously as he dumped more cream into is coffee.
"I haven't enough faith to believe otherwise," said Father.
"What do you mean?"

Father sat back in his chair. "To believe the Shroud i
counterfeit, I would have to accept that a medieval artist, al
those hundreds of years ago, somehow harnessed the radian
energy necessary to project the image onto the cloth—a three
dimensional image, mind you. I would have to accept that thi
forger would use such knowledge and expertise in this pecu
liar way, and not in some other, more profitable venture."

"After all," interjected the gardener, "considering th
weaponry prevalent at the time, he could have rallied an arm
and conquered Europe."

"The whole world, for that matter," said Father. "I woul
also have to believe that this charlatan understood moder
photography centuries before its invention, so that he woul
cast a perfect negative image. Furthermore, I would have t
embrace the notion that he understood the specifics of Roma
torture and crucifixion, centuries after virtually all knowledg
of such things had been lost. Not to mention that he somehov
acquired first-century pollens indigenous to a few hundre
square miles around Jerusalem, and painstakingly imbedde
them in the fibers of the cloth, suspecting that centuries henc
such microscopic biological fingerprints would be detectabl
and classifiable. No, Sergeant, I haven't enough faith to be
lieve all that. It's far easier for me to accept that the thing i
exactly what it appears to be: the burial cloth of Jesus Christ."

Wickes remained silent.

"Apple," announced Millie, holding out plates of steamin
pie and quickly melting vanilla ice cream. "For a job wel
done."

"Why thank-you, Millie," said Father, smiling broadly.

"You've outdone yourself," said Taper.

"As usual," added Wickes.

"But," said the gardener, contrarily curious as usual. "
have to ask. Millie, Father Baptist and I were under the im
pression when we left this morning—"

"Oh that," she said, preening her apron. "I'll admit I wa
acting the witch—or something that rhymes with it, which yo
won't dare speak at this table, Mr. Feeney."

"Of course not," I agreed. "The lady of the house is pre
sent."

She snorted pleasantly. "But then I got to reading tha
book of Father's. That *Mallerus Maligeruptum*, or howeve
you pronounce it—"

"*Malleus Maleficarum*," said Father.

"Whatever, and I got a gander at what real witches are like—"

"And what can happen to them," I interjected.

"—and to folks that interrupt," she snorted. "But being a good Catholic woman I figured I'd best stick to what I know. And I know I belong here at St. Philomena's. Heavens, somebody has to look after Father Baptist, after all." She turned to strut away. "And you, too, Mr. Feeney."

Father and I beamed at each other.

"I thought you might like to know," said Taper, digging in, "that since the case is now wrapped up, with all suspects accounted for, I plan to bring my wife, Lucille, to Mass here next Sunday."

"Really," said Father Baptist. "That will indeed be cause for celebration."

"How about you?" I said, prodding Wickes with my spoon. "Do you plan to start attending Mass again?"

"It's just," stammered Wickes, rubbing the palm of his left hand with the knuckles of his right, "it's just that I don't go in for organized religion."

"That's a tired old shibboleth," I sighed. From his expression I could tell he didn't know the word, so I tried again. "Funny how everyone I've ever heard utter that excuse sounded as though they were saying something original, something profound, even enlightened. But it's nothing of the kind. You denounce organized religion, the apex of which is the Catholic Church. Are you telling me you would seriously prefer—what?—a disorganized religion like witch-craft?"

"I can't accept a God who would condemn anyone to Hell."

"Oh? You think you'd be comfortable in the same Heaven with Adolph Hitler? Or Stalin, maybe?"

"I don't know."

"Funny, I do."

"And what about 'Catholic guilt'? You know how screwed up some people get with it."

"History would have been written differently," I said sagaciously, "if Hitler and Stalin had been privy to a little 'Catholic guilt,' don't you think?"

"Speaking of new additions," said Father, clearing his throat and producing a letter from the mysterious folds of his cassock, "this arrived in today's mail. It's from Monsignor Havermeyer."

"Oh?" I said around a mouthful of dripping pie. "What does "Ol' Lucky Soles' have to say?"

"It's a copy of a letter he mailed to the Chancery from the hospital. Long story short, he has officially requested reassignment to St. Philomena's during his recuperation. He says, 'With all due respect, Your Grace, I have much to learn, and a lot more to unlearn.'"

"Fulbright won't like that," I said.

"Archbishop Fulbright has bigger problems at the moment. I doubt he'll object. Besides, Martin, you still do have that photograph."

"Yes," I said. "That I do."

"What photograph?" asked Lieutenant Taper.

"Father," I said, setting down my spoon, "you told me not to tell them until you directed me to do so."

"Consider yourself so directed," said Father.

From a pocket in my own not-so-mysterious jacket, I pulled out a four-by-five glossy and handed it to Lieutenant Taper. He looked at it, guffawed, and handed it to Sergeant Wickes, who also shared in the merriment.

"Fulbright and Brassorie," mused Taper. "Caught in the act with the statue of St. Rita. No wonder he never shut you down."

"Quite right," said Father. "Our dear friend, Martin Feeney, is a man of unexpected and invaluable resources."

"I have a grand teacher," I said. "For example, Father, taking your spare cassock to the ceremony was a stroke of genius."

"Hm? Oh, that. I knew you'd never agree to another disguise, but Arthur was about the right size. He made a good decoy, didn't he?"

"Amazing." I hefted my spoon for another attack on the pie.

"There is another matter," said Wickes, a tinge of the ominous in his voice. He pulled an envelope out of his jacket. This was a day for deep pockets.

"What now?" I asked.

"The motive," said Wickes, unfolding some pages. "We all listened to Cheryl Farnsworth's speech about 'power.'"

"Yes," said Father.

"By the way, Martin," said Taper, "you make a fine interrogator."

I shrugged. "You were saying, Sergeant?"

"She asked if you remembered her, and that somehow it
as pivotal to the whole thing."
My mind flashed on the conversation in the interrogation
om:

> "Don't you remember me?"
> "Remember you? I don't know what you mean."
> "Until you do, you won't know how it started. But I can
> tell you where it ended up."

"But I don't remember her," I stammered. "I don't know
hat she was talking about."
"But I do," said Wickes. "You'll recall when we were at
e hospital I was looking at her chart. I noticed that her full
ame was Cheryl T. Farnsworth. I did some checking.
arnsworth was actually Jymmy Thinggob's legal name.
ames Timothy Farnsworth. They were married back when
e was associated with that rock band, Bombing Fluid. Ap-
arently the police were called in on three separate occasions.
ife beating. But she never pressed charges. It's obvious
ow that she arranged a spectacular form of justice instead.
stant divorce."
"That's interesting," I said, "in an unsettling sort of way.
ut what has that got to do with my memory?"
"You remember the watercolor you showed me in your
om. The eerie drawing by the little girl, Frances Marie
hompson. You said that she had at first been attracted to
ister Veronica Marie, and then Bishop Brassorie when he was
e pastor here. But something happened. She stopped at-
nding Mass, and became terrified at the sight of them."
"Yes."
"This was about the time that Brassorie invited the witch,
tarfire, to talk to the children."
"What are you getting at?"
"I can't prove it, but I suspect that Starfire got Brassorie
d Sister Veronica Marie involved in a coven of some sort."
"Way back then?"
"I think the drawing in your room is the child's impression
f the night they took her along."
"You're not serious."
"Some forms of demonology," noted Father, "require the
resence of an innocent child as 'receiver.'"

"It fits," said Wickes. "The drawing tells all. The lit
shape in the corner, running away. The robed figures, t
leader wearing a medallion. The medallion, as I recall, w
roughly triangular."

"Come to think of it, you're right," I said.

"Frances turned to you for help. And for a while, she w
okay. But then one night she disappeared, leaving you
painting of her worst nightmare. I think they somehow c
erced her into going back one more time. You said y
found the watercolor on May first, right? Well, according
that wiccan calendar we found yesterday, May Eve is call
Beltane, one of their 'greater sabbats.' I think Frances w
drawn into the ceremony somehow. Then, in utter terror, s
ran away."

"Did you find out what became of her?'

"No. But I've been reading the police reports from the i
vestigation. The child lived with an aunt who was so bu
holding down several jobs that she hardly knew what was g
ing on. I came upon a confidential memo written by one
the investigators from Social Services who, after goi
through the child's belongings, was convinced of an occ
connection. You were never told because the investigato
kept a lid on the details. Scandals were avoided back in tho
days. Apparently your drawing is only one of many simil
things they found in her bedroom."

"But you said this somehow ties in with Cheryl... Mi
Farnsworth?"

"Yes," he said, running his fingers through his ragged ha
"Cheryl's maiden name was Thompson. She was France
older sister. And, though you don't seem to remember, s
was a novice in the convent at the time, under Sister Veroni
Marie."

I dropped my spoon. "Right here at St. Philomena's?"

"Cheryl Farnsworth—Sister Mary Gemma at the time—w
in a perfect position to discover what was going on."

My mind was racing again, replaying snippets from the co
versation in the interrogation room:

    *"Stephanie Fury you knew about: a former nun who had
been oppressed by a male-dominated religion. I could tell you
things about her, things that would curdle your blood, but not
now ... and Starfire ... was a con-artist and a charlatan."*

    "For that she deserved to die?"

"No, not for that."
"Then for what?"
"Not now, Martin ..."
"And the triangles carved in the hands and feet?"
"'The Bible says, 'An eye for an eye, a tooth for a tooth.'"
"So?"
"Not now, Martin."

"The triangle medallion in the painting," I whispered. "Cheryl knew all about it. And she finally got her revenge, all these years later."

"I suspect Brassorie or Starfire was wearing it that night," said Wickes. "Perhaps Frances told Cheryl before she ran away. At this point it's all conjecture. We'll interrogate Miss Farnsworth further, but I think we've got a general idea 'how it started.'"

"Incredible," I said, trying to remember Sister Gemma amidst the gaggle of habited nuns as they strolled from their convent to Mass each morning. She would have been about twenty. I strained to imagine her face framed in the white bonnet they used to wear. Her red hair would not have been visible. No, I had no recollection of Sister Mary Gemma at all. But to think that we must have passed each other, nodding "Good mornings" every day. How strange.

"From bits and pieces I've been able to fit together," continued Wickes, "Cheryl Farnsworth never took final vows. She left the religious life when the convent was dissolved and entered the entertainment field. Then, a few years ago, she came back to Los Angeles and worked her way into the Chancery bureaucracy. By then Starfire was well known, having published several books, and had gained notoriety in several celebrated police cases—I know, I know, I was taken in, too. I don't know how she persuaded Sister Veronica Marie, then Stephanie Fury, to accept her as a wiccan mentor, but we know she's fiendishly clever. She managed to draw in all the major women movers in the Chancery. Once in their confidence, she engineered this whole bloody thing."

"What about the other bishops? How did they figure into her revenge?"

"The friendship between Archbishop Fulbright and Bishop Brassorie was well publicized. Whether Fulbright knew of these horrid events involving Frances Marie Thompson, we've yet to find out. I suspect that he did. But he certainly knew

about Brassorie's other, uh, vices. And we know that Ful
bright promoted all the others, knowing their tenuous regar
for the Catholic Faith. Five men, all in all, a clerical Pentoven
In any case, our vengeful Miss Farnsworth took it from
there."

"When did you know?" I asked Father.

"When did I know what?"

"When did you suspect Cheryl was the murderess?"

"I don't remember exactly. It grew out of other suspicions
Her lack of an alibi for the first couple of murders, and he
coolness about it, caught my attention in a miss-matched sor
of way. At the time I just filed that away under 'things t
ponder.' On the other hand, I was deeply concerned by th
behavior of the other women. Sister Charlene Vickers wa
most uncooperative from day one. Remember the first day w
interrogated her at St. Philip's?"

"Sure," I nodded.

"She was close to Madeline Sugarman and Marsha Dukes
As our amateur detectives, the Tumblars, discovered, Siste
Vickers not only worked with them on the TV show, but so
cialized with them in bars. Their behavior was even more sus
pect."

"How so?" asked Wickes.

"You'll remember that on the Monday when Archbisho
Fulbright was almost arrested at the Chancery, I tossed a few
insinuations in Marsha Dukes' direction, and she responded
with acute nervousness. At the time I criticized Chief Bil
lowack for revealing items of evidence in her presence. Then
the following Thursday, when we were having dinner a
Darby's, these same clues—the knives, the triangles carved i
the victims' hands and feet—came as a complete surprise to
Bishop Ravenshorst."

"He was rather upset when he heard about them," said Ta
per.

"An understatement," said the gardener.

"But that raised a question," said Father. "Here was a mar
surrounded by Marsha Dukes' friends, and they hadn't sai
anything about these shocking clues to him? Surely, I
thought, Marsha Dukes must have told her associates. Why
hadn't they talked about it with him?"

"You mean women can't help gossiping," said Taper.
"Forgive my saying so, but that sounds a bit sexist."

"Women are women," said Father. "And people are people."

"News is news," commented the gardener, "and tongues is tongues." It was fun not having to maintain any more.

"I would have thought," said Wickes, "not knowing what I know now, that perhaps they didn't want to alarm him. He was already pretty stressed out."

"Or," said Father, "these things were not news to them. And since he was part of the gathering plot, it was essential that they not alert him to his peril. I admit it was not conclusive, it was merely supposition. But it certainly aroused my suspicions."

"And you certainly blew their mutual alibi sky-high," noted Taper.

"Don't remind me," said Father, "of the Slap-Happy-Bappy Latin Hour."

"Never," said Taper.

"As for Cheryl Farnsworth," continued Father, "I just couldn't understand why she was poisoned along with the archbishop at Darby's. I suspected that he had been so attacked to keep him away from the Rosary ceremony at St. Barbara's, but why her? The deciding moment came when I saw the list of phone numbers she called from the hospital."

"Ah," I said. "Last Sunday, when you were in your room, I heard you setting the phone down before I came in. You had that blue print-out in your hand."

"Yes," said Father. "I had called the number marked 'mobile' on the bill. I got a message that said, 'This pager is currently out of service.'"

"Of course," I said. "It was destroyed in the fire at St. Barbara's."

"And just before you came in, I was speaking with the phone company. They confirmed my suspicions. Miss Farnsworth had called her own pager from the hospital at the precise time that things went wild at the Rosary."

"Why didn't you tell me?" I asked.

Father Baptist looked at me. "Wanda Hemmingway came to see me not long after Cheryl came here for Mass two Sundays back."

"Why?"

"She told me that she thought you were interested in Cheryl, and suggested I intervene."

I was embarrassed beyond words.

"Martin, we are all friends here." Father reached out a hand and put it on my shoulder. "I wouldn't bring this up in front of Sergeant Wickes and Lieutenant Taper if they hadn't listened to your conversation today with Miss Farnsworth. But you did ask. And men understand one another. We've all experienced unhealthy attractions. That goes with the territory."

I glanced around the table, meeting their eyes, and knew that he was right. "I must've feared the Lord," I said, swallowing hard.

GARDENING TIPS: Sirach, who wrote the Book of Ecclesiasticus several centuries before the Birth of Christ, knew what he was talking about when he wrote:

"A faithful friend is a strong defense; and he that hath found him hath found a treasure. Nothing can be compared to a faithful friend, and no weight of gold and silver is able to countervail the goodness of his fidelity. A faithful friend is the medicine of life and immortality: and they that fear the Lord, shall find him. He that feareth God, shall likewise have good friendship: because according to him shall his friends be."

Chapter six. It's easy to find in my Bible. The page is frayed.

                                        --M.F.

"Come again?" asked Wickes.

"Nothing," I said sheepishly, looking at Father. "So, Wanda approached you."

Father gave my shoulder a nudge and removed his hand.
Wanda gave me copies of the same materials she also gave
ou."

"But you didn't say anything."

"I noticed that you had a funny way of never quite getting
ound to looking at them. A part of you simply didn't want
know, I suppose. But I knew from experience that such
ings have a way of unraveling themselves."

"That they do," agreed Taper.

"You're not going to tell me," I said, "that you planned
r me to be the one to deal with her at the dedication cere-
ony."

"Not if you don't want me to," said Father.

"Then that's why you had me take the path into the woods
y myself."

"Not specifically, no. But I had a feeling—no not a feeling,
ore like a conviction—that you were going to play an im-
ortant part in the outcome. Call it a hunch. Whatever, my
ith in you was vindicated beyond all expectation."

I bowed my head. "I don't know how to take all of this."

"Like you do everything, Martin: as the movement of
od's Grace in your life."

"This is getting too deep for me," said Wickes, rising to his
et.

"We've got a ton of forms waiting to be filled out in the
orning," said Taper, also rising. "Millie, thank-you for the
onderful meal."

Millie acknowledged the compliment with a resounding
atter of pans.

Father and I accompanied the detectives to the front door.

"I hope you get a good night's sleep," said Taper to Fa-
er, clasping his hand. "Jack—Father Baptist—it's been an
onor working with you again."

"Thank-you," said Father. "And it will be a great honor to
ve you and your wife Holy Communion this Sunday. Ser-
eant?"

"No, not me. I'll take a rain check."

"Fine, fine. But don't get struck by lightening while
ou're stalling in the downpour," said the gardener, opening
e door.

"Hurrah!" shouted five blustering lads in tuxedoes on the
oorstep.

"Good Lord," said Father.

"Yes, He is," said Pierre. "We all pitched in and boug Joel here some new apparel, complete with tails. Nice touc don't you think?"

"White tie," said Arthur.

"White vest," added Edward.

"And white gloves," noted Jonathan with a twinkle.

"I guess I've been 'assumed,'" laughed Joel.

"Precisely," nodded Pierre. "And we thought we'd con by for your blessing and a nightcap."

"Of course," said Father wearily. "Come on in, gentlemer The evening's young."

Thursday, June Twenty-second

Feast Day of Saint Paulinus of Nola (431 AD)

∞ Early Morning Epilogue ∞

95

"FATHER BAPTIST," I HUFFED as I hobbled up the brick walkway through the garden. I was huffing and hobbling more than usual because I was just returning from carting a heavy cardboard carton to my room for storage. All the papers, files, and reports that had been piled on Father's desk in the study were now safely secured on the shelf in my closet, along with five ominous bottles of liquor and a plaque about a dog and his vomit. "Father Baptist, is that you?"

I had to ask because it was so dark outside. The illuminated clock on the stove said 12:05. I could see it through the kitchen window. Thursday was only five minutes old. Millie had turned all the lights off when she went to bed, except for the one in the dining nook. Its dim glow faintly penetrated the stained-glass window that Mrs. Magillicuddy utilized for her Friday evening confessions. It looked cozy, the ambers and reds. But other than that colorful but faint source, the garden was cloaked in blackness.

Yes, there he was, seated in his neat but somewhat threadbare cassock on the wooden bench facing the statue of Saint Thérèse the Little Flower. Through the tranquil gloom he looked up at me with those glistening eyes that seemed to whisper, exhausted but triumphantly, "Considering that God is in Heaven with His Angels and Saints, and everyone with a modicum of sense is fast asleep in bed, Martin, who else would it be?" Exhaling slowly, he folded his arms across his chest and said, "Come, my friend, sit with me."

As I groped for the cement birdbath, my cane bumped the rigid, porous bird perched on the pockmarked rim. The poor thing toppled off into the ivy with a plop. Sighing, I started to stoop to retrieve it but decided the effort could wait until morning. With a tired groan I settled down on the edge of the birdbath and listened for a while to the sounds of the evening.

It wasn't really quiet, but it was peaceful. In the middle of a huge city, there is never silence. The background drone of restless traffic is ceaseless, even after midnight. The pulse of motorized life and the crackle of neon advertising does not stop, even when the giant seems to be asleep. But that, at least was beyond the walls of our small sanctuary. Within, crickets were chirping merrily from their secret hiding places in the rose bushes. A couple of cats were frolicking in St. Joseph's gardenias, and a squirrel was chasing his tail among the ripe avocados near the front gate.

The moon was hiding behind a high, feathery cloud, conversing conspiratorially with Venus and Mercury. Few stars were bright enough to penetrate the canopy of the electric metropolitan aurora. The Angels were guiding them all in their macrocosmic dance above, maternally nudging us in our microcosmic fatigue here below.

The pattern turns upon itself.

And the Endless Knot goes on interweaving within itself forever.

"A penny for your thoughts," I ventured.

"I have several," he said, resting his hands on his knees. "For one, I was just thinking that in the new Church calendar today is the feast of St. Thomas More. As Traditionalists, we normally wouldn't acknowledge this as his proper day—but any excuse, I say, to thank our dear patron."

My thoughts drifted to the statue of the Lord Chancellor of England, standing beside St. Anthony near the far edge of the now-uncluttered desk, DO WE WALK IN LEGENDS between them.

"For another," continued Father, "I was just marveling at the symmetry of God's unfolding plan."

"How so?"

"Well, on the dark side, we had two 'Pentovens.' I dislike the contrived term, but for want of a better word we'll make do. Five witches, five bishops, and the notorious 'plus one.'"

"And on your side?"

"Considering myself as the 'plus one,' I had five wonderful Saints: Philomena, patroness of our poor but rich parish, St

Thérèse here in the garden, St. Jude the Patron of Things
Despaired Of watching from within the church, and Sts.
Anthony and Thomas More in the study."

"And the other five?"

"Why, the Tumblars, of course. Fine lads all."

"I see. And where does the gardener fit in, I'd like to
know."

"Why Martin, need you ask? You're my chauffeur, my
valet, my right-hand man, my cook when Millie's away, not to
mention a remarkable gardener in your way."

"Well then," I said, rubbing my hands together, "on that
less than auspicious note, I have a request to make."

"Such as?"

"As you know, I took the pledge many years ago, before
you came here. On that fateful evening, I set aside a case of
wine which I keep in the closet in my humble room. I've
never opened a single bottle since, but I had a hunch that there
might come an event or two in my life when I might want to
seek a dispensation in order to make a special toast."

"Are you asking me to absolve you of your promise?"

"Well, Father, you know as well as I that a personal oath
doesn't carry the same weight as a solemn vow. A priest does
have the power to suspend it, providing the situation warrants
it."

I produced the bottle I had secreted under my coat.

"Ah." Father Baptist fished around in the mysterious folds
of his cassock. He brought out a pair of things which
sparkled and clinked in the dim light. "I was wondering
when you might ask."

I blinked. "Are those wine glasses?"

"Yes."

"You knew about it then."

"I am your confessor, Martin."

"But you forget everything said under the Seal of the
Confessional."

It was too dark to see, but I'm sure his silhouette winked.
"I must have lapsed. With what fine wine do you wish to
temporarily—and I stress 'temporarily'—suspend your
pledge?"

I held up the bottle, though neither of us could read the
label. "Lacrimae Christi."

"'The tears of Christ,'" translated Father as I peeled off the
seal. "A fitting wine, under the circs."

I pulled the cork and poured out the old but obliging liquid.
A little bit dribbled onto the ground.   A lizard skittered
between my feet, waving his tail in scaly thanks.

Father and I looked at each other's outline through the
peaceful darkness.

"To His tears," I said, as we clinked our glasses. "May we
be worthy of His concern."

"To His tears," said Father.

THE END

—July 6th, 1996:
The Traditional Feast of St. Thomas More;
Rock Haven.

Made in the USA
Monee, IL
18 August 2020